Ed, Hope you enjoy reading...

Statehood of Affairs

Best, Dan

STATEHOOD OF AFFAIRS

◀◀◀◆▶▶▶

DANIEL R. CILLIS, PHD

iUniverse, Inc.
Bloomington

Statehood of Affairs

iUniverse books may be ordered through booksellers or by contacting:

iUniverse
1663 Liberty Drive
Bloomington, IN 47403
www.iuniverse.com
1-800-Authors (1-800-288-4677)

ISBN: 978-1-4620-5084-0 (sc)
ISBN: 978-1-4620-5085-7 (hc)
ISBN: 978-1-4620-5086-4 (e)

Library of Congress Control Number: 2011915959

Printed in the United States of America

iUniverse rev. date: 09/22/2011

Timeline...

1821 - Mexico wins Independence from Spain

1829 - President Jackson offers to buy Texas—Mexico rejects offer

1830 - Valtura, New Mexico founded

1835 - Americans in Texas announce intentions to secede from Mexico

1836 - Battle of the Alamo/Texans defeat Mexico/The Republic of Texas formed

1844 - James Polk elected president

1845 - Texas obtains U.S. statehood

1846 - Mexican War/U.S. occupies Santa Fe with annexation of New Mexico

1848 - Treaty of Guadalupe Hidalgo ends Mexican War/ Mexican Cession yields 500,000 square miles of the Southwest to the U.S.

1852 - Franklin Pierce elected president

1853 - Treaty of Mesilla designed to settle unresolved issues from the Mexican War

1856 - James Buchanan elected president

1861 - Treaty of Mesilla amended with Article X, the Revert Document

1861 - Chaco Canyon Expedition led by Colonel Alvarado - Revert Document hidden

1878 - Fire destroys Washington Archive building

1898 - Battleship Maine explodes in Havana starting the Spanish-American War/Adoloreto Centori wins Medal of Honor for action on San Juan Heights

1900 - Valtura Journal founded

1903 - Mad Mady Blaylock arrives in Valtura

1905 - Circle C Ranch founded in Corona County by Adobe Centori

1908 - William Taft elected president

1910 - Adobe Centori becomes New Mexico statehood delegate

1910 - (June) President Taft signs Enabling Act, allowing New Mexico to call a state constitutional convention

1910 - (Oct.) Delegates draft and frame a state constitution for New Mexico

1911 - Renewed interest in the Revert Document caused by approaching deadline

1911 - (Jan.) Territorial voters approve the state constitution

1911 - (Nov.) Territorial voters ratify the state constitution and congressional conditions

1912 - (Jan.) New Mexico statehood

Dramatis Personae

Adoloreto "Adobe" Centori - Circle C Ranch owner, Corona County sheriff and New Mexico statehood delegate

Gabriella Zena - Cuban freedom fighter, the object of Adobe's affection, co-conspirator

Elizabeth "Mad Mady" Blaylock - owner of Mad Mady's Saloon, friend of Adobe Centori

Santa Fe Sharon Blaylock - Mady's sister, co-conspirator and femme fatale

Antonio Santos - member of Chaco Canyon Expedition, prominent Valtura citizen

A.P. Baker - Circle C Ranch Foreman

Berta Brandt - Mady's friend and saloon worker

Johan Morgenstern - newspaper editor, Valtura Journal

Klara Morgenstern - Johan's daughter and opinionated beauty

Henry Anthony Ellison - Circle C ranch hand

Bill "Black Eye Pea" Blackstone - co-conspirator

Madame Francine Fournier - Santa Fe finishing school proprietor and boastful vamp

Albert Hietmann - German ambassador to Mexico, co-conspirator

John Murphy - Adobe's Army friend, captain of New Mexico Rangers

Carrie Carlson - friend of Sharon, co-conspirator

Dr. Thornton N. Trumble - Medical Director, Territorial Insane Asylum

Darcie Denton - Head Psychiatric Nurse, Territorial Insane Asylum

Coyote - A wild dog and cultural hero who can be humorous and dangerous

Prologue

Chaco Canyon

Two columns of horse soldiers cross the vast, high desert landscape toward Chaco Canyon. The mounted men, armed with Brown Bess muskets, flintlock pistols and lances, are creating a legend in the year 1861. As they ride deeper into the broad canyon, the hot, harsh climate increases the challenge of the mission.

Located in northwestern New Mexico Territory, Chaco Canyon sits on the Colorado Plateau, enclosed by the grand Chuska San Juan and San Pedro Mountains. The remote canyon is the site of significant archaeological ruins. Chaco Pueblo, built into caves in a precipice, is a dramatic cliff dwelling. Almost a thousand years ago, Chaco Pueblo was a habitat and cultural center for a population called the Anasazi. These white soldiers with black beards, riding strange, large creatures would have appeared extraordinary to the pre-Columbian Anasazi.

Twenty-five hard riders enter Chaco Canyon heading toward Chaco Pueblo. The sky grows darker, and a ghostly strong wind creates a sense of peril. A mystical world unfolds, revealing strange secluded ruins. The riders become increasingly aware of the canyon's spiritual nature. Although hardened by war, they share glances of anxiety.

The men are Mexican cavalry troops commanded by Colonel José Bautista Alvarado. Their colorful uniforms provide a stark contrast to the earthen tones of the desert. They wear cropped, green jackets with yellow turnbacks and piped yellow lapels. Their trousers are grey and their helmets are black, with brass visors and red plumes. It is the first time in Chaco Canyon for the men, but not for Colonel Alvarado.

Resplendent in his uniform and officer's saber, Colonel Alvarado is a tall, forty-four-year-old veteran soldier. Mounted straight and stoic on his stallion, there is nothing in the colonel's bearing except a strong sense of purpose. Yet he has doubts about the number of men required to complete the mission. His force must be big enough for security yet small enough to avoid detection.

The Mexican cavalry is a long way from home and is, in fact, an invader of the United States. If caught in the territory of New Mexico, the soldiers would cause embarrassment, at the least, for Old Mexico. Despite the risk, Alvarado, driven by duty and some sort of instinct, believes that the gravity of the mission outweighs the risk of the border-crossing. Ironically, his assignment is more about foreign policy than war. Alvarado carries an intergovernmental document that could exacerbate Mexico's relationship with the United States and even change history.

The desolate location, appropriate to the clandestine mission, provides a fantastic view into the past. Many of the men marvel over the sacred archeological sites that were homes for an advanced society. Some soldiers wonder why the Ancient Ones abandoned this place. A long drought in the twelfth century was probably the cause, but that is something these men could not have known.

Rain clouds appear and swirls of dust devils develop into huge funnels as the riders get close to Fajada Butte and Pueblo Bonito.

Pueblo Bonito, a complex of 650 rooms, is four stories high. A wall bisects a central plaza that contains a circular ceremonial room—the Great Kiva. The dusty, weary men squint against the remaining sunlight and wonder at the spectacular sight. They slow down and stare open-mouthed at the ancient dwellings carved out of the sandstone—on top of Fajada Butte.

At the base of the high-reaching butte, with a gesture of his hand, the colonel halts his columns and in a strong voice, says, "*Capitán Santos, hemos llegado a nuestro destino.*" (Captain Santos, this is our destination.)

Santos answers with an interested look, "*Si Coronel.*"

Alvarado dismounts, opens his saddlebag, and asserts, "*Desde aquí tenemos que seguir a pie, Capitán.*" (We must proceed on foot from here, Captain.)

Captain Antonio Santos shifts uneasily in his saddle. A strong, seasoned soldier in his late twenties and highly trusted by Alvarado, he wonders about the mission. He has some awareness of the Mexican government's long-term strategy, but not of the thinking behind the Chaco Canyon operation. He looks over at Alvarado, a man with whom he plays chess, knowing the game reveals an officer's strategic competence. The colonel is a brilliant chess player, but Santos still wonders.

Alvarado pulls a thin metal box containing a document case from his saddlebag, turns to Santos and asks, "*Capitán, se siente cómodo para cruzar la frontera*?" (Captain, are you comfortable crossing the U.S. border?)

Santos dismounts, takes the colonel's horse, hands the reins of the two horses to the closest soldier and replies, "*Coronel, no hemos cruzado la frontera, la frontera nos ha cruzado!*" (Colonel, we did not cross the border, the border crossed us!)

Alvarado smiles to display his understanding of the sentiment, and then turns his attention to the fine document case with solid brass hardware and a flap-over buckle. The colonel knows about its markedly valuable contents and the momentous implications it holds for Mexico and the United States. The men will not be part of the final journey; he will finish the assignment alone.

The leather case contains a diplomatic pouch with a manuscript copy of the Treaty of Mesilla signed by President Pierce and the recent Article X signed by President Buchanan. The original treaty, which clarifies the boundaries created at the end of the Mexican-American War, has nine publicly-known articles. The tenth, the new Article X, a potentially explosive political agreement, is unknown beyond the walls of government, a secret agreement made between American and Mexican leaders. The version of the treaty ratified by the United States Senate contains only nine articles, omitting Article X, at least publicly.

Should other manuscript copies secured in Old Mexico disappear, there will be a return to Chaco Canyon. The act of hiding a manuscript copy inside the United States is hard for Alvarado to resist. Somehow, the irony seems appropriate to him.

At the last moment, Alvarado ignores orders from the Mexican government to ascend Fajada Butte alone and deliberately says, "*Vamos, Capitán.*" (Let's go, Captain.)

Surprised by the sudden change, Santos replies, "*Si Coronel.*"

Both men go up the prehistoric trail on foot. The climb to the summit is difficult and dangerous. There is only one possible path and Alvarado knows it well. As a boy, he grew up in the north when New Mexico was part of Old Mexico.

Toward the middle of the climb, Santos becomes aware of many dwellings along the higher cliff bands. Noticing signs and symbols etched into the sandstone, he says, "*Este sitio es interesante, mi Coronel. Ya entiendo porqué usted lo escogió para esconder el maletín.*" (This is an interesting place, Colonel. I can see why you chose to protect the case here.)

"*Interesante y seguro.*" (Interesting and secure.) Alvarado pauses for a breath and continues, "*La parte superior del cañón está más de 134 metros por encima de la parte inferior.*" (The top rises over 440 feet above the canyon floor.)

The two officers climb in silence for what seems like a long time. Then Santos stops to examine the strange lines and shapes in the sandstone. These petroglyphs, marking solar and lunar cycles with light and shadows, are a mystery.

"*Mi coronel, ¿qué son estas figuras y marcas tan increíbles?*" (Colonel, what are these amazing pictures and markings?)

At that time, Chaco Canyon had not yet been identified as an observatory. The colonel replies, "*No se.*" (I do not know.)

They continue with unwavering determination. Finally arriving at the summit of the butte, they admire the breathtaking landscape from the high elevation. The commanding views of Chaco Canyon distract them from their purpose, but they refocus on the mission and search for a suitable place.

Scanning the area, they find a large crack in the sandstone that will conceal the leather case. Santos clears away brush. Alvarado places the case deep within the recess, followed by small rocks. He reaches for a knife and carefully scratches a distinct marking above the opening. The marking blends with the petroglyphs; it is an image of a coyote.

High above the canyon, the summit of the butte becomes a time capsule. The case will stay hidden there until the document becomes politically relevant. They carefully walk back down the summit on the same path. Alvarado descends without looking back, but Santos hesitates and looks back. The officers go down and rejoin the men who are anxiously waiting to leave this unsettling place and return to their side of the border.

No one has seen the activity of the two officers at the summit—no one except a lone coyote. Now the task is to return to Mexico unbeknownst to the Americans.

Alvarado quickly mounts and orders, "*Vamos, Capitán*," and leads the columns out of the canyon. Suddenly, a distant rumble blends with the noise of fast-moving horses. They cannot see the source of any movement but hear it, a sound that Alvarado and his men take as a warning. Alvarado stops his columns to reconsider their direction. The rumble changes to a loud roar and a wall of large rocks comes crashing down, narrowing the escape route.

The colonel commands what the men already instinctively know. The riders have only one option. They must outrun this deadly rockslide. The troopers desperately kick the flanks of their mounts and gallop away, riding low in the saddle, at breakneck speed, hooves fiercely pounding the earth. Horses and men, breathing heavily, confront violent dust devils whirling wildly. Branches breaking, snapping, and cracking reach a grand crescendo. Then it stops as abruptly as it started.

The colossal rockslide is a force of nature, but Alvarado knows that rockslides are uncommon in the canyon. When water gets into the rocks, they can slide, but Chaco is one of the driest places in the world. Perhaps ancient spirits haunt the canyon and are responsible. The men entered a sacred space as one European-American group in conflict with another European-American group, over land inhabited by native people for thousands of years. In the future, the mystifying vanishing of the Anasazi from Chaco Canyon will connect to the mystifying vanishing of Article X.

With relief, Alvarado and his men continue riding hard through the unforgiving desert, quickly moving away from any powerful presence that may have caused the danger. The colonel senses the rockslide was more spiritual than geological. Alvarado rides on, doubting whether Chaco Canyon is the best hiding place for Article X.

1

New Year's Eve 1910

All three men sitting in the Circle C line shack on the open range had arrived on the strength of their character, having met the physical and emotional challenges of the day. More than two feet of snow covers the range, the result of a blizzard that has blanketed the central New Mexico Territory. The blizzard has exposed cattle to the most severe winter of the new century. Snow-covered grass is beyond reach and time is running out.

When the storm hit the territory, ranchers had found it nearly impossible to help their drifting cattle. Yet the three men of Circle C have led a valiant effort to save many animals and will continue their work at daybreak. Since the three men had arrived at the shack, the temperature had dropped and the wind had worsened.

Exhausted, wet and chilled, they are dressed in heavy coats, with their collars pushed up and their hats pulled down. The small, one-room structure houses an old rough-hewn table, a few bunks and a stone fireplace. The flames dance wildly as the Circle C men sit around the table. Line shacks across the range provide shelter to men protecting invisible boundaries. Tonight the cabins protect against nature's wrath.

Inside, the fire gives the line shack a slight smoky smell. Outside, lingering clouds conceal the sky; the darkness is absolute with no visible moon or stars, and the air is getting colder. Intermittent coyote cries shatter the otherwise complete silence. According to legend, the coyote gave man fire; on this night, the men are especially grateful for the gift of the crackling blaze.

One man offers coffee, cigars and appreciation to the two other men for their courageous and decisive action out on the range. He is Adobe Centori, sole owner of the Circle C Ranch. The vast ranch, with thousands of cattle on thousands of acres, is located near the town of Valtura, in Corona County, New Mexico Territory.

The conjunction of the Sandia Mountains to the east and vast mesas and plains to the west distinguish Valtura, the county seat. Established along the Rio Grande, the high desert town is elevated 4,800 feet above sea level. Although there are many sunny and dry days, the winters here can be unpredictable.

Adobe Centori is forty years old, intelligent, educated and romantic to the extreme. At times, practicality pushes his romantic view of the world to the back of his mind. Today was one of those times. The handsome leader is square-jawed with a slender, square-shouldered build. He wears a long brown coat, a big tan hat and an ivory-handled, silver-plated Navy Colt pistol.

As Centori drinks black coffee, his cool blue eyes see the cigar smoke and fireplace smoke intermingle. His thoughts turn to his responsibility as a New Mexico statehood delegate. He thinks, *Will the economic impact of this winter have an adverse effect on statehood? There always has been some reason that stops the process short.*

The people in Valtura appreciate Centori's integrity of character, expressed by his public-spirited work and his willingness to provide territorial leadership. A rising star in New Mexico politics, he will probably do nothing in the New Year to spoil that promise.

Centori has lived a life encircled by honor and has placed his trust in men based on intuition—experience has confirmed his feelings. Earlier, the other men had displayed their true mettle and clear devotion to the Circle C Ranch.

"Thank you for all you have done," Centori says. "There's no doubt that Circle C men are the best in the territory. This is risky business, yet you came through with skill, confidence and, above all, friendship."

The two other men nod in support of the emotion. Suddenly, the blizzard intensifies, sending a violent wind roaring across the range and slamming the cabin. The strong blast causes the door to crash open; the loud noise and the cold wind rushing through the quarters surprises the men. Centori jumps up, causing his straight-back chair to fall over with a crash. He pushes the door closed and places two heavy pieces of firewood against it as a defense against the howling power of the blizzard.

That night, the stockpiled firewood and stone fireplace shield against raging winds and frigid temperatures. That day, there had been no defense against a blinding snow driven horizontal by high-speed winds. The horses, with steaming breath, had staggered through poor visibility, fighting the deep drifts, with shards of ice flying up as they had struggled for footing. Pressing on, the men had screamed to communicate over the deafening roar of the brutal winter winds.

Sitting directly across from Centori is twenty-one-year-old Henry Anthony Ellison. A strong young man with long, wild hair, he has a devil-may-care attitude. Although he had little ranching experience, Centori had hired him and helped him to learn the job. On the surface, Ellison is loyal, but known to trust the wrong people. Nonetheless, at the Circle C, he has been a good cowboy.

The oldest in the group, A.P. Baker, has gray hair and slit eyes. An honorable person with a general good character, he is friendly and dependable. He drives a hard bargain and takes risks for a good cause. At one time, he was one of the youngest to ride the Chisholm Trail, driving longhorn cattle from Texas to Dodge City's railhead. A dedicated cowboy, he moved herds ten miles a day for bread, beans, bacon, coffee, son-of-bitch-stew and $30 a month. Upon his arrival in Valtura, the fast-growing Circle C had needed help. Centori had hired A.P. based on his notable ranching skills and had soon promoted him to line foreman.

It is the first decade of the twentieth century but this is not the first big snow of the century. According to A.P., this snow is similar to the blizzard of 1901, making it one of the worst winters in New Mexico's recorded history. Although the exact snowfall is unknown in Valtura, one thing is obvious: the unrelenting snows had started in December and had created a hard winter.

Although the men had spent the last several days focused on their jobs, they were also aware of the closing of the west. In the last century, men had protected invisible boundaries around the open range. The new century had increasingly called for more fencing, causing sweeping changes in the cattle business. The most significant sign was barbed wire—a stark symbol of the end of an era.

Centori reaches into his pocket to look at his watch while thinking of the doom that had fallen upon many unsuspecting animals. His thoughts return to New Mexico's long struggle in seeking statehood. He draws on his cigar and thinks, *Will this disaster hurt our chances again? We have sought a self-governing state for so many years with so many failed attempts.*

Coyote cries shatter the silence again, jarring Centori from his thoughts. The coyote is an amazingly adaptive animal known for shortcuts; but there are no shortcuts for the cowboys on the open range and there are no shortcuts to statehood.

Americans in New Mexico remain without self-government, a condition that has existed since Mexico ceded the territory in 1848. For centuries, New Mexico had been a Spanish province and then a Mexican territory, with Santa Fe as a significant trading town. Yet New Mexico, a low priority in Washington, was still a territory.

It is 11:58 p.m. Centori turns, pulls out a bottle of whiskey and three dusty old glasses from a not-so-hidden box and considers his role as Corona County statehood delegate. He thinks, *Since the first attempt in 1850, New Mexicans have been continually disappointed, but I am resolute that the territory achieves statehood in the New Year. This year our destiny will be different.*

The latest statehood procedure had started in June with a referendum vote by the people and then a petition to Congress. An enabling act, signed by President Taft, had allowed the territory to hold a convention to create a state constitution in compliance with the U.S. Constitution. Centori and delegates from each county had assembled in Santa Fe where they had drafted and framed a constitution for the proposed new state of New Mexico.

In the New Year, the people will vote on the constitution and, if approved, the territory will be able to seek congressional and presidential support for statehood. Another election can follow for ratification and approval of congressional conditions. If Congress passes a joint resolution accepting the territory, the president can sign the bill for statehood.

Centori and the delegates know the statehood process, but a dormant political time bomb hidden in a time capsule is unknown. The time-sensitive Article X that could awaken with far-reaching repercussions for the United States, Old Mexico and New Mexico is nearing its deadline.

In the middle of a frigid, windswept blizzard, Centori pours, raises his glass and says, "Happy New Year."

"Happy New Year to you too," Ellison says.

A.P. says, "Boss, any wishes for the new year?"

"Same wish as last year, New Mexico statehood."

"Well, with you involved as a delegate, New Mexico will finally become a state."

"Thanks, A.P. but many others have tried before."

"You will do more than try, you will succeed," A.P. insists.

Centori pledges, "I'll do my best for statehood."

A.P. smiles and says, "Happy 1911."

2

VERONA TO VALTURA

The people of Valtura are accustomed to his big tan hat and frequent walks along the town's wide streets and plazas. Adobe Centori, who is serving his second term as Corona County sheriff, flashes brilliance stemming from a family history in Verona, Italy. Valtura is a long way from Verona, but his story begins in the romantic Italian city.

Adobe is descended from a formidable European family founded by a powerful seventeenth century Renaissance man, Donato Centorius. Based on a vast banking empire, Donato occupied the commanding heights of Verona society. He was a scholar, a poet and a philosopher and was wholly involved in Machiavellian politics. As the patriarch of Verona's richest and most influential family, Donato supported artists and financed a public fountain system.

During the eighteenth century, Donato's great grandson Aldo turned away from family tradition. Seeking to distance himself from stressful city life, he sought relief in the Apennine Mountains of Southern Italy, where he found a town called Pietragalla. The small mountainous village with wonderful views overlooking the Basento River valley appeared to be a good place to live.

As heir to a financial fortune, Aldo planned a return to Verona; however, a woman changed his destiny. His diary reveals his love for a woman called Flora and an enduring passionate romance. All of his words about their walks along Traversa Giardini and their talks in the cafes on Via Serra showed that love yields more treasure than Verona riches. Besides, Flora's dowry was more than enough. Consequently, Aldo's break from Verona became complete; he married Flora and never returned. The couple had one son, Dante.

As a young man, Dante felt a clarion call for Verona and the family banking empire. He was, though, in love with the mayor's daughter Franca, a young beauty of sixteen years. The mayor, prominent and involved with many powerful allies, was against the marriage of his too-young child. Given the mayor's connections, an elopement would be mortally dangerous for Dante, but he was in love and he was determined.

One night Franca told her sister about the imminent plans and fear of their father. Then Dante entered their second-floor bedroom via the balcony to offer reassurance. Franca agreed to elope and then events quickly unfolded. Her father stormed in with sword drawn, challenging Dante. The young lover grappled with the mayor, causing the older man to fall out of the window. On the ground, hurting and outraged, the mayor cursed the couple and cried out, "*Vendetta*!" This proclamation forced the lovers to flee from Pietragalla.

To complete their escape, they became part of the first large group of Italian immigrants to America. Upon their arrival in New York, Dante's surname became Centori. He married Franca and worked as an unskilled laborer. They lived in lower Manhattan and enjoyed a long, happy marriage that produced three children, six grandchildren and ten great-grandchildren including Aldoloreto Centori.

Born a third-generation American in 1870 to Dante Centori's grandson Giacomo Centori, Aldoloreto Centori spent his youth within the confines of the New York melting pot. His father, a local politician, entertained many distinguished visitors, who discussed political, social and economic issues. This childhood experience sparked a desire within the ambitious Aldoloreto to embrace the wider world. He entered New York University to study the new discipline of political science and then attended a few classes at New York University Law School, the first of its kind in New York. After several academic years, he could no longer contain his desire for adventure.

Following an instinct for excitement, Aldoloreto dropped out of school and joined the United States 6th Calvary Regiment in 1890. Although Giacamo did not condone the enlistment, it did not matter. When the regiment moved west and roamed the wide-open spaces, the army offered Aldoloreto a chance to fulfill his adventurist dreams.

In 1898, the regiment sailed to Cuba for the Spanish-American War and participated in the San Juan Hill assault. Aldoloreto received the Medal of Honor for heroism and an official citation:

> Aldoloreto Centori. Rank and organization: Captain, Troop A, 6th U.S. Cavalry. Place and date: At Santiago, Cuba, 1 July 1898. Entered service: Brooklyn NY. Birth: 8 August, 1870 New York, NY. Date of issue: 6 July 1899. Citation: Facing heavy enemy fire, Centori showed extraordinary bravery and coolness throughout the battle. In addition to performing gallantly at his command post, he carried several wounded men from the line to the rear, despite heavy fire from Spanish positions and great exposure to danger.

Aldoloreto met a special woman in Cuba who affectionately called him Adobe. The adoring name continued, as a constant reminder of the romantic escapade and the love shared—but lost.

After the war, the horse soldiers returned to the United States to patrol the Mexican border in the territory of New Mexico. Upon finishing his military service, Centori settled in a town twenty-five miles north of Albuquerque called Valtura. The town, not much more than a dusty crossroad, provided wrangler work on a cattle ranch. Based on his superior horsemanship, the range boss promoted him to cowboy.

On the open range, Centori would dream of romance and loving the right woman beyond the lost love of his life. That was a dream; reality was a completely different story. Most nights around the campfire, he favored the sound of crickets to the talk of men who wanted to hear about Cuba. He often dispelled the San Juan Hill cavalry charge myth. In fact, infantry and dismounted troopers stormed and captured the heights. Although he downplays his role in the war, his bravery in Cuba was absolute.

Eventually, Centori acquired and amassed good land and ultimately established the Circle C Ranch. For two dollars an acre, he bought over 10,000 acres of ranch land about six miles north of Valtura. Increases in animal agricultural production improved the local economy, with the Circle C as a core catalyst for growth.

Based on his reputation for honesty and bravery, Centori became a candidate for Corona County sheriff in 1908. His superior military record, strong sense of justice and penchant to do the right thing—even in the face of adversity—helped him win the election. His star continued to rise in 1909 with an appointment as the Corona County delegate to the constitutional convention. Unbeknownst to Centori, his positions as sheriff and delegate will intersect when he faces a substantial challenge from the Revert Document.

Adobe Centori, descendent of the powerful Centorius family, founder of the Circle C Ranch, Corona County sheriff and statehood delegate is a respected prominent Valtura citizen. Most people in Valtura like him—especially Mad Mady Blaylock.

3

CIRCLE C

A circle is eternal; it has no beginning, no end. Some native people see a circle as symbolic of divine power. The circle is the sun, the moon and the integration of energy and earth for enhancing spiritual awareness.

For Centori, the circle has a different but equally profound significance that began while looking into the stunning large eyes of a woman he loved and lost. The circular grandeur of her emotionally charged gaze magnified her exquisiteness, fixed his fascination and inspired an adventure of a lifetime. Naming his ranch Circle C gave him a lifetime of adventure—she is never far from his thoughts.

After enduring the winter, the spring of 1911 is a welcome relief for central New Mexico, Valtura and the Circle C Ranch. New twentieth century science provides a system to measure snow depth, compaction and temperature to verify a winter's harshness. The Winter Severity Index in Santa Fe confirms what the people of Valtura already know. It was a hard winter that rolled in early, hit hard and stayed into March. Then the snow melted, flooding many arroyos and exposing a shocking loss of cattle for many ranchers.

The precise loss is difficult to determine, especially because there are rumors of ranchers using the blizzard to explain cattle lost to other reasons. When Centori reported his actual cattle losses due to the winter rather than cover up all losses, his men were not surprised. Centori's leadership and the Circle C cowboys, all men of bravery, saved many head of cattle and protected the ranch from what seemed to be certain disaster.

During the hard winter, in January 1911, the voters throughout the territory approved the state constitution. The statehood process began the previous year when Congress authorized New Mexico to call a state constitutional convention. Now, the territory waits for Congress to pass a joint resolution for statehood.

Adobe awakes as usual in the pre-dawn hours with a sense of sadness about an old romantic misfortune. Since his army days, he has taken his coffee very strong. While hand grinding the beans, he anticipates a happier mood. Nights are the loneliest time for him. At times, he walks around the spacious Circle C lamenting the emptiness and he fears that he will always be alone. Although he could easily be with a woman, mythologizing the past clouds his decisions. He pours a full cup of strong black coffee. The mawkish moments never endure beyond his second cup of coffee.

Looking out the large windows in the great room that face the mountains, Adobe cradles the cup of black coffee. Spring has arrived, yet a thin white blanket of snow still covers the landscape. The snow will be gone before noon as the strong spring sun takes control.

The Circle C commands magnificent mountain views. The rugged Sandia Mountain range to the east, located in Corona and Bernalillo counties, is over nine thousand feet above sea level and more than fifteen miles north to south. Over the Sandia Mountains, the sun appears and angles across the valley, casting mystical shadows. With his full cup of coffee, Adobe steps outside to the portal of his Spanish Colonial house anticipating a full day.

The Circle C ranch house is a sprawling structure, a one-level construction with many fine architectural features. Like most houses in Corona County, a region with little precipitation, it has a flat roof. The impressive house has projected wooded roof vigas, thick plaster walls, a colonnade of hand-hewn vigas and Oaxacan doors.

Adobe has designed and built a great home filled with attractive cultural aspects, including an array of Mexican tiles. Saltillo tile, terracotta tile in red, yellow and orange hues, and ornately hand painted Talavera tile, create a bright environment. Interior plaster walls painted with shades of terracotta provide texture. Exposed pine ceiling beams with carved corbels and woodwork show the intricate detail of his design.

A stoic figure, Adobe pours a second cup of coffee and goes back inside to the great room. The room's massive floor-to-ceiling kiva fireplace, decorated with vibrant Mexican tile, has a large mantel and heavy iron andirons with a decorative C. The kiva is the focal point of the room and faces a leather sofa, wing chairs and a colorful hand-woven Navajo rug.

Looking into an empty fireplace, Adobe savors his coffee as his thoughts take over. *I don't know if it's time invite Mady to the Circle C; she is different from other women and she certainly indicated interest. An original personality, she loves a chance to disagree. Mady is an attractive, friendly and smart woman. That is more than enough reason to invite her to the Circle C, but Valtura is a small town. If things didn't work out, it could be awkward—better to remain alone than to start a romance I can't finish.*

Restless, Adobe enters the stately Circle C library, a room with large leather wing chairs, an ottoman and another kiva. There are shelves covering two walls and filled with hundreds of books, many purchased at the Union Square Brentano's Bookstore in New York. He always says that if a man reads he will never be lonely—but saying and believing are two different things. On a table between the two chairs is a leather-bound copy of *Ben-Hur, a* novel by Lew Wallace. Wallace was a Union general and a former governor of New Mexico Territory.

On a large desk, Adobe maintains a stamp collection that includes the first appearance of Lincoln on a stamp, issued in 1866 on the first anniversary of the assassination. He sits in a large executive chair; puts down his cup and examines the pride of his collection. Behind his desk, a New York City map hangs on the wall along with a New York Tribune headline reporting the first underground subway in October 1904.

On the opposite wall, a painting called Tugboat with Black Smokestack shows a smokestack emitting golden smoke and an American flag flying. Adjacent to this 1908 Edward Hopper painting is a framed 1905 World Series Program signed by managers John McGraw and Connie Mack.

The New York Giants beat the Philadelphia Athletics with pitcher Christy Mathewson emerging as a star. Looking at the program, Adobe reflects, *Major league baseball seems so far away. Even the most western team, in St. Louis, is over a thousand miles away.*

Drifting to a table with a Victor Talking Machine, he pauses and looks at its picture of a terrier dog that appears to be looking and listening to a phonograph. Sitting on the machine is a recording of "Alexander's Ragtime Band" by Irving Berlin. The song has given the young songwriter immediate fame.

Recordings by the great Caruso and Stephen Foster are among his collection. He plays Caruso's recording of *Pagliacci* and sinks into a large chair. *At times, I feel like a clown when it comes to women,* he thinks. Then the Victor scratches out the aria, "*Recitar! Vesti la giubba.*"

During his time in New York, Adobe saw Enrico Caruso in Verdi's *Il Trovatore* at the Metropolitan Opera on Broadway and 39th Street. After the aria, Adobe plays another recording. He is especially fond of Foster's song "Beautiful Dreamer" with the ballad's poetic lyrics, melody and lullaby sentiment. *What wonderful lyrics praising a sleeping woman. How many more dreams of her waking unto me will I have?* he contemplates.

After his second cup of coffee, Adobe thinks of the success of Circle C—a source of pride. His business sense and good cattle markets have made the Circle C a brand leader among New Mexico cattle ranchers. However, recovering from the winter losses will test his skills.

The spread has a good water supply and good grazing land, providing an economical source of nutrients for cattle. In areas that become drier in the late summer, dams on creeks create ponds of water—critical in the arid high desert. Clumps of trees provide some shade during hot spells and some shelter from bad weather. Each horse has ample stall room in the ranch's fine stables.

At the end of "Beautiful Dreamer," Adobe walks outside to his hand-made lumber bench under the main portal. He scans the Sandia ridge and looks into the coffee steam as a large coyote appears and stares. With sharp pointed ears and nose, the light gray animal is nearly five feet long. The wild dog, about 25 pounds, with a long, bushy tail, symbolizes the open range. Some native cultures respect the coyote as a creator that can be both humorous and dangerous.

The coyote's presence can bring a lesson in balancing wisdom and folly that may help Adobe in the challenges ahead. They have a variety of calls to defend their territory and enhance communication, including howling, yelping and barking.

On this morning, it is not the call that attracts Adobe. He leans forward on the bench as the coyote marches past the portal with confidence and a dead rabbit clenched in his teeth. In legend, some native peoples suggest that the coyote helped God create the earth and the first humans. It is no wonder that this one walks with a certain swagger. Coyotes are adaptable and capable of survival in the harshest conditions. Many have endured the hard winter. For some of the other wildlife, it was the end of the line.

Adobe finishes his second cup of coffee as A.P. and Ellison walk up with three horses in tow. Two horses, Minuteman and Mars, are new to the ranch. The other is Adobe's horse, Patriot, his beautiful stallion and trustworthy companion.

"Good morning, Boss, thought you would be ready," A.P. says.

"I'm ready," he answers while inspecting the new cutting horses for the roundup.

The men and horses are highly skilled in moving and sorting cattle. In the spring, the Circle C and other ranches engage in open range roundups to assemble their branded cattle and identify unbranded cattle. Adobe and the Circle C cowboys will search every part of the ranch for their cattle. They will gather and brand the young calves with a Circle C mark.

"Another roundup, A.P."

"Let's get to gettin'."

Adobe mounts Patriot and leads the cowboys to the open range, his favorite place—and his smile makes a full recovery.

4

MISSING NEW YORK

New Mexico's windy spring season continued, with gusts above twenty miles per hour. On any day in Valtura during the spring, the odds are that the wind will be blowing. Sometimes the wind occurs just before thunderstorms.

With the successful completion of the roundup, Adobe returns to his other responsibilities. The distance from the Circle C to Valtura is fewer than six miles. He usually takes an hour for the trip. Mounted high on Patriot, he slowly rides toward town, passing the familiar landscape. He is a beautiful rider who moves stylishly in the saddle. Together since the army days, Patriot is a trusted companion. The stallion, a reddish brown bay with a black mane, tail and lower legs, is intelligent, playful and loyal. Although past his prime, the old warhorse is not easily frightened and has an uncanny ability to adapt to changing situations.

Adobe stops at the top of a low hill and bends to whisper something into Patriot's ear as Valtura, covered in sunlight, comes into sight in the distance. Valtura Plaza is more of a rectangle than a square; the surrounding buildings show the town's Spanish Colonial origin. In the nineteenth century, most of the houses clustered around the plaza. Corona Street, the main public passage, extends from the plaza and runs east toward the mountains, becoming East Corona Street. The thoroughfare goes directly in front of the plaza's north side. Beyond the plaza and west toward the mesa, the street becomes West Corona.

Adobe enters town on East Corona Street and moves past an old familiar weather-beaten sign and wonders about its accuracy.

VALTURA, NEW MEXICO,
POPULATION 1460

A period of steady development for the community and an expansion of the town limits marked the first decade of the twentieth century. The 1910 census results are sure to show population growth in Valtura.

At the turn of the century, the earth around Valtura yielded almost $10 million in silver, and newspapers printed stories about the silver strike. During the boom, saloons, brothels and gambling places were common sights around the plaza. Those with good luck found fortunes but many more found disappointment.

When the mother lode ultimately faded, Valtura was no longer a boomtown, but it was far from a ghost town. As a silver mining town, there was more time for economic development than many short-lived gold rush towns. Ambitious men and women embarked upon new enterprises and developed non-silver based businesses. Valtura prospered from the foresight of leading citizens and from the surrounding ranches.

Railroads reduce travel time and cost, stimulate consumption and production, and promote prosperity. Even though the rail station is five miles from the plaza, Valtura's growth has been good. During the last decade, the town boundaries had pushed away from the plaza in all directions. Nevertheless, the poorly located rail station needs a rail extension into town.

The growth created three sub-villages: Valtura Plaza, the old village around the central plaza; Valtura Park, the area on West Corona Street toward the mesa; and Valtura Heights, the area on East Corona Street toward the foothills. Today, the town map shows ten north-south and eight east-west streets.

Electric lights are gradually supplanting the old gas lamps and horsepower is replacing horses. Since Henry Ford's automobile assembly line initiatives in 1903, Valtura has been entering the twentieth century. Horse-drawn traffic is fading as automobiles emerge, along with the familiar sounds of *Ah-ooo-ga, Ah-ooo-ga* from the horns of the Ford Model A and other motorcars.

Small shops and houses, some that are affluent homes, line fashionable East Corona Street. Progressing along the street, Adobe passes the old mission church and waves to Padre Morales before crossing Mission Road. Franciscan Friars established missions from San Francisco to San Antonio, including Valtura.

"Buenos dias."

"Padre Morales. How are you?"

"I am fine, but how are you? I see you much too infrequently."

Adobe never joined a church. He smiles and says in a low voice, "I'm tolerable."

Crossing First Avenue on Patriot and approaching Valtura Plaza, Adobe sees several people, all well-known faces, standing near the center gazebo engaged in conversation. They stop talking to wave and acknowledge the renowned rider. Iron benches shaded by old cottonwood trees that are in bloom encircle the plaza. Under the largest tree, three young women—all dressed in Edwardian elegance—stop their discussion and call out in harmony, "Sheriff Adobe!"

"Good morning, Ladies."

The women share a knowing smirk, as Adobe turns left away from his office, forgetting their existence. Klara Morgenstern is their current rival for his affection, or at least his attention. The Union Hotel and the Valtura Journal, both timber-framed structures, are located on the east side of the plaza. The idea of Klara working in the Valtura Journal office is a strong stimulant—he takes the romantic road.

Almost on cue, Klara gracefully steps outside and using her most charming voice declares, "*Guten Morgen*, Sheriff."

"Klara," he says with a smile.

In her late twenties with fair skin, she has a slight German accent—when speaking Engish—and a well-defined face.

"It looks like another beautiful bright blue sky day," she says.

"Yes, it does."

Klara is a curious, smart woman, five feet seven inches tall, with deep blue eyes and flowing light brown hair framing fine features. Although slow to smile, when she does, she unveils perfect white teeth.

"And the future is bright too."

"It's a great day, but I don't speculate about the future."

Of course he does.

She wears an unadorned black skirt and a sophisticated blue blouse. The blouse, opened at the neck, reveals turquoise jewelry and an alluring nature.

"*Adios* for now, Klara."

On the edge of the plaza, two Civil War field guns sit as a silent reminder of New Mexico's involvement in the war. Confederate forces from Texas entered New Mexico and defeated the federals at Valverde. After the victory, they took Valtura, Albuquerque and Santa Fe. Yet, it was a reversal of fortune for the confederates at Glorieta Pass, forcing them back into Texas.

The two-story stately masonry brick county courthouse is dominant on Corona Street, towering over the other buildings on the plaza. The sheriff's office, a one-story building made of mud bricks, is adjacent to the courthouse at the corner of First Avenue. The county attorney's office and town hall are on the second floor of the courthouse.

The First National Bank of Santa Fe, the oldest in the territory, with a strong brick facade, is on the west plaza, beside the timber-framed post office. Off the west plaza stands the telegraph office with the mercantile off the east plaza. Spanning the entire south side of the plaza on National Street is the spacious Mad Mady's Saloon.

Adobe stops, dismounts and tethers Patriot to a post in front of his office on the plaza's northeast corner. This geographical point sometimes causes his thoughts to turn to New York. *I love New Mexico, but those fine hotels, fancy restaurants, high-class saloons and high-class women in New York...and the women in their new revealing bathing suits in Coney Island.*

The Southern Railway in El Paso makes New York in five days. During Adobe's last New York visit, he arrived at Pennsylvania Station. The grand structure, completed in 1910, is a masterpiece of Beaux-Arts architectural style and a monumental entrance to New York. Through the colossal waiting room, inspired by the Roman Baths of Caracalla, Adobe entered New York feeling like a king.

During that visit, he was among the first to see the Edison Company's movie, *The Great Train Robbery*, at the Eden Musee on 14th Street. There is talk in Valtura about building a motion picture theater off the plaza on National Street. For now, the people go to Albuquerque to see a picture show.

Mady is from New York too. We should travel the rails home for a while, but I guess I am home, he thought.

New York is now a teeming metropolis of almost five million people and hundreds of motorcars. Auto-taxis replaced the hansom cabs with the motorization of fire wagons, sanitation wagons and the mails. There is a cacophony on the streets of New York that bursts with energy as the cadence of street life speeds up.

I guess I miss New York, but the spirit of freedom surges in New Mexico, he thinks, while glancing at a sign surrounded by a multicolored pattern of Mexican tiles.

A. CENTORI, SHERIFF,
CORONA COUNTY
NEW MEXICO TERRITORY

Adobe dismounts as his long duster flaps open in a sudden wind, revealing his ivory-handled, silver-plated pistol. Swinging open a creaking door, he finds the Spartan two-room office cold. A cast-iron stove, sitting on a wood plank floor that is clean most of the time, will soon remove the chill.

A portable Remington typewriter and a new telephone with the number 3222 sit on his desk. Old copies of "Collier's Weekly, An Illustrated Journal" obscure a sepia photograph of a fine-looking dark-haired woman. The woman in the photo holds a special place in his heart, a role many mistakenly attribute to Mady Blaylock. The lockup, empty most of the time, accommodates four guests.

Adobe goes to a table under a wall-hung Corona County map, and makes a pot of coffee. There, he sits in a swivel chair behind a roll-top desk and looks at the photograph of his mythologized woman. Although he is in a maelstrom of romantic ambiguity, he keeps the photo from the past.

5

Mad Mady's Saloon

As spring turns to summer, strong hot winds and dust storms swept through the Circle C Ranch early this morning, driving most prey underground. It could be a tricky day for the coyotes, but they are tenacious, adaptable, opportunistic predators with a variety of hunting techniques. The coyotes survived the hard winter; today's dust storms should not be a problem.

Adobe arrived early at his office, thus avoiding a ride to town in the heat. Savoring his cup of coffee, he breaks from a feeling of indifference and walks to the front windows to study Mad Mady's Saloon. Across the plaza on National Street, Mady is probably working on her saloon books.

Much of Mad Mady's life, shrouded in tall tales, has inspired curious stories. She resents questions about her eastern origins and often answers with obscure replies. Consequently, it is hard to sort fact from fiction.

Mad Mady—born Elizabeth Mady Blaylock thirty-five years earlier in New York City—is coolheaded, with a superb mind, and speaks as if she obtained an education back East. She is an attractive woman who stands at five feet five inches, with wavy black hair and hazel eyes. She usually wears the same outfit of blue pants, a red shirt with a blue vest, and a dark brown hat. The hat is a trademark for Mady; it has a flat round brim and top with a black ribbon, a leather cord hangs loosely under her chin.

As a child, her sister Sharon, a constant antagonist, called her Mad Mady. It did not make sense; it just hurt. Elizabeth countered by adopting the name Mad Mady to neutralize Sharon's insult. Overall, she is self-assured and inclined toward the sunny side of life.

Most accounts agree that Mady arrived in Valtura in 1901 and worked downstairs at McNeely's Saloon. Jake McNeely's saloon was one of the first structures built during the silver rush. As a capable negotiator, Mady saw an opportunity after McNeely's death and bought the saloon from his widow. She became an active proprietor and renamed the place, Mad Mady's Saloon.

The downstairs at Mad Mady's Saloon supports a long bar, a variety of unmatched chairs and tables, a stamped tin ceiling and gas wall fixtures. The timber floor foundation is askew, but is as strong as the proprietor's personality. In the far corner, strategically placed to survey the entire room is Mady's table. She holds court, works on her books, and watches the saloon activity. Only a few select people sit at her table; Adobe is among the fortunate ones.

Mad Mady's Saloon was an established business before Adobe arrived in Valtura. After a few encounters, the former New Yorkers became fast friends with chronic romantic tension. Mady loves Adobe's clear, blue eyes, his intelligence, his physical strength and his bravery as a war hero. She is attracted to his free, friendly and charismatic nature, but at times sees his independence and self-sufficiency as egotistical and isolated. Sometimes his charming smile provides Mady with a sense of confidence. Most of all, he seems to be genuinely interested in her thoughts and feelings.

Mad Mady's Saloon offers whiskey, cigars, gambling and more.

Upstairs, at the saloon, the rooms are small and crowded each with a wardrobe, a dressing table and a chair. Not intended for long-term use, the cramped accommodations each include a washstand and a bed of iron or a brass bedstead with four-posters in hardwood. The least kept secret in town is the perfumed, painted women and their upstairs transactional and, in most cases, transformational services.

There are no discreet brothels in Valtura. The commerce is profitable and visible. Such enterprises exist at the law's discretion. Mady's doves arrived during the silver rush and before the virtuous women, so they are unlikely to leave. Sheriff Centori ignores the upstairs business, believing that we all create our own moral universe.

Mad Mady's is the social center of Valtura, where people share happiness and commiserate. Tonight is no exception. While the piano player bangs out barely recognizable tunes, Adobe walks into a loud room clamoring with voices. The crowd is larger than usual, but Mady notices Adobe's arrival and his magnetism that lights up the room. Many people turn their heads to acknowledge him—and respect his importance as statehood delegate. Ben, the piano player, turns around and smiles. Men of charisma can become the center of attention. Adobe strives for freedom; yet women see a certain romance about his life.

The bar, the poker, and the faro tables are thick with Valtura denizens, cardsharps and spectators along with the obvious doves. Drinks are flowing and waiters move swiftly around, balancing trays filled with bottles and glasses.

Adobe sits down at the table with Johan Morgenstern and A.P. Baker and immediately orders more drinks. Being generous is an attractive quality to Mady—who is still watching from her table. All three men have cigars and clink their whiskey glasses.

Johan is editor-in-chief of the Valtura Journal. Well versed in

German, he is of medium height and frame, in his mid-fifties with gray hair.

"Congratulations on creating a new state constitution, Adobe." Johan calls out.

The hullabaloo makes conversation difficult. Adobe strains his voice, "Thanks Johan, I'll be happy when statehood is a reality. It has been a long road with many delays. Geography, economics, culture and politics have all played a part in preventing statehood." Adobe looks around for Mady and goes on, "Regardless of the explanation, it's long overdue. TR said, while in the White House, that we should achieve statehood and self-government and not stay in a condition of tutelage."

A.P. adds, "Yes, sir. As a state, we can make as much racket in Washington as we need to serve New Mexico."

Adobe agrees by saying, "Yes, the Territorial Clause of the Constitution says 'Congress shall have power to dispose of and make all needful Rules and Regulations respecting the Territory.' As a state, we will at least have *some* tangible influence on the national game in Washington."

A.P. offers, "I hear towns across the territory are holding Territorial Statehood Fairs to support and encourage statehood. Valtura should keep up with the times."

Adobe nods and looks up at the tobacco smoke filling the space between the huge vigas. He thinks about the fresh air in the plaza but instead of going outside, he adds, "We can obtain representation in the House and Senate and an opportunity to secure the boon that every free American citizen desires. As a territory, New Mexico has long been without the self-government inherent in statehood."

"Statehood has been an issue all of my life," A.P. says.

"That's right, even before your time. The first attempt occurred within a few years of the American occupation. To the credit of those first constitutional framers, they wanted to prohibit slavery and that killed the bill."

"We should all carefully read the statehood bill," Johan advises. After remaining silent a moment, he presents a concern, "The federal system is considered permanent."

Surprised by the statement, Adobe and A.P. look at each other.

Adobe, compelled to respond, says, "That's right. The national Constitution was created by *we the people* and it binds the states to the Union."

Johan counters with, "Yet it is argued that the Constitution was a compact between sovereign states who can decide to be independent."

A.P., quiet too long, says, "It seems to me that my daddy and the rest of Mr. Lincoln's army settled that argument over fifty years ago."

Before Johan can reply, Adobe states, "The Supreme Court said the Constitution, in all its provisions, looks to an indestructible Union composed of indestructible states."

"But, Sheriff, federal control is clear in article 1, section 8 of the Constitution. It gives Congress the power to collect taxes and provide for the general welfare," Johan counters.

"That's true, Johan. Yet I point you to the Tenth Amendment, which states that powers not delegated to the U.S. by the Constitution are reserved to the states or to the people."

"Okay, Sheriff, but do you think the general welfare provision can't be applied by Washington to implement powers *beyond* those listed in the Constitution?"

"Johan, there are limitations on the interpretation of the general welfare clause. Madison said that if Congress can do whatever *can be done* with money, the government is no longer limited."

"Exactly my point, the federal government can and will grow." Johan is adamant. "There are many in government and in the general public that support limited federalism. Many consider internal improvements, taking money from one region to finance another, to be wrong."

"Johan, the national defense and the preservation of the country's economic integrity are limited matters involving the general welfare of its citizens," Adobe stresses.

"Perhaps I can provide some general welfare," a soft, seductive woman's voice suddenly interjected.

The men stop their conversation and look up at Mercy, an attractive, petite woman with long brown hair. She is in her late-thirties, somewhat old for a dove. A.P. appreciates the interruption more than the others do. A leading upstairs woman, Mercy leans over the table smiling and continues, "Enjoying the evening?"

Before anyone could answer, Mady rushes to confront her, "Mercy you know the sheriff and his friends do their own inviting. Isn't that right Sheriff?"

Adobe enjoys Mady's accent—he misses New York. He smiles an implied agreement, but A.P. exclaims, "Speak for yourself, Boss!"

There is a bray of laughter. After another round of hilarity and drinks, Johan—hiding his lechery—says goodbye. A.P. goes upstairs with Mercy, and Mady and Adobe sit alone at Mady's table.

"You have quite a crowd tonight, Mady."

Mady, dressed in her usual blue pants, red shirt and blue vest, says, "Yes, business is good on both levels."

After glasses of whiskey, Adobe says, "You were pretty adamant with Mercy; the lady doth protest too much."

"I guess your fancy education forgot to inform you that the meaning of protest in Shakespeare's time was to *declare,* not object."

"Whether you declare or object too much, a person's credibility is at risk."

"Stop flattering yourself, Adobe."

Adobe laughs and says, "I don't mean anything by it."

"That's the trouble; I don't know what *you* mean, but I have large ideas about us."

He removes his hat, suddenly feeling uncomfortable with the direction of the conversation, but says, "You know I care about you. I admire how you go after what you want. You wanted this saloon, you were determined to get it and now you got it."

She looks at her glass for a moment then coldly says, "Thanks. I always thought we could be more than friends, but I'm not so sure." Mady goes on, "You make me feel inferior to that unknown woman in that cheap frame on your desk."

"Damn it, Mady," Adobe slams his fist on the table.

Perhaps he was directing his anger toward an easier target than the one in that cheap frame. The noise causes a few people to turn around. He quickly laughs to conceal his reaction from the crowd and says, "You are genuine about what you say, without caring what others may think."

Ignoring his laughter and words, she responds, "Why keep the mysterious photograph visible if you wish not to discuss her? You could keep it at your precious Circle C. Few people visit there."

She may have pushed too far. His tight smile offers reluctant approval of her rant. He keeps her at a safe distance and avoids other women in her presence. After ten years, this attitude is rather ridiculous to Mady. Will Adobe ever destroy the photograph? No one knows the answer, least of all him.

"Look, it's none of my business," Mady continues, "but you seem to measure any possible romance against Miss Mystery in a Woolworth frame. In your social world...." She stops and waits for his reaction. Adobe, knowing he needs to change his attitude toward women, stares and says, "You are doing fine."

"That woman is keeping you stuck in the past, preventing you from seeing a bright future, or any future," she states aggressively.

"Now who's flattering themselves?" he chuckles.

"Adobe, forget about me. How can you compare every other woman to Miss Mystery? Is she really the one and only ideal?"

"Could you please stop calling her Miss Mystery?"

"I would if you gave her a name! However, you are the one that placed her on a pedestal and mythologized her. No woman could ever be as good as your perceived perfection of Miss...."

"Are you done, Mady?"

"Yes, I'm certainly done. You have charisma, but no brains when it comes to me. Remember, we are all unique. I have a saloon to run. Enjoy the rest of the evening, Sheriff."

Mady briskly walks away. She admires the respect he gives others, but not the way he treats her. It is all he can give, at least for now.

Johan is putting his paper to bed, A.P. is doing the same with Mercy, and Adobe sits alone. He decides to get out of the smoky saloon and head for the brisk air of the plaza. The night air is particularly sweet. *"Mystery woman in a cheap frame," that hurt, but I guess I deserve it for treating women in an incompetent manner.* He thinks, *I know people show who they are, yet often it's ignored because we tend to see others as we wish them to be—not as they really are. Why do I still see that photo as I wish her to be?*

Adobe's affairs of the heart will soon be complicated with affairs of state. His personal problems are about to be placed in perspective by the Revert Document. He looks at his watch. *It is time to return to my precious Circle C,* he thinks.

6

La Guerrillera

Back at the Circle C, Adobe sits on the portal and stares at the stars above. Thousands of crickets scream zaa-zee, zaa zee, disturbing his thoughts. At times, he feels his attitude and behavior toward Mady are unfair. Tonight was one of those times.

During conversations with Mady, he often thinks about another woman, who is a mystery to her, but painfully known to him. After ten years, she is still part of his thoughts—and Mady has certainly noticed his mind wandering back in time. Adobe frequently recalls his army time in the Spanish-American War. It was a long time ago, but remains fresh in his memory.

It was January 1898. An American battleship, the *USS Maine*, arrived in Cuba to protect U.S. interests during a time of revolutionary fervor. A month later, she exploded, and swiftly sank, killing 274 men. Although the cause was initially unclear, the United States Naval Court of Inquiry in Key West said that a mine had caused the explosion. The U.S. blamed Spain, which was trying to suppress the Cuban revolt. This conclusion precipitated the Spanish-American War.

In April, the American army, including the 6th U.S. Cavalry, sailed from Tampa Bay, Florida, to Havana Harbor, bringing the cavalry back into action. Afterward, the 6th joined the 1st U.S. Volunteer Cavalry, Roosevelt's Rough Riders, as part of the 1st Brigade of the dismounted cavalry division. In July, the division moved against Spanish positions on San Juan Heights.

Captain Aldoloreto Centori and Sergeant John Murphy of the 6th U.S. Cavalry led two batteries of Gatling guns close to the Spanish lines. They opened up with heavy fire, while the Rough Riders poured additional fire on the flanks. This forced the defenders into the jaws of hell, igniting the charge up the hill and ending Spanish resistance. Both soldiers fought brilliantly and received the Medal of Honor for heroism. The Battle of San Juan Hill was decisive and the most famous battle of the conflict. In the same month, the battle in Santiago ended the Spanish naval presence in Cuba, preventing resupply of the army and leading to Spanish surrender.

In August 1898, Spain accepted President McKinley's terms and the Protocol of Peace between the United States and Spain ended the war. America had overwhelmingly defeated Spain in a few months, the expected outcome. As a declining power thousands of miles from Cuba, Spain was no match against an emerging power ninety miles from Cuba. As a result, the U.S. acquired the Philippines, Puerto Rico and Guam, whereas Spain was paid $20 million.

After the hostilities finished, the American army waited for its return to Tampa Bay, allowing time for the soldiers to explore Havana, one of the oldest cities in the western hemisphere. On a late summer day, Centori and Murphy, looking dashing in their blue cavalry tunics and khaki pants at the Plaza de Armas, the center of Havana life, were drinking café cubano—so strong and black it would surprise the uninitiated.

The coffee was so powerful Centori expected to be awake for hours, but nothing prepared him for the awakening that was about to happen. Halfway through a Havana Perfecto, Centori became intrigued with a woman sitting alone at another table. He waited for a chance to see her face. She was a female guerrilla fighter or guerrilla girl, a revolutionary woman determined to liberate Cuba from injustice.

Gabriella Zena, a young, stately, gracious and strong leader of an independence movement, would change his life. She instinctively turned toward him and smiled. About her face was a splendid beauty that framed a charming smile, revealing a confident attitude. Mysterious, glowing eyes missed nothing and appeared filled with passion for her country and perhaps the right man.

Centori saw a special woman with a bold heart and a brave mind. *She is a descendent of the goddess Athena who clashed with the Giants,* he thought. Guerrilla fighters are often from the indigenous peasantry class, but *La Guerrillera* was from a family of financially successful planters and was educated at the National Autonomous University of Mexico in Mexico City.

Gabriella's black hair was straight, long and wrapped in a band bearing the words *Cuba Libre.* Although dressed for war, her inviting sensual lips signaled love. The Cuban revolution had ended, yet when their eyes locked for the first time, a quiet revolution began in Centori's heart. Her large eyes were dramatic and of circular splendor. Centori was immediately fascinated, discovering that the arrows of Eros can be sharper than the arrows of war. She was more than mesmerizing, compelling him to speak.

"*Buenos dias, Señorita. Soy Capitán* Aldoloreto Centori."

"*Hola Capitán, soy Gabriella Zena.*" She spoke with a striking voice.

"*Usted parece estar disfrutando de este hermoso día, Señorita Zena.*" (You seem to be enjoying this beautiful day, Miss Zena.)

"*Nuestra victoria hace cada día hermoso.*" (Our victory makes every day beautiful.)

He raised his cup to salute the victory; John Murphy took his leave.

Gabriella smiled and said, "*La Guerra de la Independencia fue mas corta de lo que se esperaba.*" (The war was shorter than expected.)

"*Afortunadamente fue solo una guerra de tres meses.*" (Fortunately, it was only a three-month war.)

To impress Centori, she switched to English with a Spanish accent. Her English was flawless.

"José Martí's leadership was inspiring. He gave the order to start the Revolution. We consider him the father of our country and I was a close advisor," she proclaimed.

Centori speculated on how close and said, "Your passion for the cause is remarkable and principle motivates you, not pay. I admire that in you, *Señorita.*"

"*Gracias, Capitán.*"

"Americans fought against Spanish rule for humanitarian reasons, and the United States is in full support of Cuban independence," he proudly said.

"Yes and American businessmen are in full support of their economic interests in Cuba," she quickly replied.

The somewhat cynical comment surprised Centori, but she was beautiful enough that he focused on their common ground as military allies and potential romantic partners.

"Americans have a history with Cuban sugar and shipping, Captain Centori."

Again, he thought, *if this is flirting I have much to learn from her.*

"There have been revolts before, always suppressed by Spain," she said. "This time the Americans made the difference."

Better, he thought. Sensing her growing interest, he found the courage, perhaps more than he needed to attack San Juan Heights, to ask about a rendezvous.

"*Señorita Zena*, would you like to meet again before I leave Cuba?"

"You are leaving soon?"

She sounded disappointed and Centori wondered if her reaction was to him or to the American troops leaving Cuba.

"Yes, troop withdrawal has started; it should be within a few weeks for my unit."

Gabriella finished her café cubano, picked up her flat black Spanish riding hat, looked deeply into his eyes and said seductively, "Is tomorrow too soon?"

The immediate willingness to come together startled him, but it was natural for her. After a few words, he watched her walk away with the instincts of a jungle cat and focused on the flowing movements of her graceful body.

They had agreed to meet at a café a few blocks from the central plaza, at *Plaza del Catedral* near Havana's Cathedral. As he walked to the café, music was emanating from the several open-fronted narrow restaurants. Aldoloreto approached their rendezvous place; it had a strong smell of tobacco.

He wanted to be first at the café to greet her, but she was already waiting. Moving through the early afternoon crowd, he saw her. Gabriella sat at a corner table that had a decanter of red wine and two glasses. Without a word, she lifted the decanter and filled two glasses. He saw eyes that shimmered with intelligence, impeccable character, and vibrant sexuality. Indeed, she was at the height of her beauty and of her power as she handed him a glass while flashing a flirtatious smile.

"Thank you, *Señorita*. You are not the shy type," he said while sitting down.

"Not in my line of work."

"And you are successful in your work."

"Our work is not done yet. We wait for Spain to formally turn over Cuba's government to the U.S. and then for the U.S. to turn over Cuba's government to the Cubans."

Sensing concern he said, "Of course, my country has no interest in staying in Cuba."

"Of course not," she said with a touch of irony. "But the Americans do control the Havana Bay channel."

"True, those old forts guard the channel entrance."

"Captain, we have been a Spanish colony for several hundred years. My country has been in an armed struggle against the Spanish Crown for thirty years."

"Thanks for the history lesson," he said, immediately regretting the sarcasm.

She looked at him hard but said nothing; she did not have to. After a few moments of uncomfortable silence she said, "Aldoloreto, you do not retreat from your opinion just to win me over. You are honest and say what you mean. You speak truthfully in a confident and bold way. I admire that."

"We may differ on certain issues, but I believe we have much in common."

"Yes we do. We are both disciplined and in control of life. Yet you seem to be more relaxed than I am."

"I'm relaxed now that the war has ended, and of course, in meeting you.

She smiled and said, "Do you like Havana?"

"Very much so," he stopped to pour more wine, "especially the narrow streets and Spanish plazas, with all those refined colonial and baroque buildings. They are architecturally appealing to me. I hope to design my own house one day."

"You would design a fine house, Aldoloreto."

"Gracias Señorita and I like the café cubano. Sure is a strong brew, but I like it."

A second decanter of red wine encouraged further discussion and at the end of their afternoon encounter, she surprised him by asking, "Aldoloreto, would you like to see my home on Sunday?"

An accelerated courtship is far from routine, but few things are routine in wartime.

"Of course I would."

Later that week in the officers' quarters, he reduced his feelings to words while he savored the anticipation of seeing her on Sunday.

> *She stopped me when the lightning bolt struck with all the power of Zeus. This flower was so grand and dramatically beautiful. Perhaps she walked a few inches above the ground, not even a whisper as she moved. Yet she could not hide her radiant beauty.*

The full silvery moon provided enough light to see the street sign: Calle Vera Cruz. Her house at number 48 was a stately two-story baroque structure. Centori stopped in front of a grand ornate door and looked up, absorbing the atmosphere. He then reflected on the words of Dante Alighieri: "*Love with delight discourses in my mind, upon my lady's admirable gifts, beyond the range of human intellect.*"

Centori was surprised to find such a fine colonial mansion. Her great grandfather, a founding member of the Havana Society, built the house. In 1791, several Habaneros from the upper stratum of Cuban life promoted agriculture, stock raising, popular industry and youth instruction. He knocked on the solid wood door and she opened it, smiling.

"Good evening, Aldoloreto. Or should I call you Adobe?"

Instantly accepting the intimate expression of her feelings he said, "Yes I like it because you like it."

He had a new name, perhaps a new life. He never told anyone about the origin of his name. That night Adobe was born in more than one way and he was about to have the adventure of a lifetime.

Gabriella, a strong woman, spoke gently as he stood in the center of the doorway.

"Please come in, Adobe."

"*Gracias Gabriella, estas mas bella que nunca esta noche.*" (You look even more beautiful tonight), he said while removing his campaign hat.

She wore a side-slit black form-fitting dress covering her full, well-rounded breasts and a gold cross around her neck. The long, dangling earrings with matching bracelets and her perfume confirmed Adobe's almost obsessed interest. Her high-button shoes had a two-inch heel, elevating her to his height. They were eye to eye and he liked it that way. It was not love at first sight, but he was definitely falling fast.

Goddess Gabriella's smile spoke volumes about how she viewed this charming and dashing cavalryman. She looked deep into his eyes and found his sincerity. Adobe broke the moment with, "This is a fine house in a fine neighborhood."

"It has been in my family for many years."

She led him to a large, comfortable parlor and he watched the gentle swinging of her hips. It was dark and a few candles provided ambient light. In this glow, she looked especially lovely.

"I am sorry you are leaving Cuba so soon," she said without concealing her sadness.

"Now that I met you, I am not in a hurry to leave," he smiled and offered, "Our pullout shows that the U.S. has no interest in colonizing Cuba."

"You are naïve. The U.S. is just 90 miles from Cuba and just as we were about to beat the Spanish, the United States declared war on Spain."

"Are you forgetting the men lost on the *Maine* at the hands of the Spanish?" he said forcefully.

"Allegedly by Spain," she said with equal force.

"The U.S. is clear on that issue."

"Are you saying I am a liar?" she asked defensively.

"No, of course not, just misinformed." Adobe added, "I'm sorry. I know there is a wider world out there with its problems. But we have a world too, right here, tonight."

"This is not about you and me, it's about Cuba."

We both love our country—too bad it is two different countries, he thought.

"What are your plans now that the war is over?" he asked.

"There still is much work with the new government, but it is difficult for a woman to enter government in Cuba. Yet I will somehow be part of the Cuban constitutional convention and the election process," she proclaimed.

"I'm sure you will be involved with the new government."

"Perhaps, but women are heard less than men in Cuba. My father taught me to be relentless and to listen to the people most upset by government policies, but it may not be enough."

"You're an important and forceful woman."

Gabriella took the comment as an accolade and an invitation, but changed the tone, sensing that further policy discussion might cause a rift between them.

Smiling she said, "I admit that confusion is common in government."

He got the hint and agreed. At that moment, he was more interested in her enchanting scent than in U.S. policy anyway.

Gabriella suddenly grabbed his hand and led the way to an elegantly decorated bedroom. The room contained a hardwood, four-poster bed with elaborately carved columns. Tables on each side of the bed held iron candleholders and lit candles. She stood near a silver-framed mirror and a large French window that revealed a bay view and a sky blanketed with stars. A breeze blew through the windows and curtains, creating a gentle noise. It sounded like music to him, perhaps an overture to her song.

Women like Gabriella, who sought intimacy without hesitation and discomfiture, were unique to him. She was not prudish and he was eager to match her attitude. Still holding hands and standing next to the bed, she said, "Do you think war heightens our savage instincts?"

With the message received loud and clear, he pulled her close and whispered his answer in her ear, creating a sense of privacy and excitement. She was a woman who would yield to a man—but only so far.

When he touched her hair, she became soothed and aroused all at the same time. Their lips met before the embrace was complete and her dominant kiss startled him. *Is this the kiss of Athena or Aphrodite?* he thought.

Gabriella closed her eyes, moving her head slightly back. Adobe's heart was about to burst through his chest and he was ready to pour out his heart, but too soon. At that moment, he loved her and knew it beyond any doubt.

Gabriella's powerful kiss was increasingly demanding. Victorian women in America would blush at such behavior. He pulled back and stared into her blazing eyes, still holding tight. Realizing it could be love, she became flooded with gentleness. Acquiescing gracefully, her once resolute mouth softened. The resistance resolved itself as she pressed her body to his.

It was ambiguous as to who was the seducer. When near-perfect lovers meet, it does not matter. In his arms, Gabriella's body communicated readiness and an ability to surrender all. She naturally knew he wanted closeness, not dominance.

"Adobe," she said softly while pulling him closer.

"Yes?"

"Love me, love me now."

Her unbridled passion was most unexpected and most welcomed by Adobe, who waited for her lead. She moved back, released her dress to the floor, gracefully stepped out and offered a smile. There she stood naked and confident—Venus incarnate.

Adobe took an involuntary deep breath at the sight of her loveliness. Magnificence abounded with a flawless figure, long legs, slender hips, wide shoulders, shapely back and supple breasts. Yet Gabriella's eyes were most alluring. The circular majesty of her striking eyes held a singular meaning. At that moment his exultation crystallizes, he would not leave her tonight.

Later, Adobe looked into her sleepy eyes, kissed her lips and said, "*Uno mas*?"

"She smiled brilliantly and said, "*Si, mi amor*."

He complied.

Her uninhibited passion would change things now and for all time.

As the days passed, they spent every available moment together walking the streets, the beaches, and learning about how they thought and loved. Gabriella was more reserved about her feelings for him—not so for Adobe. Although he wondered if she really loved him at all, he reacted to her inspiration by evolving into a better person, into a better man.

One stormy afternoon, while drinking café cubano at the Plaza de Armas, Adobe brought up a painful topic. "You know, the 6th Cavalry can get orders to ship out at any time."

Gabriella knew that an agonizing decision waited. Adobe accepted her silence and changed the subject, "I am going to miss this strong café cubano." It was a poor choice of words.

With a soft, sad smile, she reached into her pocket, "I want you to have this photograph."

Her unmistakable meaning caused Adobe's eyes to well up. The sepia photograph captured the essence of Gabriella's beauty. He placed the photo inside his shirt pocket. Then the skies darkened.

They spent the rest of the day at 48 Calle Del Vera Cruz, loving in tune with the rhythm of the waves crashing on the shore.

It was mission accomplished for the Cuban expedition; departure preparations were underway, with time running out for Adobe and his love. While sharing limited time, they anticipated the fateful day. One night on the beach, connected by a lovers' embrace, he spoke the inevitable words, "The regiment will ship out. I must leave Cuba in three days."

"I know, Adobe. You were distant tonight."

"Gabriella, please come with me. I love you."

Then, in that moment, she became cold and lapsed into silence.

"I love you too, but my country needs me."

"I need you and I want us to have more than memories. We have *every* reason to expect our romance to have a happy ending."

Something about her expression was unclear, perhaps a warning, when she said, "Don't you mean *one* reason?"

He stroked her cheek and gently moved her hair away. "Yes, one all important reason."

Her eyes narrowed and she said sharply, "Is love always enough? My life in Cuba is complicated; my country needs me now. Perhaps I am unlike the women you know in America."

"You are unlike any woman in the world. Come with me to Tampa Bay. I will resign my commission and we can start a new life in America—in New York or out West." His words were rapid fire.

Gabriella was silent for what seemed like an eternity. She finally said, "Adobe, you are tender, warm and kind to me." With tears about to fall, she says, "The more I know you the more I want us to be together. You value and even want a strong woman—I love you most of all for that. I never met a man who respects and accepts me as I am. I will go with you to America."

It was early on the morning of departure and time ticked away. The sun was hot, but the sea breeze from the harbor offered some relief. Adobe waited at the dock with Sergeant Murphy. The ship was about to depart.

"Murph, she's late and this ship will not wait."

"Don't worry, sir; she agreed to travel to Tampa Bay with you. She'll be here."

"Wish I was as sure as you."

The ship's horn blew, piercing human thought. The sound gained the attention of all except Adobe, who stared at the path leading to the ship. No sign of Gabriella. Then a boy appeared selling flowers.

The boy yelled, "*Flores para la venta*." (Flowers for sale.)

Adobe yelled back, "*Chico, aquí, ahorita*." (Boy, come here quickly.)

He grabbed the flowers and boarded the troop ship. Leaning over the rail with Murphy at his side, Adobe strained to see her in the crowd. She was not there.

The final horn blew and the ship departed on time. He released the flowers to the harbor, but kept the sepia photograph. As the flowers fell, every loving link between Adobe and Gabriella seemed to vanish. In an instant, they were strangers again.

Adobe went down hard, with a mind full of thoughts and a heart full of anguish. He could not bear to leave Cuba alone, but suppressed an instinct to jump ship—her absence was painfully plain. Besides, an officer never deserted his men. Gabriella chose her country over him. A new independent Cuba and involvement with the constitutional convention proved to be more exciting than an American soldier and love.

The power of love infected his imagination, projecting Gabriella to the zenith of romantic idealism. She appeared as a princess, but princesses live in storybooks; women live in the real world. Their relationship was a shooting star, an amazing burst of light streaming across the night sky. Yet a shooting star is not a star at all. It is burning dust and rock falling to earth. Perhaps their love was not love at all, or at least not the kind that lasted.

Adobe had gone to Cuba for war, found love on the breathtaking romantic island, and departed in despair. He was leaning over the ship's railing, watching the waves when he turned to Murphy and said, "There is no protection against the distress of love, now that she is gone."

"Sir, as the good book says, let not your heart be troubled, you have survived this war to love again."

"Murph, you're right. I survived this war, and for that, I am eternally grateful."

The ship slowly moved away, with Cuba fading into the mist. Adobe turned to his friend, "All I can think about is Gabriella. The more I turn over thoughts of her, the more distressed I become. Love is merely madness, a poet said. I am feeling much less than sane."

"Yes sir. I understand."

"She is a fiery free spirit, probably not one to settle down. I guess a man in love sees what he wants to see. Don't believe everything you dream, Murph."

"I suppose so, sir. But women are only human."

"Are they?" Adobe shoved his hat down low in indignant silence and spoke no more. As the troop ship departed Havana, he stared at the bay and at an empty future. *Good-bye, my lady.*

The two stoic figures on the ship's rail receded into the horizon. Gabriella's impression on his heart was indelible. It was a cautionary tale that changed Adobe's philosophy on women. From that moment, he would never trust happiness and would keep women at a safe distance. She gave him a name and changed his character. Adobe Centori was made in Cuba.

When the 6th Calvary reached Tampa Bay, the officers and men received orders for New Mexico Territory. They would patrol the U.S.'s southern border with Old Mexico. Once the regiment settled in, Adobe roamed the entire New Mexico Territory and sometimes vanished for days, but always returned on time for his responsibilities.

Spanish New Mexico reminded him of Spanish Cuba—and of Gabriella. He felt at home in New Mexico and if she had second thoughts, the regiment would not be hard to find. The emotional wound was deep; at times, missing her became the air he breathed.

That was the point at which Adobe usually ended his daydream. Still sitting on the Circle C portal, he waits for the bad feeling to subside. He has tried to forget the Cuban experience, but recently the flashbacks occur with increased frequency. Fumbling with the whiskey bottle, he seeks to accelerate the return to the present.

Adobe walks away from the portal and scans the Sandia ridge and the night sky. The beautiful stars stare as if to mock his aloneness. Then, in the shadows, a familiar coyote appears. He is the same wild dog, marching the same familiar path as the humorous and dangerous trickster.

Smells like a rare rain is coming, he thought.

Adobe walks to the placita wall, prompting the coyote to howl, yelp and bark. He finishes his drink and answers the coyote, "Okay, I know I am a fool."

He may be a fool about women, but the trickster can be a portal to renewal.

A.P. approaches the house. "Hey, up late tonight," he ventured.

"Yes, and I see Mercy has not kept you out too late."

"Like you always say, Boss, things start early here at the Circle C."

He smiles. "That's right. See you in the morning, A.P."

"Good night."

Then an odd, large, crested bird with short wings runs by—fast. Roadrunners seldom fly, but when in flight they provide quite a sight. This brown, black and buff roadrunner is almost two feet long including a twelve-inch tail. He pauses in front of Adobe, flashing a curious stare, and rapidly dashes away.

The roadrunner has limited flight, but great speed. Sometimes a weakness can have an impact on strength. Although Adobe is down, he searches for his strength.

7

CAPITAL WOMAN

Adobe leaves the Circle C early in the morning in a futile attempt to escape last night's vivid memories. Although his affair with *La Guerrillera was* over ten years ago, it takes time to get over the unwelcomed memories about Cuba. In his office, recovering from the ghostly visit, he makes a pot of coffee and picks up the new constitution.

Last fall, Adobe and delegates from every county convened in Santa Fe, and drafted and adopted a state constitution. In January of the current year, territorial voters approved the charter. He reads the new constitution:

CONSTITUTION OF THE STATE OF NEW MEXICO
ADOPTED JANUARY 21, 1911
PREAMBLE

We, the people of New Mexico, grateful to Almighty God for the blessings of liberty, in order to secure the advantages of a state government, do ordain and establish this constitution.

ARTICLE I

Name and Boundaries

The name of this state is New Mexico, and its boundaries are as follows...

Remembering the animated conversation with Mady, he places the constitution down and thinks about her. *It is clear enough; she is available to me. All I need to do is ask.* Feeling restless, he abandons the coffee and walks across the plaza to Mad Mady's place. He enters the saloon to the aroma of coffee brewing and wonders if Mady is there.

Unlike last night, the saloon is quiet. He looks around the room of vacant tables. Berta Brandt, a pleasant woman in her forties, is behind the bar reading the Valtura Journal and Mady sits at her corner table poring over papers.

"Morning, Mady," Adobe says carefully, wondering if she holds residual irritation from last night's tense conversation.

"Good morning, Sheriff. Coffee?" she smiles without any hint of anger.

"Sure. That was some revelry last night and lively statehood debate."

"That's true. I'm sure the political debate divided into predictable positions." Mady says, while pushing the papers aside.

"We all know where everyone stands on issues of the day. So, Mady, upstairs was darker than usual last night."

"Oh, really? I didn't notice."

"Did you happen to notice the scantily clad women lining the stairs? Come on, Mady, admit it—you like the upstairs dim so people can pretend it doesn't exist. But the darkness can't conceal the reality behind the doors."

"Sheriff, come down from your high horse. I know you were no stranger to the upstairs life when you first arrived in Valtura." She laughs to herself.

"That has changed," he states firmly.

"Now, that I *did* notice."

Caught in an awkward moment, Mady raises the corner of her mouth, stopping short of a smile. Adobe, captured by a private thought, smiles ever so slightly. Moving away from the subject, he says, “It seemed like most of the town was here last night.”

Mady stares and says, “A few new people too.” Her unusual intonation revealed the first clue of trouble.

“And so?” he says, noticing the worried look on her face.

“One unfamiliar person had something curious to say to Berta.”

Adobe sees her demeanor change and asks, “What’s that?”

“The stranger said there’s a woman in the capital, at the Plaza Hotel.

Mady stops to regain her composure and Adobe wonders what is so upsetting.

She goes on, “This woman was asking questions of anyone who came from Corona County.”

“What kind of questions?”

“About Valtura, the saloon…and me.”

“Do you know why?”

“Berta asked the stranger if he knew the woman’s intentions but he said he never stays anywhere that long.”

“I’m sure it’s nothing,” Adobe says to reassure her. “What’s her name?”

“Santa Fe Sharon,” smiling tightly she continues, “maybe it’s nothing, but it kind of makes sense.”

“What are you talking about, Mady?”

“My sister’s name is Sharon, or I should say my estranged sister. I lost touch with her after I left New York. The last I heard, she was in Old Mexico.”

“Old Mexico, are you sure?”

“I don’t know, as sure as I can be. I mean the telegram came from Mexico City.”

“There is all that ongoing political unrest.”

“I don’t know much about that.”

"President Diaz allowed an election and Francesco Madero won, but Diaz imprisoned him."

"I thought that was last year."

"Yes, but then Pancho Villa and Emiliano Zapata defeated Diaz and Madero assumed the presidency. Right now, Madero is at odds with his former allies, Villa and Zapata."

Instead of contributing to Mady's fears he says, "Old Mexico is a long way from Santa Fe, but how do you know this woman in the capital is your sister?"

"I don't know for sure, but I believe it."

"If Santa Fe Sharon is your sister, what exactly is the problem?"

Mady's voice changes to a certain pitch filled with concern, "Growing up, Sharon was immune to Victorian values, and nouveaux-riches middle class morals were lost on her."

"Okay, but what are you concerned about now?"

"We had a big falling-out back East over Mother Blaylock's estate. My sister is deceitful and not one to forgive and forget, especially when it comes to power and money."

"Forgive and forget?"

Mady ignores the question and continues the preamble, "We are not speaking, but haven't completely cut our ties. One day, I expect her to walk into my place. If she does, our relationship will probably fall back on old conflicts, reducing us to hurtful childhood roles." Mady stops and drops her head.

"What is it?"

"A New York doctor once diagnosed her with some kind of personality disorder; it probably helps her to escape the past."

Adobe looks a little confused so Mady continues, "It disrupts her sense of identity or her ability to maintain an identity. And *now* Sharon Blaylock is Santa Fe Sharon!"

"And her new personality concerns you?"

"It's not her identity so much, it's her intentions!"

"I'm not sure what she has against you, but have you tried to view each other in a new way, Mady? The road to redemption could be open."

"Not likely. Our relationship has always been volatile and our attempts to improve things have never amounted to much. The issues have changed, but I'm afraid our old behavior patterns and emotions have not."

"I wondered why you spoke so little about your New York time, especially since it's my hometown too. I would like to know more about you two. Maybe there are exceptions to the conflict."

"I told you, Adobe, it's doubtful. There are strong motives that act as obstacles with no apparent exception." She says defensively.

"Are you sure you want to talk about this, Mady?"

Mady glances at Berta, who is pretending not to listen, and says, "You see, I was favored over Sharon, and Mother carefully raised and educated me. People back East thought I was an eligible debutante. Mother saw me as a better investment and tended toward my way. This created resentment in Sharon. Then our mother left me $25,000 in her will."

"That's a large amount of money, Mady."

"Yes, I admit that I may have encouraged favorable treatment from mother, but Sharon saw only the bad. The money made everything even worse. She viewed the inheritance with bitterness and stopped hiding her anger. Even small issues caused a fight. Jealousy turned to rage, changing her so much that she was unrecognizable. The more she challenged me, the angrier I became. When there was nothing left to fight over, she fled New York and her negative feelings about me. That was over eight years ago."

"No word in all that time?"

"Every few years I would get a letter saying that she is coming to Valtura—she never did."

Adobe is listening, but looks around for Berta with his coffee. This morning, she is not moving fast. He does not ask for much, but insists on freshly-brewed, strong coffee. Mady continues unabated, "I guess part of her behavior comes from childhood experiences. She could never bear Mother's close scrutiny."

Adobe responds, "Mady, this is the wild west. No blaming mothers here."

"Whatever the cause, Sharon is insistent, scheming and bad-tempered. I'm more accommodating."

This comment surprises Adobe. *Mady is friendly but independent and somewhat detached. Then again, I keep my distance too. All of this is fascinating, but I still need coffee,* he thought.

Pushing back from the table, he again looks for Berta. Mady pauses for a second, and then continues, "Some problems were ignored, but one issue that will never be resolved is Mother Blaylock's treatment and her money. Sharon feels I received an unfair amount of both. Ultimately, she needed relief from her obsession and disappeared, but I knew she would be back one day."

"So before the Santa Fe Sharon story, the last word came from Old Mexico?"

"Yes, about a month ago. She asked for some of mother's money."

"Did you send any?"

"Yes, I thought a part of the $25,000 should go to her."

"What part?"

"I sent $7,000 to her in Mexico—I hope she left Mexico City."

Adobe, still waiting for coffee, says, "Given the political instability with opposing factions and armies posturing for control, what is Sharon doing there—if she is still there."

Mady replies, "I don't know and can't be sure. Could she be in danger?"

Deflecting her concern he says, "Don't worry. You think she's in Santa Fe. I'm going to the capital to see Governor Jackson on July 1st about statehood issues. I will see if the governor or anyone in Santa Fe knows anything about this woman."

"You're leaving," she says, while shuffling papers.

"I'll be back for the Fourth of July celebration," he smiles, "the territory is long overdue for statehood and this year promises to have the best opportunity. Statehood is a top priority, but I will also discuss our rail line extension."

This news hits Mady with a sense of apprehension. Suddenly she feels alone and says, "Thanks, Adobe, but I wouldn't want you to make an enemy of Sharon."

"That's my concern. You and I are friends. More to the point, it's my job."

"It's only your job if she comes to Valtura for wicked purposes."

"You should take it easy today, Mady. Stay away from the worry for a while. Now, what about that coffee?"

Mady presses her lips, nods in agreement and waves to Berta for coffee. Berta serves while trying not to notice Mady's consternation. Mady taps her coffee cup and goes back to her papers thinking, *I can handle my sister.*

Adobe grasps his cup with two hands and tries to make sense of the situation. *Mady is not prone to endless ruminations. Is it a sibling rivalry or is this Santa Fe Sharon business real trouble? Why would she go to Old Mexico? Money clouds human affairs, but my money is on Mady,* he thinks.

Mad Mady myths are long and strong. She may have spent time in mining towns gaining a reputation as a character who likes drinking, gambling and shooting. Adobe has heard it all before, but now the story is coming directly from Mady. *She has uncharacteristically shared much, and I wonder if her new openness is driven by fear or an attempt to draw closer to me. Perhaps both are motivating forces.* Standing to leave, he declares, "When I return from Santa Fe, I'll have information on Santa Fe Sharon."

"Thanks, Adobe."

Finishing the last of the coffee, he tips his hat to Berta and says, "*Adios*, Mady."

Adobe exits and turns left on First Avenue toward the Union Hotel and an inviting aroma of good cooking from the hotel restaurant. From the corner of his eye, he sees a young, confident coyote strutting along Mission Road carrying an old grain sack in his teeth, looking much the role of a trickster. He wonders, *What is in the sack—it looks heavy. Where is the coyote going with that sack and why is he carrying it so resolutely? It looks like a bit of a struggle yet he is so strong-minded, or perhaps just ridiculous. That's what separates the coyote from the wolf—silliness.*

Adobe enters the lobby and smiles at desk clerk James Clarke.

"Good morning, Sheriff," Clarke says.

"James." He replies with a nod.

Continuing across the lobby and into the dining room, he finds a table and sits with his back against the wall. The service is always fast.

"What can I get you, Sheriff?"

"I'll have flapjacks, bacon, eggs with hot green chili, and strong black coffee."

"Right away, Sheriff."

While eating breakfast, he thinks about Mady, who has never been to the Circle C. *She does not know the extent of the story behind the photograph, but I guess the picture speaks for itself.*

When it comes to affairs of the heart, Adobe is a little gun-shy—the ghost of Gabriella sees to that. Yet it is plain to see that Adobe and Mady have a warm relationship. Although their friendship remains devoid of intimacy, the people of Valtura assume otherwise. Swirls of rumors surround them, but he does not care about the gossip.

8

Santa Fe Sharon

While Europe was experiencing the medieval period, Santa Fe was home to Pueblo Indian villages. During the Early Modern Baroque age, Conquistador Coronado claimed New Mexico for Spain in 1540. In 1609, with the Renaissance in bloom, Governor-General Peralta established Santa Fe as the capital, making it the oldest capital in America.

Santa Fe's history of conquest, culture and civilization includes many colorful personalities: Spanish soldiers, American soldiers, French trappers, Franciscan Missionaries, Pueblo Indians, nomadic Indians—and, at the moment, Sharon Blaylock.

Sharon Blaylock is a beautiful, vibrant woman with a keen sense of purpose; she is older and more glamorous than her sister Mad Mady. She perceives Mady as a scoundrel who will get her just deserts—and the long wait could be over. Sharon's involvement in the Old Mexico organization will lead to Mady's fall.

At age thirty-seven, Sharon stands five feet six inches, and has brown eyes and brown hair. She lives near Santa Fe Plaza, alone, without any visible means of support. Some see the Gibson

Girl beauty with a slender body and full bosom as combative, manipulative and a master of the art of self-promotion. Others agree she is opportunistic when it serves her ambitions. She often acts beyond the margins of socially acceptable behavior and from an ego-driven perspective. Sharon has no vision beyond her desires and uses her rapacious sexual appetite to get her way.

When she arrived in Santa Fe, Sharon hastily acquired the image and personality of a New Mexican, adopting her colorful appellation, Santa Fe Sharon. Whether fact or fiction, some say she has been a whiskey peddler, horse thief and cattle rustler, and that she cheats at every turn. Others say she was a part of the great ostentation age in Edwardian New York, her lifestyle defined by all the extravagance of grand balls, dinners and estate parties. Some say she killed her husband back East and fled to New Mexico to escape the law.

This background might have been encouraged, if not fabricated, by Santa Fe Sharon herself. Although the Santa Fe image is now prominent, Sharon has had other distinct personalities. Her multiple personalities become especially evident when it suits her agenda.

Sharon has never stopped long enough to develop a lasting romantic relationship, but there have been many non-romantic physical liaisons. In those instances, she has enjoyed manipulating men in sexual affairs. On occasion, she has found intimacy with women.

Santa Fe is usually cooler than Valtura. Today, Sharon is sitting in the plaza dressed in blue pants, a red shirt and a blue vest, and feeling a little chill. Her dark brown hat, made of felt, has a flat round brim under a flat round top with a black ribbon around it; the leather cord hangs loosely under her chin. Next to her is a slim woman who has ash-blonde hair and sorrowful eyes.

"But where will you go, Sharon?" the woman asks.

Sharon takes out a pack of cigarettes from the new Philip Morris Corporation in New York. Using a paper matchbook, she lights a Marlboro Red Tip with a double-headed match. After a puff she answers, "I told you, I have important business in Albuquerque," she lies.

"What about me?"

"You'll be fine," Sharon curtly replies.

With that, Carrie Carlson approaches the two women. Carrie, a tall blonde woman with blue eyes, is young and eager to make a living away from the brothels of Calle Montano.

"Carrie, this is Dora. She was just leaving." Sharon says dismissively.

"Hello," Carrie replies.

Dora dashes back into the Plaza Hotel.

"Something I said?" Carrie chuckles.

"No, she has the wrong idea about something. Anyway, I understand you're looking for opportunities to get out of Calle Montano."

"Yes, what do you have in mind?"

Concealing her overall purpose in terms of sibling rivalry, Sharon offers, "There's a place in Valtura called Mad Mady's Saloon. Mady is my sister."

Sharon fakes a sentimental moment. Carrie, drawn in, says, "Go on."

"Sure. I'm sorry. I vacillate between a complete break from Mady and exacting payback. Lately, I'm leaning toward revenge."

Carrie, wide-eyed and interested, declares, "What did she do to you?"

"Mady manipulated Mother Blaylock for favorable treatment, more money and inequitable amounts of everything."

As an only child of hard luck, Carrie says, "At least you got something."

"But I didn't get close to what I deserved."

"In life you don't get what you deserve; you get what you negotiate."

Sharon thinks about the comment and says, "You're right, and I plan to do some strong negotiating. Now I understand she's cozy with Sheriff Centori, an important man in Corona County and in the territory."

Carrie inquires, "And this fuels your lust for retribution?"

Failing to mention that associates in Old Mexico support her propensity for payback, she says, "Mady has been feeding my green-eyed monster for a long time and encouraging my actions toward revenge."

"You want her man?"

Sharon answers a question with a question, "You want out of the cat house?"

"So how do I fit in?"

"Well Carrie, now that we've established your interest, meet me tomorrow morning at San Miguel at 8:30. I should have more information and details for you then."

"Okay, Sharon."

"Don't be late, and enjoy your remaining time on Calle Montano," Sharon mocks with pleasure.

"Good day to you too!"

Swaggering through the plaza, Sharon is satisfied that the timing is on target and that the events are moving forward. She made progress by enlisting Carrie, but the prospect of removing Mady and corrupting Centori is more satisfying.

While in Old Mexico, Sharon learned that her Valtura connections are valuable resources to those interested in the Revert Document. All the politics that she does not care about are a welcome pretext for striking at Mady. *Mady's supposed relationship with Centori will end, as will her saloon—in grand style,* she thought with satisfaction, believing that her sister would be shocked. As the proverb says, *vengeance is a dish best served cold.*

The international plot and the need to remake Mad Mady's

Saloon in her own image have trigged another personality crisis. This time Sharon imagines morphing into a sophisticated woman who is fascinated with all things French, a fervent Francophile with interest in French culture, couture and language. Based on the Old Mexico trip, the time has come to advance this ego state—and destroy her sister in the process.

It will be the role of a lifetime, and Sharon is determined to play it to the hilt as a stylish French woman. Decorum, elegance and societal *savoir-faire* are assets for Sharon's assignment. She will rise to the occasion with assistance. There is one place to pursue this change in Santa Fe: Madame Francine Fournier's Salon.

9

EAGLE EYES

Colonel Antonio Santos' well-built brick house, a half-mile and a ten-minute walk from Valtura Plaza, is among several large homes on fashionable East Corona Street. His Victorian-era building, far from being in a state of good repair, has wide eaves, ornamental brackets and some gingerbread trim. The porch provides good views of the Sandia Mountains to the east and of Valtura Plaza to the west.

Each week Adobe takes the road toward the Sandia Mountains to play chess with Antonio Santos. He values the time spent with Santos, especially when he needs to talk. Santos is long past military service, yet he maintains an honorary title of colonel.

At 81 years of age, the colonel has a failing body, but a strong mind. He was born a few years after Mexican independence from Spain in Las Cruces, New Mexico. Founded in 1598, the former Mexican town is one of Spanish colonial architecture—and is similar to Valtura. Following a stellar military career, he settled in Albuquerque in 1880 to write about Mexican history. When the rail line extended, he discovered Valtura. The small town reminded him of Las Cruces at the time of his birth. It was reason enough to make Valtura his home.

As a long-term resident of Valtura and native New Mexican, the colonel has an uncanny familiarity with the people, the culture and the history of New Mexico. He served as a member of the Valtura town council for years, and values his community position as a leading citizen. His opinions on the major issues of the day, which matter to the political class and to the people, make him sought-after for quotes by the Valtura Journal.

Although the colonel usually wins their chess game, Adobe enjoys the old man's company and his wisdom, but most of all the special bond that military veterans share. Both men are former cavalry officers, although from different and, at times, opposing armies.

On the front porch of his two-story house, the colonel, dressed in black, sits at a small, square table covered with a white cloth. He slowly unbuttons his jacket and draws a watch from the vest pocket. The silver watch has a coyote image and two letters engraved on the cover. It is past 1 p.m. Before he can return the watch, he hears, "*Buenas tardes.*"

"Right on time as always, Adobe," he says with a Spanish accent.

"Why would I be late to suffer another defeat at the chessboard," Adobe says while putting down a dry goods sack and a whiskey bottle.

"You have come close to beating me many times."

"Sure. So how are you feeling, Colonel?"

Adobe knows that the colonel never complains, but he asks anyway. In fact, the colonel suffers from many old-age ailments including a debilitating joint disease that restricts his movement.

"No problems." He positions the chessboard on the table between them and they place the beautiful chess pieces on the squares. Qualities such as majesty and pride are apparent in this chess set. The wooden hand-carved work of art is the colonel's prized possession.

When the colonel attempts to stand, Adobe jumps up and says, "Open the bottle, I'll get the glasses."

Once settled in, the colonel pours two drinks and waits for his opponent's opening gambit. Adobe moves his king's knight forward. Carved with skill, the mane on the knight gives life to the piece.

"You are so predictable," the colonel says with affection.

"Some call it dependable, Colonel," he replies with equal warmth.

Openness is an integral part of their friendship. Adobe has shared his New York, Cuba and New Mexico experiences with him.

"Yes, as dependable as an old cavalry officer."

"Maybe that's right. It takes one to know one, Colonel."

The colonel smiles sagely and says, "You always move the knight first because you are partial to mounted soldiers."

"Or because knights are better than bishops," Adobe counters. "They can alternate colors with every move; guard squares of both colors and, by jumping pieces, can occupy positions in your camp."

The colonel, a former mounted soldier, counters with his bishop, implementing its greater scope and mobility as compared to a knight. In terms of strategy and tactics, chess and war are related. The colonel is well versed in both; his renowned military record started as a young soldier during the Mexican-American War.

After a few more moves, the colonel gains a quick advantage in pawn structure and in developing more pieces than Adobe.

"You've obtained the better chance of winning again, Colonel."

"Adobe, you know the fortunes of chess can change as fast as the fortunes of war." He is speaking with authority, credibility and as a veteran of the Battle of Chapultepec. The battle was a U.S. victory at the defended strongpoint of Chapultepec Castle in Mexico City.

Adobe studies the board and notices the colonel is setting his strategy on the right, where his queen is close to his bishop and rook. Staring at the chessboard seeking an answer, he reflects on his friendship with the colonel. In many ways, the colonel is like a father to him. Yet they are on equal footing as ex-army officers and war veterans. Adobe moves his king's knight.

The colonel counters his opponent's probe by moving his pawn forward two squares. Adobe quickly moves his queen's knight forward.

Shifting in his chair the colonel says, "Protecting your queen, I see. You must be in love again."

All the pieces are magnificent, weighted, and felted, yet the queen looks stunning, carved in the highest-grade hardwood.

Adobe looks up with curiosity, not surprise, and says, "What do *you* know about women?"

"True, I have slowed down in pursuing women a little, but I do know *you*."

Adobe has confided his innermost feelings about love, women and especially his Cuban adventure. The colonel is the only one in Valtura who knows about *La Guerrillera*.

"Okay Colonel, you probably know I'm visiting the newspaper office more often these days."

"Of course I know. The press is an important part of your public service job. As a statehood delegate, you should be involved with the Fourth Estate."

"The Fourth Estate? You are being droll."

The colonel tends to obscure an issue until he is sure Adobe is comfortable with discussing the topic, allowing an avenue of retreat. Over the years, talk of women has veered to the negative.

"Not droll, historical. The term Fourth Estate is from the medieval estates of the realm, the church, the nobility and commoners. The press, as a separate entity, is the Fourth Estate."

"Colonel, it's all right. We can talk about Klara."

"Ha-ha, Valtura is not that big. Yes, I know about your interest in Klara Morgenstern." Now the colonel has the material advantage in more and more valuable chessmen, while Adobe has the advantage in the safety of his king. "She is very pretty, a good enough reason for visiting the newspaper. Or are you weary of my counsel and seek Johan Morgenstern?" he added with humor and a friendly grin.

"No one can replace you, Colonel, but can anyone ever replace *La Guerrillera*?"

"That's up to you. She is in your mind, as a filter to your world. You allow the Cuban woman to enter your heart and stay without charging rent. That is fine when you are in love and in each other's arms, but not for a lifetime. She is gone."

As the colonel feared, Adobe drops his head down for a second, indicating the ongoing pain.

"*Mi hijo*, take her from your mind. Make peace with the past. Bury *La Guerrillera* in an unmarked grave in some far away, forgotten place. And when you find a woman to love—hold on to her."

Adobe breaks his gaze with the colonel, studies the chessboard and says, "She is able to rip a man's heart out without a tear."

"Are you sure of that? Or is it a convenient defense against allowing another woman to get close?"

Adobe did not feel the need to confirm or deny the statement.

"Remove the armor forged in Cuba, *mi hijo*. That war is over."

The colonel knows when to stop, and after a pause, asks, "Will Klara make your heart come alive again?"

"Nice to imagine, but I am not sure. It is no secret on the plaza that I see Klara in a new light."

"That light may be her loveliness; have you told her how you feel?"

"Not in so many words, probably not at all."

"You may not be in love. I remind you of a similar conversation about Mady."

"You love to confuse me with the facts, Colonel."

The colonel has heard this story before about other women, starting with Adobe's interest in Mad Mady Blaylock. Nevertheless, he remains a good listener and a good friend.

"Klara is very attractive. We have much in common, with some dissimilar opinions, especially about politics and the territory's quest for statehood."

Adobe moves a pawn two squares and as a conversation gambit says, "Colonel, when we obtain statehood, you should be the first U.S. Senator from New Mexico."

The old man's reaction is less than enthusiastic. The colonel walks the razor edge with dual loyalty to Old Mexico and New Mexico. He does his best in reconciling conflicting emotions. The latest push for statehood stirs old, complicated feelings.

Noticing his lack of reaction Adobe says, "You seem to avoid talking about statehood, Colonel."

Again, the colonel does not react, but finally says, "We both know I am too old to go to Washington. I wish to see you in the Senate."

"Fine, but what about statehood in general?"

"Adobe, have you ever studied the New Mexico territorial seal?"

"Sure, I've seen it, eagles and a Latin motto."

"Yes. There are two eagles, a Mexican eagle and an American eagle. Do you know which eagle is bigger?"

Adobe knows the colonel likes the Socratic method of asking and answering questions to stimulate thinking and illuminate ideas. He accepts this and plays along.

"I never thought about it that way."

"The American eagle is clearly bigger. The coat of arms is the Mexican eagle grasping a serpent in its beak and a cactus in its talons. It is shielded by the American eagle with outspread wings grasping arrows in its talons."

"That's interesting, Colonel."

"Interesting *and* significant—the Mexican eagle is the smaller of the two and watched over by the larger American eagle."

Following a long silence, Adobe says, "Remarkable, I think it symbolizes the territory's acceptance of New Mexico's history, heritage and culture. All of which are part of the new constitution."

"Some have a different interpretation, Adobe. They see the seal as a war trophy representing the strong-armed change of sovereignty in 1846. The American eagle is dominant, with arrows in its talons, wings widely spread, and piercing vigilant eyes when compared to the Mexican eagle."

Before Adobe can respond, the colonel smiles and slowly whispers, "Checkmate."

"*Salud, mi compadre,*" says Adobe.

10

AWAITING INSTRUCTIONS

It is early summer in New Mexico and the high desert is in full bloom. It is early morning in Santa Fe and the bells of St. Francis Church are loud as Sharon walks toward the telegraph office on San Francisco Street. A young man of no more than twenty sits behind an old desk. Sharon gives him a piece of paper and tells him to tap out a message to her Valtura contact: *Start work, remove barrier, SFS.* The telegraph keys began to click rapidly.

"I'll be back later," she announces, "thanks."

"You're welcome, Miss Sharon," he says with curiosity.

Destroying the outgoing message, she steps outside, takes out a pack of cigarettes and lights a Marlboro Red Tip. She feels fashionable smoking a cigarette designed especially for women. After a few deep inhalations, she walks from the telegraph office to the plaza and past the Palace of the Governor. A short distance ahead, the sound of a piano is a harbinger of personal transformation. The music comes from Madame Francine Fournier's salon.

Before seeing Madame Fournier, Sharon has an important meeting that will advance the plan. A previously arranged rendezvous with Carrie is set for 8:30 a.m. at the San Miguel Mission Church. San Miguel is the oldest church in America, but she is not looking for history. The church is located off the plaza and away from any curious eyes. Sharon paces under the Missions' San José Bell with a Red Tip Marlboro clenched in her teeth, waiting. Carrie remains unaware of the Old Mexico connection and Sharon will keep it that way.

Glaring from under her flat-brimmed hat at the approaching woman, Sharon throws down her cigarette and snarls, "You are late!"

"I'm here now," Carrie snaps back defensively.

"The time will soon come to act on what we discussed."

"Good, I would be better prepared if I knew what you want."

"Just prepare to leave Santa Fe. You will take the train to Valtura in Corona County on my orders."

"Valtura?"

"Yes, Valtura. The station is about five miles outside of town. You will meet an associate named Bill Blackstone."

"To what end?"

"Blackstone will help you become established in Valtura and claim Mad Mady's Saloon."

"Claim Mad Mady's Saloon? What are you talking about?"

"We have been over this, Carrie. I told you about my sister and you told me to get what I deserve—so are you ready or not?"

"Yes, but how can I claim her place? She is sure to resist me."

"As next of kin, I give you the authority to act as my agent in taking over Mady's place."

"What about Mady?"

"Let me worry about her."

"But will she be in Valtura?"

"She will not. After you establish your authority, you will begin to receive shipments of fine furnishings that will help in refining Mady's low-class saloon. Take these instructions." Sharon hands her a sealed envelope containing her vision for the new saloon.

"What are they?" she says submissively.

"Particulars on how you should arrange the goods when the shipments begin to arrive. Follow these directions closely."

"Are you coming to Valtura?"

Becoming annoyed, Sharon yells, "Yes, of course. I will be in Valtura as soon as I can."

"But how will I take over Mady's place?"

"Carrie, I told you, Mady will *not* be there. As next of kin to Mady, I will run the show when I arrive. In the meantime, you will act as my agent."

"But why can't you come with me?"

"I can't come *because* I'm incapacitated from the auto accident," Sharon shouts.

"What auto accident?"

Sharon clenches her teeth and snarls, "Damn it, just go to Valtura when I say so, or do you want to stay in the brothel?"

Carrie reluctantly accepts the situation and says, "Okay. Is there anything else?"

"Yes, remove anything that would remind me of Mady and her bawdy house, keep me informed of your progress, and one more thing—change the name to Chez Beau Sharon."

Sharon returns to the telegraph office and hears a message click back: *Will act to remove barrier first opportunity*, signed EL.

"Please send another message to this name and city."

The telegraph keys click rapidly again. The message reads, *Started things, awaiting instructions.*

Sharon, smoking another Marlboro Red Tip, meets one of her male supplicants in the plaza.

"Miss Sharon, I missed you."

He moves in to kiss her, but she pushes back, "Just be ready to drive me to the rail station on short notice. I will be inaccessible for a while. For now, keep your eyes and ears open on the plaza."

The fool tolerates Sharon's abuse just to be near her. The supplicant's name, background and identity are unimportant to her. Yet as a source of cash and meals for Sharon, he is important. He provides service; she provides apathy—at best.

Once again, Sharon returns to the telegraph office. She hears the keys clicking a coded message intended for her: *Confirm confinement, wait for next message.* She stashes the unsigned note into her pocket and tells the operator to acknowledge receipt. Old Mexico is almost ready.

11

Madame Francine Fournier

Madame Francine Fournier, a French National, has been popular in Santa Fe social circles ever since her arrival at the turn of the century. People in the plaza often hear her on the piano, playing and singing "*La Marseillaise*."

Francine Fournier is a woman of forty-two years, of medium height and with a perfect figure. Educated at La Sorbonne, the prestigious University of Paris, she was the epitome of haute couture and an icon of elegance in France. Over time, she has developed a reputation of being a snob toward American women. Many people on the plaza refer to her as "Miss Frenchy" behind her back.

Renée Reynolds, her assistant and very close friend, attributes Francine's haughty attitude to a psychological defense relating to a secret past. Renée, a petite woman around forty from New Orleans' French Quarter, thinks that Francine is projecting her undesirable thoughts, feelings and experiences onto her clients instead of resolving them. Whatever the case, the difference between Santa Fe saloons and Paris salons has Francine dreaming of returning to France and to high-class endeavors.

Madame Francine Fournier's salon, uniquely distinguished in New Mexico, provides a structured and coherent analysis of French culture and its social significance within a cosmopolitan world. Excruciatingly correct behavior drives the salon concept, with etiquette lessons on how women should stand, how they should walk and how they should speak for the elegant life. The program within the proper and prestigious salon consists of instructions in language, in fashion and in seduction.

Francine is singing at her piano when Renée interrupts, announcing, "*Madame Fournier, votre rendezvous de trois heures est arrivé.*" (Madame Fournier, your 3 p.m. appointment has arrived.)

Francine smiles in anticipation of their evening ahead and Renée simply looks down. In many ways, Francine dominates Renée and some people on the plaza believe that they share secrets together.

"*Merci, Renée. Comment s'appelle-t-elle?*" (Thank you, Renée. What is her name?)

"Santa Fe Sharon."

"*J'ai entendu parlé d'elle,*" (I have heard of her) she says with sadness.

"*Madame Fournier, vous avez l'air, malheureux. Est-ce que Paris vous manque?*" (Madame Fournier, you seem unhappy. Do you miss Paris?)

"*Oui, plus que vous pouvez savoir.*" (Yes, more than you know.)

Renée laments, "*L'idée d'être sans vous me fait beaucoup de mal, Madame. Je n'ai jamais visité la France.*" (The prospect of being without you is distressing, Madame. I have never been to France.)

"*Dites-lui que j'arrive maintenant.*" (Tell her I will be right there.)

"*Oui Madame.*" Renée quickly turns to leave.

Sharon, waiting on the settee, looks less than resplendent in her Western clothes and dusty boots as Francine reluctantly enters.

Francine has become increasingly wary of her situation in Santa Fe and this appointment is unlikely to help matters.

Francine enunciates, "*Bonjour. Entrez, s'il vous plaît.*" (Hello, please come in.)

"Hello, Miss Frenchy."

"That's Madame Fournier. How may I help you?" she says sternly with a heavy French accent.

"I plan to transform an old saloon into a fine place with a decidedly French atmosphere. I will start with myself."

"*C'est une très bonne idée, mais ce sera très difficile*!" (Good idea, but this will be hard!)

"What's that, Miss Frenchy?"

"Please, my name is Madame Fournier. I said it will be nice to help you."

"That sounds fine."

"Would you like an aperitif, Mademoiselle Santa Fe?"

"A pair of what?"

"No, no. It is a drink, a fine French drink," Francine says with a sigh.

She pours the aperitif into crystal glasses and is appalled to see Sharon down hers in one gulp.

"That tastes good; I think I'm going to like all these French things."

"*Oh la la*," Francine moans.

Having recovered from Sharon's shockingly tawdry behavior, Francine sips her aperitif and considers her options. She could end the session but needs the income to return to Paris. Resigned to the situation, she accepts the difficult job with this offensive woman.

"*Alors! Notre programme consiste à enseigner la langue, la culture, les bonnes manières et comment séduire un homme,* er, I mean our program consists of language, culture, manners and how to seduce a man."

"Most men around here don't need much seducing, Miss Frenchy."

Francine stares at Sharon, rolls her eyes and wonders why her life is so dreadful. Realizing that Sharon is a challenging client, she exclaims, "*Ce sera beaucoup plus difficile que je n'aie imaginé.*" (This will be harder than I thought.)

"What's that?"

"I said we are off to a good start."

"That's wonderful."

"*Ces Américaines sont vraiment sans culture*!" (Americans have no culture!)

"What's that?"

"I said I love working with American women."

Sharon smiles and says, "I am so happy with my decision to meet you."

"*Alors, commençons avec la langue française*, er, let us start with language."

"Okay."

"*Bonjour.*"

"Bone jar."

Francine spontaneously exclaims, "*Je dois absolument m'enfuir.*" (I must get out of here.)

Sharon repeats this in poor French, further exacerbating Francine's sensibilities. After an hour, it is painfully clear that Sharon is ill-equipped to master the French language. Nevertheless, Francine declares, "*Très bien*," she can no longer tolerate such violence to the language and suggests they move to fashion.

"*Alors, Mademoiselle Santa Fe, vous étiez une si bonne étudiante en langue,* er I mean you were a good language student."

"Why thank you, Miss Frenchy. You are too kind."

"I told you, call me Madame Fournier. Now, shall we work on fashion?"

"Yes, let's move on to fashion."

"Please come with me."

With Francine's experience, her eye for fashion and her knowledge of chic, her salon enables women to achieve the most flattering look. An extensive wardrobe session transforms her client.

Santa Fe Sharon emerges from an interior room as Mademoiselle Sharon, swaggering in all her glory. Francine has provided a fabulous red dress. The one-piece corset with adjustable halter straps and off the shoulder-ruffled sleeves enhances Sharon's saucy manner. The skirt is bustled with a large bow. Underneath the beautiful costume is an attached black petticoat providing fullness and excitement.

Sharon has achieved the image she believes will distract those who think women have little involvement with the political world. This stereotypical perception is an advantage for her and a disadvantage for curious foes. She pays her bill with crisp greenbacks and says, "Thank you, Madame Fournier."

"You are welcome I am sure, Mademoiselle Sharon."

Sharon is pleased with the sound of her new name and becoming a flamboyant Mademoiselle, but Madame Fournier is less than satisfied. The stressful session weakens her tolerance of unsophisticated American women. From her perspective, few women in New Mexico can rise to her standards and there may be more ruffians seeking to be refined. Sharon has been too much for Francine, prompting her to return to Paris sooner rather than later.

Proceeding to her white adobe casita off the plaza, Sharon notices two men staring. Her first instinct is apprehension. *Did I somehow compromise the plan?* Government agents never arrest suspects near their homes—it alerts other agents who could destroy evidence. The men are probably attracted to the new beautiful Mademoiselle Sharon.

The first responsibility of a conspirator is to remain in a covert role. People in this line of work know the danger of publicity and do their best to avoid attention. Ironically, Sharon loves being flamboyant and playing the beguiling woman who will not be clandestine. Hiding in plain sight has been her modus operandi and she is unlikely to stop now. Furthermore, the co-conspirators in Old Mexico will tolerate her high-profile appearance based on her important connection to a statehood delegate.

Once inside her casita, Sharon starts packing her new fashionable dress into an old trunk. Then seeking considerable attention, she dyes her hair red. At the appropriate time, her disarming nature and confident attitude can serve her well in the dangerous seduction game that lies ahead. Her ability to engender openness from others can secure information and corrupt men for political purposes.

Sharon returns to the telegraph office to find an encrypted message originating from Old Mexico. She deciphers the following: *If your engagement allows acceptance of service, depart for Valtura.* The message is clear—the time to act is now. She immediately writes a reply: *Leaving Santa Fe soonest.*

12

NEW MEXICO TERRITORY

The Circle C is a big ranch in an immense territory. New Mexico Territory is more than 120,000 square miles. On the eastern border is the new state of Oklahoma. Texas is to the east and south and the Mexican states of Chihuahua and Sonora are on the southern border. The western and northern boundaries are with the states of Arizona and Colorado, respectively. Within the territory, rich in minerals, agriculture and optimism, the population is less than 300,000.

In 1596, when New Mexico was part of New Spain, Cabezada Vaca explored the region seeking gold in the Seven Cities of Cibola. Following this early expedition, Spanish colonization was established. Then, the 1821 Mexican revolution ended Spanish rule in the Southwest.

New Mexico, acquired by the Unites States as part of the 1848 Mexican Cession, originally included Arizona. In 1850, the U.S. Territory of New Mexico was created. The Confederate Territory of Arizona emerged from New Mexico in 1861. After Union victories, it became the Territory of Arizona. In 1863, President Lincoln signed a bill separating Arizona from New Mexico.

Over the years, Adobe has traveled to almost every corner of the territory, a distance of almost 400 miles from north to south. Today, he is going 60 miles north to Santa Fe. A staunch unionist, he is eager about the new statehood opportunity presented by President Taft, an Ohio Republican, who authorized New Mexico to convene a state constitutional convention.

Things always start early at the Circle C Ranch, especially today. It is another fine day of blue skies and bright sun. Adobe is waiting for his morning brew, while donning his Arkansas toothpick in its leg sheath—standard travel gear for him.

A.P. is in the horse barn saddling Patriot when Adobe enters and says, "Good Morning."

"Morning, Boss. Looks like it rained a little last night." A.P. observes.

"Good, should be less dust on the road to Santa Fe."

"Even less dust on the train," A.P. states the obvious.

"I know, but the meeting is in two days and sometimes I like to take the long way on Patriot."

"You are a dying breed, Boss."

"Maybe I am," he states. "Governor Jackson has arranged to meet the delegates from each county to discuss the upcoming election to ratify the state constitution—it will be a big day. He is also assessing men for important posts."

"That sounds fine. New Mexico will require representation in the National Congress. Jackson knows how to make good appointments and I'm sure Adobe Centori from Corona County is at the top of his list."

Adobe laughs and says, "You're in charge around here for a while."

"Leave it to me, Boss, and good luck with the governor and all the statehood issues."

"Thanks. We properly answered the economic, social, political and natural resources questions that caused delays—and we hope *at last* to attain success. It is almost 1912 and New Mexico is still a territory. You know, every state except for the original thirteen, Vermont and California, were territories. So that's the American way."

"Yes, I knew that, Boss!"

Both men laugh aloud and Adobe says, "It's my job to know these things, but my point is we have waited too long."

"From what I understand, it's a straightforward process, with the National Congress having full discretion to admit a new state," A.P. opines.

"It may be straightforward, A.P., but every step in the process has potential setbacks. So far, the people, through the legislature, petitioned Congress for an enabling act spelling out the constitution requirements. Congress authorized a constitutional convention and delegates convened in Santa Fe to debate the issues. Then we created a state constitution and formed a state government. Voters throughout the territory approved it in January."

"And the time has come to secure the final steps," A.P. says.

"That's right. Now, we wait for an election to ratify the state constitution."

"Congratulations again, Boss," A.P. proudly says, honored to know an important man in the statehood quest.

Smiling, Adobe says, "Thanks, but the draft must be approved by the voters, those with the real power."

"I'm sure you and the other delegates have written write a fine constitution."

"Even so, Congress must approve it with a joint resolution of admission, and then the voters can elect state officers."

"Senator Centori. That has a nice ring."

"Nice fantasy, too. Anyway, the last step is President Taft issuing a proclamation declaring New Mexico a state and member of the Union."

"Amen. Anyway, have a good trip. I'll take care of things around here."

"Thanks, A.P. I know Ellison is off his mark these days. Perhaps you can be temporary undersheriff along with him."

"I'm no lawman. Ellison is a good Circle C cowboy but a little distracted. Don't worry, he'll be fine."

"If you say so. He may be spending too much time in town with too many doves. The folly of youth," he observes.

A.P. does not reply. As far as he knows, Adobe does not seek the company of doves.

Adobe signals to Patriot to move out and says, "*Adios*, A.P."

"Good luck, Boss."

"Thanks."

Cabezada Vaca explored New Mexico seeking gold. Adobe often explores New Mexico too, not for gold, but for the absolute beauty of the land. He has spent more years in New Mexico than in his native New York, yet never tires of riding the range, with landscapes of rose-colored deserts, broken mesas, high plains and snow-capped mountain peaks. New Mexico consists of intriguing mountain ranges rising into high peaks separated by fertile valleys. The Rocky Mountains, before entering the territory, divide into two ranges. One range ends in Santa Fe; the other, of lower elevation, extends to the Sierra Madre of Old Mexico. The most significant rivers are the Pecos, Canadian, San Juan and Rio Grande. Running north to south along the Rio Grande are the Sangre de Cristo Mountains.

There is something special about New Mexico's environment. The territory has a glorious mild and arid climate with plentiful sunshine and temperatures that vary based on terrain. Despite an arid environment, the territory has heavy forests in mountain wilderness areas, especially north of Valtura. The majestic mountains, grand mesas, vast high deserts and big skies blend to create a dignified and magnificent world.

New Mexico is a habitat for many plant and animal species. Sagebrush, cactus and the mesquite express nature's variety and beauty. The same is true for the cottonwood, aspen, piñon and juniper trees. Wildlife is also plentiful, with mule deer, antelope, hawks, roadrunners, eagles and coyotes. Each mile offers new perspectives on natural history and wildlife. The experience is not lost on Adobe, a slow rider.

As Adobe and Patriot near Linden Lake, the northern border of the ranch, and ride past colorful red rock cliffs, an alpha male coyote appears. Some native people believe that the coyote changed the course of rivers and moved mountains to improve the earth.

The wild dog keeps his distance, but Adobe speaks to Patriot in a low, even voice. He knows that composure is important in dealing with a startled horse, even an old warhorse like Patriot.

In an instant, the coyote vanishes among the heavy trees along the northern bank. Alpha male coyotes are bold leaders from a strong social support system. Adobe has shown bold leadership skills and has many supporters. Coyotes are instructive, inspiring and dedicated team players, skills that Adobe will need as a member of the U.S. Senate. Horse and rider continue the two-day ride to Santa Fe.

13

Plaza Hotel

At the end of his second day of travel, Adobe enters Santa Fe on Cerrillos Road and rides toward Santa Fe Plaza. During the Mexican-American War, General Stephen Kearney raised the American flag over Santa Fe Plaza. After the war, he announced the intention to establish a civil government on a republican basis leading to statehood. Yet New Mexicans remain without self-government, a condition that has existed since Mexico ceded the territory in 1848.

The famous plaza marks the end of the Santa Fe Trail that extends all the way to Missouri. After the Mexican Revolution of 1820, the trail came into existence as an important trade route, essential for economic development, until the arrival of the railroad and the telegraph.

Adobe arrives at the architecturally distinctive central plaza, where flat-roofed buildings, made of unburnt sun-dried clay bricks, blend into the earth. He ties Patriot to a rail, grabs his saddlebags and enters the lobby of the Plaza Hotel. At the front desk, he registers with the hotel clerk, who recognizes him as a delegate.

The tall, slender woman turns the registration book around and says, "Welcome to Santa Fe, Mr. Centori. We were expecting you."

"Thank you, Miss."

"We're seeing many delegates from all over the territory these days."

"I'm sure of that. The great statehood issue is bringing us to Santa Fe."

She is a tall, pretty thing with ash-blonde hair and grey eyes.

"Enjoy your time at the Plaza Hotel and in Santa Fe, Sheriff."

Adobe appreciates a fine-looking woman who seems not to be an innocent maiden. Revealing his approval he says, "I am already enjoying the hotel."

Her slight smile projects a thinly veiled invitation—he hopes. He returns the smile, completing the circle with interest established and action to be determined.

After sending his saddlebags to his room, Adobe goes into the quiet bar, finds a table, and waits. The service here is slower than the service in Valtura. Finally, a waiter comes to his table.

"*Si, Señor?*"

"*Cerveza, por favor.*"

"*Bueno.*"

The quiet does not last long. Sounds of guitar and castanets signal the Fandango, a suggestive and colorful courtship dance with highly skilled dancers.

"*Cerveza, Señor.*"

"*Gracias.*"

"*De nada.*"

Adobe drinks the beer while watching the serious, sensuous movements. Then the dancers and music suddenly stop. They stay frozen as the female's short, vivid skirt settles. The evocative dance causes his thoughts to return to the tall pretty creature at the front desk.

She could make this trip more interesting. At least I would like to know her better—a lot better—and she may know something about Sharon, he rationalized.

Regaining his good sense, he wonders if Sharon has somehow betrayed Mady. *Beyond sibling jealousy, there could be something more—if this Santa Fe Sharon is her sister at all.*

After the beer, Adobe returns to the lobby. Sitting nearby is a man with a wide brimmed hat, who looks up as he walks to the front desk.

"Pardon me, Miss," he says while admiring her face, "do you know of a woman in town called Santa Fe Sharon?"

"No!" She snaps quickly, her eyes wide.

Adobe walks away, startled at her reaction. *Her unpleasant attitude conflicts with my desire to know her better. Perhaps it can be reconciled, he thinks. Then, there is the possibility she knows something about Sharon.*

Before going to his room, he leaves the hotel, walks across to the historic plaza, which has shady trees, benches and a war memorial obelisk. In the middle of the plaza, he stops to scan the inscription on the obelisk, but the implication of the desk clerk's protest still resonates.

Adobe continues to the stable behind the plaza to check on Patriot. The stallion is secure and has been fed, watered and groomed. After being in the saddle so long, he takes an extended walk beyond the plaza. On impulse, he follows a familiar route from West Palace Avenue to Lincoln Avenue to Paseo de Peralta to Calle Montano. He ignores the Calle Montano women and returns to the hotel.

Adobe ascends the carpeted steps to the second floor and approaches his room. The door is unlocked and slightly ajar, prompting concern. Drawing his Navy Colt, he slowly opens the door. Before entering, a female voice says, "Hello."

"What in the world are you doing here?" he says with shock in his voice.

"Use your imagination."

No need to imagine, smiling from behind a sheet pulled to her chest, the woman from the front desk is clearly and completely naked under the sheet.

"You want me to leave?"

"I didn't say that—I'm just surprised by your apparent intentions."

He holsters the gun and thinks, *Acting on impulse could be costly; but when I asked about Sharon, she reacted too quickly. There could be an opportunity to help Mady, or at least me.*

"Are you sure you don't know Santa Fe Sharon?"

"Given my compromising position, I'm the only woman you should be concerned about right now."

Appreciating her willingness to share so much so soon, he says, "You are a very desirable woman," he agrees, and asks, "How long have you been in Santa Fe?"

She sits up, allowing the sheet to fall slightly, and gushes about how she came to Santa Fe and obtained a job usually held by a man.

Reaching for Adobe's arm, she reluctantly says, "What really brings you to Santa Fe?"

"From this view, luck I guess." He thinks of the irresistible secrets that lie under the thin sheet.

"Thank you," she smiles widely, and goes on with personal stories almost to the point of Adobe's fatigue.

"Are we going to talk all night?"

"Relax, you won't be disappointed." Pulling off the sheet, he instantly knows she was right. Her stunning body convinces him to touch her flat stomach. She reaches up, removes his shirt and says, "What broad shoulders you have. That's not the only measure of man, but a good one."

She embraces and pulls him down with little resistance; he kisses her full lips.

At midnight, she is a little nervous and says, "I don't know what to say."

"You can tell me what you know about Santa Fe Sharon."

"Sharon again?"

"Yes, her very name seemed to spark fear in you."

"Okay, at the front desk you asked about Santa Fe Sharon, too loudly I'd say."

"So you do know her."

"Most people in Santa Fe at least know *of* her."

"But why did you say no?"

"I don't like to discuss my personal life in public, especially while at work."

"I can only assume you are off duty now. Look, who is she?"

"Sharon displays a strong brassy presence on the plaza. She loves showing off by traipsing around the plaza," she says with a curious smile. "I must admit she has a slender shape even *without* wearing a corset. Most days, she looks good wearing tight blue pants and vest, a red shirt and a stylish brown hat."

"That may explain a few things, but not *who* she is."

"Sharon is high in flair," she smiles again," but sadly, low in character."

"Okay, did she ever mention having a sister in Valtura—or Valtura at all?"

"Not to me. She kept to herself about personal things like that."

"But not all personal things."

"Look, she tries to cozy up to *anyone* who can help her. In some ways, I'm glad she's gone. She is a very good taker, but a very bad giver."

"Gone?"

"Well, she told me about some important business in Albuquerque."

"Albuquerque? What kind of business?"

"Do you have to continue talking about her? Because I sure don't."

"One last thing. Supposedly she was here at the hotel talking to people from Corona County."

"At times she frequents the hotel bar, but not lately. She seemed interested in anybody involved in the statehood movement."

Adobe takes exception to the comment. *Why would Sharon care about statehood? Mady never mentioned Sharon being interested in affairs of state. Perhaps Mady knows more than she says.*

"Why is she interested in statehood?"

"How would I know?" she says with annoyance.

"Okay, is there anything else?"

Exhaling, she says, "Last week she was seen entering Frenchy Fournier's place. After that, she may have left town. That's all I know... Oh, and she carries a strategically placed single-shot pistol."

"Frenchy Fournier?"

"Yes, Madame Francine Fournier. She has a salon on the plaza."

"Salon? What do you mean?"

"Go see for yourself," she snaps. "Look, I don't want you to think I am a shameless hussy; a woman should be modest."

She is far from modest, he thought.

"Don't suppose I have expectations after one night."

Taking her hand, he says, "I don't."

"I could get fired for this."

"Don't worry; this is our business."

She stands and, looking a little sad, puts on a homespun dress. Adobe, sensing her distress, kisses her gently and says, "Sometimes things come together to create perfect moments and memories. You are a fine woman."

"But you don't even know my name," she says cuttingly.

Adobe stiffens, "Let's keep it that way." He instantly regrets his words spoken in self-defense. There is a wistful look in her eyes, but he is not constrained by guilt. She has nothing he cannot live without.

As she walks out of the room, she turns and says, "My name is Dora."

Adobe believes that a man's life is incomplete without love, but his emotions are unavailable to women. Drifting to sleep, he thinks of Dora. *At times, I want a woman and at times, I will have a woman. I have behaved well, always one woman at a time, ended as painlessly as possible. I have been honest and kind...well, perhaps not so kind.*

The next morning Adobe returns to the dining room and reflects on the night, relieved to see that Dora is not at the front desk. Although uneasy about the intimate encounter and unable to focus on the imminent meeting, his appetite is not lost.

The service is still slow—Valtura is a long way from Santa Fe.

"Sorry for the wait, busy morning," says the waiter.

"No problem, I'll have eggs, salt-cured ham, green chili, hot biscuits and a pot of strong, black coffee."

Compared to Circle C coffee, the hotel brew is only tolerable. After breakfast, a man wearing a wide-brimmed hat and a heavily embroidered short jacket that partly conceals a pair of six-shooters approaches his table.

Interrupting Adobe's thoughts, he says, "*Buenos dias, Señor.*"

"*Le conozco?*" *(Do I know you?)*

"*No, Señor, pero y sé que Usted es de Valtura.*" *(No sir, but I know you are from Valtura.)*

"*Tiene razón.*" (You are right.)

There is nothing subtle about the man. During his military service, Adobe developed sensitivity to danger; he flexes his hip to feel his revolver.

"You are *Señor Centori*...I understand you were asking about Santa Fe Sharon," he says in accented English.

"Maybe that's right; does it concern you?" Adobe speaks in a measured manner.

"May I sit down?"

"Suit yourself," he says with a poker face.

"*Gracias.*"

Because the man may have information, Adobe tolerates the company and is comforted to feel the coolness of his Arkansas toothpick in its leg sheath. The man draws on his cigarette and lets the smoke flow out of his nose.

"*Señor,* you are curious about Santa Fe Sharon and maybe some of her ideas and people who can be of service to you."

Adobe folds his arms across his chest and says, "What makes you think so?"

"Your interest in Santa Fe Sharon tells me so, *no es verdad?*"

"It is *not* true, but what can you tell me about her?"

"*Mucho*, but I must be paid, *Señor.*"

"My answer is no."

"Think it over."

"I don't have to; now excuse me, my breakfast is getting cold."

Glancing at his plate, he counters with, "But it looks like you are done."

"Let me tell you again, but differently. *We* are done."

The man laughs angrily and does not leave.

"Done! Is that clear? Because if it isn't, have someone else draw you a picture, I haven't got the time."

"Perhaps there is some mix-up. *Adios amigo.*"

14

Palace of the Governors

Walking across the Santa Fe Plaza to the Palace of the Governors, Adobe admires the largest building on the plaza. He glances at Madame Francine Fournier's Salon, still thinking about the stranger. *Santa Fe Sharon may not be Mady's sister, but she seems to be involved with something.*

Adobe arrives at the Santa Fe Plaza. In the plaza sits the Palace of the Governors, built in the early seventeenth century by the Spanish. It is the center of New Mexico government and the oldest public building in North America.

When New Mexico became a U.S. territory, the palace continued as the territorial capitol. In 1909, the territorial legislature created the Museum of New Mexico, with the palace becoming the site of the history museum. As a result, Governor Jackson will be the last to serve in the historic building.

Reaching the unornamented adobe brick building that occupies the entire north side of the plaza, he sees the new activity under the long porch. Two years ago, the Museum of New Mexico reserved the long porch for Indians to market their wares; they sell baked goods, and decorative works such as pottery, metalwork, weavings and stone jewelry. Adobe thinks about buying jewelry for a woman. He settles for a piece of oven bread instead.

In the palace courtyard, a young, attractive and elegant woman sits on a bench near a stone fountain, reading an old manuscript. She wears a long turquoise skirt with black embroidery at the hemline, a white shirt and silver bracelets. Adobe stops to look at her profile and lovely image. When she turns, he gasps at the sight of someone so lovely that the light of life is in her face.

The gracious woman has dark eyes and shoulder length, perfumed black hair. A gold cross hangs around her neck. He immediately conjures Gabriella and rises to his full height. The two women are similar in appearance, yet this serene beauty is taller than Gabriella—and more poised.

"*Hola, Señor.*"

When she speaks, Gabriella falls from his psyche like a rock from a bridge. She has an affectionate and cultured voice with a charismatic Spanish intonation.

"*Hola Señorita. Soy Sheriff Centori de Valtura.*"

The young woman stands from the bench and pushes the old parchments under a few books.

"*Soy Juliana Martinez de la Villanueva Galvan Madrid, huespeda del gobernador Jackson.*"

"Is it all right if I just call you Miss Madrid?"

"*Sí, por supuesto.*" (Yes, of course.)

"*Es un placer en conocerla,*" (It is a pleasure meeting you.) Have you been in Santa Fe long?"

"No, I recently arrived from Spain," she says in English with her soft Spanish accent.

"You sure are a long way from home."

"Home is the reason for coming to New Mexico."

"What do you mean by that, Miss Madrid?"

"Spain has a history of colonizing the Southwest. Long before U.S. independence from England, Spanish soldiers and colonists established towns in California, Texas and New Mexico."

"I'm not a native New Mexican, but I do know that the Spanish were the first Europeans to enter New Mexico in the 1500s."

She continues, "More than New Mexico, the Viceroyalty of New Spain included most of the Southwest before Mexican independence and U.S. involvement."

He takes notice of her U.S. comment, but says nothing.

"King Alfonso sent me to investigate Spanish Land Grant Claims in New Mexico. As you may know, land grants to individuals and communities for the establishment of settlements occurred here from 1598 to 1846."

"I'm aware, Miss Madrid. U.S. involvement started in 1846." He cannot resist the comment.

She smiles politely and says, "Spanish hidalgos and royalty received extensive land grants in the Southwest for large ranches. Many seventeenth century Spanish documents in New Mexico are missing or destroyed. This incomplete historical record has created legal conflicts."

"Yes, Miss Madrid, but I understand that after New Mexico became part of the U.S., the Office of Surveyor General ascertained the validity of land grant claims."

"That is correct, Sheriff Centori, but that office had limited success and led to the Court of Private Land Claims. That is why I am in Santa Fe. My job is to observe the legal battles over land grant claims in New Mexico's district courts."

"That's impressive. You have an important job, especially for a woman. I mean, society is lagging behind women, who can do any job. In Valtura, we have Mady Blaylock running the biggest business on the plaza and Klara Morgenstern running a newspaper."

He decides to quit while he is slightly behind. Adobe's words are awkward, but not meant to offend.

Realizing his embarrassment, she changes the subject by saying, "Yes, it is an important undertaking for anyone, and the governor is cooperating by allowing me to stay in the palace."

Cooperating, he thinks. *What man would turn away a beautiful, intelligent, gracious woman like Juliana?*

"We have much in common, Miss Madrid. New Mexico accepts many Spanish traditions."

"Of course, the tradition began in the 1530s when the Viceroy of Mexico sent Anvar Nunez to seek New Mexico's mineral wealth."

"Right here in Santa Fe a permanent settlement was established; soldiers were stationed here to protect the missionaries," he says, to acknowledge the cultural commonalities while hoping to have much in common on a personal level.

"We hope the tradition will continue with fairness to those seeking justice for land grant claims in New Mexico's district courts."

What about the justice for the native inhabitants who were good in the civilized arts, tilled the soil and lived in communities until the Spaniards' heavy hand changed things? he thinks. *There is no point in mentioning the 1680 pueblo revolt. I want to bring her closer, not drive her away.*

"You have a good sense of history, Sheriff Centori."

"You're the expert, Miss Madrid. Perhaps we can talk more about it later. I have a meeting with Governor Jackson."

"The governor is in his office. I'm sure he will see Sheriff Centori of Valtura."

"Thank you Miss Madrid. I do have an appointment."

"Yes, of course. Please walk across the patio and through the first door."

"And, Miss Madrid?"

"Yes?"

"Good luck in New Mexico."

"*Gracias.*"

Como estar de bonita, Adobe thinks, "*I have never seen a woman prettier than Gabriella—until now.*

Juliana Madrid could be the one to penetrate his armor. However, she would certainly be reticent about romance and even require marriage before allowing a man to see her charms. Any designs on Juliana would have to wait. It is time to see Governor Jackson.

The sumptuously appointed governor's office has lavish carpeting and fine furniture, including a large desk made of strong hardwood with carved accents. A nameplate with one-inch-high gold letters and a large Stetson hat are on his desk. Behind the desk, which dominates the office, is a sizeable and comfortable leather chair. There are two other chairs facing his desk, and his black greatcoat is draped over one.

Governor Jackson, a well-known businessman and economic contributor to the territory, is heavily involved in investment companies, oil promotion and real estate.

The governor greets his guest, "Welcome to Santa Fe, Sheriff Centori," and walks to his well-stocked bar.

"Thank you, Governor."

"Would you like a drink?"

"Well, Governor, I'm no day drinker, but since you're the one asking, sure."

Governor Jackson, wearing a well-pressed gray worsted suit with a heavy gold watch chain running across his vest, points to a big, overstuffed, leather chair, reaches for a bottle of preferred whiskey and pours out two glasses. Adobe removes his hat and settles in the chair without the coat over the back.

"Here you are, Sheriff, or should I call you senator?" he says while sitting down.

Taken aback by the Governor's statement, he says, "Adobe is fine. I'm sure there are better qualified men in New Mexico for that job."

Adobe sips the whiskey. The Jameson, one of the best brands of single-malt Irish whiskey, goes down smoothly.

"You would be a good choice for senator, Adobe, a big job for a big man. You are an ardent patriot, respected public servant, successful rancher and a war hero."

"I'm no war hero, Governor, but I did wear the uniform."

"You are too modest. New Mexico is proud of you. Your appointment as a statehood delegate is only the beginning for you. Our new state will need good representation in Washington."

Adobe nods and says, "That is flattering but the bigger story is New Mexico joining the Union on an equal footing to every other state." He finishes his Irish whiskey and considers his political future. *Senator Centori*?

"Sheriff, I want to be the first state governor of New Mexico and I want 1912 to be the year."

"I am sure the joint resolution will pass in Congress."

"Don't forget the election for state officials, including governor—and I need you to bring in the Corona County vote."

Now I see the Senator Centori possibility, Adobe thinks, but says, "We have acted in accordance with congressional provisions."

"Indeed and we have been successful at previous steps. I met with the Chief Justice and Secretary of the Territory to consider the enabling act and I ordered an election in which delegates voted," the governor says over his second Irish whiskey.

"Forming a constitution and a state government was successful. I expect our achievements will continue all the way to statehood."

"Yes, Sheriff, but if history is an indication, the process can fail at any point. Let me read from the statehood bill:

The constitution shall be republican in form and make no distinction in civil or political rights on account of race or color

> *and shall not be repugnant to the Constitution of the United States or the Declaration of Independence.*

"That's fine, all will agree," says Adobe.

"Yes, but the next passage could be a little contentious, Sheriff." He continues:

> *The people inhabiting said proposed state disagree and declare to disclaim all rights and title to the un-appropriated and un-granted public lands lying in the boundaries of the territory.*

"We resolved the public lands issue in convention, Governor."

"But can I trust the voters to agree in November?"

So you can be the first governor of the new state, Adobe thinks.

"Everybody in the county knows my position, Governor."

"I hope so; I don't want the public land provision to be a roadblock. The people should know that we can obtain improved public protection with land policies and agriculture."

"Yes, Governor, and we need better soil, water, forest, minerals and wildlife conservation."

"Of course, I know you admired TR's environment policies. We all want to use natural resources in the best possible way. If you were senator, you could vote on these and other issues."

A.P. was right. Senator Centori does have a nice ring to it, he thinks.

"Perhaps you think I am being overly cautious, but I intend to be…"

Adobe finishes the governor's words to himself.

"Sheriff, I know you're a proponent of education. The new constitution says that a system of public schools for all children be free from sectarian control and should be conducted in English, provided that nothing in the act precludes the teaching of other languages in public schools."

"What does that mean?"

He laughs, "I'm no lawyer, Sheriff, but I want to ensure the voters will approve this provision. Statehood is inevitable; but I want it to happen while I'm in office. There are many issues such as finance, taxation, trade and commerce and debt management that can block the positive vote."

"As I said, we addressed those issues in convention, and the territorial-wide election to ratify the amended constitution is scheduled for November."

"Statehood in 1912," the governor repeats, "—but we need support from every corner of New Mexico. We are getting more support from both Republicans and Democrats." The governor fumbles with a few newspapers on his desk. "The Santa Fe New Mexican, a Republican paper, is quite to the point:

> *The people are anxious for autonomy; they desire a voice and a realization of a government of the people, for the people and by the people. It is a condition and not a theory that confronts us. Shall we continue to be represented by voteless delegates in Washington or shall we obtain two whole senators and two members of the House of Representatives with full authority to vote for the best interests of New Mexico?*

Returning the newspaper to his desk and looking at Adobe, he says, "Most territorial newspapers run editorials in favor of statehood. There are exceptions; the Valtura Journal seems reluctant to endorse statehood and often equivocates on the issues. Perhaps you can convince your Democrat friend to be more supportive."

"This is why you are concerned about the Corona County vote?"

"I am concerned about all votes throughout the territory."

"Johan *is* in favor of statehood, but not unconditionally. He stresses decentralization, allowing states to govern themselves and worries about Federalism."

"Washington confines itself to the important role in protecting our freedom from foreign powers; our system of Federalism has many benefits. We get uniformity in national affairs, while the states control internal affairs."

"Great in theory, Governor, but some resist a strong central government, especially over business. The statehood debate is a reflection of the national debate about excessiveness of laissez-faire capitalism versus federal control."

"I don't see it as a key statehood issue, Sheriff. We have no proof that New Mexico industries would be in danger of a federal regulation overload."

"You believe the federal government has only enumerated powers."

"You speak of article 1, section 8 of the U.S. Constitution. Yes, I do. Governor, it is little known, but what about the last clause in section 8 that gives Congress implied powers?" Adobe pulls out a copy of the Constitution from his pocket.

"You carry a copy with you?" the Governor exclaims.

"Only for important meetings," he quips. Then he turns to section 8 and begins to recite, "'*To make all laws which shall be necessary and proper for carrying into execution the foregoing powers, and all other powers vested by this Constitution of the U.S., or in any department or officer thereof.*' From this clause we get the implied powers from Chief Justice Marshall's interpretation."

"And he was a nationalist, not a states' rights proponent," the governor conceded.

"You make my point. The clause has increased and can continue to increase federal control over the states and regulation of business."

"Sheriff, I'm sure you are aware of the Tenth Amendment that says powers not delegated to the states by the Constitution are reserved to the states."

"Of course Governor," he says while looking through his Constitution, "but article 6, section 2 says that the laws of the U.S. shall be the supreme law of the land with the states bound."

A knock on the door interrupts the meeting and without waiting for an answer, Julia Madrid enters, "Pardon me Governor, when I finish with the Land Records of New Mexico, I will need access to the Spanish Archives of New Mexico."

"Yes of course, Miss Madrid, you have my full cooperation."

"*Gracias*, Governor."

After she leaves, Adobe says, "She is a little forward, breaking into our meeting."

"Well, she does represent the King of Spain."

"This is America, we have no royalty. But I guess she is beautiful enough to forgive," he jokes.

Getting back to business the governor continues, "Sheriff, your concerns about a potential strong central government can be allayed by the powers states have now; such as state tax, chartering corporations and the making and administrating of civil and criminal law."

"Perhaps, but the delegates themselves are divided on the implied powers clause and on the appropriate overall role of government regulation of business." Adobe says, with a little anger, "You know, the railroad, steel, coal, telegraph and the even the new telephone industry are targets of greater national regulation."

"And, of course, Washington has no business at the Circle C Ranch."

Defensively, Adobe replies, "I supported TR's Pure Food and Drug Act of '06. I am not against federal inspection of meat products."

"I know you are a fair minded man, Sheriff. In my position, one can get cynical. There are no monopolies in New Mexico ranching, unlike Rockefeller, who held monopolies over drilling, transportation, refinement and the sale of oil, showing the dangerous power of big business."

"That is true enough, Governor. Monopolistic practices have caused business and government conflict. Many industries have accumulated vast wealth and power; and the Supreme Court decision to break up Standard Oil shows the power of Washington."

"These issues can contribute to delaying statehood, but you are not clear. Where do you stand on all this, Sheriff?"

"Well, Governor, business is essential to the American way of life. It is the creator of wealth in our society. The market economy is a dominant force for material and social progress."

"Good assessment, but we are no longer a country of small shops with few workers in local markets. Twentieth century America is a much different country, with giant corporations and thousands of workers in national markets. There are reasons to question laissez faire capitalism. Adam Smith himself said wherever two businessmen meet the conversation ends in a conspiracy against the public or in a contrivance to raise prices. And don't forget, Sheriff, as big business becomes increasingly powerful, we get more popular demand for government protection against the power of big business."

"I agree. We need more competition, not less, for better products and prices. But more people are concerned with defining its appropriate role in America and in New Mexico. My concern is with Washington taking on too much business regulation."

"I'm still not clear where you stand on this, Sheriff."

"I love America, but believe in states' rights—that's why I strongly support statehood. The way I see it, our government should not go beyond the basics to influence the free market. If they do, liberty may be at risk, leading to the probability of corruption and economic depression. On the other hand, I believe that the free market has a place *but it must be kept* in its place.

"So it comes down to how its *place* is defined."

"Governor, business has fiduciary financial obligations to their stockholders. This is one of its primary places, yet serving only stockholders' wealth and interests excludes social obligation to our overall society."

"That's right, Sheriff. Some people are alarmed about the force of industrialization on the political process and society's values."

"Of course, but don't forget the progress made and wealth created by the concentration of mechanical power: steam, electric and furnace. We have a great standard of living. America specializes in the business domain of human affairs as a nation of great industrial and commercial success."

"Some say at the expense of workers and culture, Sheriff."

"I agree there is room for improvement for worker conditions, but we can see culture and art in the new colossal skyscrapers. The Woolworth Building under construction in New York resembles a European Gothic Cathedral. And I've experienced other artistic sensations in New York architecture, where imposing structures go straight to the heavens!"

"Others say they were built with wicked and excessive profits."

"Governor, profit is *not* a bad word, but too few men may control these resources. Besides, other economic systems can undermine our rights as free people."

"So it falls to government to control the systems."

"No, I disagree, Governor. There is nothing wrong with capitalism as a system, but some capitalists are corrupt and greedy."

"Okay, but men are the trustees of the public, not capitalism per se." The governor moves to his humidor, pulls out two large cigars expertly rolled into perfect cylinders, and continues, "Look, Sheriff, the point of government is to protect the public regardless of your subtle distinctions."

"Governor, we must protect workers from the dangerous and unhealthy conditions in factories and mines. But in practice, we have a struggle among forces. The main issue is *how much* control by the federal government?"

"Sounds like a fair question, Sheriff. Some feel any control is too much and with others no amount is enough."

"Exactly! We need to find a balance."

"So where do we draw the line?"

"Governor, it must be debated in an open forum between business and government. We need a constructive partnership, not adversarial groups, a balance between profit and people."

The governor snips the ends of the two cigars and suppresses a smile. He is impressed with Adobe's mind and may *even* like him.

"As I said, Governor, the free market has a place but *must* be kept in its place."

"Damn well spoken. Have you read the report of the National Monetary Commission that was published in January?"

"No, but I know its purpose. Since Andy Jackson ended the U.S. Bank, we have been without a central bank, making our economy vulnerable. The commission's proposed solution could help in periods of low cash reserves."

"So you agree with a central bank's ability to extend the money supply?"

"If it has enough control of credit resources to prevent money panics, and no more, than yes."

"*Enough* you say?"

"Well, the legislators are debating the level of control a central bank should exert."

"A Federal Reserve Bank would put the free market in its *'place,'* Sheriff!"

"Governor, I admit that the 1907 panic is a good example of the free market being *out* of place."

"Fair enough, Sheriff. Now, have a fine cigar."

"One more thing about the territory legislative assembly—

Corona County expects an additional member in the Council and in the House of Representatives."

"I understand. Now, let's have a Partagar Havana."

A Cuban cigar—the pain of an old emotional injury ripples through Adobe. Both men fire up and savor their cigars.

As the governor pours another drink, Adobe thinks, *The timing is right to bring up the railroad question. A rail station in Valtura proper would provide an economic stimulus.* "Governor, you know how important the railroad is for a town's growth and development?"

"Yes, I anticipated this topic."

"We need that line extension and a station in town to join the twentieth century. Our rail station is miles from town and the railroad is reluctant to build a switch line."

"But, Sheriff, when the railroad arrived in Albuquerque, away from the plaza, it created a separate, new town. Why not use the same master plan for growth?"

"The Albuquerque rail station is less than a mile from the old plaza. In Valtura, the station is five miles away. The separation of two towns would take years to unify, with too much duplication of effort. We're counting on the line extension for continued growth."

"First, let's become part of the Union. Then we can see about your rail line and secure a prominent position for Valtura. I know you see Valtura as a town of considerable importance."

"Okay, Governor, you are a man of your word," he replies, for insurance rather than as a compliment.

"Another drink?"

"Sure."

Sensing that the meeting is over he says, "Governor, that Miss Madrid is quite a beauty."

"Be careful. We do not want another war with Spain," he chuckles.

Adobe takes his meaning and a long puff, *She's probably too much lady and not enough woman,* he rationalizes. Dropping the topic, he says, "Do you know of a woman here called Santa Fe Sharon?"

Startled, the governor responds with a pithy comment, "She is a self-absorbed amorous woman." He will not betray sexual intimacy, albeit he has knowledge of the fact.

Respecting his privacy, Adobe continues, "Any reason to suspect her of dangerous or criminal activity?"

"It's not the criminal that is hanged; it's the one who is caught."

"Thanks, I understand. Governor, you can count on the Corona County vote. And don't worry about the Valtura Journal."

After a final round of drinks, Adobe leaves the palace, reluctantly says goodbye to Juliana Martinez de la Villanueva Galvan Madrid and sits in the plaza near a marker in honor of the Santa Fe Trail. Drawing on his fine cigar, he reads the inscription:

This stone marks the end of the Santa Fe Trail, 1822-1879
Erected by the Daughters of the American Revolution
and the Territory of New Mexico 1910

Directly across from the marker is another sign: Madame Francine Fournier.

Adobe thinks, *Dora provided more information than the governor did about Santa Fe Sharon. However, the governor's cryptic warning is revealing. Perhaps this French place can add a piece to the puzzle, but first things first.*

Adobe finishes his fine Cuban cigar.

15

TIME TO TIME

A visit to Madame Francine Fournier could help in understanding Sharon Blaylock's threat. Adobe walks through the plaza and toward her salon. Renée, surprised to see a man calling, opens the door.

"*Bonjour.*" Renée says with an unsmiling face.

"Oh, uh, I'm Sheriff Centori from Valtura to see Francine Fournier."

"I see. Please come in and wait here."

"Thank you."

When Francine learns of her male caller, she immediately reaches for a fine bottle of French perfume. Unknown in Santa Fe, she spent her early years in a Nice brothel. The brothel women raised Francine until she was old enough to return to Paris, the city of her birth. As a result, she is comfortable seeing unknown men.

As Francine parades into the reception area, her eyes widen with surprise at the sight of an interesting-looking man. She gives a dazzling smile before saying, "Bonjour, I am Madame Fournier, and to what do I owe this pleasure?" she almost sings the words.

Adobe becomes aware of a tantalizing fragrance and says, "I'm Sheriff Adobe Centori of Corona County, and the pleasure is mine."

Francine, who looks younger than her years, has a commanding presence as a desirable raven-haired beauty. She has brown eyes, fair coloring and wears a sophisticated dress that shows off her shape. Under her dress, silk and lace undergarments beautify her body.

"Excuse me one moment please," she says.

Walking away and back to her office, she informs Renée, "That will be all for today."

"Yes, of course, Madam," Renée says, and then, somewhat offended, mutters, "*Quelle femme arrogante,*" (What an arrogant woman) while reaching for her hat.

"*Je suis désolée, ma cheri.*" (I am sorry, my dear.)

Although annoyed, Renée accepts Francine's dominance and storms out. Francine thinks she can get any man she likes. Renée thinks Francine would like any man she can get.

"Now, Sheriff Centori," Francine's alert eyes show delight, "what can I do for you?" she says with a smile, while tossing her hair haughtily.

Francine is elegant despite her conceit and speaks perfect, though accented, English. Her speech pattern causes Adobe to become increasingly fascinated with the exotic French woman, causing him to stir.

Despite curiosity, he remains cool. After all, the business of investigating Santa Fe Sharon comes before any potential rendezvous.

Adobe takes a deep breath and states, "I understand Sharon Blaylock was a recent client here."

"Oh, I see. Mademoiselle Sharon." Francine fakes a dramatic pause and continues, "Is this a police matter?"

"It could be. What can you say about her?"

"She seemed like a person not given to notorious criminal pursuits."

"Really."

"Yes, Sheriff. I can't image why you would be interested in her, unless being a frisky female is a law enforcement priority," she says, again flipping her hair over her slender shoulders.

"Did she mention a sister in Valtura?"

"No. Our relationship was purely professional."

"I see."

After an extended silence, Francine ventures, "You are unlike the usual men found here. A lady can become quite frustrated by the lack of gentlemen."

"You are, indeed, quite the lady, Miss Fournier."

A beautiful woman of education and breeding impresses him, or at least the beautiful part, she thinks, and smiles to herself.

Overture received, thinks Adobe, but he delays taking the implied offer and says, "Perhaps you miss France, Madam Fournier."

"Shall we go into my parlor? We can have Champagne."

This could be the only way to learn about Santa Fe Sharon, Adobe jokes to himself.

He follows her into a well-appointed parlor, watching the view all the way. Once in the parlor, Francine produces a bottle of Champagne and two fancy flutes. With great skill, she pops the cork, pours and says, "This wine is exclusively from the Champagne region of France, from which it takes its name."

"Yes, of course. So why are you in Santa Fe?"

Although Francine's passion is beneath the surface, it fills the entire space as she hands him a glass and says, "New Mexico has a wild aspect I find invigorating. I can say no more about Mademoiselle Sharon, but please sit down and tell me about yourself."

Believing Francine has told all she knows about Sharon, Adobe becomes open to her overture. Sitting across from her, he explains his job as delegate to the state constitutional convention.

"Your job as delegate sounds like an exciting position."

"So is running the Circle C Ranch."

The Circle C is a topic he likes to discuss any time, but given the current opportunity, Francine will be the topic.

"You sound very proud of, how do you say, Sea Ranch?"

"That's *Circle C.* Yes, I am proud of it, having built it with my own two hands."

"Perhaps one day I will see your Circle C."

I don't know about that, he thinks, and then says, "I'm sure France was fascinating. You must have exciting stories to share."

Francine's eyes flash shut, her head dips downward, and then she faces him with a smile and whispers, "Perhaps we can evoke excitement tonight."

Demurely grasping her hands, she smiles again, unclasps her hands and pours more Champagne without asking. Although more than ready to take all of Francine, he senses her need to create sexual tension. He accepts the second glass, the intelligent conversation and the quantum leap to Francine's femininity.

"At seventeen I entered *La Sorbonne,* the University of Paris, and dreamt about being the very image of sophistication. Have you been to Paris, Sheriff?"

"No, Miss Francine, but I'm from New York, so I do know big city lights."

"Oh yes, New York. I knew you had a certain eastern appeal. I, too, have been to New York. While at the *Sorbonne*, I was determined that Fournier would become synonymous with French high class. Upon graduation, I achieved immediate fame in Paris, with many successes that revolutionized haute couture. I was the epitome of the type of glamour that personified the dreams of all young French women."

"That sounds exciting, but Santa Fe is a long way from Paris."

"I am completely and painfully aware of that fact. I had to leave France," she says mysteriously.

He sips his sparkling wine and waits for her to continue, wondering about her unwillingness to share her reason for leaving Paris.

She reads his mind. "I had to avoid an unfortunate situation."

Francine had a torrid love affair with a married French Minister. When it was exposed, she fled Paris to avoid a major scandal. She sailed to New York, hoping to start over. However, fashionable Fifth Avenue knew about the affair. Some believe there was a murder involved. What else would compel Francine to seek a new life in far away Santa Fe?

"So you came here from New York," he supposes, while moving closer.

"Yes," she says, smiling widely, "far enough away."

"Way out west to Santa Fe, I hope this town is not a millstone around your pretty neck."

Then, she announces, "I have been thinking about returning to Paris despite the scandal."

"Scandal?"

"Yes, well that is another story for another time. For now, I will tell you that I must change my name to return to France, but it will be worth it to be back."

"Sounds like more than wishful thinking."

"Yes, I have decided to leave in a few weeks."

"I'm sure you're making the right decision."

She touches his arm and says, "Yes, but I am still here for now."

The decisive moment arrives as he moves even closer. Expressing a wave of excitement, he says, "Francine, you are very captivating."

Feeling equally energized, she grins and says, "Do you like Shakespeare?"

"Yes, I do."

Francine stands and smiles with her arms akimbo. She carefully selects a story that she believes he would care about and recites:

Captain of our fairy band,
Helena is here at hand,
And the youth, mistook by me,
Pleading for a lover's fee.
Shall we their fond pageant see?
Lord, what fools these mortals be!

Adobe marvels at her tone, pronunciation, cadence and crescendo. Francine found the right guise to present her meaning and artistically choreographed her movement for seductive effectiveness. It worked—almost anything would have. The message from the movements of her body is one word from the many; the one word is *yes.*

"That was a wonderful recital, Miss Francine."

"Thank you. Do you agree with Shakespeare that love is madness, causing lovers to act foolishly?"

Consumed by obsession he answers, "I happily agree with Shakespeare and his assessment."

They sip champagne, talk and laugh. Then he is surprised to see Francine gently remove her shoes and say, "You are unlike any man I have known in Santa Fe. *Now* I find something to miss about New Mexico."

"As you said, you are still here for now, Francine."

"Yes, I am, Adobe."

Without warning, Francine luxuriously peels off her black stockings, revealing her shapely naked legs. His glowing appreciation of the exciting show encourages her. She boldly removes her dress showing her finest French lingerie. Perhaps when she dressed she sensed that a man would visit and would adore her alluring outfit. Adobe definitely does.

Francine stands and reaches for his hand and squeezes hard. He stands and moves closer, embracing her full body in his arms. She steps back, places her hands on his shoulders and whispers, "*Pense à moi de temps en temps.*" *(Think of me from time to time.)*

16

BUENA SUERTE

The man who had approached Adobe earlier at the hotel restaurant anxiously arrives for a meeting at St. Francis Street, off the plaza. Santa Fe Sharon waits with a cocked Winchester, held at the ready. The rifle is not the best weapon for close range, but it can do the job.

"You wish to see me?" the man asks.

"What gives you the right to talk about me—to a delegate! What's his name?" Sharon shouts.

"Centori."

"Here in Santa Fe? You should have told me immediately! Damn you!"

"*Loco en la cabeza*."

"Your first mistake was approaching Centori without permission; you were under no orders to do so. Your job is to identify delegates in the hotel, that's all! Your second mistake is meeting me here."

"*Charla grande para una mujer,"* he says. (Big talk for a woman).

She quickly decides his fate.

"Might this change your mind?"

He finds himself looking at the barrel of the Winchester. She fires at point blank range, destroying his midsection and taking his life. Sharon steps over the dead body and says, "*Buena suerte* in the afterlife." She pulls out a Red Tip, which conceals lipstick but not blood stains, and disappears into the night.

Competition between predator and prey is part of the natural order, with life as the reward. The predator sharpens senses with experience, patience and skill. Santa Fe Sharon grows strong and perhaps unstoppable.

Back at the Plaza Hotel, Adobe takes a late dinner alone and thinks about the afternoon rendezvous with Francine. *Too bad she is returning to France, it would be a good to see her during future Santa Fe trips. Dora should still be here, but she means nothing to me—I get lost sometimes.*

"*Señor?*"

"Whiskey, fried chicken, biscuits and gravy."

"*Si Señor.*"

The waiter returns quickly with whiskey and tortillas with chopped tomatoes, onions and jalapeno peppers. *The service has improved,* he thinks. Adobe, who is usually friendly, accepts the refreshments without a word; he has other things on his mind.

The way Francine expressed her sexual aggressiveness was an exceptional experience, not true love but a delightful detour. The road to happiness is unclear. Does the path go through love or lust? Sometimes there is no time to decide.

Twenty minutes later, the waiter returns and says pleasantly, "*Aqui esta tu comida, Señor.*"

"*Gracias.*"

Ten minutes later, looking up from his dinner and his thoughts, Adobe sees a tall man in a tall hat. It is City Marshal Johnny Romano. He figures it is a courtesy call, one police officer to another. He is wrong.

"Hello, Sheriff Centori."

"Evening, Marshal Romano, have a seat and join me."

Adobe signals for another whiskey glass.

"Thanks, and welcome back to Santa Fe. I understand you're the Corona County delegate to the statehood convention."

"Yes sir. It will be one fine day when New Mexico becomes a full part of the U.S."

He pours Romano a drink from his bottle.

"Amen. Say, I understand you were talking to a man this morning at this table."

Adobe puts down his biscuit and says, "Yes, he is a complete stranger to me."

"Well, he was no stranger around the plaza, and he is dead."

Startled by the news, Adobe stares and says, "How?"

"Killed, shot dead outside of town on St. Francis Road. Mind if I see your gun?"

Adobe palms his Navy Colt and hands it to Romano. He takes a perfunctory look and gives it back.

"You consider me involved with the killing?"

"No, but you spoke to him. What can you tell me?"

"Not much. He was concerned about my Santa Fe Sharon inquiry and offered some information about her for money. I don't deal that way."

"Santa Fe Sharon," Johnny echoes. "My office is aware of her."

"Marshall, this news is most concerning. Who was that man? Who killed him and why? Was he involved in some sort of criminal behavior?"

"I'm working on it, Adobe."

"Sure, I understand. You said you are aware of Santa Fe Sharon. There could be connections to Valtura. Do you know Mady Blaylock?"

"I know the famous Mad Mady's Saloon on the plaza."

"Mady has a sister named Sharon Blaylock."

"Blaylock? I don't know Sharon by that name. Are you sure Santa Fe Sharon is Mady's sister?"

"Not yet. There may be no relation, but there is a concern. Mady feels threatened by Sharon."

"Threatened?"

"It's a long story. I asked around about Santa Fe Sharon—that probably attracted the stranger to me."

"Okay, I will keep you informed about the killing and any news on Santa Fe Sharon—I'll see if she uses the name Blaylock."

"All right. Thanks."

"Hope you had a good trip up here."

"Yes, Santa Fe proved to be eventful, but I'll be happy to get back to the Circle C and Valtura."

Adobe thinks about the two female encounters and keeps them to himself.

"When you come back to Santa Fe, I'll buy the drinks."

"You got a deal. *Adios*, Johnny."

"*Buena suerte, Amico.*"

Adobe returns to his dinner and his thoughts, *The governor understands my politics and the Senate seems like a real possibility. We made progress on the rail extension, two women were much more than kind, there was some information on Santa Fe Sharon, but the killing was troubling. Overall, it was damn well worth the time. There will be an early start to Valtura in the morning; I hope Dora is out of surprises.*

17

FOURTH OF JULY

Two days later, Adobe rides past the Circle C and goes directly to Valtura, knowing Mady has been anxiously awaiting his return. A patriotic Independence Day celebration, organized by the Valtura Merchant Association, is underway as he enters town.

The plaza illuminations are on a grand scale. The people are smiling, delighted by the outdoor lighting. Most Valtura residents and many visitors from other Corona County towns are present. Patriotic music, readings and songs—including the "Star Spangled Banner"—are part of the party. Adobe smiles as he rides past people dressed as Uncle Sam, the Goddess of Liberty, Revolutionary War figures, and American founders.

When he enters the crowded Mad Mady's Saloon, Mady drops everything and rushes to him. "Welcome back, Adobe."

"It's good to be back, Mady. Look, I know you want to hear about Sharon, so I will get right to it."

"Go right ahead!" She signals Berta to send over a bottle then leads Adobe to her table.

"Your sister—or at least a woman known as Santa Fe Sharon—is in Santa Fe.

Berta arrives with a full tray and says, "Welcome back, Sheriff."

"Berta," he replies with a smile.

He waits for Berta to leave and says, "Many people there have heard of Santa Fe Sharon. Some say she is a shady character who carries a pistol."

"That could be my sister."

Ben, the piano player, strains to overhear the conversation. Mady turns her head to express her privacy; Ben shrugs and turns his head back to his music sheets.

Adobe continues, "We don't know for sure and she could have left Santa Fe. I also learned that she seems to be interested in statehood."

"Statehood? Sharon cares nothing of politics," she says with surprise. "Do you know what this woman looks like?"

"Only by description, of course. A woman named Dora said Sharon loves showing off her beauty."

"Who's Dora?"

"She's just the hotel desk clerk. She said Sharon has a slender shape even *without* wearing a corset. Have you known your sister to have close female friends?"

"I don't know!"

"Okay, it doesn't matter. We need to determine if this woman is your sister. Most days she wears blue pants and vest, a red shirt and a stylish brown hat."

It strikes them at the same time—*Mady* tends to wear blue pants and vest and a red shirt.

Mady looks at her stylish brown hat that is hanging on an adjacent chair and says, "Santa Fe Sharon is my sister."

"She is a very good taker, but a very bad giver."

"That sounds like Sharon, all right,"

Mady pauses and continues, “Is there anything else?”

“She visited a fancy French salon.”

“A French salon…. What is she up to now?”

“I don’t know, but the woman in the French place felt that Sharon does not have a criminal nature but the governor implied the opposite is true.”

“You spoke to the governor about this situation?”

“Yes, as I promised.”

“So where does that leave us? What should we do?”

“Not much, Mady. Except be ready for your sister—if she shows up in Valtura.”

”Okay, what can I do to thank you?” Mady smiles.

Adobe comes close to acquiescing, but reluctantly says, “Let’s watch the fireworks together.”

“I will be glad to do so.”

They walk outside and wait for the show.

“Mady, this will probably be the last Fourth of July we celebrate as a territory.”

“Good point, Adobe. Even with the slow pace in Washington, we should be a state before next summer.”

Mady notices Klara Morgenstern in the crowd and says, “We can have a better view from the roof of my place.”

He turns around to look up at the big Mad Mady’s Saloon sign.

“Okay, Mady, let’s go to the roof.”

Adobe and Mady stand behind the parapet that holds the sign for Mad Mady’s Saloon, and watch the crowd in the plaza. At sundown, the much anticipated fireworks show begins.

A thousand points of light and sparkling trails illuminate the sky over Valtura Plaza. Aerial shell bursts fall slowly in erratic patterns. Mady turns to Adobe and points to the single and double rings of red, white and blue stars that are erupting with a fabulous flash. Then the large stars fall for a short distance and burst again.

The display of brilliant skyrockets dazzles the people and ends in a blaze of patriotic glory and applause.

"That was quite a celebration, Adobe."

"Yes, it was. Happy birthday, USA!"

They embrace, but not for long. Adobe returns to the Circle C, alone. There will be no further fireworks on this Fourth of July.

18

Sears and Roebuck Catalog

Mademoiselle Sharon grudgingly agreed to meet Carrie at San Miguel's Church.

"How much longer?" Carrie asks with uneasiness.

"When I say so—that's when! Don't pretend you dislike your work on Calle Montano."

"Oh, and you can get by on your brains?"

Sharon steps forward and growls, "I don't have time to waste on you. You will be in Valtura when the shipments begin to arrive—not before and not after. Now meet me here in one week. All should be ready."

Carrie storms away, but she will return as ordered. Another issue is delaying Carrie's departure. To complete Mademoiselle Sharon's fancy attire, Sharon has been purchasing satin dresses embroidered with floral patterns and small ribbons in various pastel shades with sewn-in sequins. Other dresses are made of crepe de chine, chiffon and mousseline de soie, and tulle. Blouses decorated with tucking and circular trimmings of fluted muslin complete the new array of fabulous clothing.

Carrie has her schedule—so does Mademoiselle Sharon. Sharon is using a mail-order catalog from Sears, Roebuck and Company to purchase her fancy dresses. The company handles mail orders economically and proficiently, but deliveries still take time. The Valtura part of the international conspiracy depends on the Sears and Roebuck catalog.

19

VALTURA RAIL STATION

July became August and the new month shows early signs of fall, with daytime temperatures reaching only eighty degrees. Yet it is hot, particularly on the open range and at the isolated rail station. The New Mexico railroads continued the economic impact that the Camino Real and the Santa Fe Trail had on the territory.

In addition to passengers, cattle and freight move via the rails. Railroads carry natural resources such as lumber, potash, coal, sulfur and copper throughout the Southwest. Towns along or near the tracks of railroad companies grew and flourished. Remote outposts similar to Valtura became small towns, and a few small towns became big towns.

The Valtura Rail Station, completed in 1900, is not in Valtura at all; it sits five miles east at a crossroads. What's more, the station is a flag stop; trains stop for a displayed flag or for a departing passenger. Despite the distance, the railroad line began to contribute to Valtura's growth as soon as the first locomotive arrived.

The rail station, a single-story building with red brick walls and a bluestone base, is vacant. Two single-room frame structures stand alongside the station. The platform has a curved verandah with cast-iron columns and a corrugated metal roof. A red, white and blue 46-star American flag whips in the wind. A loud whistle announces the locomotive, breaking the eerie silence of the open range.

The train huffs and puffs as steam spews out of the stack, then stops, allowing passengers to depart. There is only one passenger. A cloud of smoke partially conceals a tall blonde woman carrying a small valise.

Carrie Carlson, who obtained a fair amount of toughness on Calle Montano, is ready to implement the detailed plan for Mad Mady's Saloon. She has been languishing on Calle Montano waiting for Sharon's departure order. It took time for Sharon to arrange shipments to Mady's saloon.

Shipments of fine furniture and accessories will allow Mad Mady's Saloon to emerge in the image of Mademoiselle Sharon and win favor in Valtura, and especially with Adobe Centori. Carrie must be in Valtura to receive shipments of those goods—but not too soon. Finally, the timing is right. Although kept under tight control and unaware of the statehood plot, she senses that there is more to the picture than meets the eye.

Her brown eyes, annoyed by the coal dust, seek the train station contact. There is no one waiting. Carrie, nonplussed, wonders if something has gone wrong and how she will travel the five miles to Valtura. She calmly accepts the challenge of the current situation without fear. Sharon thought she had it figured, but this impediment could hurt the plan—a plan that demands efficient timing.

White smoke shoots from the engine's stack into the clear blue sky as the train starts to move again. The whistle blows, and the big, black, steam engine slowly picks up speed and heads toward the horizon. After the deafening departure, the desert reverts to motionless quiet. It is the last train to come through until tomorrow morning.

A screaming eagle soars above as Carrie stands alone on the platform weighing her options. The eagle's wingspan is massive, reaching at least ten feet. Eagle eyes look down, harshly watching the world from a high position. Under a hot sun, Carrie feels the presence of something and turns to see a lone coyote at the end of the platform. She is anxious and walks away, but when she turns again, the animal is gone.

Coyotes pursue their goals persistently—so will Carrie. She decides to hide her bags in a clump of trees and starts on foot. If the train station contact is coming, perhaps they will cross paths. Besides, there will be other trips to the station for the shipping crates.

Within several hundred feet of the station, the sound of a coyote disturbs Carrie. Although he is no longer visible, he is audible. *Why is he howling?* she thinks.

In the Southwest, the coyote howl is well known; a cry in the wilderness calls for the salvation of the world. Yet the purpose of the howling could be to add enervating stress to Carrie's life. If that is the reason, it has worked. Carrie walks faster without looking back, feeling the sweat on her back. She looks left and right—surrounded by wide-open spaces—she studies the view in each direction. Carrie heads west as the only person on the face of the earth.

In less than two minutes, Carrie reconsiders and returns to the station for refuge. She retrieves her trunk and settles in suspense, hoping for the contact to arrive.

20

FOURTH ESTATE, FIRST INTERVIEW

When Louisiana was French, many hardworking Germans immigrated to St. Louis, including Johan Morgenstern, who worked as a clerk for the *St. Louis Post-Dispatch.* After his wife Klara died during childbirth, he channeled all of his energy into journalism and into raising his daughter.

To the surprise of many in the city with a growing German population, Johan and young Klara abruptly left St. Louis. They arrived in Valtura before the turn of the century, where he started the Valtura Journal in 1899. Editor-in-chief Johan Morgenstern and his daughter Klara are dedicated publishers.

The Valtura Journal is widely read in Corona County and the publishers want to expand readership to territorial-wide coverage. To help in this goal, Johan is planning a series of articles on the history of New Mexico's quest for statehood. It is a compelling story, one that the editor intends to share with his readers.

The insights of the people who have lived through certain times can be as valuable as historical documents. Oral history accounts provide a narrative about the people, the leaders and the challenges of the past. Through stories gained from interviews, the Valtura Journal will document and preserve knowledge of the road to statehood. Colonel Santos is an important historical resource with much information. More than most, he has a depth of knowledge about the territory and a unique perspective into New Mexico's past.

The colonel sits on his porch at a table with a jug of wine and a loaf of crusty black bread, anticipating a quiet afternoon. Then the sound of a four-cylinder, 20-horsepower engine in the distance catches his attention. It is Johan's Model T Ford driving along the rough road of East Corona Street.

"Colonel," Johan shouts from his motorcar.

"*Bueno dias.* Welcome to my humble home."

"Colonel Santos, I am the one humbled to be in the presence of Valtura's most respected citizen."

"You are too kind."

The colonel invites him to sit down and says, "Would you like a glass of wine?"

"No thanks, it's a little early for me."

"You don't mind if I do? It helps my joints."

"Of course not, Colonel."

"What brings you here today?"

"As editor of the largest paper in Corona County," he boasts, "I am preparing a series of statehood articles. Our territorial status has lasted longer than most other U.S. territories. But statehood is close, so we would like to publish the history of New Mexico's quest for statehood."

"That is a good idea, but what do you wish from me?" he asks unassumingly.

"You could help write the long, admirable story of New Mexico's fight for statehood. I am here to ask you about an oral history, an interview for the newspaper. You could tell our readers about your experiences in the territory, the past attempts for statehood and perhaps your current position on statehood."

"Johan, you place too much trust in me. I am an old man with fading memories."

"You are too modest, Colonel. You have witnessed much of territorial history. Your knowledge can provide an extensive background."

"As a fine journalist, you naturally seek interesting stories about New Mexico."

"Yes, I do, and the power of the press can help tell those stories."

"There are such stories that should be retold now that we are close to statehood."

"Yes, indeed. In view of the latest efforts, may I have the honor of recording your oral history?"

The colonel pauses for a moment and then declares, "I will try to help you."

"Excellent! I would like that glass of wine now."

Watching the colonel pour, he states, "We are both from countries other than America and now we work together on her behalf."

"Countries other than America, that's amusing. I was born in Las Cruces, New Mexico, when it was part of Old Mexico and before it became a U.S. territory. New Mexico was Spanish much longer than it has been American. In fact, *my country* is within the current U.S. boundaries."

"No offense intended."

"None taken, but it is true that many New Mexican laws are of Spanish beginnings and the names of many towns are Spanish," says the colonel, thereby starting the interview. "After the war, the U.S. acquired New Mexico and California by occupation and then cession."

"I understand. New Mexico is great because of the Spanish and American cultural inheritances."

"The cultural legacy goes back more than 400 years. The story of statehood has its roots in Spanish-American history. Before the Mexican Cession, and independence from Spain, we were a Spanish colony with missions and settlements throughout New Mexico."

"Colonel, you mention the Mexican Cession. You were a soldier who fought and witnessed the war and then your home was in a ceded region."

"Yes, Johan, I was among the over 100,000 Mexican citizens living in the ceded territories. After the signing of the Treaty of Guadalupe-Hidalgo, Mexican citizens were granted American citizenship and assured language, religion and land protection. However, land protections fell short of expectations. So you see I am not exactly from another country."

"I know there is a long history, Colonel. I meant that the American political philosophy is different from Germany and Old Mexico."

"On that I can agree, in part. After the war, Mexicans who remained in the ceded lands for a year could become American citizens if they wished. Then the U.S. Senate changed the language from 'admitted as soon as possible' to 'admitted at the proper time.' The *norteamericanos* had a way with words."

"It was a subtle, but key distinction," Colonel."

"Ahem, they were not so subtle about Mesilla. The village started after the war as a reaction to the border moving south of Doña Ana, placing it in the U.S. Some people were not happy being in the U.S. and moved south of the border to Mesilla.

Johan looks up from writing and says, "That was a decisive move."

"But not without consequences. A few years later, when the people, north and south of the border, needed protection from Apache attacks, the U.S. built a military post north of the border in Mesilla Valley."

Writing and speaking at the same time, Johan says, "And the military post was welcomed help."

"Not exactly. The norteamericanos declared the Mesilla Valley part of the U.S., creating a boundary dispute."

Putting his pen down, Johan looks up and waits for the colonel, who takes a drink of wine and cuts his black bread.

The colonel continues, "The boundary dispute was resolved with the Gadsden Purchase. Mesilla and the southern regions of Arizona and New Mexico became part of the U.S."

"Both parties were satisfied with the resolution?"

"No. The issue was far from being resolved. In fact, border issues became…." He stops short and changes direction. "Johan, do you know that Mexican-Americans were a majority in New Mexico until 1900?"

"I did not know, Colonel."

"Some argue that Washington delayed statehood due to Mexican-American political leadership, denying the basic American principle of self-government. Think of the words, 'we the people of the United States.' Are we not *all* the people of the United States?"

"Yes, but not completely. The people of the territory of New Mexico are without self-government."

"That is correct."

"Self-government showed the way for our long road of statehood."

"A very long road; no other American territory has waited as long as New Mexico for statehood, no other territory has framed more constitutions and no other has had more enabling acts from Congress. Discriminatory attitudes against Hispanic, Roman Catholic and Spanish-speaking people stopped many attempts at statehood. No full citizenship for such people," he laments.

Johan barely looks up as he quickly writes every word down on a long pad.

The colonel goes on, "You said the American political philosophy is different from those of Germany and Old Mexico. Ironically, a majority of men of Spanish descent wrote the first New Mexican constitution in 1850."

"Colonel Santos, that information is exactly the type of insight I knew you could contribute."

The colonel smiles and sips his wine. Johan follows his lead and says, "Many are aware that the U.S. acquired New Mexico in 1846, but we remain a territory. There must have been compelling reasons for this delay, reasons that we should explore."

"Johan, lack of trying is not one of the reasons. Ever since the American era began in the 1840s, we have attempted statehood. Yet we have fought for and resisted statehood at the same time. Many people feel a strong tie to their rich history and to their culture. They believe that New Mexico is a very distinctive land. Some even believed that the territory could revert to Mexico."

"What?"

The colonel stops cold for a moment and says, "I mean that they had little experience with the U.S. government."

Johan nods and says, "That is true, but what about territorial government?"

Colonel Santos reaches for his glass, drinks and realizes that the conversation could take an awkward turn. He offers, "The first New Mexico legislation started in 1847 with Antonio Sandoval of Bernalillo County as president. Their first official position was a call for education, with a school in every town."

"That was a good start. Democracy and self-government require educated citizens," Johan adds.

"And statehood could promote education and other aspects of the public good. "Would you like more wine?"

"No thank you, Colonel."

"If you don't mind, I'll take another glass."

After the colonel provides details of the educational issues, including teaching English in all schools, Johan sees his physical discomfort and says, "We can continue this another day."

"Perhaps that would be best."

"That's fine. Thank you for your time and thoughts, Colonel Santos."

"Buenas tardes, Johan."

The colonel pours another glass of wine and thinks about the uncomfortable moments of the interview. While in the Mexican Army, he was part of a highly confidential mission. He could be the only surviving member of that long ago expedition, an event that gave him a secret and a special interest in Mexico's former province.

21

LITTLE PURPLE FLOWERS

It is midsummer in New Mexico. At the Circle C, Adobe watches the faint hint of daylight from the portal. The scent of sage fills the Sunday morning air. *She loves the sage plant and its little purple flowers,* he thinks.

Their bedroom is elegant, with polished hardwood furniture and a colorful down comforter. The entire Circle C became complete when she arrived. The fine touches of new paint along with curtains and rugs from Mexico created warmth. He believes that her radiant presence can transform any empty room into a warm place.

Although Adobe is up before sunrise, waking next to her is like waking up to sunshine. He cherishes the mornings and tries not to wake her—she looks too beautiful when asleep. At times, she feels uncomfortable with his deep loving gaze. She warned him about placing her too high on a pedestal for fear of being beyond reach. Since angels belong in the heavens, he does not care.

Standing on the portal, a gentle breeze flows down from the mountains. Soon she will be up brushing her silky black hair with morning sunlight illuminating her beauty. Thinking of the day to come, he looks forward to sharing it with his queen: the Queen of Circle C. Their quiet morning will start with coffee and kisses. Perhaps they will ride the range today; she takes pleasure in racing her young mare against the old warhorse Patriot.

Returning to the bedroom, he finds her in a different, more inviting position. Walking to the bed ready to accept, he feels warm at the thought of intimacy. A kiss is only seconds away, but first a few more moments of watching a living dream. Then a sound in the distance. *The mission bells peal in Valtura,* he thinks. *No, the bells are too far away.*

Then the quick beating of a horse pounding the ground causes him to turn around. When he turns back, there is no Gabriella, no woman—only an empty bed. Jolted by the sound of a horse on the long path to the house, he jumps out of bed. The rhythm of hoof beats on the dust intensifies, returning him to reality, and his heart sinks. Another dream of the imagination...she is gone again. A dream that expressed a life desired as opposed to the life he has.

As he pulls on his pants, he hears his name, "Adobe, Adobe, Mady is gone!" the rider yelled. Rushing outside, still flush with unrequited passion, he sees an out of breath woman with a face distorted by anxiety running toward him. It is Berta Brandt.

"Calm down, calm down, you are hysterical. Take a breath, Berta, and come in. What are you talking about?"

"Just what I said, Mady is missing," she announces, still breathing hard.

"Are you certain?"

"When I arrived at work this morning I found the saloon locked. I stopped asking Mady for a key a while ago. After banging on the door with no answer, I went around back, up the stairs and looked into her room. It was empty; her bed hadn't even been slept in."

"What does that prove?"

"Well, at first I thought she might be here at the Circle C, having spent the night."

"Oh, that old rumor again. Don't listen to idle gossipers."

"Okay, but we both know it is unlike Mady not to leave word, especially when it comes to her saloon. She always left me in charge whenever she left Valtura. What should we do?" her voice is uneven with emotion.

Adobe is crestfallen for missing a dreamy rendezvous with Gabriella and irritated at Berta for killing his vision. However, it is time to deal with the real world. *Berta is right; this is unlike Mady. She could be in some kind of danger.*

"Let me get dressed. Why don't you make some coffee in the meantime?"

"Okay," she says, glancing at his strong, naked chest.

Berta prepares and waits for the brew; Adobe goes back to the bedroom to dress and looks at the vacant bed. *God, I miss you and only see you in my dreams, but reality has a way of suppressing dreams.*

A minute later, he enters the kitchen. Berta has two cups out waiting for the coffee when A.P. bursts in, "Everything okay?"

"It's Mady. She's gone, perhaps missing," says Berta, still frantic.

"Missing?" A.P. turns and nods to Berta, who grabs another cup.

"We're going into Valtura. Please saddle up Patriot."

"Okay," A.P. says, without waiting for coffee.

Adobe turns back to Berta and says, "Ordinarily, I wouldn't be that concerned, but Mady was worried about Santa Fe Sharon. In a strange way I'm not surprised Mady is gone."

"It doesn't sound like a coincidence," she agrees while pouring out cups of coffee.

"No it doesn't."

Taking his coffee to the window, Adobe shakes free of Gabriella's ghost and notices a coyote on Little Hill Top. The coyote is a mesmerizing animal, filled with paradox, combining wisdom and folly for a successful life. Some believe the coyote controls dreams to calm, cure and make sleep overpowering. Perhaps the coyote used his magic to conjure the beautiful dreamer.

Sometimes the gloom of disappointment lingers, but there is no time for self-pity today. Adobe downs the last of his coffee as A.P. returns with Patriot. He looks at Berta and says, “Let’s ride to Valtura.”

“Okay. I’m worried about Mady.”

“So am I.”

22

Territorial Insane Asylum

After Arizona separated from New Mexico in 1864, the new territorial legislature viewed mental issues as a government responsibility. Counties confined insane people in county jails or in places deemed best for the person and for the town. In 1908, when the jail system failed to handle the volume, the legislature met to appropriate funding for the construction of an insane asylum in a remote part of New Mexico.

Under the legislature's direction, workers cleared thirty acres of sagebrush in Rio Arriba County near Loma Lake for construction of the facility. The newly established board of directors appointed Dr. Thornton N. Trumble as medical director.

The New Mexico Territorial Insane Asylum opened with a capacity of seventy-five patients with a small staff, including Head Administrative Nurse Darcie Denton. The complex, built as a Gothic Revival Castle, has turrets, towers and buttresses flying across four attached buildings. The main building contains a kitchen, dining area, industrial workshops, auditorium and many small rooms.

At the discretion of the medical director, policies regarding declarations of insanity, confinement and release are informally established. With no legal process for confinement, people are committed for many reasons, such as old age, tuberculosis and feeble-mindedness. In some cases, there is no reason at all, except perhaps duplicity.

As sunset nears, two tired riders travel toward the New Mexico Territorial Insane Asylum and search for its landmark, Loma Lake. The woman was combative during the first hours of the trip and then fell silent as the trip lengthened. Fatigue won over persistence and the man likes it that way. The male rider, clearly in charge, breaks the long silence between them and asks, "Are you all right?"

"What the hell do you care?" She looks over, eyes burning with rage.

"Well, since we're traveling together, we could be civil."

"What? *Traveling together*? *Civil*? You kidnapped me at gunpoint!"

Ellison ignores her comment and retreats into silence. At times in his life, he has struggled to maintain his moral compass and has succumbed to lawlessness—this is one of those times.

After sunset, as twilight grows deeper, the dusty and exhausted riders finally arrive at Loma Lake and water their horses. The other rider is Mad Mady Blaylock.

"Adobe will not be happy about this. I thought you were his friend."

"What makes you think he'll find out?"

Mady, with unflappable resolve, says, "He *will* find out. And when he does, it will be the end of you."

"He might agree with me."

"You're crazy! Why did you do this?" she demands.

He does not answer.

They approach the fortress-like main building and Ellison

pounds loudly on a brass knocker attached to a large door. No one responds. Accustomed to dealing with stubborn cattle, he simply pounds harder. Soon, sounds of metal rattling come from behind the heavy door; it squeaks, swings open and a tall, medium-built woman dressed in white stares at the late arrivals.

At first glance, Head Nurse Darcie Denton appears to be a cold, sadistic tyrant and most avoid a second glance. In her position, she reports directly to Dr. Trumble and provides balance to his erratic behavior; she is invaluable to running the questionable organization. She is empowered to maintain order, control patients and prevent escapes. Standing behind Nurse Denton, ready to receive the new patient, is Ray Raton, security chief.

"Hello, Nurse, I'm Henry Ellison and this is Mady Blaylock."

"Yes, we are expecting you."

This frightens Mady, who glares at Ellison and yells, "This is a horrible mistake!"

"Good evening, Mr. Ellison. Miss Blaylock, please come in."

"Nothing good here, and I won't stay!"

Mady's resistance is not surprising to Nurse Denton. Lately, the asylum has received several prominent women from around the territory.

"He had no right forcing me here," she appeals to Nurse Denton. "You must release me and stop this unauthorized confinement."

Nurse Denton enjoys the corrupt power and ignores Mady's protest. She studies Mady and pushes the heavy door open.

"Dr. Trumble doesn't see new arrivals after sundown, but in your high-profile case he may make an exception. Follow me."

High profile? That is a strange comment. Maybe this will straighten out once I see the doctor, Mady thinks.

Mady, an inconvenience to Santa Fe Sharon, was spirited away by Ellison, as arranged by Sharon, who believed he was corruptible.

She was right. Having completed the job, Ellison takes his leave, rides away and thinks about how he came to this day. Previous jobs have straddled the fence of right and wrong, but he has second thoughts about this one. Committing Mady violates Adobe's trust. *I hope Santa Fe Sharon is right about Mady not returning to Valtura,* he thinks.

When Ellison pauses beside Loma Lake, he sees a coyote out of the corner of his eye. In mythology, the coyote gave man the greatest gift, the ability to think. Ellison acknowledges the trickster and rides by, feeling a great burden.

Three nights earlier, Ellison entered Mad Mady's Saloon after closing and before Mady went upstairs, and announced that they would be taking a trip. Mady made a big protest to no avail; Ellison pointed his gun at her and forced her to ride out of town. Despite his ambivalence, his job is now done.

Nurse Denton and Ray Raton escort Mady into the medical director's office. Dr. Trumble grew up in Manhattan's Lower East Side, home to urban working-class and poor immigrants. As a youth, he worked grooming draft horses at Bellevue Hospital, known for its psychiatric facilities and training of medical leaders.

Dr. Trumble studied Freud and adhered to his theory that some experiences had not happened at all but were memories based on early fantasies. His empirical research on false memory is suspect. He is semi-competent with questionable ethical standards. With his dubious psychiatric knowledge and his claim to have a medical degree from a Canadian college, he sought opportunities in the West. Given the shortage of qualified psychiatrists in New Mexico, he was able to acquire the position of medical director of the asylum.

Despite a cloud of suspicion, Dr. Trumble keeps the authorities at bay while engaging in diagnosis and treatment of mental disorders. Although he hits the jug around sundown, his therapeutic technique of long-term treatment has proven to be successful—for his personal agenda.

"Dr. Trumble, meet our new resident, Miss Blaylock, also known as Mad Mady Blaylock of Valtura," says the nurse. Ray stands guard at the office door.

"That's Mad Mady!" Dr. Trumble exclaims.

Another strange comment, she thought.

The office displays a medical library and various medical items. His cluttered desk has many files, papers and more than a few bottles.

"Please sit down Miss Blaylock. I am sure you will be comfortable with us."

Mady is ready for a calm conversation to argue her position, but loses control and explodes, "What the hell am I doing here?"

Her wild eyes, bamboozled behavior and volatile demeanor are a self-fulfilling prophecy. Acting the part of a person needing treatment, she screams, "Let me out of here, I have a saloon to run, a payroll to meet. This is a terrible mistake!"

"I'm sure your saloon will be fine, perhaps even better."

Better? What does he mean by that? Mady thinks, while searching for answers and her composure.

"I was kidnapped by Ellison," she screams.

"Miss Blaylock, you were not kidnapped, as temporary undersheriff, Mr. Ellison was well within his authority."

"I tell you, he took me here by gunpoint!"

"Miss Blaylock, that *experience* did not really happen, it is a memory based on an early fantasy. It was all a proper commitment, I assure you."

"But I don't belong here!"

"I'm sorry, but based on your file you are a candidate for our institution."

"What file? You don't even know me."

"It is my professional opinion...."

"That's it, let me out. This can't be legal."

Dr. Trumble is annoyed with her protest, especially since it is jug time. He glances at Nurse Denton to blame her for this inconvenience. Mady is not going along with the program. Nobody in her situation would cooperate and she will never submit without a powerful protest.

"Miss Blaylock, we can take you here against your will; involuntary commitment *is legal* as part of our territorial laws. Ellison is an authorized agent of the law and has the right to commit you," Dr. Trumble explains.

"For what?"

"For reasons we deem appropriate."

Unconvinced, Mady becomes infuriated. She jumps up to escape and Ray blocks the door. She turns, stares at Dr. Trumble and says, "Do you want to see *why* they call me Mad Mady?"

"That will not be necessary and would be an unwise decision on your part. Allow me to explain your situation more carefully. A lawman can request a commitment for psychiatric evaluation."

"But you have no warrant."

"We don't need one," Dr. Trumble boasts. "You are here for a short time. If after your evaluation we determine you need further treatment, we will get a court order. Fear not, Miss Blaylock, involuntary commitment is limited and requires re-evaluation. We must have a court order for more than short-term treatment."

"Evaluated for what?"

"We have been informed that you were exhibiting dangerous behavior that allows us to hold you for evaluation. You see, your brothel is a threat to the fabric of society."

"What? That's crazy. I mean no one has ever complained and everyone knows the difference between upstairs and downstairs operations!"

"Nevertheless, your upstairs business is illegal."

"But not insane!"

"It is irrational and subject to insanity."

"It's the world's oldest profession!" Mady screams like a maniac.

"Then it's the world's oldest irrational profession."

"Because it doesn't conform to *your* idea of rationality?"

"Yes, my idea—and every sane person's idea. Look, government agencies have yielded to the theories and practices of the psychiatric field. Perhaps the laws and rules are somewhat ambiguous, but you are clearly under my supervision now."

"I want to call Sheriff Adobe Centori in Valtura," Mady demands. "Do you have a telephone?"

Ignoring her demand, Dr. Trumble says, "We shall start observation and treatment in the morning. You should accept your short-term situation. If you do not, there could be another serious legal issue relating to the new Mann Act."

"What man?"

"Congress passed the Mann Act forbidding the transport of women across state lines for irrational uses."

"What does that have to do with me?"

"It is alleged that some of your upstairs women are from Texas and Colorado. If this is true, your situation can change for the worse. Nurse, please ask *Señorita Valdez* to take Miss Blaylock to her room."

Valdez, a patient attendant, is sympathetic to those who are involuntarily committed, and powerless to help patients in cases of wrongful confinement.

Mady jumps up abruptly, shaking with anger, and says, "This is maddening!"

She starts toward the door with a burst of energy, but Ray blocks the way. Mady attempts to shove him aside with surprising strength.

He braces and holds his ground. Overwhelmed, she realizes that further resistance is crazy. After firing him a murderous look, Mady regains her composure and reluctantly yields to her captors.

Nurse Denton takes her arm and leads her away under Ray's watchful eyes. Dr. Trumble smiles at Ray, who knows the medical director accommodates requests to remove inconvenient people—at a price.

Mady moves through the austere halls with all-consuming questions racing through her mind. *Why did Ellison do this? Why am I here?* She misses the most important question of all—who could be so cunning?

Nurse Denton unlocks the door to a small space containing a steel frame bed with a thin green mattress. Mady freezes in the doorway.

"No point in complaining," Nurse Denton says, "your days of saloons and cantinas are over. You are a psychiatric patient now, stop acting like one. Accept your situation, or you could get lost in the confusion."

Nurse Denton shoves Mady in and slams the door.

23

MAD MADY MISSING

Adobe and Berta waste no time in getting to Valtura, racing to town in record time. Galloping down East Corona Street, they pass early churchgoers and then a deserted plaza. Turning left on First Street and right on National Street, they pull up hard in front of Mad Mady's Saloon.

Berta follows Adobe as he tries to open the front door, but no luck.

"I told you, Sheriff, when I arrived this morning I found it locked."

"Ever think of asking Mady for a key?"

Exasperated, she says, "I told you, I stopped asking for a key."

He draws his Navy Colt and breaks the closest window with the grip. They enter and survey the saloon and at first glance, see no signs of trouble.

"Let's go upstairs to her room and try to reconstruct last night," Adobe said.

Berta follows him up the staircase and into Mady's room. Looking around, it hit him immediately. *This is my first time in*

Mady's private suite. Well, I wanted it that way, still, the idea of being in her inner sanctum is exciting, he thought.

"Everything looks in order."

"Just as I said, her bed is empty, never slept in last night."

Adobe, ignoring the latest round of I told you so, offers, "Nothing is disturbed, including $20 in silver coins on her dresser," he observed.

"I better put that money in the safe."

Staring at Mady's four-poster canopy bed made of mahogany, he thinks. *Is it me, or Mady that keeps us at arm's length? Perhaps it is a combination of two forces seeking avoidance, but it feels natural to fall into bed with her. It is not a big bed, no room for haunted memories of a mythologized woman.*

"Sheriff!"

"Sorry. Yes, put it the safe," he says, with visible concern about the situation.

"You all right?"

"Yes, fine. I always believed Mady would return to New York one day, but not without saying goodbye to anyone," Adobe states to which Berta agrees. "Well at least she would have said goodbye to you."

Adobe, who never suffers from low self-esteem, turns to her and laments, "Mady may have found it hard to say goodbye to me."

"We may as well face the facts, Sheriff. There is little reason to believe she went back to New York. She is gone without a word."

"I know," he states, while staring at Mady's music box.

He opens the lid of the wood and brass box and is startled to hear "Beautiful Dreamer" fill the air.

Being emotionally faithful to a ghost is a fool's play. All the more foolish since Mady is a willing woman....

"Sheriff, are you all right?"

"Yes. There's not much more we can do here. I will explore up at the foothills; she may have decided to camp out for a while."

He does not believe it for a second, but goes on, "Let's start asking around the plaza."

"I'll start with James Clarke at the hotel. Someone may know something."

"Good. If she doesn't turn up soon, I'll notify the rangers.

"When will I see you again?"

"I have ranching business at the Circle C that should take several days."

"Oh, despite the excitement, I noticed that you have a very nice place," Berta says playfully.

Not amused, he replies, "Just come to the Circle C when Mady shows up."

"You mean *if* she shows up."

He stares and says, "In the meantime, see if you can have that window fixed."

"Is that it, Sheriff?"

"No, there is something else."

"What's that?

"Remember the night a stranger told you about a woman up in the capital?"

"Yes, a woman called Santa Fe Sharon. She was asking unusual questions about Valtura, the saloon and Mady," Berta says with a feeling of revelation.

"That's right. Do you remember anything else unusual about this stranger?"

"No, he was an ordinary man. You think there's a connection to Mady's disappearance?"

"It's worth considering."

"What should we do about running the saloon?"

Considering the uncertainty, he says, "Nothing. I guess we can survive without it for a few days or until we understand what happened to Mady."

"Okay, Sheriff. You know, it seems strange that nothing in the saloon or in Mady's room has changed. It looks like she is still here."

"Sure, if she's invisible."

Adobe calls Johan on the telephone and asks him to meet at the gazebo. He arrives first and then Johan rushes up.

"Sheriff, what is it?"

"When did you last see Mady?" he asks, stepping closer.

"I saw her yesterday walking in the plaza. Is she okay?"

"No. In fact, she is gone."

"What?"

"It's extraordinary, but Mady has utterly vanished."

"What are you going to do, Sheriff?"

"Play the cards dealt to me."

The next day, the Valtura Journal runs shocking banner headlines:

MADY BLAYLOCK MISSING

Mad Mady's Saloon Closed

Sheriff Centori Investigating

24

AUTOMOBILE ACCIDENT

Carrie waits for dawn and still alone, attempts to walk to Valtura again. It is a hard walk from the train station, but it is easy to find Valtura. Carrie arrives in town exhausted, but ready for the challenge ahead. Entering on Junction Street, she walks past the back of Mad Mady's Saloon. At Second Avenue, she turns right, walking toward the plaza, and observes the courthouse and the adjoining sheriff's office on Corona Street. Standing under the shade of two large trees, Carrie looks around the plaza, turns to National Street and sees her target destination.

Spotting Mad Mady's Saloon, she walks through the plaza with a sudden wind ruffling her hair. She arrives at the front door, looks up at the parapet and the Mad Mady's Saloon sign. Since the plan calls for Mady's absence, she expects not to find her. However, Carrie will have to deal with Berta Brandt.

Entering the saloon, she sees Berta polishing the bar, working hard while hoping for Mady's return. She has tried her best to keep up the saloon since Mady vanished. All efforts to learn anything about Mady's disappearance have failed, until now.

"Good morning, Miss, Do you work here?"

"I run the place," Berta says without eye contact.

But no more, she thinks, as Berta looks up.

"I'm Carrie Carlson from Santa Fe."

"Morning," she states, looking puzzled. "I'm Berta Brandt."

"You're probably wondering about Mady Blaylock," Carrie said.

Berta rushes around the bar and confronts Carrie, "Yes, I am wondering—and so is most of Valtura, including Sheriff Centori. What are you saying? Is she all right?"

"Oh, she's fine. I have some papers for you. Take a look at these documents."

Berta takes the papers while Carrie explains, "Mady rushed to Santa Fe to attend to her sister, Sharon, who was hurt in an automobile accident."

"Automobile accident? Mady's sister…wait, why didn't Mady tell me?"

"No time, I guess. She hurried to Sharon's side. You know, she's very close to her sister."

"Right now, I don't know anything, except that there must be underlying reasons for all this. It's not like Mady to disappear without a word. I don't ever remember her leaving Valtura that way. Not one time!"

"Listen, Berta, all I know is what I said. I'm sure Mady will talk to you as soon as she can. In the meantime, I have the authority to run the saloon during Mady's extended stay in Santa Fe."

"I can run the saloon without you while Mady is gone."

"I'm sure you can, but that's not how the sisters want it. Berta, you're invaluable to Mady and I'll need your help with interior changes to this place."

"What changes? We like the saloon the way it is just fine," Berta states defensively.

"Sharon wants to thank Mady by improving her saloon."

"Is that so? Mady loves this place the way it is and she never talked about any alterations."

"Don't worry, Berta, Mady will approve of the changes."

"I wouldn't count on that," Berta says sternly.

Carrie, losing her composure, exclaims, "I'm in charge now. Are you going to help me, or not?"

"Listen, this is a big deal. I'm sure Mady would have told me!"

"Yes, it is a big deal. I have instructions on just *how* big. A plan for the new saloon is in these papers, directions on how we will arrange things when they arrive."

"I don't care what you have, Mady would have told me."

"No time. As I said, she rushed to Sharon's side."

"I need to talk to Mady—to make sure she's okay. Does Sharon have a telephone?"

Carrie encounters her first barrier to implementing the plan and shouts, "I have answered your questions, but now I'm getting annoyed."

"Aren't you the sweet type?" Berta smiles derisively.

Berta's resistance is clear. She may ultimately comply, but with time a factor, Carrie decides not to wait. After staring down at her, Carrie declares, "Berta, there's one more thing. You're fired!"

Berta becomes livid and screams, "You can't do that. What are you talking about?"

"I've finished talking."

Expressing her pent-up frustration over Mady's disappearance, Berta upends the table, sending objects flying. This shocks Carrie, who pushes her to the floor. Berta comes up with a clenched fist and attempts to roundhouse Carrie. A gun barks, the punch stops in midair and Berta drops dead. Before she can start her assigned tasks, Carrie needs to find her contact, a man named Blackstone—whoever and wherever he is.

"Are you Carrie Carlson?"

Carrie glances up over Berta's dead body and gives a weak nod.

"I'm Bill 'Black Eyed Pea' Blackstone. Sorry I missed you at the rail station; looks like you wasted no time in finding trouble in Valtura."

About forty years of age and of medium height, he wears rough boots, wrinkled clothes, a black vest and black broad brimmed hat with a gun strapped down low.

"Lucky for you no one noticed the gunshot—I thought it was a motorcar backfiring, myself."

"Look mister, you're late and I had to walk from the station. First job is immediate disposal of this body. Then we will eradicate all things related to Mad Mady's Saloon; remove anything reminiscent of Mady Blaylock."

"Whoa, whoa, slow down, lady."

"I have much work for you," she shrieks.

"You know, you look familiar to me—could be you *worked for me* up in Santa Fe."

Carrie does not remember all her male clients on Calle Montano, but Blackstone remembers her well.

Carrie swallows hard and meekly says, "Those days are over."

"Too bad," he says with a grin.

"Are you going to help me?" she glares.

"I'll move this body to the back and take it out at midnight. You clean up this mess."

Returning from his grisly task, Blackstone pours a drink and asks, "Care to join me?"

"No. I am expecting crates and will need them transported from the rail station. We also need to dismiss anyone loyal to Mady; resistors could be trouble. I'll select the doves that will stay."

"I'm sure you will make good decisions about the doves."

"Fuck you."

Laughing aloud, Blackstone says. "Don't worry; I will send good men to help you get ready for Santa Fe Sharon."

"You mean Mademoiselle Sharon."

"Sure. When the shipments arrive at the rail station, my men will transport the crates to the saloon."

"Sharon wants to avoid detection and questions until her grand opening."

"Okay, we will work at night and make all deliveries through the saloon's back door on Junction Street."

"Good."

Now that she had the saloon secured, Carrie's job is to bring charm to Mady's run-down place and to Valtura. She immediately locks the place to prevent anyone from seeing the activities that will soon change Mad Mady's Saloon. In anticipation of any public curiosity, Carrie places a sign in the window:

Closed for Renovation

At midnight, Carrie lies awake in Mady's bed, reviewing the days' events and second-guessing her decision about coming to Valtura. Off in the distance, the yipping of coyotes is especially shrill tonight, with a negative edge. The coyotes are expressing a sinister side.

Two days later, the first shipments arrive. With the help of Blackstone and his men, Carrie spends all her time unpacking crystal, fine linens, sterling silverware, vases, goblets, candelabras and hand painted china. In this fashion, she begins the transformation of Mad Mady's Saloon to Chez Beau Sharon, a much better defined place, with a French touch.

After a final series of shipments of furniture and much time and effort behind closed doors, Chez Beau Sharon is born. In the middle of the large main room, a chandelier extends from the second-story ceiling over a new luxurious environment. Dark mahogany tables, plush chairs, dark curtains and rugs fill the room with Edwardian inspired colors, and oil paintings in gold gilt frames hang on the red walls. Sharon spent Mother Blaylock's money well.

25

Fourth Estate, Second Interview

The success of the initial oral history interview encouraged Johan to return sooner rather than later. The colonel sits at his porch table and looks up when he hears the rumbling of a motorcar.

"Good day, Colonel Santos. As predicted, you are a valuable resource for understanding New Mexico's past. Your interview increased readership of the newspaper by more than ten percent. This will help to expand the Valtura Journal to territorial coverage."

The colonel smiles, invites him to sit down and says, "Would you like a glass of wine?"

With excitement trumping thirst, Johan answers, "Our first interview was popular with the readers. Your experiences and knowledge in and of the territory are fascinating."

"You are a fine writer and you made my stories interesting."

"Thank you, Colonel, but we both know the truth."

"I am just the storyteller." He smiles softly.

"Yes, so please continue the story. And I would like some wine."

While pouring a glass, the colonel says, “In the beginning of American rule, the people wanted to move from military authority to civil government. Civil authority was a driving force behind the 1848 convention.”

“Of course, Colonel. Civil authority is a major part of the American political philosophy. Executive power is vested in a governor or a president—a civilian, not a general.”

“That is correct, but enabling acts from Congress that allowed the people to call constitution conventions failed over ten times for various reasons.”

Johan reaches for his glass without looking and knocks it over, spilling the wine over the table.

“Oh Colonel, I am sorry.”

“Don’t worry; this old table can use a little wine. It is small thing, but when President Polk wanted to bring New Mexico and California in the Union the issue of free or slave territories entered the debate—it was a big thing. Then a petition to Congress called for the prevention of slavery in New Mexico territory.”

“I imagine that caused a stir between northern and southern congressmen.”

“Yes, the New Mexican people offended pro-slavery senators. As you may expect, the petition failed and divided New Mexico into two groups—one still seeking statehood and the other willing to settle for a civil territorial organization.”

“Colonel, it sounds like New Mexico was a pawn in the national game.”

“That is exactly correct. When California entered the Union as a free state in 1850, other acquired regions became territories without mention of slavery. The statehood issue was quiet for several years, most content with a civil territorial government.”

“What started the renewed statehood interest?”

“It was a perceived invasion from Texas and Indian wars that caused many to take another formal look at statehood in 1866, to no avail. Then the 1872 bill had support from large towns, but people in rural areas were apathetic."

The *Ah-ooo-ga, Ah-ooo-ga* from an automobile interrupts the colonel, who laments, "East Corona Street is getting more motorcars these days."

"Should I come on a horse next time?"

The colonel smiles and continues, "The leading newspapers during that period wanted statehood for avoiding annexation, preventing the division of the people, sustaining the culture and history and, of course, obtaining self-government."

"They are all important reasons."

"But not enough for success. There was more reason in the 1874 Enabling Act that claimed New Mexico had a population of 130,000 with great natural resources. In addition, we had small public debt."

"Of course, something went wrong."

"Yes, personal and regional conflicts stopped this attempt," the colonel says while looking at his gold pocket watch.

Johan notices the magnificent watch with the distinct marking of a coyote on the case and says, "Are you getting tired, Colonel?"

"No, let's continue."

Staring at the watch, Johan says, "That is a beautiful watch. What is the CC under the coyote?"

"Oh…, the double C is for two colonels. Colonel Alvarado, a superior officer during the war, gave me the watch. He believed I would one day become a colonel, like he did."

The story sounds unbelievable to him and probably to Johan as well. The colonel made a mental note not to flash the watch in the future.

"Interesting story. Your colonel was right about your army career."

Quickly returning to the interview, the colonel goes on, "In the early 1880s, the growing population of 150,000, new towns and increased mining activity distracted people from the pursuit of statehood—for a while. The next serious attempt was in the late 1880s. Congress stopped the bill, with some calling Santa Fe a primitive and depressed town and maintaining that the people were not ready for statehood."

As the colonel continues to provide details of false statehood starts, Johan wonders about his watch and his implausible explanation.

Noticing the loss of eye contact, the colonel says, "Are you okay?"

"Yes, fine. Please go on."

"In other statehood attempts, congressional recess and too short sessions stopped the bills. Then, in 1890, another promising attempt failed when divided opinions of New Mexicans weakened the case for statehood. The next bill never reached the Senate."

"It sounds like there was a series of mishaps, Colonel."

"And a long history of failure. Sometimes congressional procedure and protocol prevented the two-thirds vote necessary to move forward. One time legislature action to frame a state constitution started, but dissatisfaction with apportionment ended the initiative. There has been continual progress, yet statehood remains elusive."

The sound of *Ah-ooo-ga*, *Ah-ooo-ga* is a chance for both men to raise their glasses.

"It seems that sometimes relatively small matters blocked the statehood efforts, Colonel."

"Yes, at times they intervened and caused delays. In fact, the very name became an issue, because many found New Mexico confusing. Foreigners and Americans from the East often confuse it with Old Mexico. There were many anecdotes of people in the U.S. sending letters to Mexico instead of to New Mexico, or of people being surprised to learn Albuquerque is in the U.S. or to see an American flag in Santa Fe!"

Both men laugh.

"Some felt the old name could be an obstacle to immigration and progress," the colonel continues.

"I see. Perhaps we should stop now. I'm sure you want to rest for your chess game with Adobe."

"Ah, is our chess game so widely known in town?"

"It is a small town, Colonel," says the journalist.

"I am free today; Adobe is at the Circle C attending to his ranch."

"He is also concerned about Mad Mady."

"I saw your headline about Mady's disappearance, a bigger story than our interview."

"Well, for now. I am sure Mady will return when she is ready."

"I have not yet spoken to Adobe about her."

"Perhaps we can stop here and continue on another day. I wish not to give my readers too much information too soon."

"As you wish; my days are not very busy. Besides, you are building anticipation with the readers which could increase circulation."

"Yes, of course. Thank you again, Colonel Santos."

"*Adios.*"

The colonel takes out his gold watch and thinks about another time. He was not prepared to reveal his involvement in the legend of Chaco Canyon—especially to a newspaperman. Chaco Canyon could play a significant role in New Mexico's history, but his lifelong secret will remain a secret.

26

Chez Beau Sharon

The new, fabulous Chez Beau Sharon is a remarkable stage from which Mademoiselle Sharon can sing her own praises, apply her role in the political intrigue and keep Old Mexico informed. She fantasizes about becoming the wife of the Viceroy of New Mexico—if Old Mexico is successful with the Revert Document.

Enthusiastic about the future, Mademoiselle Sharon is risking everything for fame and fortune—hurting Mady along the way is a bonus. In any case, Chez Beau Sharon is a wonderful environment for Mademoiselle Sharon, a grand court befitting a queen and a forum for fancy parties. For now, the future sovereign is in Santa Fe, packing her own trunk, with a ticket to Valtura.

After searching for Mady in the Sandia foothills to no avail, Adobe notified the New Mexico Rangers, but they have too few men for such a vast territory. Having done all he can do, he retreated to the Circle C to focus on ranching business—with Mady's disappearance on his mind.

The next morning, Adobe turns his attention to ranching

matters. It is getting close to the time for the roundup crew to start cattle gathering on the open range. The problems beyond Circle C will have to wait for a while. Over the last week, Adobe and A.P. had discussed how the winter cattle losses decreased the profit margin per head and how more cattle could reduce the average cost of production. Due to economies of scale, the Circle C needs to expand the herd for greater efficiency.

As a result, Adobe decides to conduct an early fall roundup. Dissimilar to the spring, in the fall, cowboys cut out marketable steers from the herd. The rider and his rope help the cutting horses, trained to anticipate cattle movements.

Satisfied with the plans for improving operations and with sending the mature cows to the marketplace, Adobe is ready to return to Valtura. He usually takes an hour for the six-mile trip to town, but today he picks up the pace on Patriot because he is afraid he may have let Mady down.

There is a peaceful feeling on National Street. Adobe gives no notice to a new sign over Mad Mady's Saloon, but he does see the window has been fixed. Something about the window bothers him. His eyes scan, looking for a reason why things seem different. Distracted, Adobe enters Mad Mady's Saloon. Remarkable renovations and alterations are obvious the instant he opens the door. Chandeliers, plush chairs, dark mahogany furniture and oil paintings exemplify the extensive transformation. The almost overnight change in Mad Mady's Saloon stuns Adobe.

This is unbelievable. Does Mady know about these changes? he thinks, while bewildered and looking for his table. It is not in its usual place, in fact, it is gone altogether.

Once again, Sharon has violated a basic tenet of clandestine work by creating a place that is flashy, even gaudy, with fancy accouterments to enhance an ornate style. Starting with her dream in mind, she financed her vision with her own money, or Mother

Blaylock's, and designed the place in her image. Chez Beau Sharon, as well as Mademoiselle Sharon herself, will be a major attraction.

Rather than sitting, Adobe moves to the bar and looks for Berta. Instead, he is surprised to see a new, striking woman. Standing at the end of the bar, she drops everything and rushes to him.

"Adobe Centori?" she says with concern.

"Yes, I am *Sheriff* Centori. Who are you?" he demanded.

She is attractive enough to engage, even to pursue in normal times. However, events in Valtura are getting increasingly strange. Adobe's priorities have rapidly changed—he stays focused on his role as a detective.

"I'm Carrie Carlson," she beams, with a pretty smile.

"What are you doing here and where is Berta Brandt?"

"Berta went to Nevada Territory to open a new business," she answers—more quickly than she would have liked.

It was a familiar story. *First, Mady disappears, now Berta is gone. This woman has no idea how ridiculous her story sounds, and now all these big changes have been made to the saloon. There is more here than meets the eye. Something is not right,* he thinks.

There are problems without answers, and his suspicions are increasing. Playing for time, he conceals his true, visceral reaction, "Really? That's news to me. She has been here almost since the start. Mad Mady's will be different without Berta."

"It's already is different, Sheriff. I know you are a friend of Mady's but this is not Mad Mady's Saloon any more, this is Chez Beau Sharon. Did you *not* see the new sign out front?"

Adobe swears inwardly. He will not learn anything with antipathy, so checking his emotions, he repeats, "Chez Beau Sharon?"

Carrie smiles as if she knows a secret worth keeping, and anticipating his next question, she says, "You must be wondering about Mady."

"You could say that. She wouldn't leave town without notice."

"Would you like coffee, Sheriff? We can talk it over. Take any table you like."

Adobe nods and Carrie steps away. While alone, he takes in the Edwardian decoration, the artwork and the elegant detail that creates a significantly different saloon.

Carrie returns with coffee and sits down next to him.

"This new environment is fitting for a fine looking woman like you." Adobe wonders if such flattery will work. He finds the coffee so strong that he thinks a bullet could float in it, but says nothing.

"Mady rushed off to Santa Fe to attend to her sister, who was hurt in an automobile accident."

"Are we talking about Santa Fe Sharon, by chance?"

"Yes we are. Sharon Blaylock."

Although her explanation is plausible, from his perspective the story and the coffee are not going down very well. At least, he knows Mady's instinct about Santa Fe Sharon was right.

"An automobile accident? It's curious Mady didn't say so—to anyone."

"Well, the urgent nature of Sharon's problem and Mady's frantic need to help…"

"Hmm, I suppose so," he says, without believing a word. "But why the fast changes here? Why has there been such widespread renovation in Mad Mady's Saloon? And all taking place while Mady is gone."

"Sharon wants to thank Mady for coming to Santa Fe in her hour of serious need. The sisters are very close, you know."

She seems to have an answer for everything. Except they are all lies, he thinks.

Adobe has heard enough, for now. He pushes away from the table and says, "Thanks for the coffee, Miss."

Walking briskly outside to National Street, he looks up to the new sign. Sure enough, it reads "Chez Beau Sharon." There is a fatal flaw in Carrie's story. *Even if all the lies were true, why would they change the name? What is so important about a saloon in a small town? Mady vanishing while all these changes occurred is no coincidence. In any case, there are many unanswered questions.* With the entire situation becoming intolerable, he is ready for the unexpected and will not be disappointed.

Back in his office, Adobe makes his own coffee and marks time pondering the astonishing redecorating measures—and his next move. The strategy is clear, but the tactics are not. He writes a few lines, walks out, turns left on Corona Street and then turns right on Camino San Antonio, avoiding National Street.

Adobe enters the telegraph office and states, "Buster, send this off to City Marshall Johnny Romano in Santa Fe right away."

Jumping up Buster responds, "Sure thing, Sheriff. Has there been any word on Mady? There has been a lot of activity at her place the last few days."

"So I see."

"What about Mady, Sheriff?"

"Don't know yet, Buster. When you get an answer from Romano, drop everything and find me."

"Yes sir, Sheriff, I sure will!" Buster feels like he is part of something important.

Although unsure of the next move, the answers are at Mady's place; perhaps pressing Carrie could be helpful. Adobe goes across Second Avenue, returning to the bar. There are three unidentified horses tethered in front of Mad Mady's Saloon—or Chez Beau Sharon.

27

Mayhem at Mad Mady's Saloon

Adobe returns to Mad Mady's Saloon—Chez Beau Sharon. He finds the place empty except for two men sitting with Carrie. They are drunk and boisterous. Before he knows it, he hears a sound from behind and feels a gun pressed against his head. A savage force is unleashed within his basic survival instinct. Adobe drops down and elbows the man hard in the stomach, disarming him and sending him to the floor. Holding his abdomen, the fallen man lurches toward Adobe, who stumbles and scrambles for footing with his .36 caliber Navy Colt at the ready.

The two men at the table draw their guns and Carrie runs upstairs. It happens in a flash. Adobe steps away as the man closest rises to his full height, his exposed chest creating a target. With speed, Adobe's six-shooter blazes two rounds, hitting and killing the target instantly. Then, the other man, less impulsive, carefully levels a rifle. The former cavalry officer sees the action, crouches down and fires, striking him dead center. The man stumbles forward, crashes into a table, sending splinters and bottles flying. He falls dead into the shattered glass.

The first attacker recovers from Adobe's elbow blow, stands and bursts outside, startling the horses; they are spooked, neighing in annoyance and kicking up dust devils. As the attacker jumps into the saddle, the horse bucks and rears, throwing his would-be rider. In desperation, he jumps on the closest horse, reins about and thunders away. A passing Valtura citizen draws his pistol and attempts to help. It is too late. When the mayhem ends, two men are dead and Carrie is looking down from upstairs, frozen.

Adobe, revolver still drawn, scans the room for further danger. All is quiet except for the noise of spent cartridges still rolling on the slanted floor. He ventures outside to see about the first man. Finding no other threats, he holsters the two-pound gun but remains alert. The Navy Colt, although discontinued in the 1870s, is still reliable. Adobe maintains his six-shooter with expert care, and he has no complaints about the old Colt's performance on this day.

The people on the plaza start rushing to the saloon and confront the caustic smell of gunpowder. There has not been a shoot-out in Valtura in the new century. Violent bar brawls and explosive gun battles on the streets are outdated. The mayhem does not reflect a town trend; it is a symptom of a new, greater problem. Adobe clears the crowd, sends for the undertaker and goes back inside to confront Carrie.

"What the hell was that? Who were those men?" he commands. "Where did they come from?" She appears clearly shaken from the pandemonium and does not respond. Carrie needs laudanum and Adobe needs a drink, or two. He goes behind the bar, snatches up a bottle of Jameson and turns around toward Carrie. Uncharacteristically forceful, he slams his fist on the bar and demands, "I said, 'Who were those men?'"

"I don't know. They came in from the back after you left," she says with an ethereal look, "they started drinking hard and asked about the women upstairs."

Carrie's desultory explanation is unconvincing. Ever since Cuba, Adobe has never fully trusted women.

"Are you Santa Fe Sharon?"

"What? No. What are you talking about?"

Frowning he says, "Get someone to clean up this mess."

Adobe abruptly walks out and goes back to the office, inspects his gun and then studies the Jameson bottle with solemnity. Not much fazes Adobe, but there are too many questions and too few answers, and the efficiency shown in changing Mad Mady's Saloon to Chez Beau Sharon is startling. *It appears to be a well-designed plan*, he thinks. *People in trouble often say things that seem irrelevant but could have a bearing on the truth. I will get to know Carrie better.*

Suddenly, Buster charges in waving a sheet of paper, an answer from Johnny Romano. As expected, there is no record of a recent automobile accident, and Sharon and Mad Mady do not appear to be in Santa Fe.

By noon, over 100 people have gathered at the scene of the shooting. News of the event went out over the telegraph wire and the Valtura Journal put out an extra edition with a banner headline:

MAYHEM AT MAD MADY'S SALOON

Sheriff Centori Kills 2 Hard Cases

New Management on National Street Raises Questions

28

The Valtura Journal

The Valtura Journal, the town's only newspaper, publishes weekly on Saturday at a subscription cost of $3.00 a year. Adobe is a close friend and frequent visitor who respects Johan and is infatuated with Klara. The mayhem at Mad Mady's Saloon prompts Adobe to see Johan, a confidant, and Klara, a potential confidant.

Klara is well spoken, self-assured and a suffragist. Sometimes she gives an initial impression of being callow, but her well-thought-out positions on business and government do not lack analysis. Some think her ideas about the role of business and government in modern society are dangerously naïve.

The emergence of scientific management, which views workers as production tools, and the overall mechanization in industry that assaults the human spirit, affronts her. Yet she is especially suspicious of government power.

"Why not print this editorial, Father? Corrupt territory officials back the governor and his financial and political monopoly."

"It is a rumor, Klara. We only print the facts."

"But he refers to robber baron tycoons as industrial statesmen! That exposes his attitude," she insists.

"Why are you so anti-business?"

"Because the powers of the great industrialists, financiers, trust builders and tycoons are sources of concern. Don't you see the inherent problems in capitalism? The greed and corruption—and don't you realize that statehood will lead to more corruption resulting from more control over business?"

"And on what do you base your fanciful theory?"

"Business will be less able to avoid taxes and regulations under a state government and that can create dishonesty, fraud and bribery between business and government."

"Klara, avoiding taxes and rules may be harder under a state, but that is not a recipe for corruption."

Klara laughs, "I don't know, Father."

"I keep telling you, Klara, I support statehood, but not unconditionally. I expect our new state to have a strong self-government."

"Sometimes you are hopeless."

"You should be in politics!"

"Father, every American is in politics, but most don't know it. Public affairs are sometimes too complex for citizens. They need to find the right way to respond to some things and not respond to many others."

"Yes, we have limits in paying attention to the entire political process and we have limits to this discussion—there is a deadline to publish the morning edition."

Adobe walks right across the plaza toward the newspaper office. The vigorous air and clear sunshine help clear his head. A traumatic event can affect mental and emotional states. No time for full recovery, he needs to consider Valtura's current state of affairs. He walks in the office under a sign above the door:

Valtura Journal

Published Weekly by

The Rio Grande Publishing Company

Entering with the clang of a bell, he finds Johan and Klara in conversation. They both turn to the opening door.

"You're okay, Sheriff!" Johan can make any statement sound like a proclamation.

"Sure," he answers with a flat and exhausted voice.

Klara holds his gaze longer than appropriate and then looks down. Adobe sees no inappropriateness, as his interest increases.

"You look under the weather with good reason," Johan continues.

"And under the gun," Adobe says with a defensive tone in his voice.

"There were shots fired. We didn't know what to think."

"Yes, a lot of shots." *I have seen worse*, he thinks.

"I'm glad you were not hurt." Klara's kind words go beyond politeness—or at least he hopes.

Overall, Adobe believes his prospects are favorable. Klara tends to rebuff the attention of men, keeps them at arm's length and appears somewhat aloof around Adobe. Even so, he fantasizes about knowing her better and she is somewhat more accessible today.

"Who were those men, Sheriff?" Johan asks.

"Not sure. But I have a suspicion they're connected to the new management of Mad Mady's Saloon—or should I say, Chez Beau Sharon."

"Well, whoever they were, whatever they wanted, they're gone now, Sheriff."

"Yes, but I have a feeling there could be an encore. That's why I'm here," Adobe says, while failing to mention the opportunity to see Klara.

"You know that Mady left in a big hurry and a woman called Carrie Carlson arrived in town." This gets Klara's attention. She imagines Mady has the inside track for Adobe's attention.

"Mady is still missing and Carrie is running the saloon right now as Sharon's pawn and she wears a pistol," Adobe said.

Johan frowns and says, "Ladies don't handle guns." His remark is for Klara who carries a derringer.

"Oh, really, Father? Now you have met a lady who does," she said with a mocking sigh and waits for Adobe. Johan cringes, but ignores the barb and turns back to Adobe.

"Go on, Sheriff."

"The last thing Mady and I discussed was her concern about her sister, Santa Fe Sharon."

"Do you think that this Carrie woman knows what happened to Mady?" asks Johan.

"If not the whole story, I'm sure she knows something."

"Right now, following the mayhem at Mad Mady's saloon, I need to discuss a defensive strategy before I can go on the offensive."

Johan is flattered that he referenced his banner headline and says, "How can we help?"

"Keep a sharp eye on the comings and goings at Mad Mady's when I am at the Circle C and if Mady shows up, send Buster to the ranch."

"We will do that, Sheriff," Johan answers for both.

"And other than that, there is not much else. We watch and wait for them to make a mistake—criminals usually do."

Thinking about his press deadline, Johan says, "Please come to our house tonight so we can continue this discussion."

Klara provides silent approval and her eyes overflow with curiosity.

Adobe, surprised by the comment, says, "I need to go up to Circle C, but I'll try."

"*Adios*, Sheriff."

29

Revert Document

Wagner's opera *Die Walküre* is playing on a phonograph. The music does not distract his attention from the steady flow of information from every New Mexico County. The latest telegram, held tightly, is from Sharon Blaylock and simply reads *Awaiting instructions.* He writes his response, walks to the balcony doors, mentally checking Blaylock's name on the list, and considers the next name, Margaret Stanton. His New Mexico network nears completion as the deadline draws closer.

Standing on the balcony of a well-appointed Mexico City apartment, he watches the crowd in the plaza. His tailor-made coat conceals a strong frame and a Pistole Parabellum known as the Luger. Designed by Georg J. Luger in 1898, the 9mm toggle-locked, recoil-operated, semi-automatic pistol is produced by the German arms manufacturer, Deutsche Waffenund Munitionsfabriken.

Albert Hietmann, a careful, systematic German National, is a tall, distinguished man at fifty years of age who wears a handlebar mustache. His harsh comportment shows a man of authority. Born in East Prussia, where he attended military school, he is the son of a German field marshal. Rather than pursuing a military career, Hietmann entered the German civil service diplomatic branch in 1905, assuming a major role in the foreign secretary's office.

In 1910, Hietmann arrived in Mexico City as ambassador to Mexico and easily ingratiated himself in the highest levels of society, including the political elite. An opportunist, Hietmann is skilled in managing information to facilitate intelligence and in developing political, financial and operational resources.

Strategic alignment is vital for success and is an essential leadership component. In this sense, he coordinates and communicates the mission toward common goals while providing a collection point for information.

Hietmann is also a man who believes in a certain legend and has a hidden agenda. He has a gift for efficiency, effectiveness and diplomacy, but no real integrity.

The German government is interested in the American Southwest and the notion of Old Mexico recovering her lost border territories. This interest flows from aggressiveness against the U.S., not from altruistic support of Mexico. In the past, Mexican presidents and top generals maintained that a takeover of former territories was not achievable. Such an attempt would provoke war with the United States. Mexico does not have the military resources, given that the only substantial arms manufacturer in North America is in the United States.

Nevertheless, Hietmann has a new plan to recapture New Mexico and Arizona for Old Mexico. The plan is extremely risky, but Germany is prepared to exercise the military option. It now appears that the goal is moving from impossible to possible, even probable, with German involvement.

Ambassador Hietmann serves as military attaché to Mexico with aspirations for recovering the border territories lost after the Mexican-American War, Mexican Cession and the Gadsden Purchase. His strategy is based on Article X of the Treaty of Mesilla—the Revert Document.

The Treaty of Mesilla, an acknowledged part of the historical record that ended the war, contains nine known articles. The tenth article was a secret agreement not intended for public knowledge. Some believe that the U.S. annulled the Revert Document. Others believe it never existed at all. In any case, copies are not in the possession of the Mexican government. Any evidence of the document or an annulment may be lost to history. If the U.S. has a copy, it is their best-kept secret.

The Revert Document has significant implications for New Mexico's destiny. The person or faction finding it would assume a commanding position. Hietmann seeks to be in that position. If his plan is successful, the great victory could propel him to the Viceroyship of New Mexico. What is more, many female conspirators would like to be part of his success, including the beautiful Sharon Blaylock.

"Are all things in place, Herr Ambassador?"

Hietmann turns to Vice Ambassador Jan Steiner and announces, "We are making progress. Sharon Blaylock has contacted me. She is ready to act and will be directed to go to Corona County."

Steiner, a tall, blond, young man who recently arrived from Berlin, walks softly around Hietmann but says, "Let's hope we don't regret recruiting her. She is high risk, having no experience."

"That is true for most of the women, Steiner. Blaylock is enthusiastic about our cause and she personally financed the Corona County part of the operation. She also has special connections to her assigned delegate."

"Yes, of course, but our people in Santa Fe say she attracts a great deal of attention."

"I am aware of this, Herr Steiner, but she has gathered and reported information with remarkable instincts."

"That's the easy part, but caution may not be her strength. Can she control her delegate?"

"Beauty is her strength and unlike many female agents, she has a solid connection to the target. That is her value. Our intelligence shows that Corona County Delegate Centori has a relationship with her sister, Elizabeth Blaylock."

Hietmann and Steiner toast the progress in building an agent organization revolving around statehood delegate leaders in New Mexico's twelve counties. Women agents facilitate the plan through their assigned delegate with several men at their disposal. Their orders are uncomplicated: influence or corrupt the delegate leader into postponing or disrupting the ratification vote, by any means necessary, to after the December 31st deadline. If failure occurs, call an assassin.

"Forgive me, Herr Hietmann. If the elaborate strategy is successful, the U.S. cannot be expected to comply—we will be provoking war."

"Of course. We are prepared to support Mexico against new American aggression."

"I hope that is prudent, Ambassador."

"Steiner, are you comparing the German military machine to the American Army?"

"No, Ambassador. We would, however, offend a strong American ideal and fight more than an army. We would face an ideal that can turn an average army into an exceedingly spirited fighting force. I speak of the Monroe Doctrine."

"Yes, Steiner, their policy warns European powers about interfering in the affairs of state in the Western Hemisphere. You see, America is against imperialism, except of course, their own. Manifest Destiny was their *right* to expand across the American continent. Our plan circumvents the Monroe Doctrine with a powerful legal position."

"Herr Hietmann, you know any legal demands will be not recognized by the Americans and be seen as a path to European interventionism, or German interventionism."

"Our action *will* cause an aggressive American reaction. However, great armies are not led by doctrines, they are led by great generals. Berlin is prepared to answer the Americans, Steiner."

"The danger of going forward with the Revert Document is clear, Ambassador."

"Not going forward is hard to imagine. This is a special chance for Germany."

"And for Mexico, too, Herr Hietmann?"

"Yes, for Mexico too. In fact, when we meet with President Madero, we both should know the history of his country, their struggle with the Americans and especially the details and implications of the Revert Document."

"*Ja, Herr Hietmann.*" Steiner says, with keenness to learn about his new diplomatic assignment.

"Following their aggressive instincts, the Americans wanted Mexico's northern lands. At the beginning of the war, the U.S. occupied the Mexican territories of Santa Fe de Nuevo México and Alta California. When Mexico resisted this loss, U.S. troops invaded central Mexico and captured Mexico City," Hietmann says with authority.

"Should we remind Madero of this?"

"Indirectly, Steiner. He is certainly aware of this old wound and how the Americans crushed resistance. The Treaty of Guadalupe Hidalgo formalized the loss of New Mexico and California in 1848."

"The Revert Document could be the remedy to the painful transfer of Mexico's northern territories to the U.S.," Steiner observes.

"That is our intention, Steiner."

"Yes, of course, Ambassador."

"As a result of the treaty, Mexico ceded over 500,000 square miles, more than fifty percent of Mexico's pre-war territory to the U.S. for $15 million. In effect, the funds came from an elimination of Mexico's large debt toward the U.S."

"I see. It appears not to be a purchase at all," Steiner says.

"The U.S. also assumed $3 million of debt owed to U.S. citizens."

"Will Mexico welcome a chance to recover those territories now? It seems like an old dream."

"But old dreams can die hard, Steiner. Certain factors created the Revert Document, and the roots are found in the treaty."

"How does the Revert Document fit into this treaty?"

"First, losing a gigantic measurement of territory was a humiliation for many Mexicans, who remained angry. Second, Mexican property rights were a major negotiation point. The treaty called for property protection for Mexicans in the new U.S. territories, including California, Nevada, Utah, parts of Colorado, Arizona, Wyoming and New Mexico."

"And this did not satisfy the Mexicans?"

"No it did not. The Americans often ignored the property rights of the former Mexican citizens in U.S. territories. A majority of Mexicans supported the new U.S. government and stayed in the ceded areas as American citizens. Although promised property protection, many Mexican-Americans lost land in the courts or through legislation subsequent to the treaty. Predictably, property rights violations created resentment against the U.S. and territorial governments."

"Can we assume that Madero holds on to enough anger for our purpose against the Americans?"

"We shall find out, Steiner. We shall find out."

A knock on the door abruptly stops Hietmann's review of Mexican history.

"Please come in," says the ambassador.

A small man in a dark suit offers Hietmann a written message.

After reading the note, Hietmann announces, "It is from Madero. He will see us at *Palacio Nacional* on September 15, Independence Day, when Mexico commemorates freedom from Spain."

"Independence Day is an interesting choice of days, Ambassador. I am sure your request for that date is coincidental."

"Of course," Hietmann says with satisfaction.

Returning to the underlying historical events leading to his plan, Hietmann continues, "The animosity between the U.S. and Mexico extended beyond the war, with both countries claiming a border area known as the Mesilla Valley. In order to maintain Mexican citizenship some residents in the adjacent areas moved to Mesilla and out of the U.S."

"Hmmm, that sounds as if they acted on their own to revert to Mexico," Steiner observed.

"That is an interesting way to look at it; Mexico expected U.S. protection from Indian attacks in Mesilla and from Americans entering Mexico. When Mexico evicted the Americans from Mesilla, the New Mexico governor acted when the U.S. did not. He deemed the region part of New Mexico Territory. His action caused the Mexican president to send troops into the valley."

"Brinkmanship."

"You could say that, Steiner, but an opportunity to address the grievance came in 1854 with the Treaty of Mesilla or Gadsden Purchase."

"Another purchase," says Steiner.

"Yes, the Americans wanted the land for a southern transcontinental railroad route that passed through Mexican territory. The U.S. Minister to Mexico, James Gadsden, renegotiated a border that would accommodate the railroad. The U.S. paid $10 million for 30,000 square miles of land south of the territory that became the extreme lower parts of present-day Arizona and New Mexico."

"That was quite a land sale, Herr Hietmann."

"Indeed. President Franklin Pierce and Santa Anna signed the treaty in 1854 that ceded the final southern regions. The Gadsden Purchase addressed this unresolved conflict from the war and reset the boundaries."

"Herr Hietmann, this land deal does not provide for the return of Mexican Territories."

"Not at that time, but in 1858, the Mexicans, still angry with the U.S. over financial claims, were winning the diplomatic war. The much bigger issue for the U.S. was the coming Civil War. Consumed by the war threat, the U.S. agreed to a special amendment to the Treaty of Mesilla, Article X. Under key conditions it provides for ceded border territory to revert to Mexico."

"But why would the Americans *agree* to such an extraordinary amendment, Herr Hietmann?"

"At first they did not, but Congress and the new president, James Buchanan, were engaged in national politics. Few wanted trouble with Mexico given the growing conflict between the northern and southern states. Wishing to avoid a clash with Mexico at that critical time, the U.S. Senate ratified Article X in 1861 and it was signed by Buchanan as he happily left the White House."

"The Revert Document." Steiner says.

"Yes, Steiner. The Revert Document requires that each border territory be returned to Mexico if that territory is *not* a U.S. state in fifty years—or on January 1, 1912."

"Agreeing to the Revert Document seems like an unnecessary risk for the Americans, Herr Hietmann."

"Not then. The U.S. guaranteed the disposition of border territories after the deadline, but they were certain that the territories would become states long before 1912."

"I see. The prevailing wisdom was wrong. The presages of the U.S. Senate and a weak President Buchanan failed. The borderlands of Arizona and New Mexico remain territories today. So the Mexicans were right to argue for Article X, but wrong in not protecting the Revert Document."

"Steiner, there is no official copy in the Mexican government, but there is a legend that an original manuscript copy of the Revert Document is hidden in New Mexico."

"Territories shall revert to Mexico," Steiner whispers.

30

Let the Dice Fly

Adobe rides Patriot from the plaza on East Corona Street. It is time for another visit with Colonel Santos. As usual, the colonel sits on the porch of his Victorian house ready to play chess.

"*Buenas tardes*, Colonel," Adobe says while putting down a dry goods sack and a whiskey bottle, "how are you feeling?"

"Never mind me, Adobe. I know much has happened since our last game. I wanted to come to the plaza when I heard of the shoot-out at Mad Mady's place."

"I'm sure you did."

"Have you heard from Mady?"

"No, nothing, but the newcomer at the saloon knows something. More than she said, I'm sure. You would not recognize Mady's place, it's completely renovated, Colonel."

"You will find the answer, Adobe."

"I'm starting to fear the worst."

"Don't give up hope. Tell me what happened at her place."

"It was a few hard cases with too much to drink."

"Are you sure of that?"

Adobe pauses while setting up his chessmen and says, "No. It could be more than drunkenness."

The colonel gestures to Adobe to make the first move. No surprise, Adobe moves his queen's knight as an opening maneuver. After a flurry of exchanging moves, he makes a frivolous pawn ploy.

"Attacking for the sake of attacking without a sound reason?"

"Are you talking about the game or the shoot-out, Colonel?"

"What's the difference?"

"Is a threat sound enough reason?"

"Perhaps, but a pawn can never retreat. Did those men at Mady's place have a chance to retreat?"

Adobe shakes his head and says, "No, they did not. They were not inclined to do so anyway." He carelessly moves his queen's knight forward and the colonel captures the knight with his bishop. "Nice move."

"You are not paying attention to our game, *mi hijo*."

"Sorry, there is much on my mind. All of these problems are occurring when I should be dealing with statehood issues—not to mention running the Circle C."

"You speak of problems and statehood as if they are separate issues."

Adobe pauses at the significance of the statement and the colonel offers, "They could be related to one another. Although statehood is inevitable and will naturally happen, there could be problems that need attention. The U.S. still believes in Manifest Destiny, a belief that was strong at the time of the war."

Adobe's focus on the game weakens; he loses three pawns to the colonel's one.

The colonel, who seldom discusses his Mexican-American War service, continues, and Adobe listens closely.

"Despite Manifest Destiny, some Americans thought it a war of U.S. aggression."

"The U.S. lost over 13,000 men in that war, Colonel."

"The U.S. also won vast territories from Mexico. During the Polk years, the U.S. acquired more than 500,000 square miles of territory."

With the game starting to fade in importance, the colonel says, "Perhaps I told you about my involvement in creating Los Ninos Heroes' monuments in Mexico City."

"Yes, Colonel, I know the story of the six teenaged cadets who bravely held Chapultepec positions against a superior force and died defending their country."

"That is true. How many Civil War memorials are there in the U.S.?"

Perplexed by the question, he thinks for a second and answers, "Hundreds, if not thousands—we have one right here on the plaza."

"Yes, the plaza does have Civil War cannons and a few plaques. Now how many Mexican-American War memorials are there in the U.S.?"

"I don't know."

"*Mi hijo,* there are none in Valtura, none in the territory and probably none in all the country."

"But the Civil War was a much bigger and bloodier affair."

"Or is it because the U.S. is not proud of how an immeasurable amount of land was acquired?"

"Colonel, the Mexican War is *not* the only American war without a memorial. Someone must take the lead in creating one. Are you saying that you're against New Mexico statehood and our right to self-government?"

"I never said that. We need statehood because a territorial government is unstable and not permanent. It has no sovereign powers and fails to meet the needs of the people."

Adobe, trying to make sense of the mixed meanings, makes no reply and moves his queen forward on the diagonal. This prompts the colonel to say, "Before you protected the queen. Now you are aggressive. Political issues, like chess, can change and be complicated."

"I think we are ready."

"Yes we are," the colonel agrees as Adobe fills their glasses.

"*Salud.* When I was a boy in the far north part of Mexico, Coahuila-Tejas, U.S. immigrants settled in Texas and with the local Mexicans won independence at the Battle of San Jacinto in 1836. Do you know that Americans helped the Texans with money, weapons and war supplies? The U.S. government supported the rebellion, but Mexico refused to recognize the new Republic of Texas and believed Coahuila-Tejas would revert one day."

"Yes, Colonel, Texas independence is well known history."

"Very well known. However, the story of New Mexico's attempt at independence in 1837 is lesser known if known at all."

Adobe shifts in his chair and pays attention. The chess game is somewhat forgotten, the whiskey and the discussion are not. He refills the glasses and the colonel goes on.

"After Texas won independence, Mexico reacted with increased government control in administrative power, taxes and voting rights in their Northern Provinces, including New Mexico. New Mexican rebels, fearing Mexico's new policies, assembled at Santa Cruz de la Cañada." The colonel pauses and begins again, "There is an old chest of drawers just beyond the door. Please get the pouch in the bottom drawer."

Without a word, Adobe retrieves the pouch. The colonel unties the straps, reaches in, pulls out an old manuscript and hands it across the chessboard. It reads:

> For God, Nation and the Faith of Christ. The principle points we defend are the following:
>
> 1. To be with God and the Nation and the Faith of Jesus Christ.
> 2. To defend our country until we shed every drop of our blood in order to obtain victory.

3. Not to admit the Department Plan.
4. Not to admit any tax.
5. Not to admit any disorder desired by those who are attempting to procure it.
   August 3, 1837

"This is very interesting, Colonel."

"It is the New Mexican Declaration of Independence and a family artifact. You see, the rebels entered Santa Fe and placed their leader José Gonzales as governor of the territory. Gonzales is my great uncle and this document has been in the family for many years."

"Colonel, it seems that your family would approve of self government inherent in statehood as they approved of independence from Mexico."

"Remember, like a chess game, political issues can be complicated. Not all New Mexicans were happy with the rebel government."

Adobe creates a bishop situation with his own pawn blocking its path and drinks more whiskey.

"Many citizens, who loved their country, called for a counterrevolution with Padre Francisco Antonio de Madariaga leading the effort. In January 1838, federal troops from Mexico arrived in Santa Cruz and prevailed in a decisive battle ending the revolt. What's more, Mexico believed the U.S. was responsible for the revolt."

"Colonel, this is the twentieth century!"

"Nevertheless, history has present-day implications."

"Are you in favor of statehood or not?"

"The past can shape us and make us who we are today."

"Okay, so who are you today?"

Ignoring the comment, he goes on, "Much of New Mexico history has a Spanish origin, including your Circle C cattle business."

"Colonel, if you have a point, please make it."

"I am making my point, *mi hijo*. Spanish cattle arrived in Vera

Cruz from Santa Domingo in the early sixteenth century. Over the years, cattle spread northward along with Spanish control. *Vaqueros,* the first men to ranch in the Mexican provinces, spoke Spanish, not English. Their cattle and horses were descendents of the livestock brought here by Spanish conquistadors."

"I never claimed to have invented the cattle business, Colonel."

"Yes, of course," he says, and tries another way. "How much do you know about the Mexican-American War?"

"You know my army experience was in Cuba."

"So you know little." It is not an insult—just a statement of fact. "You are not alone. The war is little known in the U.S."

"Let me guess," Adobe says with slight annoyance, "because we are not proud of ourselves."

The colonel, who never questions his friendship, smiles, "The hostility and suspicion between the U.S. and Mexico continued when Congress approved the Republic of Texas, never recognized by Mexico, for statehood in 1845." He pauses for dramatic effect and continues, "Then Polk moved to acquire New Mexico and Upper-California, provoking the Mexican Minister to the U.S. to claim aggression and the Mexican government to break diplomatic relations, a harbinger of war."

Adobe moves his bishop forward and says, "So it was a statehood issue."

Capturing the bishop, the colonel says, "A statehood issue based on a historical dispute. Remember, Mexico did not recognize Texas as an independent country, and statehood compounded the issue. Also, a border location dispute persisted and added to the pressure."

"I know of the old dispute. Mexico said that the boundary was north of the Rio Grande, but the U.S. said it was south," Adobe says while withdrawing his knight from impending danger.

"Old dispute," the colonel replies with irony and goes on.

"The U.S. countered the diplomatic break by placing troops near Brownsville, *south* of the Rio Grande."

"Colonel, I appreciate the intrigue, but are you saying Old Mexico will object to New Mexico statehood in the same way she objected to Texas statehood?"

"Not in the same way. Unlike Texas, New Mexico was never an independent country. Yet events that caused the war set into motion the creation of New Mexico as a U.S. Territory."

"But they may object just the same. You said federal troops from Mexico ended the New Mexican revolt."

"That was a long time ago when New Mexico was part of Old Mexico." The old man points at the chessboard and says, "Political issues can be complicated. After President Tyler annexed Texas, President Polk exacerbated tensions by offering Mexico an offensively low price for Upper-California and New Mexico. He also covertly supported California, should a revolt occur there."

The chess players exchange several quick moves while clearly distracted by the conversation, especially Adobe. At the end of the exchange, the colonel has captured four pawns, one knight and one bishop.

He continues, "The California-New Mexico purchase was rejected and international relations got worse. Polk deployed General Taylor's army along the Rio Grande—into an area claimed by Mexico. It was a provocative move on the part of the norteamericanos, leading to Mexican troops firing on U.S. soldiers. The U.S. claimed they were attacked on American soil."

"But you said the Americans crossed the border."

"That is precisely right. And when the predictable skirmish occurred, Polk had his war. He wrote to Congress, claiming that notwithstanding U.S. efforts to avoid it, the war existed by the act of Mexico. Within a year, American troops advanced into Mexico City and held all of New Mexico and Upper-California."

The two former soldiers linger over the table. There are many captured pieces, more for the colonel, and a half-full bottle of whiskey on the side of the chessboard.

"As you said, political issues can be complicated."

The colonel, smiling at Adobe's attempt to defend his country says, "I know you are an admirer of Abraham Lincoln."

Adobe looks up and says, "Yes, the power of Mr. Lincoln's speeches inspired the country as he led America through the gravest crisis. His view on the Union is a major factor in shaping my own view."

"So you respect Lincoln and his opinions?" the colonel asks.

He pauses and answers, "Very much, and I will go to Washington when his Monument is built."

"What if I told you Congressman Lincoln opposed the war with Mexico?"

"I thought he voted for the war," Adobe says inquiringly.

The colonel explains, "Lincoln accused Polk of violating the Constitution in declaring war and voted against the war. Once the U.S. was committed, however, he voted to fund the war. With unwavering support for the soldiers, he voted to supply the army."

Adobe, the war veteran, understands the importance of government supporting troops in the field. The colonel moves his queen like a rook and says, "Check."

"Nice move, Colonel."

Not replying to the compliment, he says, "Lincoln contended that the disputed Texas territory did not extend to the Rio Grande. In his 'Spot Resolution' speech, he asked Polk to show the *spot* that proved the war began in Texas."

"Using Lincoln to make a point is a clever tactic," he says. "Nice move, Colonel."

Again not replying to the compliment, he continues, "Lincoln was unconvinced that the Mexican army crossed into the U.S. to start an armed conflict. Questioning Polk's motives, he maintained that the war was unprovoked and unnecessary."

Escaping the check with a clever move, Adobe offers an explanation, "Perhaps both sides wanted the war, given the vast territories that were in the balance, and there was also the old Texas issue."

The colonel makes a castling move, preparing his queen for attack. Adobe, distant from the game, goes through the motion of moving his knight and says, "*No es verdad*?"

"Opinions varied. New York newspaperman Horace Greeley predicted that the U.S. would win the war," he answers.

"But was Greeley for the war?"

"Regardless, we know the Fourth Estate's power to influence opinion and sometimes outcomes," the colonel says. "On the other hand, Mexican military strategists and some European observers believed that Mexico would win, but Mexico never had a chance at winning."

Adobe presses, "History is not always so clear. How can you be sure?"

"Because I was at Palo Alto where the Americans won a decisive battle followed by victory at Resaca de la Palma. When General Taylor marched on Monterrey and defeated seven thousand soldiers and forty guns, the inevitability of America winning the war emerged."

Adobe pushes back from the table with little interest in the game.

"After the war, the U.S. created territories to govern the acquired land and most became states in the late nineteenth century and early twentieth centuries, but Arizona and New Mexico, the two territories that border Mexico, remain territories." Exhausted by his long answer, the colonel falls back in his chair.

"Colonel, we know the fortunes of war can change fast."

"Yes, but it did not change the outcome for Mexico. General Scott's expedition of 10,000 men to Vera Cruz provided another

American victory. Simultaneously, General Kearney marched on Santa Fe and captured San Diego and Los Angeles. The final blow came with General Scott's successful attack on the Fortress at Chapultepec and his capture of Mexico City."

"You have an excellent recall of these events."

"I recollect it all very well, even the exact dates. On September 14, 1847, American Marines guarded the Halls of Montezuma."

Impressed with his experience and knowledge Adobe says, "You are quite a student of history."

"And a student of truth, *mi hijo*. The U.S. ended the war by occupying California, Texas and the Southwest. This placed the Americans in a powerful position to negotiate the Treaty of Guadalupe Hidalgo. In January 1848, the treaty gave Mexico $15 million and the U.S. acquired California, the disputed Texas border to the Rio Grande and the vast area of Utah, Nevada, Arizona and New Mexico."

The colonel moves his queen, "Check," he announces. "The U.S. Senate approved the treaty on March 10, 1848."

As Adobe scans the board searching for a way to save his king, the colonel goes on, "Some American politicians, at the time, said the aggression against Mexico was a political and moral crime."

Adobe looks up from the board and says, "The two countries had much to justify and some things to hide, each offered self-serving reasons."

"But the U.S. went beyond the purpose of securing Texas and seized additional territories."

"Colonel, to paraphrase Caesar, both sides said let the dice fly."

He finds a way out of check, giving the colonel time to rest his case and return focus to the game. The colonel is reluctant to develop his points further, at least not for now, and thinks, *Mi hijo, what am I to do now? I know what is right to do, but what is best? The Revert Document is taking on greater significance as we approach the deadline and it is Mexico's legal right, but at a great cost—for both sides of the border.*

There are more captured chess pieces and an empty bottle of whiskey on the side of the chessboard. Adobe scrutinizes the board and says, "Colonel, you still have not answered my question. Are you in favor of New Mexico statehood?"

The colonel finishes the last bit of whiskey and thinks, *I am in favor of peace.* He puts his glass down, moves his castle and with authority proclaims, "Checkmate."

"Well done, again. So what about statehood?" Adobe persists.

"The goal of chess is to capture your king; the goal of the Chinese game GO is to control more territory than your opponent and not destroy him. The U.S. did not attack Mexico for independence or for real provocation—it was for territorial expansion. The unjust war fulfilled the American dream of manifest destiny. Does the powerful U.S. play chess or GO?" the colonel exclaims.

The explosive statement startles Adobe who sips more whiskey and takes time to understand the most contentious time he had ever spent with the colonel. After the Mexican War, Spanish possessions in the new world were gone. An empire that had started in 1565 and had included Florida, Texas, New Orleans, the Southwest and California was now the U.S.A.

31

KLARA MORGENSTERN

Laws of attraction flow from what a man sees *in* a woman. At times, attraction flows from what a man sees from a woman's perspective. Adobe sees a curious political world through Klara's ardent eyes. At times, he questions her judgment but never her beauty or spirit. He is falling for her, but finds no need to show her any emotion now—or ever.

Adobe enters dangerous territory as a man romantically adrift and haunted by memories of a lost love. Romantic standards developed in Cuba persist and comparisons have doomed past relationships. Klara is different from Gabriella in image and intellect. Both are smart, but Klara's introspective expression is superior. Klara's dedication to politics and a free press is akin to Gabriella's passion for freedom. Gabriella was quicker to become irascible than Klara. Both are strong in substance, with Klara more reasonable in manner.

A flirtation with Klara could be imprudent. Unlike the women in Santa Fe, Klara's affection would certainly require greater involvement and her feelings are at risk, he thinks. *Does heartbreak turn all men into cynics? Why be emotionally faithful to a specter? Klara is a living, breathing woman. Being physically faithful to a memory is irrational. A better man would not see Klara with so much uncertainty.* He decides to see her anyway—so much for being a better man.

The Morgenstern house is on Junction Street and Camino San Antonio. The modest cottage is a short distance from Valtura Plaza, yet prior to now Adobe has kept his distance. He dismounts Patriot and walks through the front gate. The house has a white fence, gardens in the back, shrubs around the porch and large trees providing shade.

Reaching the front door, he looks for Johan's Ford motorcar. The Model T, with its hand-crank ignition, wood-spoke wheels, acetylene lamp headlights and brass horn, is *not* here.

Klara opens the door before he can knock and says, "How are you, Sheriff?"

"I'm all right," he says.

She smiles, but senses it is not true. Although he received the Medal of Honor for action in Cuba, a man never is accustomed to hot lead flying around his head. The mayhem at the saloon has him on edge, but his confidence is unshaken.

Klara wears a black silk blouse with embroidered flowers, a long gray skirt, and a sparkling necklace of turquoise and onyx set in sterling silver on a leather cord. The night air is cool as they sit on her front porch. She pours two glasses of tequila and quietly watches him. Her blue eyes, which miss nothing, are introspective and curious.

Aware of Adobe's frame of mind, she says, "The shoot-out at Mad Mady's place is enough tension for anyone. Not for you, of course—I mean with your experience at San Juan Hill."

"TR's boys did most of the work there."

Adobe lowers his eyes to her pretty neck and fine necklace. In the past, he has not pursued, placing her at a certain distance. That distance is rapidly dwindling as she moves slightly closer.

"Klara, we haven't heard gunshots in Valtura since the turn

of the century. My instincts tell me that recent events are related. It started with a stranger from Santa Fe asking about Valtura. Then Mady was worried about her sister, Santa Fe Sharon, and then Mady disappeared. The next thing we know, Mady's sister has commandeered the saloon. Then there's Berta Brandt."

"What about Berta?"

"The woman at the saloon claims she went to Nevada Territory, but I don't believe it for a second."

"There is more than your instinct that suggests a connection," Klara tries to help.

"That's true. As night leads to day, these events are connected. I just don't know what the links are yet."

"You think Santa Fe Sharon has created an elaborate plot against her sister?"

"With the killings, it is a diabolical plot, part of something bigger, more than sibling rivalry. Don't you see that?" Adobe admonishes.

"I'm not a fool. I was educated in St. Louis," she says with a small reproach.

Looking a little irked, he says, "Yes, of course."

She is progressive, professional and acutely aware of men disregarding intellect in favor of femininity. However, Adobe's attitude is far from condescending; in fact, he appreciates smart women.

In an attempt to repair the damage, he says, "I meant no disrespect. Your role as a newspaperwoman is an important part of informing the public in a democracy. Our constitution of limited government confers substantial power to the people—and they must be informed."

It works. The compliment more than quells the unintentional offense.

"It is exciting work and it is satisfying to work with my father, a man I admire, who is an advocate of the press that provides information needed for freedom."

"I know the newspaper business can be hard work."

"And long days, but I never quit until the paper is printed. I have the ability to work like a man," she says with a coy smile.

"Yes, you do." *And you have the wisdom to know when to be womanly*, he thinks.

They take a moment to refill their glasses and gaze at the stars in the sky.

"Klara, whatever's behind the string of unusual events must be explained and stopped. I don't know what else to do about Mady. She has always taken care of herself, but this is different. One thing is for sure, something is not right. I need to know what that something is."

Klara senses a difference in Adobe; he is concerned about Mady, but seems open to new possibilities. She sees an opportunity and decides to speed things along and talk plainly about their relationship. The willing woman says, "I hoped one day you would have feelings for me."

Startled, he takes a moment to reply since most women use metaphor as an invitation to romance, but he answers with a question. "Do you really want to talk about this?"

Speaking openly about her feelings, she says, "I need to know what's happening between us. I have a right to know the truth about our potential."

He will not talk about the past. Rather he offers, "I can't say how I feel about that, but my admiration for you is becoming absolute."

"You've never lied to me Adobe, but not knowing how you feel still hurts."

"I never wished to be misleading."

He wants to tell her about his heartbreaking experience in Cuba, but a man should never discuss a former love with a current woman.

"Yes, I know," she says with a slight, sad smile.

Changing the subject, he says, "The fight for statehood is growing to a grand conclusion."

Klara, agreeing to talk about something else, replies, "Do we really need more government in our life?"

"What? You know that New Mexico has sought statehood for a long time with good reason."

"For what reason—more control over personal liberty?"

Surprised by her quick and strong reaction, he says, "The free market is an economic system that promotes and maintains personal liberty."

Klara remains unimpressed but continues anyway, "Even Hamilton, who was not strong on state checks on Federal power, warned about a central government with too much power. He said we would regret the Constitution if it allowed the national government to penetrate and control all areas of private conduct."

"Klara, I strongly believe in states' rights and a limited role for Washington. The idea of checks and balances is not just to keep any branch of the federal government from getting too powerful; it also applies to the states and the federal government."

"And the states have a responsibility to push back against an overaggressive federal government?"

"That's exactly right, Klara."

"Good, so let's start pushing back *now*!"

"Fine," Adobe draws backs. "You may not trust the motives of Washington, but the statehood bill should please you on suffrage. The current bill says that the new state shall never enact any law restricting or abridging the right of suffrage because of race, color or previous conditions of rectitude."

She laughs bitterly, "Oh, a woman's previous condition of rectitude is in question? We need full and immediate participation in the political process or none at all." Couching her meaning in other words, she goes on, "Right now, women have only psychological participation in politics without voting rights. Opinions without action at the ballot box have little relevance to the political process."

"Klara, I agree that citizenship is only significant in the context of voting."

"You speak of citizenship. Citizenship holds that people have a role in society and government as opposed to strict individualism or small-group autonomy."

Adobe sees her fiery, disturbing look as she reveals her political philosophy and says, "As a citizen, I connect to issues that have consequences beyond an individual, such as statehood."

"The distinction between private and public matters can be vague," she admits.

Seeing common ground, he adds, "Whether private or public, personal needs can be satisfied through the political process."

Finding his remark troubling, she replies, "You assume a person can only satisfy private needs through government. Many people are concerned about a central government that can increase in size and in strength."

"Klara, states have considerable autonomy from the tenth amendment that says state governments have all powers that aren't reserved for the federal government."

"Are you certain that Washington will exercise limited powers that the states relinquish and only create laws that suit our needs? Moreover, how much control are we giving up?"

"As I said, I am for states' rights." He adds, "*And* I am a strong advocate for New Mexico statehood."

"You did not answer my questions. Washington is a long way from New Mexico. Can they hear us from such a distance and be responsive to our needs? Are you so sure there's no potential for oppression?"

"Klara, the U.S. has implicit representation in its documents and institutions."

"Implicit in conceptual haziness about democracy and political equality," she counters with satisfaction. "And what are your standards for measuring inalienable rights of majority rule?"

Unsure of her meaning, he thinks she will continue. She does.

"The American political philosophy of inalienable rights and consent of the governed seems wonderful, but do we preserve the natural law for all people in the face of a majority?"

"How do you see that, Klara?"

"I see that dissenting individuals can be oppressed by the tyranny of the majority."

"Can you consider the position of the greatest good for the greatest number of people?"

"I know. The good of the many outweighs the good of the few. That says natural law has no place in government—and some feel government has no place in private life."

Another political philosophy revealed. This time the anti-government reference increases his concern about her fiery look.

"Face it," she says, "the founders preserved the influence of wealth and education at the expense of those that, presumably, have fewer stakes in society."

"The Constitution has evolved with amendments."

"Has it? Has it really? Besides, as Jefferson said, 'each generation has a right to choose for itself the form of government it believes the most promotive of its own happiness'."

"He also wrote that a government long so established should not be changed for light or transient reasons," he rejoins.

"And you think my arguments are light or transient?"

Sensing a conversational impasse, Adobe says, "Okay, it's getting late. You know things start early at the Circle C."

"Oh, yes, the Circle C. I've heard of that place." Her tone filled with withering sarcasm.

Mildly embarrassed, he thinks, *The woman who sets foot on the Circle C Ranch will be the love of my life, or no woman at all.*

Ignoring the comment and certainly not inviting her to the Circle C, he says, "Thanks for the visit, Klara."

Not conceding the point, she replies, "Sure, perhaps you'll return the favor one day."

Adobe absorbs the hit in stride.

Klara backs off and says, "Good luck with finding Mady. We telephoned other newspapers in the territory about her."

Unaware of Gabriella, Klara believes that Mady is her only competition for his affection.

"Thank you."

"Playing it safe, I see."

"Klara, safety was removed from the equation the moment I saw you." He wants to know her much better and prepares to walk away, but Adobe, a mortal man, turns to the Sandia Mountains and says, "Have you been to the top?"

The Sandia Mountains are immediately to the east of the Morgenstern house. Many people believe that Sandia, Spanish for watermelon, refers to the reddish color of the mountain at sunset. This visual effect is from feldspar crystals in the granite.

"No, I haven't, but I would love to go."

"How about tomorrow at noon? We can meet at the plaza."

"I'll be there," she says with a slight smile.

"Good night, Klara."

On Patriot now, Adobe moves along to East Corona Street, visually inspects the colonel's house and briefly considers returning to Klara. Patriot, reading his mind, stops. "Too late, let's go home."

So much passion in her eyes about the world and perhaps us, he thinks. *I guess tomorrow will be soon enough.*

32

TROJAN WOMAN

With Adobe gone, Klara returns to a copy of *Mother Earth* magazine. Founded by Russian immigrant Emma Goldman in 1906, *Mother Earth*'s economic concerns focus on remaking the political world. The magazine is a significant part of American radicalism. Although readership is only about six thousand, it is a forum for isolated people to share their thoughts and feelings.

Men and women sometimes have secrets from one another. Klara is resolute in keeping her real political views from Adobe. However, she may have revealed ideas that a war hero, a government official and a statehood leader would never understand. Especially a man with a horse called Patriot.

Adobe continues to Corona Street past the office of the Valtura Journal. Seeing the Model T outside his office, he remembers Johan mentioning a deadline and incorrectly assumes it is a newspaper deadline.

Unknown to anyone in Valtura, except Klara, Johan is working on his magazine, *Freedom.* His political philosophy centers on individuals or small groups managing the affairs of life. *Freedom* contains articles against centrality, power and bureaucracy inherent in state socialism. The polemic journal and its two thousand adherents agree that the state is not needed and is even dangerous. Instead, Johan's editorial position promotes strong individualism, libertarianism and a market economy within a stateless society—anarchy.

Anarchy does not have widespread support in the U.S. In the American mind, anarchism is terrorism. Americans blamed anarchists for a bombing that occurred at a rally in support of striking workers in 1886. At the Haymarket Square in Chicago, a bomb killed eight police officers and a number of civilians. Then, the attempted assassination of industrialist Henry Frick revealed the anarchists' call to end big business. *Freedom* magazine supports the idea that coercive laws are unnecessary for communities. Without government, people would control their means of production with goods owned and distributed to small independent groups based on need. Johan Most, a German revolutionary, brought this doctrine to America in the 1880s and had a major influence on Emma Goldman.

Emma's experience as a low-wage factory worker in Troy, New York, nurtured her criticism of capitalism. Feeling exploited, she began to fight for the spiritual freedom of the individual and advocated the end of tyranny in wage slavery and marriage. Her first issue of *Mother Earth* contained articles on the fundamentals of anarchy that attacked nationalism and feminism. A later issue expressed support for Leon Czolgosz, the killer of President McKinley, and resulted in a large drop in readership.

While working at the St. Louis *Post-Dispatch,* a fight with the editor ended Johan's time at the newspaper and in St. Louis. By this time, Johan was secretly publishing his anarchist magazine. His editor discovered and destroyed the entire stock of publications, manuscripts and publishing plates. As a result, Johan and his daughter left St. Louis for New Mexico. He learned to keep his political views much better protected in Valtura.

Adobe stops at National Street then continues to First Avenue and slows down the pace when a coyote crosses his path. The cunning canine symbolizes continuous improvement and can be a mirror held in front of humans. Sometimes, Adobe prefers not to look in a mirror for fear of his folly.

The moon, strikingly visible, soon reveals the Circle C in the distance. With the ranch in sight, he remembers Klara's fury. *So much rage reflected in a moment about her strong interest in fundamentally changing America.*

33

SANDIA MOUNTAINS

The next day, Adobe meets Klara on the sunlit plaza. All of Valtura can see their rendezvous.

"Thanks for joining me, Klara."

"I'm sure it will be an enjoyable trip."

They start on horseback from the plaza, riding through East Corona Street, toward the beautiful mountain range.

Adobe turns to Kara and says, "I love sitting in the saddle through miles of wooded trails. The mountain meadows, streams, ancient trees and canyon vistas will be enjoyable, but there is something even more special."

"What's that?"

"This is the first time I've been to the Sandia Peak with a woman at my side."

Toward the foothills, they stop to admire the ultimate destination 10,000 feet up in the clear blue sky—the Sandia Crest. The west side of the mountain has a gentler slope and is easier to ascend than the east side with its steep and rugged rock walls.

They journey beyond the foothills and up a forest road, watching the spectacular explosion of late summer foliage—shades of red, orange and yellow. As Adobe and Klara ride the winding trails from base to summit, they travel through four different life zones that vary with elevation, temperature and rain.

The first zone contains mostly juniper trees and a mixture of piñon, juniper, evergreen and oak. Ponderosa pine and cold-tolerant oak trees are in the second zone. A mixture of conifers and gambel oaks are in the third. The highest zone contains spruce and fir trees.

Three hours after leaving the plaza, they arrive at Sandia Crest, dismount and walk along the ridge to the top. The breathtaking aerial views of the plains, the mountains in the distance, the towns of Albuquerque and Valtura, capture the romantic heart of the Southwest.

Finally, at the highest point, Adobe says, "Thoughts are free up here, Klara. They can travel uninterrupted."

She smiles contentedly, feeling the thrill of the panoramic view of rugged canyons and cliffs and says, "It is a beautiful environment."

"Yes, as far as you can see."

"It is a phenomenal, picturesque view," Klara agrees, "and we could find elusive harmony here."

Adobe believes he has won Klara's romantic interest and that the trip will be eventful. His fantasy will fade away all too soon.

"You look more beautiful at 10,000 feet," he says.

She hands him a setback by saying, "You must have high-altitude sickness."

Staring beyond the horizon, he says, "Oh, I was being descriptive."

Her implied rejection resolves his ambivalence about holding her hand.

So much for romance, he thinks, *lucky the Cuban experience has prepared me for such absurdity.*

Klara seeks expression of her romantic ideals, but not now.

"May I ask you a question?" she sheepishly says.

Adobe leans in and says, "Sure Klara. What's on your mind?"

"Mady Blaylock."

A hawk zooms overhead, stirring the horses.

"What about her?"

"I think you know. Who is she?"

"She 's a popular saloon owner on the plaza," he says evasively.

Klara insists, "What does she mean to you?"

"Mady is my oldest friend in Valtura and she is missing right now—and that is difficult for me. I know many people on the plaza think we are romantically involved, but it is not true."

"But it could be true in the future," she challenged.

"Look Klara, we are together in one of the most romantic places on earth."

She smiles and says, "I am by no means romantically inexperienced, but will not be made irrational by you. Many on the plaza believe you have a mysterious romantic past, some sort of inconsolable love tragedy."

"I don't know about that."

"You do sporadically show traces of a medieval knight. That's what keeps me interested in you and that is not likely to end." After a brief meditation she adds, "You know that the women on the plaza whisper about some nameless competition for your affection."

Adobe starts to smile reminiscently then says, "We should start back. It will be dark soon." The downward ride is quiet, with a stark desert sunset providing shadows resonating secrecy.

In the saddle, riding side-by-side Adobe brings up another proposal.

"Klara, I would like to write an article for your newspaper about the free market."

She is impressed that he did not go to Johan, but suspicious all at the same time.

It was a strategy not an objective—and it worked.

"Tell me more about the theme of your article."

"Well, for a century America's free market has created great ideas and new products. We have been the greatest force for prosperity the world has ever known."

Klara gives a quick frown. "Yes, I know your position."

"The point of my article is that the free market is the way to continue our success as a nation."

Klara allows her horse to slow down, suggesting he has lost her interest, but she continues to listen.

"You may be surprised to know, I feel that one reason the free market has worked is government control—that is a proper balance."

She moves her mount up to face Adobe and says, "I would love to know what you mean by balance."

"Perhaps you would like to be a co-author."

Klara gives a noncommittal smile and Adobe gives an opinion, "We need freedom of commerce while welcoming government involvement to protect the people from health and safety threats—without placing unreasonable demands on business."

"And you have the magic formula for this?" she mocks.

"No, but the point of the article is to start thinking about ways to ensure government protection from any business abuse while promoting the benefits of the free market."

"Benefits, did you forget about the financial panic that occurred four years ago? The runs on banks and trust companies were widespread throughout the country! All caused by greed!"

"Klara, it was a retraction of market liquidity by New York banks and a loss of confidence for depositors."

"Fancy talk for banks and businesses going bankrupt! Greedy capitalists tried to corner the market on that copper company stock."

"You mean the United Copper Company."

"Yes that one. When their plot failed, the banks that advanced cash for the scheme had runs that spread fear all over New York and regional banks withdrew their cash reserves."

"Klara, it was significant economic disruption, with bank panics, falling stock prices, big drop in industrial production and many bankruptcies. However, did you forget that J.P. Morgan and other New York bankers put up millions of their own money to support the banking system—and stopped the panic?"

"J.P. Morgan, ha! Officers of the Morgan Company sit on the boards of over a hundred corporations who control billions of dollars."

"We can include different points of view, Klara. I would like to work with you."

In a moment of humility, Klara says, "Thanks for coming to me; I know you could have easily talked to my father."

"Is that a yes?"

"Let me think about it."

Adobe escorts Klara home and returns to the ranch. The Circle C coyotes are active, as they are every night. Some native people believe that the coyote changed the course of rivers and moved mountains to improve the earth. Some nights they show their boldness by standing on Little Hill Top.

Adobe sits on the back portal, just outside the library and watches the canine company. They represent a balance of wisdom and folly, sometimes more wisdom, sometimes more folly. He wonders which it is tonight.

34

Next Stop Valtura

Autumn is nearing, along with the Revert Document deadline. All of Mademoiselle Sharon's Sears and Roebuck deliveries have arrived and Chez Beau Sharon is nearing completion.

After her meticulous preparation, and with a sense of satisfaction that plans are progressing according to *her* schedule, Sharon leaves her casita when two men appear, cross her path and stare. *Are these men attracted to the new beautiful Mademoiselle Sharon or interested in other matters,* she wonders. No time now, she quickens her pace without looking back.

Returning to the telegraph office, she stares at the young man behind an old desk and says, "What's the matter, have you not ever seen a beautiful French woman?"

"Sorry, Miss Sharon. How can I help you?"

Mademoiselle Sharon tells him to tap out a message. The telegraph keys click: *Arriving Valtura tomorrow.*

Arriving after the creation of Chez Beau Sharon is part of her overall game, but there is more to it than meets the eye. Santa Fe Sharon, now Mademoiselle Sharon, has waited for the creation of her palace. Sharon Blaylock knows how to make an entrance.

Sharon, chain-smoking Marlboro Red Tips, rides to the rail station in a motorcar driven by her supplicant. Some men endure bad behavior to be near a beautiful woman; she successfully manipulates men with her attractiveness, nothing more and nothing less. Sharon knows that her currency is fading and there is limited time to be a big winner. She is on the move.

Although badly treated, he gives her the benefit of the doubt and drives her and a large trunk to the rail station.

"Will I see you when you return, Miss Sharon?" the supplicant says.

"Look, I'm bad with goodbyes, so goodbye," she says unemotionally.

The supplicant watches the train leave the station and thinks, *I have to give myself a good talking to.*

About two miles south, Sharon looks around the railcar. In the rear, two familiar men are reading newspapers. *Are they the same men from outside my house and on the plaza? Did they intercept my telegrams? They're well dressed, not too fancy for government agents; it must be the new beautiful Mademoiselle Sharon that attracts them.* The conductor enters the car, calling for tickets. When he reaches the men, Sharon listens to learn their stop, but their response is incomprehensible.

Hours later, the conductor returns and calls out, "Valtura, Valtura, next stop is Val tur raaaa."

The train comes to a screeching halt, jolting Sharon. She jumps from her bench seat and looks toward the rear. The men are engaged in conversation, but the earsplitting steam locomotive muffles their words. *Perhaps they are working for untrusting people in Old Mexico,* she thinks, *or working to know the new beautiful Mademoiselle Sharon.*

As a flag stop, the Valtura station is usually vacant. Unlike Carrie's arrival, however, Sharon's contact is waiting. Standing on the platform next to the 46-star American flag is Bill Blackstone.

One year ago, Sharon met Blackstone in Las Vegas, New Mexico, when he was known as Bill "Black Eyed Pea" Blackstone. Las Vegas is a town that has had a significant part in territorial history. In 1846, General Kearney claimed New Mexico for the U.S. in Las Vegas Plaza—a turning point in New Mexico history.

Las Vegas has come a long way from those transitional days with the influx of hardcases, desperadoes and outlaws, including a young Bill Blackstone. Many new businesses and respectable people arrived with the new railroad in 1879, creating an economic boom leading to today's electric street railroad, an opera house, a Carnegie Library, and a Harvey House Hotel.

Blackstone spent time as an undersheriff, but may have done as much to break the law as to enforce the law. He was engaged in illegal activities, and eventually arrested for murder, but despite the best lawyer in Las Vegas helping the prosecution, they could not win a conviction. Some attribute the acquittal to jury composition. However, Blackstone did spend six months in the territory prison for larceny. But he quit Las Vegas for Santa Fe and for Santa Fe Sharon.

"Welcome to Valtura, Miss Sharon."

"Let's get going," she says, walking past him without eye contact.

"Why so unfriendly? After all, you should be glad to see me."

"I don't have the time."

"Ha, if it weren't for me, you would have plenty of time."

Santa Fe Sharon and Blackstone ride to town in a wagon pulled by a two-horse team. The train leaves the station, restoring the quiet. Then, the sounds of howls; some believe coyotes can announce if a friend or foe is coming in the distance.

"How are things here?" Sharon inquires with arrogant authority.

"We had a little problem at the saloon. There was a shoot-out with Centori. Men were killed."

"What!" her screech startles the horses. "Were you trying to destroy my entire plan before I even arrived?"

"You seem to forget who helped you with your great plan. Anyway, the sheriff returned abruptly and the men thought he was looking for trouble."

"Tell me exactly what happened; start with Centori. Is he all right?"

She fumbles for a cigarette. Blackstone tries to light her smoke, but she brushes him away.

"Centori is fine. He was poised in the face of fire, and handled himself well with that Navy Colt. You ever see what that gun can do at close range? The men we hired are not so fine—two are dead, one has disappeared."

"The men *we* hired," she says mockingly. "And what were *your* instructions to these bungling men?"

"As we agreed—if you are unsuccessful in influencing Centori, he is to be killed."

"Exactly, *if* I am unsuccessful, but I have not even met him, let alone failed in influencing him!"

"I know, but these men were drinking hard and...."

Before he can finish, she yells, "Stop working with fools! You have made the job harder, if not impossible!"

"It will send him a message."

"Damn you." Sharon feels the same kind of rage that ended a man's life on St. Francis Street. That killing was for far less than Blackstone's transgression, but there is already enough unwanted attention and she needs him. Blackstone is lucky, for now.

They enter Valtura on Junction Street, turn right on First Avenue and stop at the Union Hotel. Blackstone shows Sharon to the hotel entrance.

As a parting shot, she says, "If you're trying to develop your image as an incompetent fool, you're doing a good job."

Blackstone says nothing and disappears, again.

Entering the lobby with an air of importance, Sharon attracts the attention of desk clerk James Clarke and those milling around the lobby.

"Welcome to the Union Hotel, Miss," says Clarke, a skulking man of fifty years with a receding hairline. "How can we help you?"

"I need a suite of rooms for several days."

"Room seven is the largest room in the hotel."

"I guess it will do."

"Please sign here, Miss."

Sharon artfully writes, *Sharon Blaylock, Santa Fe, New Mexico.*

Clarke spins the book around and declares, "Blaylock!"

"Yes, I'm Sharon Blaylock."

"Are you connected to Mady Blaylock? She runs Mad Mady's Saloon on the south side of the plaza."

Sharon thinks, *You mean she used to run Mad Mady's Saloon*, but says, "Mady and I are sisters."

"I see. I never heard her mention a sister before."

"You will hear more about me now that I am in Valtura."

"Are you here for Mady? Sorry to be the bearer of bad news, but she left town without a word. Some say under mysterious circumstances."

Ignoring the comment, she lights another cigarette and orders, "Please have my trunk sent up to the room." Sharon turns away from the front desk and parades by several men in the lobby who are pretending to be reading newspapers. Wasting no time, she departs for the saloon.

Clarke rings the bell to summon the porter.

"Take this trunk to room seven."

"Yes, Mr. Clarke. That woman sure is attention grabbing. What do you think she brings to town?"

"Probably bad weather—she showed no interest or emotion about Mady being gone. By the way, make sure the room has a 'do not disturb' sign. This one looks like she'll need it."

While walking through the plaza, Sharon sees a sign on the building next to the courthouse that provides the location for her ultimate target.

A. CENTORI, SHERIFF
CORONA COUNTY
NEW MEXICO TERRITORY

Carrie is setting up hand-painted china behind the long bar when Sharon comes in and immediately expresses disapproval.

Surprised by the abrupt entrance, Carrie cries out, "Sharon!"

"I told you, the china goes in the curio cabinet."

"But, I thought…."

"There are two rules around here. First, I am always right, and second, see the first rule. Remember, I got you out of those dove establishments on Calle Montano."

"You make it hard to forget."

"Speaking of forgetting, didn't I tell you to have Chez Beau Sharon completely done before I arrived?"

"Yes, but it takes time. We are almost done. I had to rely on Blackstone, who did *not* meet me at the station! People around here are not that excited about helping me. They seem to be loyal to Mady and concerned about her absence."

"Did you offer enough money?"

"Not everything can be measured in money."

"You dream, Carrie."

"Anyway, welcome to Valtura, Sharon."

Without warning, Sharon slaps Carrie across her face, causing her to fall back. In shock, she knocks the table over and glasses crash to the floor.

Carrie looks up, searching for an explanation and her gun.

"That's for not controlling the drinking of Blackstone's men, who caused an outrageous display, drawing attention to us. If you had handled things right it would not have been necessary. Did you have to explain to Centori?"

Rubbing her face, Carrie glares and slowly replies, "I told him the men were strangers to me and very drunk."

"Did he believe you?"

Silence—Sharon has her answer.

"Centori is distrustful even before we meet. Are there any other problems to report?"

With her face still smarting, Carrie says, "I fired Berta. She was too loyal to your sister."

Carrie would not dare reveal another major blunder by admitting to the shooting. Instead, she says, "Sheriff Centori is loyal to your sister. Some say in a personal way, and he was here asking questions about her."

"Really? Whatever does he see in my manly sister anyway?"

"Manly or not, he thinks she's good."

"Yeah, good to haunt a house."

"But Centori is suspicious about Mady's disappearance."

"You better pray that Centori doesn't discover that I forced Mady into the asylum, but don't worry. He'll soon forget Mady when he sees me." She steps aside in a seductive way.

"What about Mad Mady's popularity in Valtura?"

"The town will also forget Mady once they see the new fabulous Chez Beau Sharon with its fabulous French hostess."

"Centori is already intervening and he is not likely to forget the shoot-out."

"Men forget about all other things when they are with me."

"But what if Mady returns? That would prevent you from establishing control in Valtura and you could be arrested."

"Her new *home* is far away. Besides, Mady's as happy as if she were in her right mind."

"Even if you control Centori with your body, will you influence him before Mady returns?"

"You sound like you want her to return to upset my big plans."

"No, Sharon, but with you taking her business she will do everything possible to return to Valtura. It's just a matter of time."

"You're such a pain, Carrie."

"Too many things have gone wrong already."

"I'm confident that Mady is away for the long term."

"Are you willing to bet your revenge on that? You have much invested in this affair. Should you leave anything to chance?"

"It's true. I've waited a long time to pay Mady back and Old Mexico is depending on my success."

"Old Mexico?"

"Never mind. Perhaps you're right. I can control any man, but Mady must not come between Centori and me. She may have already told him too much. Our next move is clear—it is vital to control Mady's confinement."

"Yes, you must make sure Mady stays in the asylum as long as possible."

"What? How do you know about that?" Sharon demands.

"A woman in the right position can learn many things."

"You and Blackstone! Why should I be surprised? Okay, tell me how to find the telegraph office in this town. We should determine the status of her institutionalization. I may have to make further arrangements to secure Mady's long-term confinement."

"The office is on National Street near Camino San Antonio. Go out and turn right."

"I'll be right back. Try not to make any more trouble."

Sharon storms out, determined to enhance her reputation as a formidable force. As a new, beautiful woman in town, she attracts attention on the plaza, has heads turning on National Street and startles the telegraph operator, Bill "Buster" Brown, by barging into his office.

"I wish a message sent to Mr. Trumble in Rio Arriba County."

Buster, a tall, skinny man who does not drink, smoke, chew tobacco or play cards, sees her beauty and submissively says, "Please fill this out."

Sharon writes a veiled note inquiring about the extent of Mady's situation at the asylum. Buster taps it out and says, "Could be a while before you get an answer. Care for some coffee?"

"No thanks," she says curtly, not softening the rejection. "Please bring the reply to me at the Union Hotel. I am Sharon Blaylock."

"Blaylock?"

"Yes, yes! I'm Mady's sister."

"The people around the plaza and most of Valtura are worried about Mady."

"I'm sure she's fine. Now bring me the reply the moment it is received."

"Sure thing, Miss Blaylock."

Sharon walks diagonally across the plaza and returns to the hotel. Unsurprisingly, heads turn, following her movement through the lobby and up the stairs. Alone in her room Sharon unpacks and tries to rest.

All the travel, excitement and her private fear of the unknown converge. Nevertheless, Sharon undresses and lies naked on the Victorian bed, restively stares at the ornate ceiling and then closes her eyes.

Two hours later, Sharon hurries back into the bar, waving a telegram from Nurse Darcie Denton. "Damn, Mady is only there for psychiatric evaluation—not long-term treatment!"

"Where have you been?" Carrie asks.

"I am staying at the Union Hotel until I can decorate Mady's room my way."

"This is Mercy; she has been helping out in place of Berta."

"Hello. Would you leave us alone?" Sharon says while looking at Mercy's long brown hair.

Mercy smiles and goes upstairs just within earshot. Sharon watches her negotiate the steps and then says, "Mady is there for evaluation, but only for a short time because she committed no violent crime. The territory requires a court order for extended treatment."

"We can't afford any more problems," Carrie says.

"Mady's return would be more than a problem! All will fail if she returns!"

"So, what are you suggesting?"

"Perhaps I should visit the Territorial Insane Asylum to make sure Mady stays there."

"Are you sure you need to go there?"

"Scared because things are becoming dangerous? You knew the risks that accompany your job."

"All right, Sharon."

"Don't be so anxious to get rid of me. I just arrived."

"I'm not anxious. Make up your mind. I'll take care of things while you're gone."

"Really?" Sharon says sarcastically. "Once I'm convinced that things are under control, I will travel to the asylum. Even if I'm successful in extending Mady's confinement, she'll eventually get out and fight for the saloon."

"I am sure you are right about that, Sharon."

"Yes, and there is one more thing. I agree there could be limited time to recover my investment. We need to quickly fire up sales, drive up the volume of drinks with lower prices and the doves must be more aggressive. Get things busy upstairs."

"Okay, Sharon. I'll talk to Mercy and she can tell the other doves."

"No, you tell each one separately. Make a strong point."

"I'll start today."

"Then, I want you to decrease the price of drinks by twenty-five percent and the price of doves by fifteen percent. That will increase consumption by the regulars and attract new people, even draw people away from the hotel bar."

"That's clever and very impressive, Sharon."

"Of course it's impressive. That's high finance. Now follow my instructions—and while I'm gone, no more mayhem."

35

MEXICO CITY

Although the U.S. won a series of battles in the Mexican-American War, Mexico would not surrender. President Polk ordered General Winfield Scott and his men to march on Mexico City from Vera Cruz. On the outer edge of the Mexican capital, the Americans faced a larger force under the command of Santa Anna—the Alamo victor.

The Americans opened up with artillery barrage on the Chapultepec fortress. Then, the Americans attacked the fort located on a 7,500-foot-high hill by storm. After a protracted fight, they raised the U.S. flag over the castle. West Pointers and future Civil War generals, including Lee, Grant, Longstreet and Pickett, contributed to the capture of Mexico City. Ambassador Albert Hietmann views this event as an asset.

Hietmann approaches Mexico City's *Plaza de la Constitucion,* called the *Zocalo.* The *Zocalo,* a great plaza in front of the Cathedral and the *Palacio Nacional,* the home of the federal executive, is the center of ceremonial activities including Independence Day. It is 10:30 a.m. on September 15, 1911.

The *Palacio Nacional* façade, flanked by two towers, has three doors made of iron and bronze. Above the central doorway is the main balcony where the president will address the people. Each year on this date, he commemorates Mexico's 1821 independence from Spain by ringing the bell. The war started as a peasants' rebellion against Spain but ended as an alliance between Mexican ex-royalists and Mexican guerrilla insurgents.

As the leader of the German legation, Hietmann enters the southern door through the Patio of Honor and goes to the president's office, prepared to discuss relevant political factors. The U.S. victory over Spain in 1898 increased Germany's interest in Mexico. Berlin saw Mexico as an answer to the growing U.S. power and hoped to improve their international position. However, Berlin feared provoking the U.S. and hurting their economic and political prospects in Mexico. As a result, German interventionist policy toward Mexico vacillated—until now.

"Please wait here, *Señor* Hietmann, President Madero will see you soon," announces the president's secretary.

"Thank you."

He gives Hietmann a nod and walks away.

While waiting, Hietmann reviews his thoughts about President Francesco Madero. *This conference must be successful; there may not be another chance to convince Madero of the practicality inherent in the Revert Document. I will be direct with him and urge him to accept the plan, to quietly strengthen his troops in border cities and remind him of America's overwhelming ambition.*

Madero is aristocratic, reform-minded and a politically shrewd leader in charge, who started a revolution against Porfirio Diaz. In 1910, Diaz ruled with an iron fist and ruthlessly stopped resistance. After decades of power, Diaz called for a presidential election and democracy that would end the exploitation of workers and the disparity between rich and poor. Madero, a lawyer from Coahuila, ran against him and won despite incumbent corruption.

Rather than honor the election results, Diaz stole the election and claimed victory. Then Madero fled and wrote the Plan de San Luis Potosi, calling for a rebellion. His formidable supporters, Pancho Villa and Emiliano Zapata, defeated Diaz in battle. As a result, Madero became president and Diaz fled to France.

"The president will see you now, *Señor* Hietmann. Please follow me."

The secretary leads him to the balcony in time for the bell-ringing ceremony.

"Welcome, *Señor* Hietmann."

"Thank you, President Madero. I am honored to be here and thank you for granting my request on such an important day for you and all of Mexico."

Hanging above the balcony is the bell that Miguel Hidalgo rang to call for rebellion. It is 11:00 a.m., and with Hietmann standing beside him, President Madero rings the same bell, but this time it is a call to celebration. After the ceremony and a standard political speech, the men retire into the president's inner office.

"I hope you enjoyed our celebration, *Señor* Hietmann," Madero says while pouring fine wine into fine glasses from a silver decanter.

"President Madero, the celebration was inspiring and befitting our meeting. Your nationalistic message to the people is appropriate now that a certain deadline is nearing."

Suspicious of Hietmann's motives and playing it close to the vest, Madero says, "Deadline, *Señor* Hietmann? Perhaps it is not a coincidence that we meet on this day."

Hietmann smiles, knowing that the irony is not lost on Madero, who needs German political power to defend against the U.S. Hietmann removes a map from a fine leather case and says, "Please look at this map." Madero allows him to continue.

As Hietmann spreads the map across the table, the president's ceremonial Spanish sword in its silver scabbard bangs against the table. Looking down at the map with its worn edges, he says, "President Madero, this is Mexico in the year 1840—before the war and the Mexican Cession.

"*Ay Dios mio.* Our lost territories," Madero whispers.

Hietmann pauses for effect and continues, "As you know, the border extended far into North America. Mexico included the American territories of New Mexico and Arizona and many states including California, and, of course, Texas—a particular sore spot for Mexico."

"This map is quite interesting and thank you for the history lesson, but I don't know what you expect from this meeting."

"May I expect a reasonable discussion?"

"*Señor* Hietmann, it is reasonable to say that the war was long ago and those territories have been American states for many years now."

"All except Arizona and New Mexico, President Madero. As you know, all former Mexican lands taken by the Americans are now U.S. states *except* the border territories."

"That is true, but still what is there to discuss?"

"We should discuss an interesting document that has historic implications. I am referring to Article X of the Treaty of Mesilla."

"*Señor* Hietmann, as a student of history, you should know that the treaty contains only nine articles."

The president's impassive tactic does not stop Hietmann, who says, "So we have been led to believe, but perhaps there is an elusive tenth article, the so-called Revert Document."

"Many articles were annulled."

"The tenth article as well?"

Realizing that further denial is foolish, Madero empties his glass and says, "Many people think it never really existed."

Hietmann sips his wine and waits for more.

"Of course we are aware of the Revert Document, provisons about border territories and the deadline. We know the annulment theory and that American agents destroyed manuscript copies. We are aware of it all," Madero says forcefully.

"Yes, President Madero, a man in your position would know much of such things."

"And Mexico is aware of the many historical grievances connected to Amercian aggression, such as the dishonoring of land grants in ceded regions and the disrespect of property rights of former Mexican citizens."

Feeling that the meeting is going better than expected, Hietmann presses, "President Madero, there is an opportunity for concerned parties. If the Revert Document exists and is discovered, the person presenting it would be in a commanding position. If you were that person, your presidency would be secure for the long term."

Madero takes exception to the suggestion of a tenuous presidency, finding the Ambassador less than diplomatic. "It is *not* an opportunity," he says, "it is a fantasy. At best, the document is missing, and at worst, it never existed. Even if we can find it and delay statehood, we would not be successful in recapturing our border territories; the Americans will never accept the Revert Document without a fight."

"It may not exist because the Americans destroyed the inconvenient document. Or more accurately, *officially stored* manuscript copies may not exist," Hietmann ventures.

"*Señor* Hietmann, you are certainty knowledgeable about our history," says Madero.

"As Ambassador to Mexico, that is part of my professional responsibility."

Impressed with the German's knowledge, if not his manners, Madero offers, "While it is true that manuscript copies are rumored to be hidden, we cannot be sure."

"I did not say hidden, but of course you are right."

Both men sense that the time has come to sort fact from legend. One fact is for sure—Arizona and New Mexico are still territories.

"But *Señor* Hietmann, as I have said, the U.S. will not accept the demand of the Revert Document and probably construe it as an act of war."

"I am sure they will insist on war, but my government in Berlin is prepared to back Mexico's claims. At my direction, German ships containing a cargo of ten million rounds, fifty thousand Mausers, five hundred cannons, and a substantial amount of Spanish pesetas will dispatch from Hamburg to Vera Cruz."

Madero's face tightens. "You are presenting a very serious proposal."

"Berlin is very serious."

"President Madero, I know you are not one to shy from a fight—your Plan of San Luis Potosí declared an election void and called for Mexicans to fight the government. It was a bold move."

"If you know our history, then you know that not all Mexican people will be in favor of your plan. This very day we celebrate independence, but the movement was without unanimous support. Our country separated into independence seekers, autonomists and royalists."

"President Madero, in 1906, New Mexico statehood attempts failed; we may have more allies in the territory than we know. We can promise the New Mexicans immediate self-government as a Mexican state, something that the U.S. government has withheld for decades."

There is a long pause and then Madero continues, "And assuming we agree, what exactly is your plan?"

Hietmann is encouraged and diplomatically says, "First, the Revert Document must be found before final statehood approval in Santa Fe and Washington. This means we must delay statehood past the December 31 deadline. Allow me to update you on our progress."

"Progress?" Madero, offended by the German initiatives before any agreement, looks angrily at him.

Hietmann answers the implied question by asking, "May I show you another chart that can provide perspective? You will see the careful proficient planning that surrounds our grand objective."

He removes another rolled up paper from a case and spreads it across the table, covering the old map of Mexico, revealing a chart of New Mexico's twelve counties, respective agents and targeted delegates. They study the chart.

"We have identified delegates to the statehood convention in every New Mexico County and have assigned women agents."

"What about Arizona Territory? They are in the same situation."

Hietmann smiles at the president's interest and says, "Yes, but we do not have the resources to aim for Arizona."

"I have not known a German to shy from a challenge."

"Very good, but given the size of our mission, New Mexico is the goal. Besides, Arizona separated from New Mexico. Those people will likely resist reverting to Mexico. Moreover, there are tens of thousands of Spanish-speaking people in New Mexico.

"Yes, of course, New Mexico is the true prize," Madero agrees.

"I understand the special attachment to New Mexico, with Santa Fe the traditional capital of your northern provinces," Hietmann says manipulatively.

The president pauses and says, "There has been much tradition in Santa Fe and New Mexico, even before we gained our independence from Spain."

"Tradition is important."

"There is more than tradition at stake. Santa Fe and New Mexico became an economic success story. With the border between Old and New Mexico removed, all of Mexico will prosper."

Playing to the president's ego, Hietmann says, "If we win, you will be the greatest Mexican President in history."

Madero is politically perceptive and does not suffer fools, especially from obvious manipulators. He finds Hietmann arrogant, but tolerates him as long as he is expedient. Madero is motivated to pursue the plan and continues to listen. Since driving out Diaz, political and social unrest threaten the stability of his hegemony and his personal glory.

"We have placed many resources into New Mexico and assigned agents to the delegates. Next, we must find the Revert Document. Then delay the statehood process, preventing Taft's signature. Then, after the deadline has passed, we can present the document to the Americans—backed up by the German military and world opinion."

"There will be a role for the Mexican military, too."

"Of course, your military will be strategically aligned at the border," Hietmann says, recovering from a diplomatic mistake.

"*Señor* Hietmann, your plan has great risk and great reward, but what exactly does Germany expect in return?"

"I assure you we seek only positive diplomatic relations with your country and a good trading partner."

"That's what France said last century," Madero warns.

"President Madero, we are in the twentieth century now."

He stares sternly and says, "*Señor* Hietmann, the war was a long time ago."

"And that long period of time is interesting. After so many decades of territorial status, it may be an omen to repair a historical injustice for Mexico."

"Or a rationalization," Madero says harshly. "This plan is all but impossible, even for you Germans."

Music and crowd noise from the celebration interrupts the moment of silence.

"Shall I continue?" asks Hietmann.

Before Madero can answer, there is a knock on the door.

"*Venido adentro*," Madero commands.

Jan Steiner and a woman appear, escorted by a palace guard.

"President Madero, may I present *Señora Zena-Marta*?"

"*Con mucho gusto, Señora*!"

The president is immediately impressed with the striking woman and ignores Steiner.

Although no longer young, the years have been kind to her. She wears a denim shirt, black Levis and riding boots, with her hair hidden underneath a wide-brimmed black sombrero. As a beautiful woman, men have been inclined to talk to her. This has not changed.

"May I present Jan Steiner, our new Vice Ambassador?"

Madero nods and turns to the beauty, "May I pour you a glass of wine, *Señora*?"

"Yes, thank you, President Madero," Zena-Marta answers without smiling.

Hietmann, seeing her strong impression, moves to exploit his new political capital and says, "Although my associate is from Cuba, she is no stranger to Mexico, your Excellency. Gabriella Zena-Marta attended the National Autonomous University of Mexico and is married to the Cuban Foreign Secretary to Mexico, Riccardo Marta."

The diplomatic couple had lived in the outskirts of Mexico City for several years. During her time in Cuba, Gabriella was always suspicious of the U.S. Now she is an enemy of America with determined opposition to U.S. aggression.

"Yes, *Señora*, I know your husband. He is a fine addition to Cuban-Mexican relations." Madero says with feigned gusto.

The marriage to the much older Riccardo Marta was one of expediency, not passion. Given the role of women in Cuban society, the marriage allowed her to enter Cuba's highest political circles. As a forceful woman with military experience and leadership abilities, she is determined to change the course of political events.

Gabriella fought passionately against European control during the Spanish-American War. Now she sees a chance to right a historical injustice: the major land grab by the Americans. Right or wrong, she has passionate dedication to her cause.

"*Señora*, I understand you are unhappy with our neighbors to the north," says Madero.

"Yes, President Madero, many Cubans feel our country is under U.S. control. After the war, the U.S. leased forty-five square miles on Guantanamo Bay. We resent the American presence in southeast Cuba."

"I am aware of the agreement that gave the Americans a continuous lease for a coaling station in Cuba, but there are conditions."

"Yes," Gabriella says, "and the Americans are in breach of the conditions. We also believe the treaty, signed under threat of force, is invalid."

"So you wish to reclaim the land."

"Oh, it is much more than Guantanamo Bay, President Madero. After the war, the Treaty of Paris transferred power over Cuba from Spain to the U.S. We had no Cuban representation at the assembly. We will never forget that McKinley said it is not wise to recognize Cuban independence."

"Yes, *Señora*, but did not the Platt Amendment transfer rule of Cuba to your people?" Madero asks.

"It also forced us to lease part of Cuba for what is now a U.S. naval station. How would Mexico feel if the U.S. had a military base here in Mexico City?"

Madero looks at Hietmann, laughs, finally offers Steiner wine, and turns back to Gabriella. "Pardon me, *Señora*, but why would the Americans need a base in Mexico? They have all of our northern provinces. But you make an interesting point; many in my government think the United States wishes to eventually expand further into Mexico."

"Of course," Gabriella says, "you have much to protest about the Americans."

Hietmann sips his wine and adds, "And we will make a bigger protest."

She finishes her wine and says, "Cuba has a new imposition that has impelled me to act. The Americans enlarged Guantanamo, covering a shared access channel used for trade."

"I share your concern," says Madero.

Growing angry, Gabriella shouts, "The Platt Amendment is imperialistic! It is an infringement on our self-rule. Do you know the U.S. can decide when our independence is threatened and choose when to intervene?"

Hietmann refills the four wine glasses as Gabriella continues, "What's more, a tariff agreement gave us a sugar preference in the U.S. market and protection to buy U.S. products. So now sugar production dominates our economy while we become dependent on U.S. products."

With Gabriella in the room, Madero glimpses the possibility of being the greatest Mexican hero, and thinks, *This plan could help consolidate my support and political power. With all the opposing forces, a great victory over the Americans would make me the clear leader, and secure my presidency for a generation.* He brings his wine glass close to his lips and says, "We have many grievances with the Americans. They have a long history of ignoring us, and certainly Cuba's reasons are apparent." Turning to Hietmann, he adds, "But somewhat less clear are Germany's reasons."

Hietmann ignores the remark and motions to Steiner, who hands him a confidential document containing a list of New Mexico statehood delegates:

County	Agent	Delegate Leader
Bernalillo	Catherine Reinhardt	Lane Sheldon
Catron	Clara James	Roger Connelly
Chaves	Isabella McCutcheon	David Wallace
Cibola	Mary Breen	James Allen
Colfax	Amanda Foster	George Taylor
Corona	Sharon Blaylock	Aldoloreto Centori
Curry	Margaret Stanton	Edmund Mills
De Baca	Harriet Reed	Henry Ross
Doña Ana	Doris Pike	Samuel Jackson
Eddy	Virginia Williams	John Hagerman
Grant	Mary Gilbert	Juan Otero
Guadalupe	Susan McClean	William Carr

Madero takes a quick look, but says nothing. Gabriella scans the list and stops halfway down at Corona County. She focuses on the sixth name and looks as if she has seen a ghost.

Madre de Dios, she thinks, as her facial expression changes dramatically.

"*Señora Zena-Marta*, are you feeling poorly?" asks Madero.

She pauses for a moment, recovering from the news, "No, I am fine," she says with a strong voice, reaching deep inside for strength.

Hietmann then produces another map of New Mexico, "This one shows the border towns that will need military strength."

"We are talking about lives, not maps," Zena-Marta yells like a shrew, shocking the two men. She thinks of the life they never shared and now of a life in danger.

She smiles, her way of expressing regret for the outburst, and yells "*Viva el Revolucion, Señor Presidente*!"

Although puzzled by her flare-up, Madero says, "Señor

Hietmann, your elaborate plans are well thought out but the most important element is still missing."

"Yes. I present the plan providing we obtain the document."

"Providing we obtain the document," Madero repeats. "Señor Hietmann, at the time of the agreement, fifty years was generations in the future, and over time the Revert Document faded from awareness and consideration. What is more, everybody believed that New Mexico would be a state decades before the arbitrary deadline."

"Everybody was wrong," Zena-Marta says.

"President Madero, we are hoping that you can help to obtain an original manuscript copy, the last piece of our plan." Hietmann says.

"But no one has claimed to see the document in many years, perhaps decades. If it ever existed, it has disappeared or been destroyed."

Deflated, Hietmann sighs and laments, "Berlin will be very disappointed with me."

Madero slowly drinks from his fine wine glass and reveals, "In any case, all that is left is lore and legend."

The two Germans and one Cuban stare at Madero, absorbing the promising revelation.

"One legend is particularly curious. It tells of a column of Mexican cavalry that penetrated into northwestern New Mexico Territory after the Treaty of Mesilla and just weeks before the American Civil War."

"So someone *was* concerned about the distant future?" Zena-Marta says.

Hietmann eagerly asks, "We must learn the names of the officers and men on that mission."

She adds, "But that information is probably lost to history, and many, if not all, of those men are dead by now."

"Perhaps there is a way," Madero offered. "I can order research of military records for missions from the period, especially vaguely-defined missions. We can look for the youngest men on the list, those most likely to have survived to this day. The records could provide a clue to their location, provided they are alive at all."

"That is excellent, President Madero, excellent," Hietmann says.

Zena-Marta restrains her approval. The conspirators continue the breathtaking conversation and then toast their common cause, knowing the plan is not perfect.

That night, Hietmann and Zena-Marta retire to their respective residences. He is thinking about Madero and she is thinking about Adobe. Lightning cracks and thunder rumbles provide an overture to the howling hijinks of exceptionally loud coyotes. Some believe that wrongdoers, upon reaching the land of the dead, return to earth as coyotes.

36

Loma Lake

A dry wind gusts across the high desert, the sun peaks and Sharon is on the move. It is her second of travel and she is determined to arrive before sundown. She travels in a two-horse carriage dressed in her old familiar blue pants, red shirt, blue vest and brown hat. In addition to her derringer, she carries Winchester's 1890 takedown-frame slide-action rifle in good mechanical condition.

Sharon stops for a smoke and a drink from her canteen. Unexpectedly, she hears the alarming hoof-beats of galloping horses. The men and horses turn out to be the U.S. Cavalry. Their red-over-white regimental and troop guidons provide a welcome sight for her. The pennant reveals the number six of the U.S. 6th Calvary. An officer and two cavalrymen ride up to Sharon. "I'm Captain Reed of Troop D, U.S. 6th Calvary, Miss. All is well?"

Captain Reed, a seasoned soldier, is leading a detachment of cavalry from Fort Union to Valtura. Reacting to Mexico's military buildup, the Army is on the move to the southern border.

"Yes, Captain, all is well. I'm Sharon Blaylock."

"Glad to meet you, Miss Blaylock. We haven't seen many women traveling alone out here. Where are you going?"

"I'm going to Loma Lake to visit my sister." Sharon feels she said too much. There is only one reason anyone goes there. She smiles to deflect any suspicion.

"All right, Miss, be careful."

"Thank you, Captain. I will."

Reed and the other two riders turn their mounts and rejoin the troop. They resume their journey on the road to Valtura, on their way south to protect New Mexico's border towns.

About a mile from the Territorial Insane Asylum, Sharon stops along Loma Lake, undresses and places her clothing on a branch. Suddenly, a fast-flying eagle shrieks and darts over her head. Undaunted, she enters the lake. After a few minutes in the water, she finds a spot to rest naked in the sun. The warmth feels good and more than a bit arousing.

The light reflecting off the surface of Loma Lake generates a flash of guilt for Sharon. Sibling rivalry is one thing, but the plot against Mady is loathsome, criminal and marginally traitorous. Sharon shakes off the guilt, as she stands naked in the wind reaching her hands to the sky. *I wonder what those troopers would think if they could see me now.* She laughs aloud.

She begins dressing in a revealing red dress with a corset and bustled skirt, and spots a coyote. Some native people see the animal as a troublemaker that lies and steals. This one coyly stares at her, and then disappears into the blowing tumbleweeds. The coyote instills another fleeting moment of guilt, but there is no time for sentiment now. When money and blind ambition speak, truth is silent.

After making the final mile to the asylum, Sharon checks her outfit. Now dressed for the task, she approaches the asylum and steps down from her carriage. Pleased with her appearance, she believes the lavish dress is more deadly than her Winchester. Mademoiselle Sharon, the irresistible seductress, is ready to play her favorite role of femme fatale.

After using the big knocker on the heavy front door, Sharon waits impatiently.

Finally, the door swings open.

In her best French, she says, *Bonjour, je suis Mademoiselle Sharon. Je suis ici pour voir le Docteur Trumble.* (Hello, I'm Mademoiselle Sharon, here to see Dr. Trumble.) Francine Fournier would have been appalled, but Ray Raton simply nods and escorts her to the doctor's office.

He knocks, enters and says, "Dr. Trumble, this is Mademoiselle Sharon can you see her now?"

"Oh yes, of course," the doctor answers, glancing up from his seated position behind the desk. The stunning woman brings him to his feet. "Mademoiselle Sharon. To what do I owe a visit from such a fine woman?"

Ray backs out of the office, turns and closes the door behind him. Dr. Trumble fusses with his tie and invites Sharon to have a seat.

Smiling and looking into his eyes, she says, "Why thank you Dr. Trumble." Then she slowly and seductively sits down, providing a full view of her low-cut dress.

Skilled at getting her way with men, she smiles demurely, brushes an imaginary hair away and waits a few seconds before speaking, "Dr. Trumble, I understand you have Mady Blaylock here."

"Yes, that's right. Miss Blaylock is here now. May I ask what your interest is?"

"Well you see, Doctor," she smiles again and says, "I am Mady's sister."

"Oh, I see." His mouth suddenly feels dry, so he reaches for the glass of water he keeps on his desk, but in his haste, he clumsily knocks it over.

"Damn," he mutters then clears his throat and folds his hands on top of the desk. "Her sister, you said?" He attempts to smile as he considers her motives and quietly says, "You are Mady's sister?"

"That's right," Sharon continues, pretending not to notice the small pool of water flowing toward the scattered papers on Dr. Trumble's desk. "And, as her sister, I know her well, as I am sure you can imagine."

Dr. Trumble nods and clears his throat several times.

Sharon ignores his nervousness and says, "I am *relieved* to know that Mady is finally in the right place to get the help she needs." She looks him dead in the eyes, leans forward and says, "Know what I mean, Doctor?"

Relieved, realizing that Sharon's purpose is not to challenge his operation, he takes a deep breath and says, "Yes, I do. And I want you to know that we will do our very best to help your sister."

"Oh, Doctor, you don't know *what* that means to me." Sharon sees an opening and goes on, "However, for her own good, I need to know she will stay for long-term treatment."

Playing the game, he says, "What do you mean? As prescribed by territorial law, a thorough evaluation determines length of stay."

"Dr. Trumble, I am sure an important person like you has some discretion. I would like you to use your judgment to make certain arrangements."

Faking righteous indignation, he says, "I have a professional responsibility and a reputation to uphold. You are asking too much of me."

This is just his opening position; he is anxious to know more about the negotiation and the ardent negotiator.

"We all know that your field is not an exact science, many unfortunate mistakes are made with the best intentions."

"What exactly are you suggesting, Mademoiselle Sharon?"

"As long as Mady Blaylock stays here, you'll see my appreciation generously expressed."

"And how do you define generously?"

Now we're getting somewhere, she thinks, and says, "I'll be in a position to control her saloon as long as she stays away from Valtura. Consider five percent of monthly profits."

"That's an interesting idea. Did you say fifteen percent?"

"I said ten percent."

"Oh, I see. Well, Miss Blaylock will absolutely need long-term treatment, but we will need a court order."

Sharon adjusts her body in a provocative manner. "I am sure that will not be a problem for you." Pinned against his seat with desire, he takes a deep breath and manages to squeak out, "Would you like to stay for dinner?"

"No, thank you."

Having obtained her goal, there is no need to tolerate his company any longer. Sharon is skilled in taking, but not so good at giving.

"It will be a lovely night," he presses.

"Dr. Trumble, it was a pleasure doing business with you."

"I'm suggesting nothing more than dinner, Mademoiselle Sharon."

Sharon stands, makes a half turn and proudly says, "*Bons chemins a vous.*"

Ironically, a greater, more insidious power controls the corrupt doctor and he had already intended to keep Mady Blaylock indefinitely. Unknown to Sharon, Dr. Trumble is extremely slow in releasing attractive women. This unnecessary meeting kept Sharon from her primary job in Valtura.

About a mile from the asylum, the self-satisfied Sharon stops at Loma Lake and undresses. Naked again, she floats her arms in the air and she screams, "*Quell plan malin!*"

There is a new moon or no moon at all, when the same lone coyote prowling along the lake suddenly interrupts her pleasurable pursuit. The coyote, who can recognize a jackal, gazes directly at the naked woman. Sharon, caught in the act, ignores the two staring eyes, dresses in her traveling outfit and continues to Valtura. The high desert can play tricks on people; perhaps there was no coyote at all.

37

Two Doves

Patriot shies away from the illuminated gaslight fixtures and loud music as Adobe approaches the saloon. Ladies, some of uncertain virtue and others with a measure of refinement, marvel at the changes brought about by Sharon Blaylock. Adobe would marvel, too, if he could get some straight answers. He ties the stallion's reins to the branch of an old cottonwood tree and enters the saloon.

Cigar smoke clouds the saloon and partially obscures the two women sitting with Carrie over a bottle of tequila. Wishing to downplay his interest in finding Mad Mady, he goes to the bar for a whiskey. The saloon has an unusually rough host of hard cases drinking and playing poker at the center tables.

Several patrons are new faces in town, including four of the five poker players. Three men and one fancy-dressed player named Skinner are sitting with Ellison around a poker table. After many losing hands, Ellison gets kings full of aces, a strong hand expressed with strong bets. Skinner calls and Ellison announces, "Full house, mister."

"It must be my lucky day, four jacks!"

Stunned by another loss and suspicious of Skinner's skill, Ellison looks up and recognizes an arriving man who distracts him. Skinner makes another fast move, but this time Ellison sees it and challenges. Before he knows it, the affronted cardsharp pulls a pistol and aims. Then a shot rings out from across the saloon. When the smoke clears, Skinner is dead. Adobe turns and runs toward Ellison.

"You okay, Kid?"

"Sure, Adobe, thanks to that man."

That man is Bill "Black Eye Pea" Blackstone. Ellison knows Blackstone from the past and their recent reconnection.

"Blackstone! *Que cojones.* Firing into a crowd and hitting your target. What are you doing in Valtura?" He knows the answer.

"I heard you were working at the Circle C and thought I would come to see an old friend."

"This here is Adobe Centori of the Circle C."

Blackstone sees the star on Adobe's shirt and asks, "Sheriff, hope I don't have any trouble with the law."

Shaking his head, he answers, "I saw the whole thing, he had it coming. Good enough for me." Adobe orders a bottle at the bar, points to the back of the saloon and offers, "Let's take that table on the far side of the room."

There has been enough center-stage activity. Adobe is ready to symbolically retreat into the wings—for a while. The men settle in with their drinks as Skinner settles into eternity.

Adobe quietly listens to Ellison and Blackstone talk about old times on the trail but his interest and eyes soon wander. Not content with the conversation or, in a strange way, with the men themselves, he spots Carrie sitting with two women. Then Blackstone turns to Adobe and says, "You seem to have your hands full these days, Sheriff."

It is a curious comment for a recent arrival. Adobe takes it at face value and says, "Things have been getting out of hand since the saloon owner left town—new faces and new problems."

"Yes and now a second shooting in as many days."

Adobe freezes. *How does Blackstone know about the shoot-out, having just arrived in town tonight? I guess the news was big enough that he read it in a newspaper,* he thinks.

Blackstone has a tendency to shoot off his mouth, a bad habit that gets him into more trouble than his six-shooter. Abruptly, Adobe slides his chair back for distance, flashes a concerned look, stands and announces, "It can be a dangerous world. I'll see you boys later."

Someone else dealt the hand; Adobe is determined to play it out. *People will reveal their corrupt purpose, if you pay attention,* he thinks as he moves toward Carrie's table.

He directs his general greeting to her, "Good evening, Ladies."

Mercy and Jane are quick to respond, but Carrie averts her furtive eyes. Adobe sits with the three women. Carrie is wearing a white cotton dress with a black tie around the waist and black boots. The doves, known to provide many visual pleasures, are wearing low-cut, suggestive dresses.

"Good evening to you too, Sheriff," she smiles, "I assume you came with more questions, but I already told you everything."

"Actually, I came over to stretch my legs, but since you brought it up."

"I'm trying to do the right thing," Carrie says, deflecting the statement.

"Most people know what's right but don't always act accordingly. So you never saw the three men before the day of the shoot-out." His voice reveals increasing vexation.

"I told you no. Never," she maintains.

"You were sure friendly to those you just met."

"I'm friendly to you too, Sheriff."

"Okay, Carrie, point taken."

Mercy and Jane start to laugh nervously, much to the discomfort of Carrie, who says, "Why don't you two go back upstairs? We'll be busy soon."

The women have been pushed to be more aggressive, which is stressful for Mercy, who protests, "There's still plenty of tequila in that bottle, Miss Carrie."

Carrie yells, "I said time for you doves to fly upstairs."

Mercy exclaims, "Mady never treated us this way. Things sure are different now that she's in the lockup." Mercy's strained voice yields somewhat indistinct words but the message rings loud and clear.

"Damn you, Mercy, shut up," Carrie screams.

"Why should I?"

Carrie slaps Mercy and says, "That's why."

Then Carrie smacks Jane too, just for good measure.

Mercy runs off sobbing. Jane stands to go with her and says, "People think a dove's life is easy, but doves know otherwise. Maybe you should work upstairs."

Although Jane has a penchant for drama, this time she is genuinely upset. Of course, the outburst is not lost on Adobe. Furious inside, he forces a neutral outward appearance and says, "What was that 'lockup' comment all about?"

"Just the babbling of a dumb drunken dove," Carrie says sharply.

"Sounded like she knew what she was talking about and it caused you to snap."

"Sheriff, I hope your inquisitive nature will not strain our acquaintance."

"Of course not. I'm sure Mady will return when she can," he says cynically.

Adobe stands up, stares down with a cold look and says, "*Adios*, Carrie."

"Good night, Sheriff."

He walks toward the front door and sees Ellison and Blackstone still in conversation in the back of the saloon. As he nears their table on the far side of the room, they stop talking.

Instinctively, Adobe believes Carrie is attending to Sharon's business and will quit Valtura when finished. He knows Sharon checked into the Union Hotel and has yet to make a public appearance in the saloon. The doves are providing a reason to close down the place. However, he will play the pawn and consider the queen's next move. Instead of walking directly across the plaza to his office, he turns right on National Street, left on First Avenue and enters the newspaper office.

An hour later, Johan arrives at the saloon with an invitation. He approaches the blonde woman in a white dress.

"Miss Carrie Carlson?"

"Yes?" she answers with reluctance.

"I am Johan Morgenstern, publisher and editor-in-chief of the Valtura Journal."

"Nice to meet you, Mr. Morgenstern."

"My pleasure, I am sure."

"Would you like a drink?"

"No thank you. This is a professional call, not social."

Carrie, nonplussed, says, "Professional?"

"Yes, I am here about an interview to appear in the Valtura Journal," he discloses.

"Are you serious? Why?"

"Miss Carrie, there is much interest in you, and people around the plaza are amazed by the changes you've made to Mad Mady's Saloon."

"I'm not sure. I don't know what interest your readers would have in me."

"If you don't mind me saying, you are an intriguing woman who is definitely newsworthy. So, may I have a little of your time?"

"Perhaps a little time," Carrie's voice changes.

"Excellent."

Flattered, she offers him a seat and says, "What can I tell you?"

"Thank you for agreeing, but it's much too noisy here. Please come to the newspaper office. The paper is diagonally across the plaza, right on First Avenue. My daughter Klara will make a pot of tea."

Carrie considers the invitation, the risk of leaving the bar and says, "Okay, let me do a few things and I'll be there in an hour."

"That's fine. See you at the newspaper office."

She smiles and walks behind the bar. He tips his hat and walks out.

Instead of going back to the newspaper office, Johan goes directly to the sheriff's office. Adobe is standing at his desk looking impatiently at his watch when Johan opens the door and blurts out, "It's done. Carrie will be in my office within the hour. Keep a clear eye on the plaza."

"Thanks, good job."

"Anytime, but why not confront Mady's sister at the hotel?"

"I'm not ready to put her in check. Besides, with Carrie at the newspaper office, I'll be more successful with Mercy."

"Sheriff, forgive me for saying so, but not everyone in town misses Mady. You should visit us more often."

"I take your meaning. If Klara is interested, she conceals it well."

"People think you and Mady are involved and Klara does not wish to fuel the gossip on the plaza."

"I'm a single man who lives alone."

"Okay, Sheriff. Watch out for Carrie crossing the plaza, I'll keep her busy for at least an hour."

"Thanks again."

"Good luck, Adobe."

It is the first time Johan has called him Adobe. The sheriff does not notice or at least does not mind. He sits back with his boots on the desk and fires up a cigar.

Johan's invitation was awkward. Klara is a provocative woman, but Adobe's cynicism filters his reaction. She had her chance at the Sandia Peak. *This cigar is not as good as the Governor's Cuban but good enough. Perhaps Klara is not as good as a Cuban woman, but good enough.* He smokes and waits.

Carrie finally emerges from the bar and briskly walks the short distance to the newspaper office.

Then the telephone rings and Adobe leaps to his feet.

"Centori."

"Johan here. She is on her way."

"Yes, I see that."

Adobe jams the cigar into a ceramic ashtray, grabs his hat and flies out the door. He does not walk directly across the plaza; he takes the long way back via Second Avenue out of view from the newspaper office.

Once Adobe is back inside the bar, he looks around, notices that Ellison and Blackstone are gone, moves to the bar, orders a bottle of Jameson and asks for Mercy.

The new bartender says, "Mercy is upstairs and free at the moment."

He walks past Ben the piano player, a holdover from Mad Mady's Saloon, and toward the stairs.

"Sheriff, I've never known you to go upstairs," says the piano player.

"Things change, Ben."

"I guess so, Sheriff," Ben says, taking a measure of satisfaction that the great stoic Adobe Centori is human after all.

Adobe climbs the flight of ill-lit stairs and he hears footsteps behind him. He turns to see Jane, who offers an immense smile showing even teeth.

"Is that you, Sheriff?" Jane inquires, knowing it is clearly Adobe in his big tan hat. He shrugs, as if he could not care less. Jane tousles her hair and pouts about his lack of interest. He walks down a dark hallway to the sounds of muttered conversations until he sees Mercy through an open door. She is smoothing black stockings up her fine-looking legs.

"Sheriff, this is a surprise!"

Mercy is not beautiful, but is pretty. Adobe likes her image, but stays focused on his goal.

"Hello, Mercy."

"What took you so long? I was beginning to think you didn't like us very much."

"I like you fine, Mercy. I brought a bottle of Jameson."

"Oh, let me pour us some drinks."

Mercy closes the heavy shades, sits back on the ornate bed and attempts to ensure his business by assuming a seductive position. She starts to speak softly from within a cozy haze, "Why don't you come closer?"

Sitting nearby, Adobe brings the relationship back to practical matters by saying, "Wait, I would like to know you better."

She shifts, seeking a perfect position and says, "Okay, Sheriff, so you're the talking kind."

He laughs in agreement and replies, "Tell me, where are you from?"

"What does it matter?"

Adobe's eyes repeated his question.

"I came to Valtura from Denver. Have you ever been there, Sheriff?"

"One time. I understand Mady has been there several times. Perhaps she is there now." Mercy looks a little vexed as he refills her glass. Having talked enough, she reaches out her arms to implore an embrace. He smiles away the invitation.

"Sheriff, I like Valtura. There seems to be a level of acceptance here. In Denver, women walked on the other side of the street to avoid me, and men who knew my name at night didn't know me at all in the day."

She drops the top of her dress, revealing her breasts and, surprisingly, her shyness.

"Mercy, I appreciate what you offer, but I would be more relaxed if I knew about Mady's situation."

She jumps up and screams, "So you're here about Mad Mady Blaylock!"

Remarkably, her rage ends quickly and, anxious to preserve the mood, she whispers, "Wouldn't you like to know my passion?"

Adobe places his hands around her trim waist. Mercy gasps with excitement as he pulls back and says, "Let's leave that to the imagination for now."

"Please touch me."

Moving his hands up the small of her back, he says, "I'm worried about Mady, and, as her friend, you should be concerned too."

Ignoring the criticism, she says, "Please touch me again."

Adobe complies, but not with a gentle caress; he grabs her shoulders and demands, "Where is she? Tell me right now! What was that 'lock-up' comment?"

Shocked by the sudden change in his demeanor, Mercy blurts out, "She was committed to the Territorial Insane Asylum."

"Territorial Insane Asylum! What the hell is going on?" he demands. "Who committed her and why?"

Mercy gives a pallid smile and says, "I don't know! You better take it up with people who know such matters."

He reassuringly touches her face.

She pulls back, glaring, and yells, "You were not honest with me."

"Mady is in trouble," he says softly. "I don't need to be honest."

When Carrie returns to the bar, she learns that Adobe saw Mercy and wonders what he managed to get from her. She fears it was everything.

Several hours later, the naked body of Mercy is on the bed, sprawled face down. She is dead, murdered, a single gunshot to the back of her head. Blackstone will be busy again tonight.

38

ACT OF SANITY

The Mad Mady affair is an uphill fight, and Adobe needs to know which hill. Mady believed she was right about Sharon; now there is proof. At the Circle C, the fireplace flames reflect his burning motivation to act, as recent events have increased his sense of urgency. He sits, watching the crackling fire shoot sparks against the inner walls of the kiva.

Mercy's distressing words about the Territorial Insane Asylum ring in his ears and play hard on his mind. Alone and languishing, Mady needs help before physical captivity becomes psychological captivity. Mady is no damsel, but she *is* in distress. Adobe is not a plumed knight in armor, but he *is* an armed warrior. She is not a naïve, sheltered woman without survival instincts, but this situation requires outside intervention. Without hesitation, he prepares to be her champion.

The next morning at sunrise, he mounts Patriot and rides from the Circle C to the madhouse. By nightfall, Adobe has put twenty miles behind him. Alone in the high desert, he stops and stares at the vastness and the billions of stars arrayed in the universe. To the

Navajo, coyotes reshuffled the stars and destroyed all but one moon from the evening sky. The coyote taught man to hunt; Adobe hunts Mady's tormentors.

Horse and rider settle down for the night. The fire warms his heart; the gentle wind suggests openness to new wonders under the above moonlight. Patriot, still and silent, allows Adobe a sense of being alone and adrift in his own thoughts. *A man walks a razor's edge between aloneness and loneliness. I celebrate my time alone but there are surges of loneliness.*

Suddenly a bright and spectacular flash travels across the sky and startles him. He leaps up and walks toward Patriot. The stallion is no longer still, reacting to the gaseous comet.

The comet, a collection of ice, dust and small rocky particles, appears to be a message in the night sky. Mesmerized by the comet, he thinks of sharing the heavenly experience, to hold her hand and stare at the cosmos. Although alone, he feels her body. It is only a dream, for a dream woman.

Reacting to the comet, coyote howls reach a high pitch. The coyote taught man to use medicinal plants, but there is no cure for his heartache. He throws more brush on the fire and wonders if the sky magic was visible in Cuba.

In many ways, Mady reminds him of Gabriella. Both women are strong, smart and attractive. He often wonders about Gabriella, but not now—no time to brood. Besides, it takes less energy to be happy than to be unhappy.

The next day, still following the same well-traveled trail that brought Mady to the asylum, Adobe sees the big building on the horizon. As he stops to consider his opening gambit, he hears the unmistakable sound of a rattlesnake, coiled in the nearby small rocks. Patriot reacts by champing at the bit in his jaws and stomping the ground. Adobe fires the Navy Colt, sparking the rocks and shattering the cactus plants, missing the rattler. Rather than continue the battle, he presses his knees into Patriot's flanks and gallops away. He pulls up quickly; the stallion still has the heart, but not the stamina.

Adobe arrives and stops short of the front door to view the large imposing building. He dismounts, ties Patriot and knocks on the door.

Nurse Denton opens the door slightly, while Ray runs to inform Dr. Trumble.

"I'm Sheriff Centori of Corona County. Open up."

"You're here about Mady Blaylock?"

"How do you know that, Nurse?"

She ignores his inquiry and says, "I realize you may think this is a terrible misunderstanding, but I assure you, all things are in proper order."

Adobe, who expresses himself with methodical self-confidence, takes the full measure of her demeanor and says, "I want to talk to the man in charge."

"Yes, of course. You mean Dr. Trumble. Follow me."

After a short walk down a dark corridor, Nurse Denton turns and says, "Please wait here."

Adobe stands in a large reception area that reminds him of the territorial prison in Santa Fe County. *The commitment papers might reveal who is behind this business besides Sharon. It may not resolve the issue, but it would be a good start,* he thinks.

Nurse Denton interrupts a private meeting with *Señorita Valdez,* the patient attendant, and says, "Dr. Trumble, Sheriff Centori of Corona County is here about Mad Mady."

"Mad Mady!" he says, jumping up.

"Yes."

Nurse Denton instructs *Señorita Valdez, "Rapidamente, busque Ray! Digale de ir a la recepcion y que espere al Sheriff Centori!" (Quickly find Ray. Tell him to go to the reception area to wait with Sheriff Centori.)*

"*Si, Enfermera.*"

Returning her attention to Dr. Trumble, she says, "Don't worry, we can handle him."

"Perhaps, but why take a chance? Let's hide these files," he says, while running around the office gathering records and other incriminating evidence.

"I told you he's here about Mad Mady only, not any of the corruption rumors."

"You mean not yet. We must cover our tracks before he understands how we manage. Write this down."

Dr. Trumble does not understand the extent of the conspiracy behind Mady's commitment and unjust imprisonment. Rather, he is content to know of nothing more than his compensation.

"Go ahead."

Dr. Trumble sits down and dictates a note to Nurse Denton:

> Medical Summary/Patient Elizabeth Mady Blaylock
>
> After an initial diagnostic interview, I find Miss Blaylock presents with symptoms of mental and emotional distress. Miss Blaylock has a clinically significant behavioral disorder that impairs her ability to function in society, both personally and professionally. Some of Miss Blaylock's disruptive disorders are manifest as significant psychotic symptoms of hallucinations, delusions and bizarre behaviors. It is my medical opinion that she has a treatable behavior manifestation of a condition classified as a mental case in the Territory Medical Manual.
>
> Dr. Thornton N. Trumble
>
> Medical Director, Territorial Insane Asylum

While in the reception room, an attendant escorts a distraught woman who is emaciated, barefoot and clad in tattered clothing. Suddenly, she breaks way, collides with Adobe and shrieks incoherently.

"Shut up," yells the attendant, at the same time Nurse Denton hands Adobe the note.

Adobe reads the note but remains unconvinced and remains determined to see Mady. Inappropriate behavior could hurt his reputation as an ethical professional, but there are bigger issues to consider. Ray is in his way. Adobe flashes his Navy Colt and pushes his way into Dr. Trumble's office.

"Thanks for the note, Doctor, but I'm afraid it isn't enough."

"Sheriff, please sit down. I'm sure we can work this out as two professionals."

"I would like to see the commitment papers," Adobe asserts.

Ignoring his request, the doctor replies, "Miss Blaylock's behavior and mental instability are not extreme."

"That's fine, but I still want to see the commitment papers," he orders.

Dr. Trumble hands him a file and continues to talk. "We have eliminated serious dementia that would affect her intellectual capacity."

Adobe examines the file, barely listening to Dr.Trumble.

"Rather, we believe Miss Blaylock is suffering from delusions of persecution where blameless remarks appear critical. In many cases, the patient tries to hide their delusions. Are you with me so far, Sheriff?"

Adobe slams down the sloppy file with its sketchy information and says, "According to this poorly prepared file, Mady was escorted here by a law official?"

Dr. Trumble stares in silence.

After a few seconds, he demands, "I want to see Mady, now!"

"Sheriff, please, the file may be lacking, but my evaluation is not. Miss Blaylock envisions that her sister is trying to hurt her in some way and imagines a plot."

"No more empty words. Where is she?"

Afraid to deal with Adobe's demand, he evades, "She may confide in others about a perceived plot and can have outbursts at times with a hot temper. Delusions of persecution are a form of paranoia. But I am sure the effects of the problem are not permanent."

"Sometimes even paranoids have enemies. Now take me to Mady."

Running out of fast talk, Dr. Trumble says, "Yes, of course."

Ray shows Adobe the way to Mady's room. The two men walk in silence until Adobe, says, "How do you feel about this place?"

"Sheriff, I just work here, I don't *feel* here."

After a few more steps and turns, Ray announces, "Here's her room."

Ray fumbles with the key, Adobe enters and Mady jumps up and yells, "Where the hell have you been? I hate this place!"

"Calm down. I came as soon as I found out where you were. How did this happen? Who brought you here?"

"You're not going to like it, but I was taken here at gunpoint by Ellison."

"Ellison!" Sickened by the betrayal, Adobe wonders how he could have misjudged Ellison.

"Is he still working at the Circle C?"

"He won't be much longer, at the least. Why did he do it?"

"He wouldn't say."

Almost from the beginning, Adobe had concerns about Sharon, but was reluctant to tell Mady. Now, it seems like Ellison could know Sharon.

"I'm afraid you are right about your sister. She's in Valtura staying at the Union Hotel."

"I told you. My instincts were right."

"There's more. Sharon and a woman called Carrie have taken over your saloon."

"What? How can they do that?"

"You're considered mentally incapacitated, so Sharon as next of kin can control your assets."

"I knew it! She's behind this commitment and she'll stop at nothing for revenge. This maddens me beyond reason. I'd like to kill Sharon," she shouted in an outburst of rage.

"Mady, wait, there's more at stake than revenge and your saloon—Berta is gone."

"What do you mean?"

"Carrie claims she went to Nevada," Adobe says while looking down.

"I don't think Sharon would be involved with…."

"Well, a man with some kind of connection to Sharon was killed in Santa Fe."

"Killed?"

"Yes, shot dead."

"But, Adobe, what was his connection to Sharon?"

"He didn't live long enough to tell."

"Oh my God! What is Sharon involved with?"

"All I know is that he seemed to know Sharon."

"What? You knew the man?"

"We met briefly while I was in Santa Fe. Johnny Romano is working on the case."

"I must see Sharon; she could be in real trouble and need my help."

Surprised to hear any concern, he says, "Why would you help her now?"

"Because she's my sister, now let's go."

"Hold on, I haven't secured your release."

First, there is tightness in her mouth and then she cries out, "Why not?"

"Calm down Mady. It's not that simple. The law is on their side, for now."

"What are you talking about?" she says, with growing anger in her tone.

"Your ordeal is part of a bigger problem in the psychiatric system that lacks legal protections against abuses."

"What? Ellison forced me here at gunpoint!"

"That is the least of it now. There is a legal vacuum with shaky standards for involuntary commitment."

"I don't care about all that—I must get back to Valtura now!"

"Mady, I can't just break you out of here, not yet. I never learned to turn my back on a friend and won't start now."

"I sure hope not," she frowns and adds, "I know I can count on you."

"Ellison *has* been an undersheriff. We need to show a judge he was *not* at the time of your commitment. In the meantime, we must keep your commitment a secret in Valtura. Right now, your disappearance is a mystery. If the people find out, they may always view you as an ex-mental patient."

"Okay, but how long do I have stay here?"

"Sharon carries a derringer, Mady."

"I am not surprised."

"What's good for one sister is good for another."

With that, he places a bag containing a single-shot pistol and an envelope under her pillow. "You will need more than courage to get out of here. Use this bag only as a *last resort.* Is that perfectly plain, Mady?"

"Yes, I understand. Use the gun only in the event of any serious surprises."

"That's right. After all that has happened, be prepared."

"I will be, but don't expect me to sit here for long."

"I'm not sure about the whole story. One thing is for sure, there is a pattern of deception and confusion from known and unknown forces."

"Unknown. That's not giving me confidence."

"Look Mady, I am resolute. I will get answers."

"Okay. There is something else, something odd, Adobe. There are rumors of women being held here for killing their husbands."

"That's not odd, considering where we are."

"Some say they were married to statehood delegates," Mady adds.

Adobe stares and rubs his two-day-old beard, "Statehood delegates," he repeats.

He stands to leave but Mady pulls him back. "This is a horrible place."

"I know, Mady, I know."

"What do I do now?"

"Endure."

While mounting Patriot, Adobe feels something in his back pocket. He reaches in and discovers a note placed in his pocket by the crazed woman in the reception room. It reads, "*Help us.*" An insane woman committed an act of sanity.

39

Kentucky Woman

Mad Mady attempts to take a meal in a large, cold dining room, sitting alone brooding over her dreadful situation. She glances up angrily when by chance someone brushes against her back. A short woman of some bulk with disheveled brown hair and a stained institutional gown approaches Mady with a tray in her hands, waiting for an invitation. After a moment of tension, Mady asks with fatigue, "Okay, do you want to sit down?"

"Yes, thank you. You're new here, right?"

"That's right, and I'm not planning to stay long."

"That's what I said. You need to accept your situation. It will make things easier."

"Easier for whom?" Mady snaps. "Who are you anyway?"

"Lilly Sheldon, but the guards call me Kentucky Woman."

"I'm Mady Blaylock from Valtura in Corona County."

"Mad Mady! News of your disruptive arrival has spread throughout the asylum! Why are you called that?"

"Tell me why they call you Kentucky Woman."

"Okay, my family had a hardscrabble farm in Haleyville, Kentucky, that produced a lot of children and a lot of bad luck."

Mady, not amused, asks, "So what are you doing here?"

"I worked at the Haleyville mill until I scraped together enough money to get out of Kentucky."

"I mean what are you doing *here*, in this madhouse?"

"They say I went mad and killed my husband." Her voice sounds strained.

"I'm sure he had it coming," Mady cracks.

Kentucky Woman looks around and says, "But I didn't do it. I didn't kill my husband."

Mady scans the dinner hall, hoping to find someone to get rid of her.

"One day," she continues, "I came home and found him dead with my knife deep in his neck. But I didn't kill him, Mad Mady. I couldn't have done it; I was back in Kentucky for my mother's funeral."

"Then why are you here?" Mady demands.

"It's easier for the authorities to call me insane and commit me to this asylum than to take me to trial with little or no evidence."

Mady's expression softens; she touches the woman's hand and draws closer. Then Ray Raton comes over to listen. Kentucky Woman's smile satisfies him.

"You see, we are watched closely. Ray can be friendly at times with the right persuasion. He said that some of us could be released in January."

"Why January?"

"How should I know?"

"I'll be long gone anyway," she says carefully. "So why did you settle in New Mexico?"

"I came here for the climate five years ago and met my husband, Lane Sheldon."

"That name sounds familiar."

"He was a prominent citizen and leader of the Bernalillo County statehood delegates."

Bernalillo County borders Corona County to the south, Mady thinks.

"Lane was a good leader. His positions held considerable appeal for many delegates and he was uncompromising on key statehood issues. So, Mad Mady did you kill your husband too?"

"No! The reason I'm here is an unjust commitment on *non compos mentis."*

Kentucky Woman knowingly says, "You see that woman over there?"

Mady sees a woman with a face etched with exhaustion and nods her acknowledgement.

"Her name is Rebecca. She killed, or they say she killed, her husband. Her husband was unloading supplies and retrieved a barrel from under a wagon, where he encountered an angry rattlesnake that killed him."

"So why was Rebecca blamed?"

"She grew up on a ranch in El Paso and studied herpetology. Since she's a rattlesnake expert, they blamed her. The guards call her Rattlesnake Rebecca. Traumatized by her husband's death and being locked in a mental hospital, she doesn't speak. It's some kind of phobia. If you aren't crazy when you come here, this place will make you that way."

Mady is still not amused, so Kentucky Woman adds, "Look, they are trying to tear down your mind and weaken your body to the point where you go crazy. You will see after you spend enough days locked in your room."

"Fine, fine," she replies unruffled. "Who is her husband?"

"He *was* George Taylor of Colfax County."

Another delegate. The rumors are true, Mady thinks.

"There's more, Mad Mady. Do you see that mysterious woman sitting in the corner with that fat nurse?"

"Yes."

"She's Maria Otero. She had an almost overnight mental collapse. Soon after getting here, she tried to kill herself. They used to give her chloride hydrate and morphine to help her insomnia, really more to help the guards. Instead of taking the drugs, she held on to them for a big final dose. It made her sick, not dead. They repeatedly rope her to her bed and now she speaks haltingly."

"Rope her to the bed?"

"Yes. She was married to Juan Otero of Grant County. He *is* dead, killed by Maria, they say. Nurse Darcie mocks her by asking if Juan had any last words before dying. Then before Maria can answer, Darcie quickly yells, "Put down that gun, Maria."

Again, Mady is not amused.

Mady pauses, rubs her eyes and says, "Your husband, Taylor and probably Otero too, were statehood delegates. I heard rumors about women held for killing their delegate husbands. You get the feeling someone does not like statehood delegates?"

Kentucky Woman looks tentative. "It's true about those women, but I don't know anything about statehood, except Kentucky was the first state west of the Appalachians to join the Union."

Mady stares coldly.

"All right, if these incidents are connected, then you might be right."

"Did your husband have any enemies, Lilly?"

"None that I know about."

Thinking aloud, Mady says, "Adobe has no enemies that I know about, but he could be in danger."

"Adobe?"

"Yes, Sheriff Adobe Centori of Corona County."

"He's your husband?"

"No. People in Valtura assume we're together. We're not. But Adobe *is* a delegate and he's a strong advocate for statehood."

"Perhaps someone is devising a way to kill him."

"Kill him?" Mady shrieks.

"Don't worry, Mad Mady. At least you can't be blamed."

Still not amused, she replies, "No matter, I told Adobe about the rumors, but now he must be warned. I need to get word to him."

"What are you going to do Mad Mady, shoot your way out?"

"If I must."

"Ha-ha. Good luck. The rules allow one censored letter a week."

Suddenly, Rattlesnake Rebecca, the woman who no longer speaks, stands up and shouts, "This is not my hell, not my sins! You will all pay for this outrage!"

Ray calls out, "Nurse! Nurse! Rattlesnake Rebecca is out of control!"

Nurse Denton runs down the hall, enters the dining room and admonishes Rebecca, "You crazy wretch, don't you know you're better off here with our professional staff? We're very sensitive to patient needs. Now shut the hell up."

"I *did not* kill my husband," she pleads.

Ray restrains and drags a kicking and screaming Rebecca to her room with Nurse Denton following behind. Ray throws her inside and slams the door.

Mady, shaken by the scene, turns to Kentucky Woman and declares, "That's it; I must get out of here."

"Are you serious?"

"Yes. Something strange is going on and Adobe needs to be warned."

Kentucky Woman looks around then faces Mady and whispers, "Ray has been known to provide extra privileges to willing women, if you understand my meaning."

"Yes, I understand," Mady reluctantly says.

She hesitates and stares across the table. The screams and shrieks from distant areas of the asylum replace tension with fear. Mady exclaims, "This madhouse nightmare chills me to the bone."

"Calm down or this place will make you crazy. I told you, they are supposed to make insane people sane, but can they make sane people mad," Lilly says. "See that old hag in the corner? Psychological counseling determined that she suffers from paranoia and low self-esteem and thinks that nobody important is out to get her."

Reacting to Mady's straight face, Kentucky Woman says, "You need a little humor to survive here."

The stress in Mady's face is palpable as she considers the situation. She thinks, *Maybe this place has made me crazy, but there could be a plot to kill Adobe. I must escape to warn him. I can't stand another moment here anyway.*

Mady makes a difficult, distasteful decision. With reluctance, she summons Ray. After a brief discussion, she accepts his terms and agrees to a laundry room *get-together* at midnight. In exchange, her room will be unlocked.

After lights out, as instructed, Mady leaves her small space and moves slowly down the gloomy hallway. She stops for a second at a common area adjacent to two passageways, one leading to the laundry. Taking the hall on the left, she feels her way down a long corridor and freezes. Mady had gone the wrong way and is horrified to stumble on the maximize security cages for the severely insane.

Not a sound or groan emanated from the cages. A muted silence, but then from the dark reaches of one cage comes a high-pitched whistle from a tormented person. It is disturbing. She retreats from the intense psychiatric ward before disturbing any more of the patients.

At the end of the correct hall, Mady sees clothing storage bins blocking the opening. Examining the obstacle, she struggles to move beyond the containers. Once through, she enters a supply room off the main laundry area. The room is dark and dank. Nervously waiting for Ray, she suddenly has second thoughts and turns to run. Someone strikes her head from behind.

When Mady regains consciousness, she sees the evil, battleaxe nurse standing over her and speaking slowly. "Careful what you say to strange women in insane asylums, Miss Blaylock," Nurse Denton snarls. She leads a staggering Mady to a subterranean infirmary room and says, "You're no better than your little doves. Now you will definitely need long-term treatment."

The slam of the door rattles Mady's already rattled brain.

The next morning, Mady finds herself in the infirmary with no idea of how much time has passed since she succumbed to the attack. She drifts to consciousness with a great headache, a big cranium bandage and much disorientation.

It is a disaster for Mady, but despite a foggy head, certain things are plain. The corruption extends beyond those who committed her to the asylum. Dr. Trumble, Nurse Denton, Ray Raton and even Kentucky Woman are part of some bizarre scheme. Through her confusion, she feels enough rage for many but thinks Nurse Denton requires special revenge.

My head hurts so much. Damn Kentucky Woman, she betrayed me. Where is Adobe? I can take care of myself. What is happening to my saloon? Is Berta okay? Mady's mind races.

An infirmary attendant detects Mady's restlessness and tightens her restraints. She groans, retreats to stillness and continues her befuddled thoughts. *Have they stopped wondering about me? Use the gun only as a last resort. Having my brains bashed qualifies. I can no longer wait; they may find the gun. Recover from the attack, get out of the infirmary, back to the room and secure the gun,* she thinks while drifting from disorientation to mystification.

Mady was overpowered, but physical strength will not be enough to hold her. She has a better strategy and good perceptive intelligence. She will need it to escape the gloomy grip of the Territorial Insane Asylum.

40

Lady Blaylock

Sharon Blaylock appears in front of a mirror in her new upstairs office modeled after Madame Francine Fournier's Salon in Santa Fe. What's more, her redesigned adjoining bedroom suite is an enormous improvement over the Union Hotel, and especially over Mady's gauche taste. Smoking a Marlboro Red Tip, she looks down over the railing to survey the new French bar created in her image.

Despite their loyalty to Mady, the people are curious about the new fabulous Chez Beau Sharon and eager for Mademoiselle Sharon to make her first public appearance. It is another night with a good crowd—and a large enough audience for Sharon's debut. The women and games of chance are busy and the whiskey flows. One heavy drinker, James Clarke, has thought about approaching Mademoiselle Sharon since her arrival. Halfway through a bottle of whiskey, he sees the object of his obsession standing over the upstairs railing. He bounds up the steps and crowds Sharon.

"Good evening, Miss Blaylock. This is what I call a saloon," says the inebriated hotel manager. "We sure miss you at the Union Hotel."

Sharon forces a sarcastic smile and steps back, but he presses anyway.

"I hope you like Valtura. You will like it much better if you have drinks with me."

"Fuck off."

Sharon pushes past him and slowly descends. No one, least of all this stunned fool, will stop her grand entrance. She is wearing a black dress, a one-piece corset with ruffled sleeves and a bustled skirt. Stepping down, she absorbs the attention and admires the efforts taken to establish Chez Beau Sharon.

All the heads turn to watch Mademoiselle Sharon as she takes her time coming down the steps, allowing her magnificence to shine on her subjects. Many certainly approve of her image, unaware of her notorious purposes.

Carrie, though pensive and looking somewhat glum, quickly reclaims her vivacity when Sharon appears. She meets her at the bottom of the stairs and points to Adobe at the bar. Sharon's eyes are riveted on him, when Carrie asks, "What can I do for you?"

"Make sure my office suite is clean and send up a bottle of whiskey with two crystal glasses."

"Right away," she smiles, conveying her awareness of the situation.

Sharon slowly moves toward the bar. Although they have never met, Adobe knows, as does everyone else, that the woman with the seductive walk is Santa Fe Sharon, now known as Mademoiselle Sharon.

"Hello Sheriff," she says with a wicked smile while slowly withdrawing her cigarette from her lips. "Allow me to introduce myself, I'm Mademoiselle Sharon."

"Santa Fe Sharon," Adobe says without feeling.

She cringes, immediately dislikes Mady's friend and roars, "Santa Fe Sharon ain't *no* more, call me Mademoiselle Sharon."

Adobe removes his hat, nods and admires her body. She is indeed a Gibson Girl image of feminine beauty. At the sight of her slender body and ample bosom, he has difficulty maintaining focus. Containing his visual interest, he says, "Pleasure to finally meet you. Your sister has said much about you."

"Is that right?"

"Yes. I've known Mady since I arrived in Valtura."

"I understand that you have a close friendship with my sister."

"Close enough to care about her well-being," he warns.

Deflecting the comment, she steps aside to show her S-curve torso.

"Miss Sharon, you seem to have recovered quickly from your automobile accident."

"I don't like to waste time," she quips while staring at his gun belt.

"How did it happen?"

"It happened at night. The autoists in Santa Fe, by ordinance, must have lighted lamps after dark. The auto that hit me did not have lighted lamps. I never saw it coming."

"I see."

Her conversation and eye contact indicate an abundance of self-confidence in the art of seduction. Returning the stare, Adobe holds her gaze a few seconds longer than she expected.

Sharon enjoys flirting and the related feelings of arousal. Pursuing a man is a matter of instinct and exhilaration to her. Adobe's defenses are up, but so is his interest in Sharon's body. Loyalty to Mady places his priorities in order, at least for the moment.

"I must admit," he says, "you've certainty brought this place into the twentieth century. It is a complete transformation. But there is one change that's troubling."

She continues offering gestures designed to control. Trusting her senses, she asks, "What change is that, Sheriff?"

"The change in management."

"We have moved beyond the less than sophisticated management that conflicted with my persona," she says curtly.

"The people liked Mady and her place just fine."

"Well, some felt her *upstairs* business was a danger to the fabric of Valtura society."

"That's not what I mean. Besides *upstairs* is still going on—busier than ever."

"Of course, but we do it with much more class." Sharon smiles, lights another cigarette and demurely says, "People have a hard time with change. Some fear the unknown. What do you fear, Sheriff?"

"I fear for Mady's safety, a sentiment that you probably do not share."

"Perhaps I can soften your hard opinion of me."

Her not-so-subtle approach has worked before. She looks for signs of surrender.

"Sharon, I have questions and I'd appreciate answers, straight answers."

"Sheriff, stop acting as if you are entitled to know my business."

"I am entitled as an agent of the law."

"Law? What are you accusing me of doing?"

"Nothing yet," he warns.

"Look, Sheriff, you must excuse me. I have a fine establishment to run. This is my debut appearance and many wish to meet me. If you would like, please join me in my suite for a drink later tonight. I could be amenable to an inquisition then."

Before he can answer, a tall female singer that Sharon invited from Santa Fe attracts the attention of the crowd. All eyes turn as the singer readies herself to perform. Full-length white gloves complement her elaborately draped black gown that has a red rose sewn to the right side, near her heart. Her raven hair is pinned into a knot at the nape of her neck to create a chignon, worn for special occasions.

She says a few words of greeting with a slight British accent, smiles at the audience and then watches the accompanist play a two bar introduction. The soprano takes a deep breath. Ben begins to play softly in a slow tempo. The song, "Beautiful Dreamer," by Stephen Foster, is written in 3/4 waltz time and offered in the key of F major. Her voice is sweet and high with a lilting vibrato.

Beautiful dreamer, wake unto me,
Starlight and dewdrops are waiting for thee...

Before she reaches the next lines, the sensual Santa Fe songbird has everyone in the room fixed on her image and voice. Even the people outside on the plaza stop and listen to the mighty soprano's rendition. All within the sound of her magical voice are entranced by the captivating and uplifting music.

Sounds of the rude world, heard in the day,
Lull'd by the moonlight have all pass'd away!

She is superb, subtle and spectacular all at once. The exciting woman sings with perfect precision and passion; more than vocalizing musical notes, she seems to feel the loving words.

Beautiful dreamer, wake unto me.

Her affectionate song transcends the music and is profoundly personal for Adobe, who dreams Gabriella will someday wake unto him. Sharon looks at him and says, "There are beautiful dreams ready to become reality. As I said, join me for a drink later tonight."

The song and Sharon's body weaken his resolve, but he says, "Thanks, I'm not sure. Things start early at the Circle C."

Sharon hands him a key to the rear entrance and says, "In case you change your mind. *Bone sore.*"

Adobe orders another whiskey and thinks about the opportunity. His allegiance to Mady and her situation weigh heavy on his mind. *I obtained information from Mercy, but Sharon is no fool. Still, I may need her for Mady's freedom and Berta needs help somewhere. Sharon is a greater challenge, for a greater good. She has plenty of cunning to outfox her prey; it is an even match so far. I wonder where Mercy is tonight.*

He finishes his drink, slips the key into his shirt pocket and goes on foot across the plaza, rationalization done.

In his office at his desk, he wonders why Gabriella's photo is still there. *Is the photo here because I miss her or is it just a bad habit?* Looking at the photo, he opens the bottom drawer of his desk, places it inside and kicks it closed. For tonight, he will go with the bad habit theory.

The coyote howls are early tonight, as Adobe reflects on the building across the plaza. He waits until closing time when Sharon is likely to be upstairs. They both have hidden agendas and not-so-hidden desires.

For some reason Adobe takes the long way around the plaza to the saloon. Outside his office, he turns left past the courthouse, left on Second Avenue and left in the alley behind the saloon. Taking the steps two at a time, he reaches the back porch of the bar and finds the door to Sharon's lair.

Reaching for the key, he stops at the sight of Sharon, who flashes a victorious grin and says, "I'm impressed that such an important man found time to see me."

"Not so important."

"Why so modest? As a statehood delegate you're among the most important men in the territory," she declares.

It is a strange comment. When it comes to politics, Sharon Blaylock is no Klara Morgenstern. Then he remembers Dora's point about Sharon's interest in statehood.

"You follow New Mexico's progress in joining the Union?"

"Very much, Sheriff, but I wonder if New Mexico is ready for statehood. There are many unresolved issues."

"The delegates have disagreements but we're working for the common good. Statehood is long overdue, in my estimation."

"Long overdue for good reason. Washington has objected to full citizenship for New Mexico's Spanish-speaking Catholic people."

"That's no longer true."

"But, Sheriff, you will admit that Washington favors Arizona, with its more English-speaking, Protestant people."

"Why all the interest in statehood?"

"Perhaps I can explain better in my new bedroom suite," Sharon says, believing she has the upper hand.

Armed with enthralling sexuality and headstrong energy, she sees an inevitable victory by tempting him into a compromising position. She thinks he is already determined to know the hidden secrets buried within her sexuality.

They walk into her bedroom suite. Adobe is amazed at how different the sisters are from one another. It is Mady's room with Sharon's imprint.

"Cigarette?" she offers, while pulling out another Red Tip.

"No thanks," he says, maintaining a defensive skepticism.

"Shall I get you a drink?" she smiles.

"How about a few answers first? Did Mady help you in Santa Fe after your automobile accident?"

"Jesus Christ, Sheriff. Mady again?"

"Yes, that's right, Mady again."

"Okay, okay. Yes, she did."

"Why so reluctant to discuss Mady?"

"I will be glad to do so, but wouldn't you rather be dancing with me?"

Already knowing the answer, he asks, "Where is she now?"

"I am just a working girl and not my sister's keeper."

"Really? She disappeared and you know nothing?"

"Look, all I know is that she started back to Valtura once she was convinced of my recovery from the accident."

"And you care nothing about her situation?"

"Perhaps some questions are better left unanswered."

"You are cold."

"Yes, colder than a witch's heart, but not now, not at this time."

Still pressing, Adobe tips his hand, "You know nothing about the Territorial Insane Asylum?"

Sharon's cigarette falls from her lips and she softly responds, "I know it's a place to avoid."

Sharon's reaction proves that Ellison knows her. Arriving at a conversational impasse, Adobe warns Sharon, "When there is so much at stake, heads can roll."

Worried now, she seductively bends over to retrieve her smoke and says, "Are you after my head, Sheriff?"

Before he can respond, Sharon plays her trump card and removes her beautiful costume. At first look, Adobe discovers an attached black petticoat that provides fullness and stimulation. Yet he stands his ground.

Smiling broadly, she says, "I can definitely tell you like what you see, so why the resistance? Nobody gets hurt."

What is a man to do now? He asks himself. *On the other side of passion, Sharon could help with Mady's release. It is unlikely, but I have to try, for Mady's sake, and she probably knows about Berta. It is all extremely inviting, but women are capable of morphing into Lady Macbeth.* Then he says, "You have no idea who could get hurt."

Sharon flashes a dark look. Adobe takes the risk and slips his arms around Lady Blaylock. Holding her waist and kissing her lips, he allows the seduction, yet he is not seduced at all, at least that is what he tells himself.

"Shall we try your bed?"

"Yes, if you prefer."

An hour later, Adobe stands to leave, out of line with Sharon's expectations. She sees his intentions and demands, "Where do you think you're going?"

"The Circle C of course," he says, while dressing.

"What? You aren't serious!"

"I'm serious. Good night, Mademoiselle Sharon."

"You can't come into my place and treat me this way."

"Your place? That is an interesting choice of words."

Revealing her mental instability, Sharon screams, "Nobody walks out on me!"

"I cannot rest until I know Mady is safe in Valtura."

"Ha! You sure found time to rest tonight," she says with anger.

"I am an imperfect man in an imperfect world," he offers as a weak defense.

"You're going to be a sorry man in my world if you leave now. I call the shots."

"Mady is still missing. Is that clear? Because if it isn't, have someone else draw you a picture, I haven't got the time."

"You better make time mister!"

"Beauty can hide a lot of sin, Sharon."

"How do you hide your sin?"

Adobe pauses, looks deep into her eyes and sees more than a jilted lover. Disregarding the threat, he says. "Why don't you admit that Mady is stuck in the insane asylum and you arranged to commit her? What the hell is going on?"

"Get out!"

Sharon is furious and fuming over Adobe's treatment, then remembers the big picture. *There may not be another rendezvous and chance to influence him.* She has lost control of him and the plot. Femme fatales can take desperate measures—he will pay for Sharon's failure.

Meanwhile, at the Circle C, A.P. and Ellison share a late night drink.

"A.P., I never told you that you're a good cowboy. You always do great work on roundups and find lots of strays for the Circle C."

"Top hands get most of the hard work done," A.P. jokes.

"You are a good top hand, the Circle C is lucky," Ellison laments.

"Something wrong, Kid?"

"I've been thinking about leaving."

"What are you talking about?

"Los Angeles. I saw a picture show in Albuquerque. A feller called D.W. Griffith made a picture show about Old California. There could be work for me in Los Angeles, in the picture show business."

"What about the Circle C?"

"I want to start a new life, A.P."

"You seem determined to go, but what about Adobe?"

Ellison looks down and says, "I hear he is busy tonight with Santa Fe Sharon. I knew her once. Slick woman."

"What are you trying to tell me?"

"She had me going, A.P. I did something I'm not proud of."

"Are you saying Adobe could be in trouble?"

"I don't know."

"Look, Adobe never trusts anyone until he knows them."

"Can we keep Los Angeles between you and me for awhile?"

"Sure, Kid."

41

FOURTH ESTATE, THIRD INTERVIEW

The Valtura Journal runs extra copies of the paper to accommodate increased readership. Demand is up based on the colonel's statehood interviews and so are Johan's spirits. The rumble of his Model T alerts the colonel, who slowly walks outside to greet his visitor.

"*Buenas tardes,*" the colonel smiles.

"Colonel, are you ready to continue our discussion?"

"Yes, please sit down. I have been thinking about starting with specific issues today."

Wasting no time, Johan pulls out his pencil and pad and says, "Please do so."

"First, let me say that each proposed state constitution caused contention. Arguments about equality of representation, land grants and money for education abounded."

Johan begins writing in his long pad.

"In addition, there were objections such as too much perceived protection for Spanish rights. On the other hand, Spanish-American leaders feared the Anglos from Oklahoma and Texas would dominate New Mexico culture and leadership as they did in California."

"Colonel, please slow down a little."

"Ha-ha, of course. How is Adobe? Any word on Mady?"

"He is concerned about the new management of her saloon but has not said anything more on Mady. Please continue."

"Overall, the delegates supported the general good and agreed on many issues, most importantly the need for self-government."

Johan resumes writing in his pad.

"Capital investment is an area of concern. The instability of our territorial status tends to prevent eastern investors from risking money in New Mexico. Most agree that a stable state government can better protect outside capital investments."

"Attracting investment is a solid reason for statehood," Johan responds.

The colonel sits back and continues, "We have solid qualifications too. New Mexico ranks high in the construction of reservoirs for irrigation and building canals to convey water to desirable farming localities. The fertile lands will attract the immigration needed to realize our potential."

"Colonel, it smells like your coffee is ready."

"Can you…?"

Johan quickly gets up to pour coffee and continues to write down the detailed analysis of the territory. The colonel goes on, "Our mineral resources are incalculably rich." The men wait for a loud motorcar to pass before the colonel says, "Railway construction is progressing with reasonable diligence as well."

"Let's hope the Valtura line actually comes to town."

"Yes." The colonel sips his coffee and says, "Despite compelling reasons and constant efforts, many appeals did not receive enough congressional action. Over the decades, Congress rejected or ignored many territorial resolutions. A state constitutional convention called by Governor Otero in 1901 focused on the right to be a free and independent state, but that version tended to be unreceptive to New Mexico."

"Did you say rejected by Congress?"

"Yes, Congress often postponed in favor of other national issues. They had their objections too, issues relating to the Spanish population by some members were weak at best and biased at worst. The critics pointed to the wide majority of New Mexicans who spoke Spanish and used court interpreters, hindering the judicial process."

"Interesting, Colonel, and now the majority of New Mexicans are Anglos."

"True. Another interesting complaint was that many country communities were isolated from the outside world. The most annoying grumble was that New Mexicans live in mud huts."

Johan laughs and says, "Even some of our best public buildings are made of adobe bricks."

"Also, there was eastern prejudice saying that we are foreign and not in tune with American ideals."

"That was an unfortunate barrier."

"Yes, we have been on American soil since 1846, and New Mexico sent seven thousand fighting men to save the Union during the Civil War. In fairness, New Mexico's good performance in the Spanish-American war increased congressional support for statehood."

Two motorcars rumble pass each other in opposite directions. East Corona Street is increasingly becoming busy with more traffic. The men wait a moment.

"Then there was a different approach. Johan, are you familiar with the joint statehood attempt?"

"Yes, Congress proposed that Arizona and New Mexico join the Union as one state."

"Both territories rejected that idea and it died quickly. The New

Mexico convention in 1907 opposed joint statehood with Arizona and called for a separate state. The voters agreed. We were getting closer."

"Closer, yet the statehood debate continued," Johan adds.

"Of course political debate persisted. Statehood advocates claimed that New Mexico had greater natural resources then other territories or states. That may or may not be true, but it is true that New Mexico erected, *without* federal funds, many public buildings such as the capital, penitentiary, university and insane asylum. In addition, many counties had stately courthouses."

"Like our Corona County courthouse, Colonel. What happened to the 1907 resolution?"

"The 1907 state bill, which passed in Santa Fe and was sent to Washington, died when the occupied National Congress gave the resolution little attention. Moreover, some newspaper editorials held that an enabling act from Congress should come before a territorial resolution."

"Another chance was lost."

"Yet we were getting closer to statehood," the colonel repeats. "Subsequent Congressional action produced an Enabling Act that went to the Committee on Territories. However, other territories were vying for statehood and the congressional sessions ran out, but there was a good foundation for future sessions." The colonel stands and says, "Excuse me a moment."

He slowly goes inside and returns with crusty bread and glasses of red wine, indicating they should end soon. Johan writes down a few more lines as the colonel places the tray on the table.

Johan puts down his pen, picks up the wine and offers a toast, "Here's to statehood."

The colonel raises his glass and adds, "And to our statehood delegate leader."

"I'm sure that shoot-out caused you some concern."

"Yes, there was some anxiety before he came here. Adobe is like a son to me."

"And I would welcome him as a son-in-law."

"You have a wonderful daughter. But perhaps we should continue."

Back on track, the colonel says, "A positive sign was the inclusion of a statehood plank in the platform of the two national parties. This favored home rule for New Mexico, but had no practical effect."

"I am sure that it at least added more respect to the statehood movement."

"Yes, it did. Then the 1910 population and taxable property increased beyond other territories admitted to the Union. This was strong evidence that we were ready," the colonel says.

"Indeed," Johan says, while writing down every word.

"At the congressional hearings held that year, main issues included the old cry for self-government promised by General Kearney and confirmed in the peace treaty."

The sounds of *Ah-ooo-ga, Ah-ooo-ga*, coming from a motorcar stops the colonel. He continues, "Despite the many challenges, last June President Taft signed another Enabling Act, allowing the delegates to draft and frame a new state constitution. As you know, the constitution was submitted to the people and the voters approved the constitution last January."

"Colonel, what were the main points of the latest constitution?"

"Okay, let's see. It guaranteed equality to children of Spanish descent in public schools and the right of all citizens to vote, hold office and sit upon juries. Land grants and money for educational and institutional purposes are good."

"That brings us close to the present, Colonel."

"Yes, and with the primary points of contention removed, the majority of the voters accepted the constitution and the congressional conditions. Now we need the territorial voters to ratify the constitution at the ballot box."

"We have the best chance ever this year."

"Yes, but we still need a Joint Resolution of Congress admitting New Mexico to the Union and the president's signature."

"Yes, of course."

Suggesting that they end the interview, the colonel says, "Shall I pour more wine?"

"Certainly, Colonel, we can continue on another day."

42

Midnight Nightmare

It is midnight at the Circle C. Adobe is in the library writing to the circuit court judge about Mady's release when he hears a terrible sound. Rushing out the library door, he sees smoke. Caustic black smoke is pouring out of the stable.

A.P. runs from the bunkhouse screaming, "Fire!" He charges into the stable, intent on releasing the horses, but lung-choking smoke hits him immediately. Violently coughing, he staggers outside and sees an indistinguishable number of men. They are shadows in the smoke fighting a losing battle with buckets of water.

Adobe races into the smoke-filled stable and sees flames running up the walls. Surrounded by thick smoke, he curves down close to the floor, seeking the little available air. Wildly, he fumbles at the stall latches then throws open the gates, freeing the terrified horses. Blinded by the smoke and pushed around by the terror-stricken animals, he finally gets to Patriot's stall. The stallion is frantically kicking at the gate to escape the imminent inferno.

The fire closes in on Adobe as he charges into the stall. Patriot, tormented by smoke and fear, knocks him to the ground. The spread of flames and heat quickly becomes agonizing. They have seconds to escape the burning building—now a death trap.

Pulling himself up, Adobe attempts to lead Patriot out, but he is a wild horse, out of control with panic. Facing certain death, Adobe has no more options. Running low and fast with the last of his strength, he finds the outdoors and falls to his knees.

With only minutes left before the stable collapses, Adobe gasps for breath and prays for Patriot, *Oh God, not this horse, not Patriot. He never failed me. Please get him out, give him a chance.*

Used up from exhaustion and smoke inhalation, Adobe does not react to the sickening crash of the stable disintegrating into a burning mound of wreckage. Then A.P., who recovered from his ordeal, helps Adobe to the front of the house. The other cowboys douse the flaming pile of wreckage, trying to end the nightmare. With apprehension, A.P. kneels by Adobe and presses a canteen of water to his lips.

"Boss, are you all right?"

Adobe looks up and whispers, "Patriot?"

A.P. drops his head. "We don't know, a few horses escaped and instinctively ran toward the river to hydrate; but the fire claimed the lives of seven. Patriot is not among the dead. I'll send a few boys to scout around down by the river; he is out there somewhere."

Adobe swallows hard and says, "I appreciate your efforts A.P., it was a futile attempt to lead him to safety. I love that horse, A.P."

"I know you do. I know."

Ellison was watching from a distance. He walks away in tears, feeling guilty about his despicable role in the Mady affair. Adobe is shaken, but able to return to the library to recover. Drained, he falls asleep in his chair.

In the early morning, A.P. returns to report his findings. "Boss, we found a few horses at the river, but not Patriot."

Adobe, having spent the entire night in the chair is slow to wake up.

"Don't worry, we'll find him."

This prompts Adobe to stand and shake off his fatigue. A.P. pauses and swallows hard then says, "There is something else you should know."

Dejected, he asks, "What's that?"

"It's the fire; it was no accident. We found this empty pack of cigarettes near the stables."

"What brand?"

"Marlboro Red Tips."

Flames can begin with careless smoking, lightening, spontaneous combustion and arson. The fast burning rate of wood, straw and sawdust in the barn causes fires to develop extremely fast. Adobe had little or no chance do to more for the horses or the barn.

Later that morning, Adobe withdraws to Little Hill Top with fantasies of choking the life out of Sharon Blaylock. He is not the kind of man who makes war on women, but she must pay for her wicked ways. On the high point of the Circle C, he tries to put the fire in perspective—if possible. A.P., who knows where to find him, walks to Little Hill Top.

"Thought you would be here," A.P. says without emotion.

Adobe looks up says, "We need to rebuild, pronto."

"We will, Boss."

"Let's ride up to Linden Lake and look around."

"I have two saddle-horses ready."

They move down the hill, mount the horses and head north at a steady tempo. After twenty minutes of solid riding, Adobe turns to A.P. and says, "We were lucky that no men were killed in the fire."

"That's right, but we came too close."

"There was a big factory fire in New York last March. More than a hundred women were not so lucky."

"I know. They died in the fire or jumped to their deaths trying to escape."

Adobe holds back tears and says, "They were young women, recent Italian and Jewish immigrants who quickly discovered there was no escape route. That factory is not far from my old neighborhood, A.P."

The Triangle Shirtwaist factory located near Washington Square Park made national news when a fire started in a scrap bin on March 25—146 were killed. An unextinguished match or cigarette most likely caused the worst industrial disaster in New York history. Working conditions and poor safety procedures contributed to the tragedy. However, the catastrophe initiated sweeping reforms in worker protection.

Adobe thinks of the Marlboro Red Tip pack found near the barn and feels the burning rage returning. The factory owners did not face criminal charges; it will be much different for Sharon Blaylock. First, though, he will deal with the Ellison issue.

Adobe and A.P. return from Linden Lake without Patriot. The two men stop at the front of the Circle C house and A.P. offers, "How about going into town for drinks and chili?"

"No time. We need to think about hiring another cowboy."

"Why?'

"I'll tell you later."

"Okay, Boss. I'll see what we can do about rebuilding."

Adobe finds Ellison cleaning up the ashes and debris of what use to be the stable.

"Boss, I'm sorry all this happened."

"I'm very sorry too. I thought you were a better man."

"What?"

Adobe leads him a few yards away and blasts, "I know about your trip to the Territorial Insane Asylum. Mady has always been good to you."

There is no use in Ellison denying his unsavory involvement. He is shocked, speechless and unsure of what will happen next.

"What the hell is wrong with you? Why did you betray Mady and me? You are involved with Santa Fe Sharon! What else will you and your gang do?"

"It was just about Mad Mady, that one time."

"And for what? Money? Draw your pay and get off this ranch. Do you understand what I am saying?"

"But…you know I never went against you."

"Stop. Shut up and don't say a damn word." Pointing to the ashes, Adobe admonishes, "Do you see what *that woman* is capable of doing? Do you know what you are doing?"

"Boss, you know I would never fire the barn."

With emotions running high, Adobe shouts, "Get out of Valtura, Corona County and the territory too."

A.P. hears the commotion, comes up in a hurry and says, "Everything okay here?

"Yes, he was just leaving—*for good*."

Dejected, Ellison walks away.

"What happened?"

"He forced Mady into the Territorial Insane Asylum. I'm working on her release now. I kept it quiet, thinking I could learn more that way."

"I can't believe he would do that."

"I have been working the margins since Mady's abduction, but now I must work within them."

Shaking his head, A.P, says. "Your trust is a valuable thing to lose, Boss."

"He was good at it."

"Too bad he destroyed your confidence. Ellison sure knew how to cowboy."

"We are better off without him."

"Sure, Boss. I know."

43

NEW MEXICO RANGERS

The U.S. government declared the frontier settled in 1890, although New Mexico Territory was not quite all that settled. In 1905, the territorial governor formed the Mounted Police, believing the force would change New Mexico's image as a lawless land. The Rangers, a name started in Texas when Stephen Austin created a ranging company for colony protection, could improve statehood chances with more law enforcement.

Adobe is enraged about what he imagines to be Sharon's view of the world, her indifference to human and animal life. He is in his office ready to confront Sharon when a tough, wiry and self-confident man enters. He wears a flat, wide-brimmed hat pulled low over his eyes, gauntlet gloves, a bandana, suspenders, a vest and a big sagging mustache. His two ivory-handled long-barrel Colts in a cross-draw holster are obvious. The noise of high-heeled boots and big spurs herald his arrival.

"Are you Aldoloreto Centori, former captain in the U.S. 6th Cavalry?"

Adobe stands with great surprise and says, "John Murphy, what are you doing in Valtura?"

"You can call me Captain, Captain!" he says with a jaunty air.

The former army officer laughs. "You can call me Adobe. My God, is it really ten years since Cuba?"

Murphy nods with a wide grin, "Twelve."

"Welcome to Valtura," Adobe says warmly, shaking his hand.

"Thanks."

Their army bond overrides the long break in time. Both instantly resume the friendship as if it had never been interrupted.

Adobe smiles and says, "A New Mexico Ranger. I thought about the mounted police, a chance to revive the cavalry days, but my ranging days are over. It sure suits you and your men well—encouraging obedience to the law and discouraging lawless characters from coming into New Mexico."

"We try. The rangers are a small force with insufficient funds, responsible for policing in a big territory."

"Try? You mean succeed. You have an excellent record; the available facts show hard work on the part of your command."

Murphy smiles his appreciation and thinks, *Last year we had remarkable results, but there is a far greater challenge at hand.*

"So, Murph, how many men are in your command?"

"We are twenty men strong."

"That's all the more reason to call you successful."

Captain Murphy's pride in being a ranger is clear as he says, "Thanks, Adobe. The TR White House supported Rough Riders for ranger jobs and since we fought with his regiment, I applied."

"Yes, I read about veteran recruitment and you as an original ranger."

"That's right; I've been with the rangers since '05."

"I'm sure your Medal of Honor helped your appointment as captain."

"As I recall I'm not the only one with that decoration."

Adobe nods in agreement and says, "So, did you ever meet that cowboy in the White House after Cuba?"

"Well, no. Too busy," he quickly adds. "I heard he is making another run at the presidency."

"Taft is not running in '12?"

"Taft *is* running."

"Leave it to TR to challenge a sitting president in his own party."

"Should be interesting."

The old army friends reminisce about Cuba, but Murphy carefully avoids talking about the last day. Then the door opens again and Lieutenant Francisco Montero enters.

"Sheriff Centori, this is Lieutenant Montero, New Mexico Rangers."

Montero, taller than the other two men, is about 180 pounds, with a measured manner. Born in Santa Rosa, New Mexico, he joined the rangers soon after Murphy and became second in command.

"Lieutenant," Adobe says with a smile.

"Sheriff, the captain has said much about you and him in Cuba."

Not too much, Adobe hopes.

"Let's have drinks," says Murphy.

Although impatient about Sharon, Adobe agrees, "Sure, that will be fine."

"The saloon across the plaza looks first class," Murphy suggested.

"True, but I have a feeling we need some privacy. Let's go to the hotel."

The sun is coming down on an already cold autumn day as the men march across Corona Street toward the Union Hotel. Sharon's moment of reckoning will have to wait.

44

Lives for Real Estate

Entering the hotel lobby, the three men cause a little stir. Adobe shows the way to the bar as everyone acknowledges him. As they pass the front desk, James Clarke stares at the men. They find a corner table.

"You sure are popular in this town," says Murphy.

"It's just the big hat that attracts attention."

All three men laugh, but Adobe is extremely well-liked and does gets fast service anywhere in Valtura. The waiter flies over to their table and says, "What can I get for you and your friends, Sheriff?"

He orders a bottle of rye whiskey, and the other men nod in agreement.

"Right away!"

In seconds flat, the waiter and a bottle appear, causing Montero to add, "As the captain said, you sure are popular."

"And everyone knows about the famous Circle C Ranch," Murphy adds.

Adobe shrugs his shoulders, pours drinks and says, "There was a depraved act committed at the Circle C, that will be infamous. We had a terrible stable fire and believe it was arson."

"Sorry to hear that." Murphy throws back his first drink and asks, "Anything we can do?"

"No, not yet." He suppresses his anger, gets back on point and says, "So what brings you two men to Valtura?"

Murphy glances at Montero and states, "Same reason the army will be here in two days' time."

"The army is coming to Valtura?"

"Well not for long, they will continue to the border," Murphy clarifies.

"What for?"

"It's the army's duty to respond to a potential crisis in a Federal Territory," Murphy said. He anticipates the next question and adds, "We may be on the brink of war with Old Mexico."

"What the hell is going on, Murph?"

He looks at Montero again and moves closer to Adobe. "Are you familiar with the Treaty of Mesilla?"

"Yes, it settled some lingering issues from the war with Mexico."

Murphy takes off his hat, fits it back on and says, "Yes, but you are probably unfamiliar with the Revert Document."

"Revert Document? I never heard of it."

"There are people in Old Mexico who have definitely heard of it."

Adobe drains his glass and inquires, "What exactly is it?"

Murphy follows suit with his glass and answers, "It is a manuscript copy of the Treaty of Mesilla's Article X relating to the border territories, authorized by President Buchanan in 1861—eight years after the original treaty."

More than a little curious, Adobe refills the glasses and says. "Border territories?"

Murphy pulls an envelope from his vest pocket, looks Adobe square in the eye and says, "This was sent from Governor Jackson's office to the New Mexico Militia and the rangers. In addition, the war department notified the governor that the U.S. Army would be on the move in New Mexico."

"The war department?" Adobe repeats.

Montero answers, "Yes, regiments of cavalry, infantry and engineers, about seven thousand men will be stationed in the southern border regions. New Mexico Militia companies have been mobilized and federalized to defend border towns. It's a big response to a big potential problem."

"What exactly is the problem?" Adobe inquires.

Murphy explains, "The Treaty of Mesilla did more than finally set disputed boundaries between Mexico and the U.S. The problem comes from Article X that says any ceded border territory acquired by the U.S. is subject to reverting to Mexico."

"Reverting to Mexico? Are you sure of all this?"

"Sure enough. The borderlands are *still* territories and could revert to Mexico on January 1, 1912, and that is exactly the problem."

Astonished, Adobe says, "That's quite an amazing story. Perhaps it is symbolic, a bargaining position for other issues, without aggressive intentions."

"Washington considers it significant, but they have not acknowledged the existence of the document."

"Not acknowledged? You said it was authorized by President Buchanan."

"That's right, he signed it days before he left office, but there's more." Murphy, pulling on his mustache, says, "The Revert Document, which changed the 1853 treaty, was a secret contract never announced to the public."

"Take a look at this old newspaper clipping from the Washington Post."

Adobe puts down the governor's orders and turns his attention to an article from 1878:

FIRE DESTROYS CITY ARCHIVE BUILDING

Flames completely consumed the Washington City Archive Building, located on Constitution Avenue, early yesterday morning. The building contained official records and private documents from Washington, D.C. history, and an extensive library of manuscripts. The City Archive was a closed, complete archive of older history.

In addition, the City Archive was the official city government repository that collected municipal records. The six-story archival building collapsed along with two adjoining buildings. All City Archive staff and visiting archive users survived, as they escaped after a warning.

The definite measure of damage to the historical records stored in the building is unknown. An extensive part of written records of Washington City's history is assumed destroyed.

After Adobe reads the clipping, Murphy explains, "Officially, there were no national documents stored in the City Archive, but given the nature of the secret arrangement between governments, the Article X manuscript was covertly stored in the City Archive, not the National Archive."

"And fire destroyed copies of the Revert Document," Adobe concludes.

"Right, and as a result, there are no U.S. copies in Washington."

"How do you know all this?" Adobe asks.

"As I said, TR is close to veterans."

"I see. You never said what you did before the rangers and after the army."

"We can talk about that another time."

"Sure. Are there copies in Mexico City? Or was there another fire?" Adobe quips.

"Not that dramatic," Murphy was cryptic. "But that's just it. We don't know for sure if they have a manuscript copy or know where to find one."

"This story gets more fascinating, but why would the U.S. agree to such a proposal in the first place?" Adobe asks.

"Buchanan was considered disinterested and incompetent by many including his own Democrat party, and in Congress, the Northern Senators probably felt that if the South won the war, the treaty amendment would be a confederate problem. What matters is that during the country's preoccupation with the looming Civil War, he signed the Revert Document. Now we have a possible serious situation," Murphy answers.

Montero adds, "With the U.S. distracted by the coming war, an inept president and strained diplomatic relations, the time was right for Mexico to push their interests."

"Gentlemen, all this is fantastic, but unlikely, since statehood is about to happen. Arizona and New Mexico are moving forward. I was in Santa Fe with Governor Jackson about statehood. In fact, we expect a Joint Resolution from Congress promising statehood. Our constitution will be resubmitted to the people in the election planned in November."

"All that is true, but there have been statehood failures for unexpected reasons many times. The November election could be delayed or fail; and even if it's successful, will Taft sign the statehood bill soon enough?" Murphy warns, "Even if the U.S. accelerates the process, there is no assurance it will be before the deadline."

"You're right, Murph. Last August, Taft vetoed a Joint Resolution of Congress admitting Arizona and New Mexico because he objected to Arizona's Constitution."

"In any event, the U.S. doubts that Mexico has the Revert Document, and if they do, well, the U.S. will never agree. So urgency is lost on Washington."

Adobe reflects and says, "So if they have the document, we need to save Washington from itself and soldiers from war. Okay, Murph, when is the deadline?"

"As I said, January 1, 1912. We have some time to resolve this in favor of the U.S."

"In favor of the U.S.," Adobe states, "there are people who think we stole that land and much more from Mexico."

"Do you think that?" Murphy replies.

"No, I guess not…as the saying goes, to the victor belong the spoils, and much of the land was purchased."

"In Mexico, the war is called the War of North American Invasion. Mexico controlled the Southwest for 25 years since breaking away from Spain," Montero says.

"I understand the provocation was unclear," Adobe defends, "and those distinctions matter little now."

"Sheriff, two countries rarely attack simultaneously, a nation has to initiate the violent, perhaps immoral, aggression and begin a war."

"We are not here to debate the virtues of a past war; we must avoid a future war," Murphy interjects. "The threat is not from Washington or Mexico City; the war itself is the threat."

"You're right. This is astonishing. I can hardly believe it," Adobe says.

"Washington may not acknowledge the document, but is responding. In fact, American agents with access to Mexican state secrets are learning more."

"If Washington is going to that trouble, there could be something afoot. Why are the rangers here telling me this?" Adobe asks.

"There are a few reasons. First, we're alerting all the sheriffs in the counties south of Santa Fe. Adobe, are you aware of the conflicts between the rangers and county sheriffs?"

"Yes, I know that some are not cooperative with the rangers. No problem here, Murph."

"I never thought so. The rangers are the first line of defense for New Mexico, but obviously no match against an army."

Adobe stares at him and says, "Do you think it will come to that?"

"Agents in Mexico City informed us of increased diplomatic bustle in the president's house. The German government is especially represented and we are aware of military activity in Vera Cruz."

Adobe processes the words that create a flurry of thoughts, shakes his head and says, "German forces here in North America?"

He waits for Murphy to continue.

"Not yet—but the stage is set. Also, the Cuban government may be involved."

"Cuba?"

Adobe looks up from his thoughts, which had transported him to Cuba.

"Yes, Cuba. I noticed her photo on your desk."

Looking at Montero, Adobe replies, "That's ancient history." He wished he had left the photo in the desk drawer.

"Sure, if you say so." Murphy has always suspected that their friendship waned over the years because he is a reminder of Cuba.

"Germany. Now the army makes even more sense."

"It wouldn't be the first time. When TR was in the White House, Germany challenged the Monroe Doctrine by attempting to buy Baja California for use as a naval base. TR changed their minds."

"I'm sure of that," Adobe says.

"There was no European intrusion from Berlin."

With that, Murphy signals to Lieutenant Montero, who hands Adobe a document.

"What's this?" Not waiting for an answer, Adobe reads:

Territory of New Mexico Adjutant General's Office
Santa Fe; October 23, 1911

The movement of organizations from home stations to attend maneuver camps near the southern border will be as follows:

Adobe looks up in astonishment and says, "Maneuver camps, that's an interesting choice of words."

"There is some diplomacy left," Montero says, "but very little."

"Diplomacy," Adobe chimes in. "I bet the saber rattling is heard all the way to Berlin."

"Mexico will notice the maneuver camps too. Their agents are in our southern towns and could be anywhere in New Mexico, including Valtura."

"Here in Valtura?" Adobe questions somberly.

"Yes, here," Montero confirms.

"Murph, you said *first.* Are there other reasons for telling me?"

"You are a delegate to the statehood convention."

"I understand. Acquiring statehood has moved from important to crucial. I will do my best to redouble our efforts," Adobe vows.

After a moment of quiet, Murph reveals another concern. "There is more than that; I heard about the shoot-out at your friend's saloon. It could be far-fetched, but your position as a statehood delegate *is* public knowledge. Those men could be associated with people who are interested in the Revert Document."

"The devil himself doesn't know the heart of man or woman," Adobe observes. "Murph, there have been other events that could be connected."

"You reported that Mady Blaylock is missing."

"Yes, I did. We now know she is in the Territorial Insane Asylum. Her sister Sharon is involved *and* has been to Old Mexico. There is much more at stake than I realized. What do we know about the army's position now?"

"So far, the army intends on increasing military positions on the southern border. Captain Reed is leading a detachment of cavalry from Fort Union to patrol the border and will be here soon."

"Now I see it all," Adobe says. "If history is a guide, the U.S. will not give up the territories without a fight. Washington will renounce the Revert Document as Old Santa Anna renounced the treaty claiming the Rio Grande as the boundary."

"That's about right, and we don't need another war with Mexico, this time it will be far worse with Germany involved," Murphy cautions.

"Gentlemen, if the Revert Document surfaces in the wrong hands before statehood and after the deadline, it would mean certain war. Many lives will be lost," Adobe proclaims.

"Yes, lives will be exchanged for real estate," Montero philosophizes.

Murphy responds, "We have seen war. When policy meets armed conflict, it is a bloody crossroad. The men who make policy and who can declare war are not the ones who will fight. Some blame the military for polices we had nothing to do with, except, of course, being ordered to fight."

"True," Adobe agrees. "Wars are used to achieve vital political goals, but should be used as a last resort. Let's make sure the U.S. does not go down that road. We can't control the statehood process, but we can control the situation if we can find the Revert Document."

"Finding the Revert Document, if it exists at all, is the best possible defense."

"Wait a minute; why all this fuss over a nonexistent document?" Adobe asks.

Montero turns to Murphy and says, "Someone must know something."

"And we can't take any chances," Murphy adds.

"Okay, you're probably right, but where in the world do we look? What are our agents telling us about location?"

"I am afraid a ranger does not get all the information."

"Even a government man like you?" Adobe guesses.

Smiling, he says, "There is an old tale about one manuscript copy hidden in Arizona and one in New Mexico."

"Well that narrows it down…no offense, Murph."

"None taken, it only takes finding one document to involve both territories. All we can do is focus on our territory. I'm sure the Arizona Rangers and the U.S. Army are doing the same there as we are here."

The men fall silent as the waiter returns. Sensing the privacy of the meeting, he moves away without a word.

"Adobe, even if we find the document, we do *what* exactly?"

"Destroy it," he says adamantly.

"Is that the right thing to do?" Montero says. "There could be a negotiated settlement."

"Why would the U.S. negotiate? The army is already on the move. Right or wrong, destroying it will save many lives and prevent a lot of suffering. The U.S. will declare war rather than return territories based on a document the public has never heard about, even though it may be legal and valid."

Montero, unmoved, offers no words.

"How many people outside of the Mexico City leadership want to enforce the document? Perhaps it's just the leaders and not the people," Adobe adds. "Few wars have countrywide support."

"And the reasons or grievances for such a document may no longer exist," says Murphy.

In a further attempt to justify destroying the Revert Document, Adobe moves his eyes back and forth to each ranger and says, "You know that no undertaking is more difficult than war. The battlefield is the place of the unpredictable. One thing for sure is that wars can be bloody debacles with ugly casualties."

"As the lieutenant said, lives for real estate," Murphy repeats.

"You are using my own words against me, but make good points. Seldom is war a worthwhile payoff for a country's investment and wars can prove to have been unjustified. While Mexico, even with the German allies, cannot beat us militarily, neither should we endure a loss of blood and treasure."

"We need to find the document and destroy it to prevent a disaster. The good of the many outweigh the good of the few," Adobe waxes idealistically.

"Adobe, you are in danger of becoming a great hero."

"Not just me, Murph. I thought we would work together again, along with Lieutenant Montero. What do you think? Are you two ready for some sort of treasure hunt?"

"I thought you would never ask, Adobe, but the rangers need a leader while I'm gone. The lieutenant is that leader."

"I understand. First, the Mady situation needs resolution. She was wrongly committed to the insane asylum and I *must* secure her release. Then I *must* see her sister."

"Adobe, you're giving Old Mexico more time to act. We are dealing with a deadline," Murphy warns.

"I'll take that chance. The world has its problems, and I have mine."

"We have no clue where to look; New Mexico is a big territory," Montero says.

"Of course, before we can act, the precise location, if it is real, must be known. We need to learn as much about the legend as possible." Adobe pauses and goes on, "I have a friend in Valtura who knows much about New Mexico history, fact and fiction."

"That's a good place to start. We will be at the Union Hotel overnight."

"No, there is plenty of room for you at the Circle C. There could be a few steaks for dinner, too."

"It's a cattle ranch—I sure hope so," jokes Montero.

The men have a good laugh and raise an elbow. Adobe says, "Follow East Corona Street out of town toward the Sandias for about six miles and look for a portico with a Circle C sign. Ask for A.P. Baker; he will take care of you. I'll see you there later."

"Thanks, Adobe."

"*Gracias,*" says Lieutenant Montero.

Adobe returns to the militia orders issued by the Adjutant General and reads the document.

> Company A leave Santa Fe on regular train on Atchison, Topeka and Santa Fe Railway, evening of October 10 and proceed to Albuquerque.
>
> Company B leave Las Vegas on regular train on Atchison, Topeka and Santa Fe Railway, afternoon of October 10 and proceed to Albuquerque.
>
> Companies A and B leave Albuquerque on special train leaving that point about 7 o'clock pm October 10.
>
> Detachments from Company C leave Roswell on Pecos Valley Train evening of October 10 and proceed to Hobbs.
>
> Detachments from Company D, E and G leave Santa Fe on regular train on Atchison, Topeka and Santa Fe Railway, morning of October 10 and proceed to Silver City.
>
> Detachments from Company D, E and G leave Lordsburg on special train leaving that point about 3 o'clock pm October 10.
>
> Company commanders will see that all equipages to accompany their commands is taken upon the same trains leaving home stations as their companies.
>
> Troop A leave Las Vegas on special train leaving that point about 4 o'clock pm October 10.
>
> By command of the governor.

Further deployment orders and final destinations will follow. The meaning is clear—the governor is taking the Revert Document seriously.

45

HIDDEN IN NEW MEXICO

Adobe is unsure of the priority of his goals, but sure about confronting Santa Fe Sharon. *Sharon's crime against the Circle C requires a day of reckoning; this is that day. Not just for me, but for Mady and Berta too. Sharon must have the answers, but the rangers have changed things; avoiding a war is the most pressing issue,* he thinks.

Patriot is long gone. With hope fading, Adobe has been riding Mars, a frisky two-year old stallion. He mounts Mars for the short trip from the plaza to East Corona Street. It will be an unscheduled visit to the colonel's house.

"Adobe, I heard about the fire and wanted to come to see you, but I had some bad days."

"I'm sorry to hear that. I know it's late, Colonel."

"It is never late for you, *mi hijo*. Do you have any news about your stallion?"

"Nothing, but he may have escaped the burning stable. A few horses got out and ran to the river. Some were found and some returned to the Circle C, but not Patriot."

"He could be disoriented from the trauma and unable to find his way back," the colonel says with little conviction.

"A.P. has men out looking every day," Adobe laments, with hope fading from his voice.

"I know what that horse meant to you." The colonel winces and regrets using the past tense.

Adobe, unfazed, says, "I don't like to see horses even mildly mistreated. It upsets my peace of mind. This was unspeakable violence to innocent animals. Colonel, it was no accident."

Shock registers on the colonel's face. "Arson? Do you know who did such a thing?"

"I know," Adobe says firmly. "I have every reason to believe that the circumstantial evidence points to Mady's sister, Sharon Blaylock."

"I have heard about her arrival in town. Why would she commit such a terrible act?"

"Besides being delusional, she thinks I overstepped my bounds. That is largely of her creation. Certain expectations failed to materialize and she does not take bad news very well."

"I have said playing with women can be like playing with fire." Again, he regrets the choice of words.

"Hell has no fury, I guess, but I'm here about something else."

"I see. What is on your mind, *mi hijo*?"

"Much. Colonel, you know more about the territory than just about anyone. I need your help with a certain piece of history. There is a legend about a government document hidden in New Mexico long ago that has become highly significant today."

The old soldier has protected the secret for a long time and expected a telegram or unannounced visitor, but the inquiry comes from Adobe. The colonel's first reaction is to resist. He says, "I know not of hidden documents."

Adobe senses the colonel knows more than he admits, but does not push.

Having recovered from the surprise question, the colonel offers more, "Let me read some of my old books and papers. Tell me, any news of Mady?"

"Yes, sorry I didn't tell you sooner, her sister committed her to the Territorial Insane Asylum."

"*Ay dios mio.*"

"I'm working on her release."

"There is no love lost between the sisters."

"Much more could be lost," Adobe probes.

The colonel has always thought about this inevitable moment and says, "Perhaps we can learn something about a document hidden in New Mexico."

"Thank you."

"I'll let you get some rest now, Colonel."

"*Buenas noches.*"

The colonel remains unsure about revealing the secret of Chaco Canyon, so his promise may be empty. Adobe's attention returns to Santa Fe Sharon.

46

She Sleeps Naked

It is very late and Carrie is closing up. Sharon is not downstairs. Adobe storms into Chez Beau Sharon with fierce determination, attracting Carrie's attention.

"What are you doing here so late, Sheriff?"

"Where is she?"

Seeing his overt anger she says, "You better leave. She can't see you now."

Not dissuaded, he yells, "I *said* where is she?"

Carrie darts a look upstairs. Involuntary or not, he takes the meaning and rushes up the stairs two at a time. Marching through the ornately papered hall, he stops at the door with the *fleur-de-lis.* Bursting into her office and then into the adjacent bedroom, he finds Sharon. She is in a big bed with decorative pillows, and she is naked.

"What the hell are you doing here?"

Sharon gets up, reaching for her robe. Furious, Adobe grabs it, leaving her standing naked in front of him. She produces a weak smile and touches herself, designed to disarm his wrath—but her wiles do not work this time.

"Is this any way for an officer of the law to act?" she asks with bravado.

Enraged, he pushes Sharon down onto the bed and strategically places his hands on her throat.

"Ready for another Red Tip?" he screams.

Sharon looks up in confusion, attempting to hide her fear.

"I know you torched the Circle C stable," he screams louder.

Panic claims her expression and fear blocks her speech. Powerless, all she can is do is pray that Carrie will burst in and shoot her tormentor.

Gently pressing her neck he growls, "I could easily kill you and not lose any sleep. You have one last card to play. Why was Mady committed? What happened to Berta? And where is Mercy?"

Sharon struggles to push him off and resorts to kicking and punching. He pins her and screams, "What was that shoot-out about? Why were you in Old Mexico?"

She continues to struggle and he tightens the death grip on her neck.

"One last time, tell me what you are doing in Valtura."

Choking, she signals a willingness to talk. Adobe retreats and waits. After a coughing fit, she looks at him and fearlessly says, "Fuck you and your questions."

She has called his bluff and won. He picks up her pack of Red Tips, takes out a couple of cigarettes and smashes them into her face.

"That's for the Circle C horses you killed."

Sharon coughs, brushes the mangled cigarettes away and boldly yells, "That's a damn lie. Get out of my place."

He pulls out his Navy Colt, presses it to her temple and growls, "So this is what a devil incarnate looks like."

"You wouldn't dare. You haven't got the cojones." She screams like a crazed woman.

She's right. Realizing the truth of her statement, he holsters his gun. Defiantly, Sharon leaps up. Adobe pushes her to the hardwood floor and storms downstairs. Carrie, frozen in fear, is uncertain of what will happen next.

A new, brutal Adobe nears the terrified woman. She fumbles to free a concealed pistol. The sight stiffens his backbone, and he warns, "I would not be so hasty."

Seizing her wrists from behind, he yells, "Get out of Valtura!"

She staggers back a few steps, and then braces in defense.

"Do I make myself clear?"

"Perfectly clear," Carrie bellows.

47

LEGEND OF CHACO CANYON

Colonel Santos rarely ventures from his house. This day is different. The old soldier walks slowly along East Corona Street to the plaza. He approaches the sheriff's office, knocks and enters.

Adobe, who expected Murphy, says, "Colonel, everything okay?"

"Yes, I'm feeling better today and I wish to see you."

"Please sit down."

He slowly sits on the closest chair and says, "The last time we met you talked about Mady's sister."

"Yes, Santa Fe Sharon."

"Are you sure she is a woman scorned and nothing more?"

"No, Colonel, there are too many things happening now. I am sure Sharon is as rapacious, cold and self-serving a woman as you could find."

"I believe that nothing in life occurs by chance; most things happen for a reason. That woman's motives require more thought."

Adobe nods in agreement. "Much more thought. In seeking the truth, I use background information and her recent behavior. When considered together they can provide a reliable conclusion."

The colonel lights an old cigar, puffs and says, "Are you sure?"

Adobe lights a cigar and offers a fresh one to the colonel. "Okay, there is a strange chain of events starting with Mady's disappearance, then Carrie's arrival, Berta and Mercy vanish, a shoot-out, Santa Fe Sharon's entrance, and now arson. This has been one hell of a time."

"More than time, it is *timing*."

Adobe, nonplussed, waits for more.

"And the events are not strange if you consider the connections."

"What are the connections?"

The colonel's answer is slow due to an inner, personal conflict: A friend in danger versus his oath as a Mexican Army Officer. He is well aware of the Revert Document and the deadline. After a long silence he exclaims, "The connection is statehood and your position as delegate."

"Murph had the same theory!"

"Perhaps it is more than a theory. Tell the Circle C cowboys, and be careful on your trips to Valtura. Vary your travel patterns to and from the Circle C."

If the colonel ever shares his lifelong secret—it will be with Adobe. He may be the only living person to know about the Chaco Canyon mission, and he struggles to reconcile conflicting forces. *Mexico could have a legal claim to the territories, but the U.S. is my country now,* the colonel thinks.

"There is another reason for my visit."

Adobe puffs and patiently anticipates the colonel's words."

"Yesterday, you asked about a hidden document and I did not help you."

"I understand."

Then the colonel lets it come out. "Have you been to Chaco Canyon?"

Adobe has been all over the territory. From Las Cruces to the south, Taos to the north, Tucumcari to the east and Gallup to the west. Under a cloud of smoke, he answers, "Yes, I have."

"Then you have seen the ancient carved dwellings in the cliffs. The Anasazi built pueblos from sandstone blocks and timber from distant places. The largest, most intriguing complex is Pueblo Bonito. The structure of 650 rooms was four stories high with three-foot-thick masonry walls. A wall bisecting the central plaza has the Great Kiva, a large circular ceremonial room, on both sides."

Adobe, impatient and confused says, "Yes, Colonel, Chaco Canyon contains the remains of many buildings. It is a fascinating place."

"It is fascinating in more ways than you know."

The colonel, still ambivalent about disclosing the secret, attempts to send Adobe a message by revealing one more clue.

"Do you know that several structures appear aligned to solar and lunar cycles?"

"Yes, Colonel, they suggest astronomical observation and adroitly synchronized construction, but what are you trying to say?"

The colonel takes a deep breath and finally says, "People refer to the legend of Chaco Canyon. Do you know about the legend?"

"Go on."

"The legend tells of a secret mission into Chaco by Mexican soldiers in 1861."

"Secret mission?"

"Yes, a diplomatic pouch was hidden in Pueblo Bonito containing an important amendment to the Treaty of Mesilla."

Adobe reflects on the ranger meeting, conceals that knowledge for the moment and says, "Yes, the treaty clarified the boundaries created at the end the war."

"There is more than that. The pouch contains Article X, a legal obligation to return the territories to Old Mexico," the colonel admits.

"You mean the border territories."

The colonel sighs and says, "The Revert Document covers Arizona and New Mexico, if they are territories after December 31."

"If the document is found and presented."

"Yes, if the document is found and presented," the colonel repeats.

"The shockwave will run through the Southwest and from Mexico City to Washington leading to another war. Colonel, I know about the Revert Document. John Murphy, captain of the rangers, came to Valtura and informed me of the entire situation. Tensions between the two governments are increasing as the deadline nears."

"And so it begins," the colonel laments.

"You called it a legend. Is the document truly hidden in Chaco Canyon?"

"Look at this." The colonel reaches for his silver watch. It has a coyote image and two letters, CC, engraved on the cover."

"CC, for Chaco Canyon?"

"Yes."

"How do you know the document is there?"

The colonel takes a deep breath and says, "Because I was there and helped hide the Revert Document."

"Ha! You were directly involved—you never stop amazing me."

Smiling, he continues, "As a young Captain, I was part of a Mexican cavalry troop under Colonel Alvarado, who had fought in the Texas Revolution and in the Mexican-American War and was selected to lead the expedition. The mission was to cross the border into the U.S. and to enter a strange place, a broad canyon gouged by Chaco Wash. The watch was a gift from Colonel Alvarado, a lifetime remembrance. Of course, I am unlikely to forget."

Adobe stops in his tracks, eyes the colonel and says, "There are many people who would like to know where it is hidden."

"I suppose you will tell the rangers."

Instead of replying, Adobe sits down and prepares to listen closely to every word.

"Carl von Clausewitz said that war is an instrument of foreign policy with military action protecting national interests. We were on a foreign policy mission, not military. We looked grand in our green jackets, grey trousers and black helmets with red plumes." The colonel pauses and takes a breath, "The most wonderful part was that we were young."

"Were you and the other troopers aware of the mission's purpose?"

"We were aware that we had crossed into the U.S. on an extremely important mission, but we knew no details. Alvarado told me the whole story on his deathbed. I have known for many years that the Revert Document holds potential trouble for the U.S. and Mexico."

"That trouble is now brewing."

"Alvarado explained that during the Treaty of Guadalupe Hidalgo, Old Mexico attempted to maintain New Mexico, given their special attachment to Santa Fe, the old capital. The Americans, operating from a position of strength, of course rejected their request. At the Treaty of Mesilla negotiations, the Americans wanted more Mexican land, for a railroad. The Mexicans still wanted Santa Fe."

"And it was of course rejected again."

"Not exactly. The two countries exchanged offers, counteroffers and concessions."

"Colonel, if I recall, Mexico settled for $10 million for 30,000 square miles of borderland along Arizona and New Mexico."

"This is true, Adobe, but *La Villa de Santa Fe,* founded in 1607, has so much history and culture that Mexico persisted in their desire to have it. With the advantage of having the railroad land, Mexico made a bold offer to reclaim a part of New Mexico, with the border north of Santa Fe. That offer, too, was rejected."

"So, as I said $10 million for 30,000 square miles."

"Mi hijo, that is the common belief, but as part of the negotiation, Mexico offered to lease their former border territories—including the highly valued railroad land—to the U.S. for ninety-nine years."

"Colonel, a 99-year lease is in effect between the U.S. and Cuba over Guantanamo Bay—but Guantanamo Bay is part of Cuba."

"That is an interesting observation. Mexico was acting as if the border territories were still part of Mexico. As part of the deal, the U.S got the railroad land, but Mexico's lease agreement stalled in Congress without ratification."

"How was that possible?"

The colonel just smiles and goes on, "However, seven years later Mexico was still unhappy, and seeing a weak President Buchanan and a divided America, called for the 99-year lease again."

"Then the U.S. countered with a ninety-nine year revert rule, putting forward Article X. Border territories that have not become states in ninety-nine years will revert to Mexico."

"That was not a risk for the U.S."

"Correct, with no harm to the U.S. Treasury. It an obvious face-saving effort with no risk at all. No one expected the border areas to remain territories for ninety-nine years," explains the colonel.

"Wait a minute. Murph said we are on the threshold of war and U.S. troops are on the move."

"Adobe wait, Mexico countered with a forty-year revert rule, the Americans said seventy. They finally agreed on fifty. It was an empty agreement and Article X was unknown to the people. Both governments decided not to publicize this extraordinary agreement that would have no practical result—so they believed. We *are* on the threshold—we are close to the fifty-year mark, with Arizona and New Mexico still territories."

"I see. It makes sense. Colonel, if all constraints are satisfied, do you think the territories should revert to Old Mexico?"

"Adobe, it is true that New Mexico was once part of Old Mexico and before that part of New Spain. Although the Spanish were not the original inhabitants, they did arrive before the Anglos."

"So you support the Revert Document?"

"New Mexico has been my home all my life. We are a unique place with a rich Spanish tradition. I am happy here and seek no change of government and certainly no war."

"Colonel, I agree with you. What is done can't be undone or should not be undone."

"Adobe, there are legal issues."

"The moral issue of avoiding war outweighs the legal issues. I must go to Chaco Canyon with Captain Murphy, find it, and burn it," Adobe asserts.

"*Ay Dios mio.* Destroy a document so important to Southwest history?"

"Do we have a choice?"

"I believe you are following your heart. This is the right thing to do, but it could prove difficult. If I could still ride, Adobe, I would be at your side."

"I know, Colonel. You'll be with me in spirit. Now, how do I find the Revert Document?"

The colonel smiles and says, "Yes, I must tell you the location."

"The exact location."

"Yes. Go to Chaco Canyon and then to Fajada Butte. At the base of the butte, you must proceed to the summit on foot. There is only one path and the climb is difficult, dangerous and over four hundred feet. At the top, you will see signs and symbols etched into the sandstone.

"You mean the petroglyphs and those marking solar and lunar cycles?"

"I am unsure. They were a mystery to us at that time. We placed the case in a large crack in the sandstone then covered it with rocks. Look for a sign."

"What kind of sign?"

"Look for an image of a coyote that we scratched above the crack. The picture almost blends with the petroglyphs."

"A coyote?"

"Yes, clear away the rocks, remove the stones and find a thin metal box containing a leather document case. The metal box was designed to protect the papers from the elements. Inside you will find a diplomatic pouch holding the Revert Document."

"I'll do my best, Colonel."

There is an uncomfortable silence, and then the colonel takes Adobe's hand as if he is saying a final goodbye.

"Be careful, *mi hijo. Vaya con Dios.*"

Like a coyote, Adobe is growing wiser. The series of events surrounding the Revert Document are coming into focus. Coyotes are adept at keeping alive, avoiding trouble, being elusive. He will need coyote skills for the Chaco Canyon mission.

48

TWENTIETH-CENTURY TROOPERS

The red-over-white regimental and troop guidons of the U.S. 6th Cavalry fly into Valtura over smartly dressed columns of disciplined, well-armed, U.S. government cavalrymen. Valtura has not seen a mounted army since the brief appearance of the Confederate cavalry during the Civil War. Everyone on East Corona Street stops to watch the grand pageantry.

The flat-brimmed campaign hats with chinstraps, khaki and olive drab breeches, shirts and puttees are markedly different from the nineteenth-century uniforms of dark blue jackets and sky blue pants. The officers wear the new Browning semiautomatic .45 caliber sidearm: the Colt 45.

Captain Reed and his men are quite a sight. He is a fine cavalry officer, quick to scrutinize, clear in decisions and unyielding in carrying out a mission. The entire troop streams in from East Corona to Corona Street and comes to a halt in front of the courthouse. Almost one hundred men on fine government horses stop at Captain Reed's command. The spectacle attracts everyone on the plaza including Adobe, who is walking out of the courthouse.

Reed sees the sheriff's star and dismounts, "I'm Captain Reed, U.S. 6th Calvary."

Adobe nods, "I'm Corona County Sheriff Centori. I am familiar with the 6th Calvary."

"Yes, sir, most people in the territory know of your service in Cuba."

"Welcome to Valtura, Captain. I have a general idea of the army's intentions these days. What can I do for you and your men?"

"Thank you, sir. We stopped as a courtesy to you and must continue to our destination."

"I understand, Captain. Good luck."

Captain Reed mounts his horse, signals the troopers and away they go, as swiftly as they arrived. In a flash, a large cloud of dust covers Corona Street and most of the plaza.

Reed's troops are among the first allocated to the New Mexico border and deployed against Old Mexico. In the preceding days, other army units have made the trek across the southern New Mexico desert. The mission is to defend the U.S. side of the border and to protect the American people. Arriving units have found nothing at the border to alert them, so far.

More deployments will follow. The army will maintain a border presence until the Revert Document issue is resolved, one way or the other. Adobe remembers the papers Murphy showed him. *The army mobilized in New Mexico in response to the Revert Document with orders to protect the southern border and defend border towns.*

Four days later the Valtura Journal runs the following story:

U.S. Soldier Shot at the Border

President Pledged to Protect American Soldiers

Pointing their rifles, Mexican soldiers confronted U.S. soldiers investigating the shooting of Private Mike Monzant of the 6th cavalry on the banks of the Rio Grande, the Army reported on October 15. Private Monzant survived the attack but his condition is unknown.

The 6th cavalry recently arrived at the New Mexico border with Old Mexico. The shooting of a U.S. soldier has exposed the distrust between the two countries and has enraged the U.S. government, which sees the attack on American soil as an act of war. Shortly after Monzant was shot, American soldiers arrived at the scene and pointed their guns at the Mexican soldiers across the riverbank.

"Things quickly got intense," Captain Reed of the 6th Cavalry said, adding that more soldiers arrived in an apparent attempt to cross into Mexico. Mexican soldiers responded with pointed guns from across the river.

The Mexican army accused the Americans of trying to create evidence on Mexican soil and threatened to kill them if they crossed the border, prompting both sides to draw their guns, said Captain Reed.

The confrontation ended with each government's accusation suggesting blame on the part of the other's soldiers. President Taft pledged to protect American soil and U.S. soldiers. President Madero, who views the incident as an unacceptable border violation, has also pledged to protect his country and his army.

Mexico is not taking the Americans' word that the soldier was on U.S. soil and had been defending himself when he opened fire. The investigation is focusing on where the shooting occurred and whether the soldier was shot on U.S. or Mexican soil.

49

Carrie On

Adobe is in his office with a fire going in the kiva and coffee in his cup, studying territorial maps, planning the best way to Chaco Canyon, when someone knocks on the door. He answers and sees Carrie, standing in the threshold with fear and anxiety etched on her face, he says, "What do you want?"

"Sheriff, I knew nothing about the fire, I swear," she says.

"Are you sure you want to bring up the fire? Why should I believe you anyway?"

"Can we please talk in your office?" Carrie asks urgently.

Adobe, skeptical, allows her to enter.

"I can't stay long." Carrie purses her lips, making up her mind to take the risk of talking and says, "I came to tell you I'm taking your warning."

"Which one?" he snaps.

"I am leaving Valtura."

"If this is true, it would be different from everything else you've told me."

"Please, I am in a bad way and alone in Valtura. I want to explain a few things."

He waits, indicating that she should explain more than a *few* things, but finally says, "Okay, Carrie, what's on your mind?"

She places her face in her hands and sighs, "I need your help. I am involved with something over my head, something beyond anything imaginable. And, Sheriff, I'm sorry for being at odds with you."

"We're way past apologies now. Go on."

"I wanted to refuse Sharon, but I was not strong enough. What do you do when you are not strong enough?"

"You act like you are," Adobe says without emotion.

Carrie, usually not one to flaunt herself, appears to have the vapors. Waiting for her to regain composure, he says, "You are no better than Sharon; you just hide it better."

"She is wicked. I'm not like her."

Adobe points to his desk and says, "These papers are waiting for a signature to release Mady."

"But…."

"You covered it up. That's as bad as the act itself. Is that clear? Because if it isn't, have someone else draw you a picture, because I haven't got the time."

"Okay, please listen to me. I'm sorry."

"Prove it by telling me everything you know about Sharon and her connections."

She looks out the window, across the plaza, and confides in him, "I don't know much. I met Sharon while working on Calle Montano in Santa Fe."

Adobe knows the reputation of the Calle Montano women and knows some of them personally. He does not pass judgment on Carrie, not for that.

"In Santa Fe, Sharon offered me a job in Valtura at the saloon. It was an opportunity to get away. She provided little detail except that the situation was personal, between the Blaylock sisters."

Adobe's opinion of Carrie begins to soften. He remains alert and asks, "You never questioned Sharon further?"

"No. As I said, it was between the sisters and I never thought she could be given over to greed, rage and even murder."

"Murder? Are you talking about the men from the shootout? I believe the assailants are known to you."

"Yes, I knew those men you killed."

"No need to embellish," he says sardonically.

"I mean, they were not chance visitors to Valtura."

"Okay, tell me everything about them."

"They rode into town with Bill Blackstone on the day of the shoot-out. Blackstone asked for Sharon and went upstairs. They were fighting; something about Mercy."

Mercy, Adobe thinks with a grimace and a feeling of responsibility. *If anything has happened to her, it has happened to the wrong woman.*

"The other men stayed downstairs and started drinking. I heard some talk about contingencies if things went wrong. They meant to kill you."

"Yes, I absolutely got that message."

"Sheriff, I mean that was their plan, but the shootout was a random act."

"Stop being cryptic, Carrie. Do you know the whole story?"

"I don't know. I only overheard a few things." Carrie is distancing herself from the facts, or the few facts she knows. "Sharon kept me in the dark," she continues. "My job was to set up the bar and run things until she arrived. After the shoot-out, I sensed a growing danger. I want out now."

"What happened to Berta Brandt?"

"Berta was forced to leave town," she lied.

"Forced?"

"Yes." Carrie drops her face to her hand and takes a deep breath. Adobe waits.

"I had orders from Sharon," she screams, to deflect culpability. "She said I must remove anything related to Mady Blaylock. Sharon's obsessed with her sister, almost in a sick way."

"Carrie, what happened to Berta?"

"Berta was suspicious and resisted my authority to run and change the saloon. When she became belligerent, I fired her."

"If you want protection, you better be honest. Again, what happened to Berta?"

"There was a brief fight that ended with Berta being shot dead."

Adobe stands and demands, "You killed Berta?"

"No, not me, it was Bill Blackstone."

"Blackstone. Where is he now?"

"I don't know."

"I think you're lying. You're so good at it, you don't know you're lying."

"What?"

"Listen, you're short on answers and long on being an accessory to murder. We will seek criminal prosecution for the murder of Berta Brandt. That's a lot to answer for, Carrie."

"But I didn't do any of that," Carrie protests.

"Perhaps there's no direct guilt but I won't forget the attempt on my life. You had better talk. Where is Blackstone?"

"Blackstone comes and goes mysteriously. There is no specific pattern; he follows Sharon's orders. That's all I know, all that they allow me to know."

Relatively convinced of Carrie's cooperation, he says, "What do you want from me?"

"Please help me get out of town without enraging Sharon. Show her an arrest warrant so she'll think I'm running from you and not her."

"You *would* be running from me. Why should I help you now?"

After a long pause, Carrie sobs and says, "I'm scared."

A woman's tears affect most men. Adobe is no exception.

"And I fear for her sanity."

"Okay, Carrie, calm down. Take a breath. I'll help you—start talking."

"All this doesn't make sense. How can I trust you?"

Adobe glares at her coldly and replies, "Because I said so."

"Sharon shot a man in Santa Fe just for talking to you."

"Sharon? Can you prove that?"

"No, but she bragged about it. I believed her."

Adobe's empathy fades. "You will learn more about Sharon and Blackstone before you go."

"I don't want to try. My bags are packed."

"You will try. I want to know when Blackstone is in Valtura. You will also sign a statement as witness to the murder of Berta Brandt. Johnny Romano will want to talk to you about Sharon killing that man in Santa Fe."

"Okay, okay, I will find out when he is returning. Then I want to leave Valtura forever."

"Remember, Carrie, if you play with rattlesnakes, you will be bitten."

Adobe has no time to wait for Blackstone or to contemplate the motives of known and unknown enemies. Finding the Revert Document is his priority.

"Sheriff, I believe the attempt on your life was political."

Adobe takes that statement as a final confirmation; there is a target on his back.

Carrie returns to Chez Beau Sharon to assess her options and decides that waiting is not one of them. She will detach herself from the plot and leave Valtura immediately, without Adobe's help. That night, Carrie travels to the Valtura Rail Station the same way she came to town--on foot and without her bags.

50

Too Late for Carnival

The crack of thunder and lightning causes Hietmann, Steiner and Zena-Marta to huddle close under the cafe's outstretched awning. Their conversation and posture are guarded, but not because of the weather. Mexico City, on a plateau over a mile high, has a relatively mild climate. Yet cool evenings and afternoon rains during summer are common.

This group has responsibility for controlling a network of agents in New Mexico. Hietmann spent the last year seeking appropriate people to delay statehood in support of the plot. He reviews the progress of the agents in the twelve New Mexico counties.

"All the women agents are now in a position to corrupt or kill their assigned delegates."

"Kill their assigned delegates?" Gabriella questions with interest.

"Yes, *Señora Zena-Marta*, the agents have orders. If they cannot control their assigned delegate, they can request an assassin."

"All delegates are potential assassination targets."

"Yes, that is correct," Hietmann continues. "Delegates from

Bernalillo, Grant, Colfax, and Guadalupe Counties have been killed, and the crimes have been blamed on their wives."

Gabriella, a political wife, darts a look but says nothing.

"The accused wives were sent to the New Mexico Territorial Insane Asylum. There is a cooperative staff at the asylum. This takes the focus off the real killers."

"Are we establishing a recognizable pattern?" Gabriella asks with concern.

"Perhaps, but remember time is our currency. We cannot continue forever, just long enough to enact Article X and see New Mexico revert to Old Mexico."

Not fully satisfied, she waits for Hietmann to continue.

"Agents in Catron, Cibola and Eddy Counties report ongoing affairs with their respective, married delegates. Operatives with unmarried delegates in Chaves, Curry, De Baca and Doña Ana Counties are also in various stages of relationship development."

Hietmann stops and waits for any reaction before saying, "We have a problem in Corona County. Sharon Blaylock is a wretched failure; she has not corrupted her delegate and there have been shootings in Valtura, bringing dangerous attention to the plan."

"We knew she was risky, Herr Hietmann," Steiner says softly.

After a quick glare at Steiner, Hietmann announces, "Blaylock has requested permission to kill the Corona County delegate, Sheriff Adobe Centori."

The words horrify Gabriella. She has kept her past involvement vague, but the present danger to Adobe is evident.

Hietmann, slowly becoming livid, complains, "Our plan in Valtura has collapsed."

"You don't have a plan," Gabriella shouts, hoping to hide her reaction to the news. "Why kill Centori? The county will just replace him with another delegate."

"For the same reason we killed the others—it will take time to appoint another delegate. The success of our mission is based on time. Of course, we cannot prevent statehood forever, but we need to delay it past the deadline."

"Are you sure about all this? We don't even have the Revert Document!"

Hietmann, resenting her question, replies, "As you know, Madero ordered a search of military records for clues. Remember, time is our currency. Blaylock could not control Centori—he must die."

Gabriella's mind races to find a plan that she *and* Adobe could live with and offers, "There are eleven other counties. We can stand a failure in Corona."

"No. We must pursue each delegate as if he is the *only* delegate. In this way, our chances of success increase. We have risked much and have much at stake. There are no exceptions."

"Centori's no fool. He is probably on alert, thanks to Blaylock's incompetence. I knew him once in Cuba during the war. Your men will not get close to him, but he trusts me. Let me contact him and do what needs to be done."

"*Señora Zena-Marta*, you would murder Centori?"

"No, never murder, but assassinations are sometimes necessary in politics."

That night Gabriella rides out of town to think about all that has happened. As a child, Gabriella wished to see the fabulous coastal city of Mazatlán during Carnival, the biggest carnival event in Old Mexico.

Mazatlán, across from the southernmost part of Baja California, is a thriving commercial seaport with gold and silver mines. French architecture is still part of many buildings in the center city, a reminder of the brief French rule. The festive season that occurs immediately before Lent is a public celebration that marks a change in life.

During Carnival, Mazatlán's celebration attracts thousands of people each year. One year, Gabriella and Adobe will be among the revelers, she wrote in letters to him after he had left Cuba. She wrote about a rendezvous to share the traditional circus-like events with costume parades, music and fireworks. Alas, the letters were not meant be sent.

Now she must see him in Mexico. Mazatlán is too far and there is little time; Juarez is closer and will have to do. It is too late for Carnival anyway. She hopes it will not be too late for Adobe.

51

All Possible Speed

The colonel has entrusted Adobe with a lifetime secret. There is no way of knowing if any other old soldiers from that mission survived to tell the tale. For now, all Adobe can do is wait for Murphy to head out to Chaco Canyon. Now it is a matter of finding and destroying the document.

Buster barges into Adobe's office with a message and shouts, "Sheriff Centori!"

"What's the rush, Buster?"

Embarrassed for reading the note, he shrugs and hands the envelope to him.

"Is there anything else, Buster?"

"No, that's it Sheriff. I better get going."

Adobe didn't argue. "Thank you."

Taking the hint, Buster leaves. Adobe, expecting word from Murphy, is surprised that the note originates from Mexico City. Intrigued, he stands and examines the twice-folded message. Unfolding the note, the shocking news freezes him. The words leap from the page as a dagger into his deepest emotional recesses:

Sheriff A. Centori,
Meet me at all possible speed in Juarez central plaza, Cantina Diablo, one week from the date of this message at 1 p.m. It is a matter of international urgency.
Gabriella Zena.

The note falls from his hand. Caught in a light breeze from an open window, it floats, spins, dances and takes several seconds to hit the floor. It is another lightning bolt from *La Guerrillera.*

Adobe takes his time returning to the Circle C. At the ranch, he goes directly to the library. Realizing that there will be little sleep tonight, he takes a cigar from the humidor and lights up. Puffing and contemplating the major turn of events, he wonders what destiny has in store.

Later, lying in bed sleepless, with the thought of new possibilities, Adobe listens to the songs of the coyotes. The coyote is a reminder not to become too serious, and that anything is possible. At times, the coyote complicates a situation more than needed. Adobe considers, *Am I too stoic? Am I am complicating what is simple? Is someone playing tricks on me?* The coyote, a way to self-examination, is an image of the wise fool.

It took a long time for Adobe to get to sleep last night. When sleep finally arrived, he dreamed of their first time together, holding her body close. After a restless night and before sunrise at the Circle C, Adobe pours his first cup of coffee, still obsessed with the unexpected telegram. Expectations fill his head as he strides outside to watch the mountains rematerialize from darkness. The sun reminds him of how the circle of her eyes inspired him to christen the ranch Circle C. A spectacular sunrise could light the way forward and decrease the burden of a big decision.

Meet her at Cantina Diablo. Ha, she never had a sense of humor. Why should I drop everything and go to Old Mexico after all these years? A matter of international urgency, she writes, but the telegram does not say she misses me, or that her heart is empty. I need to wait here for Murph to find the Revert Document. What could be more important? Juarez is over 300 miles away, but much closer than Cuba. Murph said the Cuban government might be involved, he thinks, as he views the sunrise.

Adobe spends the day preparing for the Chaco trip while agonizing over the decision between professional responsibility and personal imperative. *I guess no one expects their life to be turned upside down, but she may not be the same person I loved years ago—just a memory and a fantasy, not love, and not worth risking my integrity. I should forget Gabriella and a chance to renew our intimacy, and pursue the Revert Document.*

Alone in the Circle C library, he decides to reduce his thoughts to words and draft a response:

> *Dear Gabriella,*
> *I received your message about meeting you in Juarez. While I recognize the importance of the meeting, I am compelled to offer my reasons for not coming. My first instinct is to comply with your request. However, my professional responsibilities and the consideration of other people prevent me from meeting you at this time. Please know that…*

He crumples the paper and throws it in the fireplace. The crossroad is clear; the decision is not. Moving to the Victor Talking Machine, he places a record on the machine. The music of "Beautiful Dreamer" plays as he examines the bookshelves. *The mind shall banquet, though the body pine, the mind shall banquet, though the body pine,* he thinks while searching for a title. There it is—a copy of

Shakespeare's *Love's Labor's Lost.* The plot centers on King Ferdinand of Navarre. He and three lords agree to abandon the pleasures of the world, including women, for three years to pursue knowledge.

Adobe distrusts her heart, seeks her company, and continues to agonize. *Feelings are not right or wrong—they just exist and, unlike behavior, are uncontrollable. Risking emotional pain for the chance to have her again is a behavioral choice. As Shakespeare says, "Therein lies the rub."*

He reads the play, looking for but not expecting, an answer. After another restless night, he walks outside the library, waiting for his morning coffee to brew. It is twilight, that morning time when the sun is below the horizon and light from the upper atmosphere reflects toward earth. The diffused light from the sky slowly reveals the landscape. Little Hill Top, the high point of the Circle C ranch, is the first visible topographical shape to appear at daybreak

Something is different on Little Hill Top. Adobe sees a silhouette or a manifestation, causing a double take. The refracted light may be playing tricks on his eyes. As the light increases, so does the shape. He shakes his head and squints to focus his eyes for a second. Patriot stands on Little Hill Top.

Adobe throws his cup away and quickly walks, then runs to the proud stallion. Patriot is reluctant to return. The ashes of the horse barn are gone but the memories are not. Adobe whispers to Patriot.

Patriot has come home. Perhaps Gabriella will too—to take her place here at the Circle C, he thinks while leading the unbowed stallion down from Little Hill Top. Adobe will leave word for Murphy about an irresistible force—the Queen of Circle C.

52

CAFÉ DIABLO

The anxious American travels to Mexico, distraught at the past betrayal, but caught in a web of intrigue. The rail journey to El Paso, Texas, is without incident. Adobe arrives, secures accommodations and prepares to meet her again. At noon, he walks across the border to Juarez, a city filled with hectic activity, unlike Valtura.

She wrote about international urgency; for him it is a romantic rendezvous. Standing at Cafe Diablo in the central plaza, he reflects on her eternal magnetism and reads a journal entry he wrote on the night they met:

> She stopped me when the lightning bolt struck with all the power of Zeus. This flower was so grand and dramatically beautiful. Perhaps she walked a few inches above the ground—not even a whisper as she moved. Yet she could not hide her radiant beauty. All will change now and for all time.

His words from long ago compound an emotional reunion and speed up his thoughts. *For the first time since Cuba, Gabriella, how dreamlike. After ten years, how could there be any romantic urgency? Will there be anything left inside to protect; anything left to lose? Will I know the truth about Cuba and our star-crossed romance? What can I do differently this time? What about that pedestal thing? Angels belong in heaven, but she selects Café Diablo for their meeting. Flowers need water, yet too much water can drown a blossom. What to do with all that love,* he wonders while nervously waiting.

Suddenly, Adobe remembers her enchanting musk and its intoxicating power. That mysterious experience of attraction to a lover's scent was a wonderful part of her allure. Then his awareness of her natural perfume becomes vibrant.

"Adobe!"

In an instant, time, place and distance transcend the moment. They do not embrace and they struggle against emotion.

"Gabriella," he whispers while swallowing hard, realizing he had been standing in dumbstruck silence.

Maintaining an affectionate stare, she says, "You are still dashingly handsome."

"And you are as beautiful as ever."

Her eyes brighten; a smile extends across her face. Black Levis show a slender body and her wide-brimmed hat frames a still beautiful face. A large silver cross on a leather rope hangs around her neck.

"Thank you for meeting me," she says with a serious tone.

Thinking of their passionate lovemaking, he says, "It has been many years and I'm not sure why we are here."

"I am here for you."

"As you were in Havana Bay?"

Immediately regretting the comment, Adobe says, "I didn't mean that."

"You have a right to be angry, but don't look at me that way. Everything I did was for the good of Cuba." Her voice has an edge of sharpness.

"That's how you define good, but what about our love? I didn't see America or Cuba help *us* in our love."

"You do not mean that either," she scorns.

"But you sacrificed our love for the good of your country."

"As a strong nationalist, I have been true to my ideals."

"At least you placed principle over pay. Unlike the royalists, you fought without pay, but why must principle be the enemy of love?"

"Adobe, as an American patriot, you should understand."

"So we were always a forlorn hope?"

"I have defended myself *enough* for one day."

Adobe changes the tenor with, "Are you happy?"

"I am not entirely unhappy, but not fully content."

"I could be happy just to watch you sleep." The woman warrior almost swoons and he continues, "I don't really blame you for what happened between us."

Gabriella says nothing in response.

"You don't believe me, but it's true," he says. "I value freedom in myself and in others, but it still hurts. I adjusted to your change of heart or mind by evading emotion or sentiment. Nor can I blame you for the memories that haunt my every attempt to find love. All of my affairs come to hasty and ill-timed ends."

"There are many things you do *not* blame me for," she cannot help but laugh. "So I made you a stoic? I know you felt abandoned. It was hard for me too, but as I said, I have defended myself enough."

"I love you. The idea of you dominates my life."

"I love you too," she whispers.

"But just not enough," he responds.

"You should know something about that," she accuses.

"So I failed *you*. Is that how you see things?" he says with indignation.

Gabriella steps back and says, "Are we here to discuss *our* failure?"

"No, I made a long journey. Why *are* we here?"

"Adobe, I was sent to kill you."

He goes on high alert and prepares to defend his life. Adobe would die to protect Gabriella's life, but will act in self-defense. She has no apparent weapon; he holds his ground and waits.

"Instead, I want to save your life. That is why we are here."

"Stop. If you have a point, make it!" It is a rare moment of aggressiveness toward her.

She answers craftily, refusing to let him intrude into her explanation, "I will tell you everything," her voice becomes serene. "I know you are not married, but I am."

At this distressing disclosure, Adobe's heart sinks, his head drops, painfully aware of what this means, but waits for more information.

Seeing his dejection, she demands, "Listen to me. I gave up love and entered a political marriage for my country. Women in Cuba can fight but cannot be part of government, especially at high levels. I married the Cuban foreign secretary to Mexico to be involved in domestic and foreign policy. We have never shared a bed, never shared our bodies—not once."

Relieved, he says, "So you used love as a route to political power."

"I do not love my husband and it was my only route to political power. I am as good with policy formulation and implementation as our male leaders."

"You are as capable as anyone, Gabriella."

"Adobe, that is what I love about you most. *How* did you become this man who sees women this way?"

Smiling at her comment, he says arrogantly, "I am happy you followed your political ambitions, but was it worth giving up our love?"

"Sometimes you are a hopeless dreamer and then you express a practical, almost cynical side." She looks down and says softly, "I am in a loveless marriage. Are we both stranded without love?"

Adobe stares with a mixture of regret and pity.

She suddenly roars, "I can see it in your face. You condemn my choice but you would *not* easily choose love over country. As an Army veteran with medals, you would *not* be free of such a moral dilemma. Yes, I know about your war record, your Sea Ranch, your election as sheriff, your appointment as statehood delegate and your friendship with Mady Blaylock."

"It is called the Circle C. I named it for your eyes. And what in the world are you involved with?"

"A historical injustice brings me to Mexico. Love brings me to Juarez." She pauses to scan the area and announces, "New Mexico Territory should be claimed as the rightful possession of Old Mexico."

"The Revert Document," he states.

"They underestimated you, but do not underestimate them. Yes, the Revert Document."

"A historical injustice, maybe, but it is not worth another war," he defends.

"You can say that, Adobe. So far your country has won much of the Southwest."

"Many of life's questions are unclear."

"This is very clear!"

"Sometimes right or wrong supplants black and white issues. Gabriella, you know that Washington will not surrender the border territories and will resort to war. Is that what you want, another catastrophe?"

"It is worth a war because your country could continue to move the border south!" she yells angrily.

"Some things are hard to define. Do you begin your thinking with the end in mind? Why must there be useless waste of life for both countries?"

"Because Americans need a good challenge occasionally, to

check their imperialistic instincts and to keep the U.S. border from moving south," Gabriella asserts again.

"Damn you," Adobe replies. "Don't you believe in anything beyond your misguided political convictions?"

"Perhaps I believe in too much. Let me quote your own history, what we obtain too cheap is esteemed too lightly."

"That was American colonists speaking against British rule. Mexico is an independent nation."

"But for how long? At the end of the war, the *All of Mexico Movement* called for the annexation of all Mexico! Texas president Mirabeau Lamar wanted an empire and looked to Mexico. After failing to move the border south with a land purchase, he encouraged insurgents in the Rio Grande Valley to form a republic. Lamar also supported the rebels in the Yucatan revolt."

"All that was a long time ago—this is the twentieth century."

"Yes, so was Polk's attempt to purchase Cuba from Spain for sugar, molasses, rum, and tobacco profits, but old dreams die hard—and good faith from the U.S. can never be counted on."

"Mexico regained the Yucatan, Gabriella."

"Exactly, and we are prepared to do the same with New Mexico."

"That's an extraordinarily reckless position."

"It is a legal position," she quickly answers.

"But think of the consequences. Many object to war on moral grounds because it results in the deaths of innocent people. You may have an interest in pursuing your political goals through war, but justice is lost when innocent lives are lost."

"We have thought of it all. As you know, liberty is worth fighting for, Adobe."

"Are you willing to wait until January 1st to see if the border territories are states? On the other hand, are your associates intervening in the process to prevent statehood?"

"Mexico has the rule of law on her side."

"You did not answer my question. Yes, the legal issue favors Mexico, but will you corrupt the process?"

"I understand that you are not the only delegate to experience strange incidents."

She confirms a territory-wide conspiracy to delay statehood. Saddened by her admission, he says, "Once again, do we need a war to resolve this?"

"I am not certain the Revert Document will start a war."

"It already has, on the border, involving the 6th Cavalry!" He touches her face and says, "Can we forget about all this for one night? It hurts to replace our love with such antagonistic behavior."

Instead of answering, she turns to the middle of the plaza. A loud brass band plays music that they recognize. The familiar song, with great passion, makes them smile, dramatically changing the mood. Suddenly, there is no reason to explain anything; the music eclipses all concerns.

"You are right, allow me an hour," she whispers.

"Of course. I'll wait here."

She walks away and he watches every move until she is out of sight.

53

Sole Survivor

Madero ordered a small army of clerks to research the records in the Mexican Military archives. The archives clerks find two vaguely defined missions from the year 1861. One mission relates to a border region and one to the northwest part of New Mexico territory. Colonel José Bautista Alvarado commanded the northwest mission. Throughout the decades, some people have spoken the words Alvarado and Chaco Canyon in the same breath.

At the *Palacio Nacional,* Madero waits nervously for the report. It has been days since his order, and as time passes his doubts about the plan increase. Then, a knock at the door breaks into his thoughts.

"President Madero, they have the report for you," announces the secretary.

"Come in, come in," he says eagerly.

"Based on the archived papers, they think the Colonel Alvarado mission is most likely to be what you are seeking. They are also looking for any journals written by Alvarado. Here is the list of men."

"Thank you. Please stand by outside."

Madero reviews the list of men who rode with Alvarado and

eliminates any man over the age of thirty at the time of the mission. The youngest man was Captain Antonio Santos. The president rushes to open the door. The secretary, as ordered, is in position.

Madero demands, "I need to know if this Captain Santos is still alive."

"President Madero, they have taken the liberty of anticipating your orders and believe Santos is the sole survivor of the Alvarado expedition. They have identified a man of more than eighty years called Antonio Santos. He retired a colonel and is alive in New Mexico."

"Do we know if he is the same man?"

"We know he had army experience and served during the Alvarado mission."

"Do we know where in New Mexico?"

"Yes, he is in the Corona County town of Valtura."

54

NUEVO MÉXICO

Adobe waits at Café Diablo, wondering if Gabriella will return. Then he spots her wearing a plain white dress with puffed short sleeves that expose her graceful arms. She looks breathtakingly beautiful, reminding him of why she has been so unforgettable.

"You look beautiful."

"Thank you. It feels like we are back in Havana."

It is not a good sales approach, but Adobe admires the understated dress hemmed in embroidered red flowers that celebrates her profound femininity.

They were lovers and nothing can change their past. The only question relates to their future. They dine at Café Diablo on carne asada, a thinly sliced marinated flank steak served in tortillas, with rice and beans.

"Perhaps one day we can go back to Cuba, to that time you made me a better man."

Most women would say his time in Cuba had made him a worse man.

She reminisces about Havana. "We always met at *Plaza del Catedral* near the cathedral."

"I remember the stormy days at your house on Calle Vera Cruz."

Adobe smiles warmly and says, "We might even travel to Washington to see the Lincoln Memorial, if they ever finish the job."

"That will be an important trip for you."

It is the wrong response. He reaches a reluctant conclusion; she does not see a future together, at least not now.

The music is a welcome distraction.

"You still dance wonderfully, Adobe." She touches his arm and places her head on his shoulder, almost hiding the tear on her cheek.

"So do you," he says, feeling his heart come alive again.

After a few moments, he remembers how elegantly she a dances, floating above the ground. Her white dress flows stylishly as she turns to his movements. The red flowers at the hem spin with precision; Adobe's head spins with passion.

At midnight, they walk across the border to El Paso, over the bridge and to his hotel. Without a word, he takes her hand and opens the door. She trembles a little to hear the sound of the door closing.

"Welcome to the U.S." Adobe says.

"You mean Texas," she parries.

"You look a bit uneasy; it is because you are in the U.S. or is it me?"

"What's the difference?" she laughs.

They both needed to laugh. It provides closeness, as if nothing separates their two worlds. She looks around and sees the bed; he begins to light candles. She slowly moves to the window and gives him a slight smile.

"There is a nice view of the Rio Grande from here," she says.

After a pause, he approaches and says, "Let me look in your eyes for a better view."

Soft candlelight creates a relaxed atmosphere and allows them to sustain eye contact. Gabriella throws her arms round his neck. Their lips touch slowly, sensually and energetically. They kiss repeatedly, breathlessly. Adobe embraces her harder, pressing her closer. She releases a slight moan but pushes away.

Adobe stops kissing her, still staring into her eyes. Seeing her expression harden, he says, "Sometimes you are closed off to me, but then a ray of light escapes from your soul. It is at those times that I feel certain you love me."

She smiles and adds, "I have always seen your love shining with the affection you have for me."

"What's wrong?"

Gabriella's full exquisite lips part, but she says nothing. Then she says, "You look like you are reading my mind and feelings."

"Yes, I see that you wish to remember our trust and acquaintance."

"Adobe, intimacy needs trust."

"And trust takes time. I understand."

After a moment of silence, he offers, "You remember my friend John Murphy?"

"Yes, I do."

"He is the captain of the New Mexico Rangers. He suggested that manuscript copies of the document do not exist in the U.S."

"Destroyed, I am sure."

"I don't know about that."

"Adobe, since the turn of the century, manuscript copies in Mexico City have disappeared."

"Then perhaps the issue can disappear from our bed."

She agrees from tiredness, not conviction. They share the bed, engage in pillow talk and embrace. An hour later, they fall asleep in each other's arms. Two hours later, Adobe moves his hand over her sleeping body. She is in a loveless, unconsummated marriage and he is no ordinary man. When his hand comes to rest, she moves closer.

In the morning, Adobe delights in her irresistible, pretty hair spread on the pillow, but he fears that caressing her cheek might wake her. Instead, he stands quietly at the open window. A gentle breeze flows in from the river. *She will be soon brushing her hair with morning sunlight illuminating her beauty.*

She wakes suddenly. "Adobe. *Buenos dias.*"

"Gabriella," he smiles.

"How do you feel, having spent the night in America? It's not so bad," he jokes.

It was the worst possible choice of words.

"We are in Texas, *no es verdad*?"

The ominous partisan issue takes on new life on this day. She jumps out of bed, all business.

Seeing her action, he wonders about the wisdom of sharing confidential information, and says, "We should work together to resolve this issue, prevent war and have a future together."

"Would you like us to have a future in the Mexican Province of *Nuevo Mexico* at your Circle C?"

In an attempt to hide his disappointment, Adobe replies slowly, "Is that the only way for us?"

"Does the idea of *Nuevo Mexico* upset you?"

"No, the idea of war upsets me."

While dressing quickly, she says, "I must get back to Mexico City now. They will be anxious to hear of my trip."

"They will know soon enough. Please listen, I don't have complete faith in U.S. policy and I admit that U.S. ambitions are sometimes questionable."

"Sometimes? There is still work ahead of us. We believe that American agents were active in destroying copies in Mexico City—we intend to find the Revert Document elsewhere."

"So you insist on intervening in the process."

"You seem to be doing the same. You must admit, the U.S. has much at stake if the document is discovered before the deadline."

"Gabriella, can you be sure that this document and all that it means is the final goal of your associates? Will it be the end of the offensive?"

"Offensive? Adobe, you always were good at twisting an argument. I see it as *defensive*."

"This is not about winning an argument. You should question the motives of your friends in Mexico City, Gabriella. If I become a U.S. Senator, I swear on my love for you that I will work against any hint of American expansionism."

"You are such a dreamer," she sighs. "You think in terms of days and years rather than in terms of history."

"I don't understand you, but I could be in a position to influence U.S. foreign policy."

"A foreign policy with a long criminal history."

"Enough! Let me hold you."

She hesitates for a moment, but opens her arms for a tender embrace.

The power of last night's intimacy overwhelms Adobe's judgment. "Gabriella, I know where the Revert Document is hidden."

Excitement registers on her face as she exclaims, "Are you sure?"

"I learned of its location from an eyewitness." Too late, he wonders if he has misplaced his trust yet again.

"Where is it?"

"Do you wish to find it together?"

Her silence speaks volumes. He drops the question.

"I was leaving to find it when your telegram came. Your unexplained message forced me to come here."

"You put me before your duty. That is not like you."

"It may be irresponsible seeing you, but a few days should not matter," Adobe hopes.

"They sent me to kill you. I will report that I did. If they learn you are alive, you may not last long. Adobe, you will not be safe until all of this is over."

"Let me worry about that," he says sternly. "But you will be in danger for lying about killing me."

"Let *me* worry about that," she replies sternly.

She knows he will not reveal the location, but presses anyway. "If I find the Revert Document, you will be of less interest to them."

Adobe looks away. They have arrived at an impasse. She drops the subject, smiles, and says, "I loved our night together."

"You are the love of my life, *guerida.*"

"Te amo también."

Adobe takes this as hope and offers, "I know you have always had doubts about us, especially now. But why must this be our farewell? Perhaps we are drawn together again because it is our destiny."

"The Revert Document is my destiny."

"When will your life in the service of liberty be complete? The Revert Document provides a chance for bold action, or so you believe—but please see the void that exists."

"I will not be tamed, Adobe."

"Gabriella, I wish not to tame you—only to love you."

They leave the hotel and go to the river. Standing at the Rio Grande on the U.S. side of the border, she says, "*Vaya con Dios, mi corazón,*" averting her eyes.

Over the bridge and across the river she stops and turns around, hoping he will follow. Adobe is frozen in America.

Once again a lover's remorse, but this time it is no shock. He walks away and thinks of a verse from Shakespeare,

> *Two households, both alike in dignity,*
> *In fair Verona, where we lay our scene,*
> *From ancient grudge break to new mutiny,*

Where civil blood makes civil hands unclean.
From forth the fatal loins of these two foes
A pair of star-cross'd lovers take their life.

We may have more an emotional than substantive conflict. Her contradictory feelings about us, not politics, may drive her obsession with the Revert Document. I do not know if the price of patriotism is too high. Does it matter if the Circle C is in New Mexico or Nuevo Mexico?

55

FRIEND OF THE FATHERLAND

Jan Steiner startles Johan and Klara by forcefully opening the front door. He caustically says, "You are Johan Morgenstern?"

"Yes, I am, and you are?"

"I am Jan Steiner, German vice-ambassador to Mexico."

Impressed, Johan comes to attention and cheerfully replies, "You can call me Herr Morgenstern."

"I understand you are a friend of the fatherland, Herr Morgenstern."

"Yes, of course, Herr Steiner. I am a good friend of the fatherland."

"Then perhaps you can be of service to Berlin."

Turning to Klara, Johan says, "Will you excuse us?"

"What does he want, Father?"

"I will tell you later," he says sternly.

Klara flashes a menacing look and says, "I'll be downstairs in case you have a big story to print." She storms out, slamming the door behind her.

"Please forgive my daughter, Herr Steiner."

Steiner draws the window shades and instructs Johan to sit down. They speak in German. After some time, Steiner writes on a small sheet of paper, folds it in half and hands it to Johan.

"*Ich verstehen, Herr Steiner.*"

"*Es gut.*"

Coyotes often employ joint hunting techniques with an organized system of attacking prey. People sometimes use this type of cooperative energy.

56

Fourth Estate, Last Interview

After dark, Johan leaves the office and walks quickly across the plaza. The editor is always eager to interview, but this time there is urgency. He turns with caution from the plaza on East Corona Street, seeking to be unnoticed. Dark rain clouds help shroud his approach as he moves toward the colonel's house. Before reaching the gate, he takes a quick look around, and then knocks softly on the door.

It takes several minutes for the colonel to respond.

"Johan, why are you here at this hour?"

"I hope my arrival is not inconvenient."

The colonel, who had settled down for the evening, is not happy about the intrusion but reluctantly invites him inside.

"Thank you, Colonel. I am faced with a deadline for the newspaper."

"It is late in the day for an interview."

"Colonel, the statehood series in the Valtura Journal is very popular with our readers. You have been very informative in providing an extensive oral history of New Mexico's road to statehood."

"Yes, but why not wait until morning?"

"Please forgive me. There is more than a deadline."

"So what is your secret intent?" the colonel says with fatigue.

"I have learned about something extraordinary about New Mexico's past. It is most remarkable."

Becoming aware of the implications of the visit, the colonel says, "But why did you rush here now?"

Johan is blunt, "Colonel, are you familiar with the legend of the Revert Document?"

A silence fell between them.

"You came at this hour to ask about a legend?"

"Sometimes history and legend interconnect."

"I am not familiar with such a legend."

"This surprises me. You are an authority on New Mexico history."

"I have heard of the legend as part of tall tales," he replies.

"Some say you know the legend well," Johan presses.

"Placing too much credence in a legend can be foolish. Fabricated stories can cloud reality, creating elaborate conspiracies."

"But, Colonel, you are wise enough to know the true history, so you can be aware of a legend when you see one."

"We should be cautious of such things. Legends can be dangerous."

"Why dangerous, if it is just a tall tale?"

Santos knows he is in check and says, "What does this have to do with me?"

"Much."

"An editor is interested in simple legend? There is no evidence that confirms such a fiction."

"But the document could exist without evidence," Johan argues.

"This is starting to sound more like an interrogation than an interview."

"I am only pursuing the interests of a free press. I understand the legend is about a secret amendment to the Treaty of Mesilla."

"Then you understand more than I do," Santos answers with a disdainful expression.

Unconvinced, the journalist says, "You are contemptuous of my suggestion, Colonel."

"I am simply not used to late callers, but why are you probing? What reason can you have for wasting time with mere legend?"

"Colonel, I know you believe in a free press and the value of the fourth estate. Is that not reason enough?"

"It is getting late," the colonel says.

Becoming more animated, Johan straightens in his chair and says, "This is for our readers and the historical record."

"Historical record," the colonel echoes, "is that reason to abandon the statehood interview, in favor of a myth?"

"Is not the Revert Document about statehood?" His voice is unfriendly.

In check again, the colonel grimaces and demands, "What exactly is your interest?"

"Colonel, were you not a military officer with access to privileged information and involved with an important mission after the war?" Years of friendship fall away, as the colonel coldly stares at a new nemesis.

On the defensive, the colonel tries to deflect by saying, "Many times the adventurer's tales surpass the actual adventure."

Johan presses his advantage. "That may be right, but I believe you were involved and have important information."

"And who would be interested in such information?" the colonel questions.

There could hardly be a more dangerous admission. Johan takes the implication and says, "Many people would be interested in knowing where to find the Revert Document."

"I don't know. Do you really think it exists?"

"Colonel, I believe you mean to protect the old secret and your involvement in hiding the document."

"That is speculation."

"Listen closely." His tone is insolent. "I have no desire to force the issue, but I believe you can be instrumental in locating the Revert Document."

"And what would you do with it?"

"The document has great historical importance. You could be in danger."

The colonel stares coldly and says, "Danger? I don't understand."

"There are people who will stop at nothing to get the Revert Document. I want to help you."

"Help me? You have become ruthless. If it exists at all, it is something I will not tell, even out of fear!"

"It is time to reveal the secret. American agents are looking for it anyway. Would you prefer they find it first? I think you will help in unlocking this secret."

"What makes you think that?"

Johan reveals a German Luger and says, "This. You will answer me. Tell me where the Revert Document is hidden."

"Johan, is this really who you are? Is your purpose honorable?"

"My purpose is as real as is the legend. Where is the Revert Document?"

"What have they promised you—an important position in the new government of New Mexico?"

"Tell me," he demands.

"Your interest is imperialistic without concern for the Mexican people. European motives in North America are suspect. Even if you had principled reasons, nothing good could come from its discovery," he urges.

"Do not test me."

"You are not a murderer, Johan."

"True, but this would be a political assassination. I cannot fail my government in Berlin. They would be most disappointed."

The colonel reaches for his limited energy and explodes, "Your government in Berlin! That is a remarkable statement!"

Caught off guard, Johan allows him to continue.

"Are we not Americans with government in Washington?"

Johan does not respond.

"Oh yes, for the fatherland." The colonel takes the offensive. "It is clear that Mexico has far greater grievances with the U.S. than Germany. I have seen Mexico torn apart, broken in two. Yet I seek not to be an enemy of this country. My life here is good. Many Americans are my friends, and Adobe Centori," he pauses to cough back tears, "is like my son."

Since Steiner's visit, Johan has a new sense of self-importance. He counters the colonel's sentiment, "Germany has commenced a military buildup that will attract attention in Europe, particularly from the French."

The colonel interrupts, "What will your government do with such military power? Will you only to conquer Europe or will you seek to conquer us? The North American people have spent centuries pushing back against the arrogance inherent in empire."

"Colonel, Berlin only seeks to keep the United States out of European affairs. Since the Cuban war, we have noticed America's emerging power."

"Power only exercised in defense of this hemisphere," the colonel shouts.

"So far that is true, but will it always be true? We have proposed that Mexico, by means of the Revert Document, keep U.S. attention focused on this side of the Atlantic."

"Proposed to Mexico?"

"Germany has offered the Mexican government a military

alliance with generous financial and material support to press the Revert Document against Washington. So you see, the Revert Document is vital to Germany's plan."

"I have nothing to tell you."

"Once again, tell me where to find the Revert Document," Johan shouts.

"If you believe I know, what would you gain with murder? You can pretend to call it political assassination for the fatherland, but, remember, patriotism is the last refuge of the scoundrel."

"Enough!" Johan chambers a round and says, "You will tell me now. Where is the Revert Document?"

The colonel repeats, "What good is it to kill me?"

"It will prevent you from telling the Americans your secret and give them a chance to destroy it."

Too late, he has already told Adobe. But the colonel will not place him in greater danger.

"Last chance, where is the Revert Document?"

"I would rather die than tell you!"

The Luger discharges. Colonel Santos falls forward to the floor, mortally wounded. Johan bends to check the body and says, "*Ja fur das Vaterland.*" He conceals his Luger and flees. With his last speck of strength, the colonel pulls himself a few feet to the chess table. Reaching up with both arms, he sweeps across the middle of the chessboard and crumbles to the floor, each hand gripping two chessmen. The colonel dies holding four chess pieces.

57

ONE HUNDRED GREENBACKS

Since returning to her room from the infirmary, Mady's thinking has been blurred, but her decision is clear. Her unendurable ordeal accelerates her need to act accordingly—now is the time to escape the lunatic asylum.

Breaking out will certainly result in more trouble if Mady is unsuccessful. In the best case, she will endure increased examination. In the worst case, she will be thrown into the maximum-security cages, notorious for cruelty, with little more care than restraint.

Mady anticipates the risk, and factors it into her decision. Still bandaged and deathly pale, she sits alone in her darkened room, carefully examining the bag that was smuggled into the asylum. Reaching inside, she discovers an envelope with one hundred greenbacks, a note, and a gun. These items have put the odds in her favor. However, who can she trust?

Communication between inmates and staff is routine, but Mady seeks a far from routine discussion with *Señorita Valdez*. Mady, taking her first meal in the dining room since the attack, is on the lookout for *Señorita Valdez*. She showed concern when Mady arrived, and she could be trustworthy—Mady hopes.

58

THIS IS THE WORST

The rhythm of the rails comforts Adobe as he returns to Valtura filled with emotion. Seeing Gabriella supplants most of his thoughts, moving the bigger problems into the background.

The Valtura Rail Station is empty except for John Murphy, who is standing next to the red brick building near the 46-star flag with a grim look. There are two horses tied to the cast iron columns under the veranda.

The locomotive rumbles into the station with its whistle sounding loudly. Adobe bounds out of the first passenger car and says, "Murph, I am sorry about rushing off and delaying our job, but I saw Gabriella. You were right about Cuban involvement in Old Mexico." Adobe steps closer and says, "She talked about the Revert Document."

"Adobe, wait, I must tell you, it's Colonel Santos." He grips his hat in his hands. "He was shot and killed."

On receiving the shocking news, Adobe stares at Murphy. Then it hits him hard. He staggers forward, near collapse, and grabs the veranda railing for support. As he steadies himself against the railing, numbness replaces shock. Then a strong, sickening feeling in the pit of his stomach gives way to rage. Composing himself, he grasps the grip of his heavy Navy Colt and chokes, "Tell me exactly what happened."

Once again, the loud train-whistle blows, drowning out any communication. The few seconds seem like an eternity for Adobe.

"Buster saw his front door open early this morning and checked on him. I know this is the worst."

Adobe is unable to move as dreadful thoughts swirl within him. Then, a paragon of strength, he quotes from King Lear, "'The worst is not. So long as we can say, this is the worst'."

"It may not be the worst, but it is an intolerable act. Are you all right?" Murphy quietly asks.

"I will be. When did this happen? Who did it? Why?"

"We don't have all the answers yet."

They mount up and ride to Valtura.

At the end of the five-mile ride, they enter town on Junction Street and turn right on First Avenue. Passing National Street, Murphy points to the right. They pass the newspaper office and stop at the Union Hotel.

"Let's have a drink."

Adobe, still shaken by the colonel's death, nods his head and Murphy leads the way to a corner table. As usual, the service is quick.

The waiter flies over to their table and says, "Sorry about the colonel, Sheriff."

Adobe nods and Murphy orders a bottle of rye whiskey.

"Right away."

In seconds flat, the whiskey is on the table.

Murphy pours as Adobe says, "This happened while I was out of town. Perhaps I could have helped him."

"I don't know about that."

"Why would anyone kill him? It doesn't make sense…unless. Murph, I know where to look for the Revert Document. The colonel…." Adobe stops.

"You okay?"

"Yes. He told me it is hidden in Chaco Canyon," he whispers.

"How could he have known that?"

"Because he put it there!"

All Murphy can do is drain his glass and say, "That's a very big place."

"Let's talk more about it later in my office."

"Okay, but one thing. There was something interesting about the colonel's hands. He had chess pieces clenched in his fists."

"Chess pieces?"

"Yes. Grabbing the pieces was probably a reflex, his last act in this world."

"Or his last word in this world," Adobe says.

Murphy looks puzzled.

"Which pieces?"

"I don't know—Buster told me four pieces were in his hands. What's the difference?"

"Maybe nothing. On the other hand, it could be a clue to identifying the killer. I'm going over to the telegraph office now."

They down the whiskey, walk diagonally across the plaza on the double quick, and go into the telegraph office. Buster, so engrossed in reading the newspaper, takes a moment to look up.

"Interesting article?" asked Adobe, wishing to get his attention.

"Oh, I'm sorry, Sheriff. Captain Murphy. Yes, quite an interesting article." He missed the derision. "It's the series of articles on statehood."

"Statehood?"

"Yes, articles based on interviews with the colonel."

"Almost posthumously, you could say."

"We are all sorry about the colonel, Sheriff."

Adobe nods and says, "I understand there were chess pieces found his hands."

"That's right, Sheriff, just like I told the captain."

"Which pieces?"

"Well I think he had two of the smaller pieces."

"You mean pawns?"

"Yes and two large pieces."

"Were they kings, queens or bishops?"

"I don't remember."

"Come on, Buster, think," Adobe snaps.

"I don't remember. The king and the queen look alike to me. I believe there was a bishop."

"Where are the pieces now?"

"I placed them back on the table."

"Can you point them out now?"

"I don't think so."

"Do you have the last two issues of the Journal? I want to read the entire statehood series."

"Sure, they're right here," he says, gathering a stack of papers and handing them to Adobe.

"Thanks."

Adobe and Murphy walk to the sheriff's office to plan their trip to Chaco Canyon. *Chess pieces, a king or a queen and a bishop, a clue to the killer. A king is nobility, a bishop the church, pawns are commoners,* Adobe thinks.

That night at the Circle C library, Adobe reads the series on statehood, absorbing every word, unsure of what he is seeking. The colonel's knowledge of history is clear, but clues to his murder are not.

59

En Nombre del Padre

Although preparation for the Chaco Canyon expedition is compete and the journey has been outfitted, Centori and Murphy will wait a little longer. They will embark on the journey immediately following the funeral.

Most of the town is present at the Valtura cemetery for a simple affair. In the front, A.P. Baker flanks Adobe on the left, with John Murphy and Padre Morales on his right. Behind them stand Johan and Klara Morgenstern, James Clarke from the Union Hotel and Bill Brown from the Western Union office, along with many Valtura citizens.

After his comforting words, Padre Morales crosses himself and ends with these words, "*En nombre del padre, del hijo y del espíritu santo, Amen.*" He turns to his left and signals for the eulogy. Adobe, with sorrow in his face, clears his throat, looks toward the grieving crowd and offers,

"Fellow citizens, our beloved friend the colonel, as we all affectionately called him, is gone. All of Valtura will miss his presence on East Corona Street. We are here to remember a fine Christian man. No longer will I go to him for advice, wisdom or chess." He chokes back tears and presses on. "It is fitting that so many people are here, as the colonel was a dedicated friend to many. In John 10:11–18, Jesus said: 'I am the good shepherd. A good shepherd lays down his life for the sheep.' A hired man, who is not a shepherd and whose sheep are not his own, sees a wolf coming and runs away, and the wolf catches the sheep and scatters them. This is because he works for pay and has no concern for the sheep. 'I am the good shepherd,' Jesus said. Our friend was a good shepherd to people on both sides of the border.

"The news of his sudden death is unbearable and difficult to soften with any words. However, this is our time to celebrate his life, a great life as a heroic military officer, a great life as the kind of friend who stands by you. It is apparent that he touched…many with meaningful friendships."

Again, he chokes back tears and says, "When the colonel arrived in Valtura, he immediately fell in love with this town and he made it his home. I appreciated the chance to understand him through our many conversations. He could place things into proper perspective whether with a complex strategy or simply by saying 'This, too, shall pass.' We should all be grateful to have known this man and he will forever live in our hearts. That gives us solace.

"What is it that we remember most about the colonel? Is it his intellect, his kindness, his integrity? I think everyone who knew him would agree that it is his sense of caring about others. He helped everyone who came into his world by offering unwavering support. That is what we will truly miss.

"We loved the colonel for his words and actions on earth. I am sure that love will continue now that he has ascended to the heavens. If, as I believe, his spirit looks upon us, we would displease his soul if we were to forget his political and spiritual leadership. The colonel faced his adversaries with courage, and at times, reminded opponents of the right path, drawing them away from mistakes. A killer ended his life; the colonel entered eternity in a violent way."

Johan shifts nervously and looks down.

Adobe continues, "There has been enough violence and conflict in Valtura during the past months. Adversity can affect people's minds, but we must face any peril ahead in the way that our beloved friend taught us—with strength and confidence, standing behind any moral imperative.

"To me he was a great man, but he would wish to be known only as a good man. In that regard, there is no question. Colonel Santos, you came into the world with nothing and you take away nothing. As the Bible says, 'Naked I came from my mother's womb, and naked shall I return there.' The Lord gave, and the Lord has taken away. Blessed be the name of the Lord."

There are few dry eyes in the group as they slowly depart, leaving Adobe alone in front of a simple tombstone that reads:

ANTONIO SANTOS

1830–1911

RESTO EN PAZ

"You all right?" Murphy asks with empathy. He knows that a part of Adobe died with the colonel.

"Sure." Adobe takes a deep breath and says, "I just need a few moments here."

"I know it is hard to accept the end of your friend. Take your time and come to the hotel, where other friends are waiting. We will have a drink to the colonel's memory."

"Okay, go ahead. I'll be there soon."

Murphy walks away. Adobe raises his head, looks up to the blue sky and says, "Goodbye, my friend. I will bring your killer to justice. I swear by the eternal."

Valtura falls under a state of anticipation, knowing that Adobe will act soon. Adobe is not reckless, but everyone knows that Colonel Santos was like a father to him. For that reason, when he enters the hotel bar, silence falls over the room. Many think Adobe will blast the killer, once found, to kingdom come. Others think he will seek justice from within the constraints of the law.

Adobe finds Murphy, who is sitting with A.P. They have a round of drinks for the colonel, and then leave the hotel. All eyes follow Adobe out the door.

The men mount up and depart Valtura for the Circle C. Before they get too far, Klara runs from the newspaper office and calls Adobe's name.

"I'm not sure where you're going, but be careful," she says.

"Might be too busy for that, Klara, but I will promise to keep ducking."

"You are good at that," she quips. They both laugh.

Padre Morales appears from nowhere, looks at Adobe and declares, "*Vaya con Dios*, my son."

60

Sea Ranch

The next night, an attractive woman wearing a headscarf arrives in Valtura. Under the cover of night, she appears in a new Ford in front of Chez Beau Sharon. Stepping from the car, she pulls her shawl closer and quickly knocks on the locked door. The driver slowly drives on, disappearing from the plaza.

Inside, Sharon is drinking alone and annoyed at the interruption. She slams down her glass and storms to open the door. An imposing female stands before her with obvious confidence and says with a Spanish accent, "Are you Sharon Blaylock?"

A bit drunk, Sharon slurs, "Yes, I am Mademoiselle Sharon. Who the hell are you?"

By pure force of personality, Gabriella Zena-Marta moves inside, slightly brushes Sharon aside and states, "We have mutual friends in Mexico City."

Stepping back, Sharon gets the message. She knew that word of trouble in Valtura would reach Old Mexico.

"I said, who are you?"

"You can call me *La Guerrillera*. I have instructions for you and you are expected to accommodate my request."

"Oh, really? You're kind of bossy, Miss *La Guerrillera*!"

"Should I remind you about working for us, and not very well?"

"Listen, you can't come in my place and talk like that," Sharon protests.

"You are in no position to oppose me."

"What? I am the great Mademoiselle Sharon, beautiful, intelligent and charming. I attended Francine Fournier's salon in Santa Fe."

"*Loco en la cabeza*," Gabriella says, and shows a pistol under her shawl.

"What do you want from me?"

"I will stay here, out of sight. You will tell no one. That means I will take a room upstairs and wait. You will get two of your men to keep a constant watch on Adobe Centori."

"Centori is a horrible man. I guess we can work together."

"Yes, of course."

Even tacit approval of Sharon's comment causes a rush of pain for Gabriella, but soldiers deal with pain.

"We believe Centori will leave town soon. We *must* know his destination."

"He can go to hell for all I care," Sharon shouts.

"Miss Blaylock, you *will* care and so will your men. When he leaves town or his Sea Ranch, I want one man to report to me. The other will follow Centori. Wherever he goes, there our eyes will go too. Do you understand?"

"Yeah, I understand, Miss *La Guerrillera*," she mocks.

"Be sure to assign capable men—no more fools and don't bother to deny your incompetence. Now show me my room."

Sharon yells up to Jane, "Show Miss *La La* room six."

Known to have a taste of whiskey now and then, Jane is drunk but able to comply. She signals *La Guerrillera* to come upstairs.

"Can she be trusted to keep her mouth shut?"

"If you mean about staying here, then yes."

"Thank you."

Reacting to *La Guerrillera's* beauty, Sharon boldly asks, "Shall I bring up a bottle of tequila and two glasses?"

Firmly, she replies, "No. That will not be necessary, good night."

61

The Readiness is All

At the Circle C, Adobe and Murphy have dinner and drinks with A.P. Then Adobe breaks out fine cigars. An hour passes as the men discuss the cattle business and the future of New Mexico. The discussion inevitability turns to the day ahead. A.P. takes it all in and says, "You sure you don't want me along, Boss?"

"Come on, A.P., who is going to run the Circle C? Well, Murph, we should turn in. Things start early at the Circle C."

"Especially tomorrow," A.P. says. "Good night and good luck."

The next morning, Adobe brushes out Patriot's coat, checks his hooves and saddles him up. Then the two former cavalrymen and one packhorse leave the Circle C and ride out together. Although their army time was short, battlefield camaraderie created a lasting friendship that provides trust for the mission. As the men keep a northwest bearing, they watch the magnificent expanses of interlocking mountain ranges.

"Are you confident we know exactly where the Revert Document is?" Murphy asks.

"Now you ask?" Adobe jokes.

"It is a reasonable question," Murphy replies without humor. "Yes, I am confident. As Hamlet said, 'the readiness is all'."

On National Street, *La Guerrillera* has been ready for several days. She receives the report that Centori and another rider are on the move towards Santa Fe.

62

Race to Chaco Canyon

Adobe and Murphy stop in Santa Fe for one night before the big push to Chaco Canyon. Entering the Plaza Hotel, Adobe quickly notices that Dora is not at the front desk and is relieved yet disappointed.

After a few beers, they dine on roast beef, potatoes and corn tortillas.

Murphy feels that he has waited long enough. "Do you want to talk about her?"

"I sure don't," Adobe snaps, but adds, "Easy to remember, hard to forget."

"When I think of Cuba, I remember our regiment and the fine men."

"You are a good friend, Murph, and you're right about Gabriella. She has a special place in my heart and I think about her from time to time."

After dinner, the men go their separate ways. Murphy goes to his room and Adobe goes to the plaza, hoping that Francine is still in Santa Fe. She is not. Disappointed, he sits in the plaza for a while.

The next morning the men see Johnny Romano about the shooting of Sharon's henchman. They continue the seventy-mile journey into a vast landscape, determined to recover the Revert Document.

After three days of travelling, they approach Chaco Canyon close to sundown. Patriot, sensing the importance of the destination, slings his head slowly. Adobe checks his pocket watch; the temperature is dropping fast. The high desert can have extreme temperature swings in one day. The weather is fair, yet cumulus clouds fill the sky. They look like puffy cotton and can quickly develop into rainclouds.

The path they take is the same that Colonel Alvarado and Captain Santos used to enter the canyon fifty years ago. The canyon becomes wider as the two riders enter, and they stop at Pueblo Bonito. In the remarkable silence, they arrive at the same winding, narrow trail as their predecessors did, and they dismount.

After tethering their horses, Adobe says, "This path seems right. Let's get going, Murph."

"I'm right with you."

The men begin their search for the historical time capsule buried for decades. As they ascend, an uninvited rider surreptitiously enters the canyon.

They deftly climb the steep incline, stopping periodically to survey the area.

Halfway into the climb and a little winded, Adobe turns and says, "I hope the colonel remembered correctly. We must find and burn the document and then it will *really* be lost forever."

Murphy ignores the comment and stops for another breath.

Turning while wiping sweat from his brow, Adobe jokes, "Come on, move it, we are here to save the world!"

"I'm right with you."

The men continue their climb as the uninvited rider arrives at the base. Adobe senses something and turns abruptly.

"What is it, Adobe?"

"Nothing. Let's go."

"Okay, but you're the one who stopped."

At each flat area, the men scan for the right petroglyph on the right kind of surface. The colonel's instructions are clear and include a sketch of the mark of the coyote.

Almost an hour passes in silence, then Adobe raises his hand, signaling Murphy, and says, "This area shows the most promise, look at all the markings."

"Are you sure this is the place?" Murphy asks.

"I'm confident that the Revert Document is in Chaco Canyon—somewhere. I'm sure about the colonel's description, but Chaco in an unsure place. Some feel there are powerful forces here."

"Do you mean natural or supernatural?"

The strange feeling returns. "I don't know, but this could be the place. The colonel was a reliable source. I'm certain we will the document."

At that point, a howl in the distance shatters the quiet. Adobe turns toward the direction of the sound and right there his eyes catch a sketch in the sandstone—an image of a coyote. At times, a coyote can compel people to see connections to nature—if they are open to see them at all.

"Over here. The colonel said to look for markings depicting a coyote covering the hiding place," he says, pointing to the sketch. He smiles, nods at Murphy and says, "This could be it."

The men barely notice the dark clouds that formed throughout the climb. Now they ignore the drops of rain that suddenly fall, breaking the profound silence of Chaco Canyon. The ascent started in sunshine, but cumulus clouds, that can create sudden atmospheric changes, are growing.

Adobe carefully tries to shake loose the tightly wedged rock, without success. He draws his Arkansas toothpick, begins to trace the edge of the covering stone, then picks, and pries.

"Don't break that blade on that stone."

At that moment, Adobe's only concern is about breaking up the likelihood of war, so he keeps working the blade. He returns the knife to its sheath and shakes the rock again. The rock starts to move and small stones fly out of the dark recess.

Then another coyote cries as the entire cover comes free. For the first time in fifty years, light touches the time capsule. There it is. Now, as it was then.

There is a low rumble in the distance and the temperature begins to drop. Ignoring the thunderhead activity, Adobe slowly pulls out the dusty, thin metal box. Reaching inside, he finds the black leather document case. The diplomatic pouch within contains a manuscript copy of Article X of the Treaty of Mesilla—the elusive Revert Document. He works the flap over buckle and stares at it for a moment, and then says, "This is it, Murph." The old parchment transfixes Adobe, who finally says, "Here you are, the Revert Document."

Raindrops turn to a light steady rain and it is getting colder. Murphy says, "We found it. What now?"

"As we planned, we burn it and save hundreds, if not thousands, of lives."

"And save New Mexico for the U.S.," Murphy adds.

"Spoken like a true New Mexico Ranger, Captain Murphy. Yes, and save New Mexico for the Union."

The men laugh as Adobe struggles to light a cigar against the increasing rainfall, in preparation for burning the Revert Document. He kicks a shallow hole in the wet ground and says, "Murph, give me the manuscript so I can erase some history."

"No, that will not be needed," says a woman's Spanish-accented voice, from behind a cocked rifle. "Hand the case to me so I can *save* history," she says, standing on a jagged ledge above the men.

Adobe stops dead in his tracks and stares. Murphy gives a quick frown and a twitch of his mustache.

Swallowing hard and touching his Navy Colt, Adobe says, "What the hell are you doing here?"

"Don't be so surprised. I think you know."

Murphy places the Revert Document in his shirt and reaches for his service pistol. Adobe's shocked expression turns stoic as he motions silently for Murphy to stand down. During times of crisis, the men have come to rely on their complete trust in each other. Murphy complies and, in a rare moment of emotion, says, "A mistake. You never left Cuba in Cuba."

It was a mistake to trust her again. He has always moved toward her with his heart, not his head.

"Gabriella, you followed me. You need to create a war."

"And you are here to keep New Mexico for America," she says, revealing contempt for his cynicism.

His pulse races and his stomach tangles as he says, "You never did anything halfheartedly and always understood the importance of timing. I trusted you. How could I mean so little to you?"

"You will never understand. You want to see your country as good, without bad or immoral impulses," she shouts through the cold rain.

Adobe looks at her rifle. Then he turns to Murphy, conveying a calm message, and says, "A nation's strengths and weaknesses are inseparable. You are unreasonable and exaggerating rather that resolving our differences. Your shortsighted tactic will cost many lives."

"I am not a warmonger."

"I believe you, but what of the war in your heart? Affairs of the heart can cloud judgment. Are you expressing what's deep inside you, a conflict about our love?"

"*Ay Dios mio*, you flatter yourself," she responds, as the temperature dropped again. "My action here is *not* about you."

Murphy turns away from a private lover's moment, remaining at the ready.

"Gabriella, whatever is driving you to this reckless act, there is more at stake than the problems of two people. Perhaps you are acting from pride, forcing your position to prove you are right about the U.S."

"Does not history support my position?"

"If you see all things as a freedom fighter, then judging America becomes more important than love."

Adobe knows his words are melodramatic, but they feel natural. Waiting for her reply, his eyes dart from her eyes to her trigger finger.

The light rain turns to a heavy shower. Raising her voice over the cascade, she says, "You are a decent man who knows little about the world. Are you unaware of the American conquest of the Southwest as part of your country's *benevolent* destiny? Let me cite your history—if they mean to have war let it begin here."

"Emotional obstacles are blinding you from the truth, but one thing is completely visible—the ultimate truth is found in saving lives. We must destroy this document."

"No, we find our truths differently. I see it through conscience and courage, not sadness or anger about our romance…my love for you is true."

Adobe takes a step forward. A long, low rumble in the distance signals a sonic shock wave made by lightning.

Gabriella tenses and her heart pounds. "Stop there. If you move closer, I will fire," she warns.

Adobe zeros in on her trigger finger. *She could never shoot me.* He believes it with every atom in his body. Murphy's heart skips a beat, hoping Adobe knows what he is doing.

He takes another step closer. She retreats from his advance and loses her footing on the wet ground. Once she recovers, Adobe implores, "Please, let's find shelter from the storm and away from this danger."

Ignoring his plea, she yells, "Let the American people see the legal truth."

"Has the U.S. failed the people in the border territories?"

"You place too much faith in the U.S. structure."

Watching with wary eyes and seeking to find common ground, he argues, "That may be true, but do you want a final frantic act between us?"

"*Mi corazón*, the danger lies in your country's Manifest Destiny ideology. You think this continent and maybe the entire hemisphere is a divine American right."

"I don't think that way."

"But your government does," she shrieks.

"So you have your justification, but I have the Revert Document."

"That is why I am here."

Heavy showers increase the danger as torrents of rain make their words almost impossible to hear. All three are soaked through and brace against the storm.

Adobe yells, "Your plan will lead to hostilities; this document will lead to another war between the U.S. and Mexico."

Reaching an inevitable conclusion, she replies, "That's up to you and to the government in Washington."

"You are willing to risk another war?"

"That never stopped me before, *este soy yo*."

With illusions of compromise gone, Adobe asserts, "Perhaps it is my destiny to stop a war."

Then Gabriella declares, "*Mi corazón*, perhaps it is my destiny to start a war."

A long, low rumble in the distance sounds closer. The sound of thunderclaps strains the already stressful encounter.

"You are flirting with war. We all have our fate and that force can motivate us beyond reason."

"Reason depends on perspective and how we interpret destiny."

Lightning bolts continue to heat and expand the air, causing stronger sonic shock waves. The sound of thunder is closer, with sharp, loud cracks.

"Gabriella, we have been lost to each other and brought together again. The men in Old Mexico have their reasons for sending you. But this play is not your destiny."

"And you know what destiny intends for me?" she questions sarcastically.

Before he can answer, more thunderclaps shake the world, this time upsetting Gabriella's footing. "Please move away from the edge!" Adobe screams.

He wipes the cold rain from his face and sees her body language change, suggesting an opening for persuasion. He does not answer her question directly and instead says, "Our conflict can be a meeting point between two hard choices." Feeling anger turn to longing, he continues, "Did I love you enough? Could any man love you enough?"

"You loved me well, Adobe." Her features soften. "I know you care very much about me. I love you for your affection and strength, but I cannot love what you stand for."

"And what do you stand for? A simple solution?" Adobe adds with heightened concern. "The world is more complex than you realize. There are many perspectives. Look, we are all imperfect beings and countries are imperfect too. We are human and not always great in understanding complicated situations. Nevertheless, this Revert Document could lead to disaster—that is clear."

The sharp cracks are louder, almost deafening.

"Gabriella, sometimes I can't get close enough to you. I know you feel my efforts to hold you as tight as possible—to be one with you, to celebrate being in love with you."

If not for the gravity of the situation, Murphy would have blushed. He tries to ignore the passionate words while watching for the danger that charged emotions can present.

Suddenly, a high-pitched coyote cry startles Gabriella and she again loses her footing on the wet rocks. She steadies herself, still holding the rifle, but it causes a brief dizzy spell.

"Move away from the edge!" Adobe screams again.

Recovering from the slip she yells, "Give me the case!"

Abruptly, piecing the rainstorm noise, another high-pitched coyote cry jars Gabriella, causing a catastrophic slide on the slippery rocks. She falls over the ledge, but manages to grasp a few jagged rocks. Frantically, she looks for a foothold but there is none. It is a sheer drop of over two hundred feet.

Adobe recklessly lunges forward, reaching to save her life. With adrenaline pumping he tightly grabs her left hand and pleads, "Hold on!"

Fully extended, he anchors his right hand into the rocks and struggles for her wrist. The rifle falls, crashing on the rocks below. He screams to Murphy, who is already extending, trying to reach the entwined hands—too far. Murphy scrambles to the other side of Adobe to reach her hand clinging to the rocks—too far.

The rainstorm turns violent, with heavy winds and booming thunder from every direction. Dangling by her fingers, she desperately tries to secure her right hand to the wet rocks. Frantically, Adobe tries to improve his grip, but she is slipping. His last chance is to pull her up, to heave as much as he can—sweat pours from all over his body and rain soaks his clothes. His grip is failing. Blood flows as the sharp rocks rip at their hands; the rain quickly washes it away. They are immune to the physical pain; helpless, he yells, "Hold on, don't give up. I never gave up on you. I always loved you."

"I loved you, too; more than I expressed."

"I would have done anything for you."

"No…not anything," she says, struggling to speak as the strength slips away from her body.

Adrenaline in the face of depleted strength is limited and she has little power to hold on any longer. With her energy drained, her hand slips from his. One second…two, then three. For an instant, she appears to defy gravity and float in the air. It could be the strange wind patterns at Chaco Canyon or it could be a projection of his angelic image of her. After all, an angel has wings. Suspended in midair, she grasps the silver cross that hangs around her neck and without a word of farewell falls to her certain death.

The hard rain continues to fall, tears fall, and Adobe falls to the ground horrified, wailing over the lifeless body in the depths below. Murphy stands speechless, eyes fixed on Adobe, and then he grabs him around the shoulders, fearing he will follow Gabriella by accident—or intention. A primordial scream bounces off the canyon walls. The guttural shrieks alert the coyotes, who answer with their own mournful chorus, accompanied by the surging rain.

Pulling him from the edge, Murphy taps his jacket pocket, looks down at the hard rain pelting Gabriella's body and says, "Yeah, there's your Revert Document." He regrets his words. Blind obsession to a grand conspiracy condemned her to this horrible ending. She was a warrior to the end, focused on the Revert Document, not love.

He drags Adobe several yards past an enclosed rocky area of an old city wall and into a small cave. Adobe clutches his tight chest and starts choking.

"Adobe.... Adobe!" Murphy struggles to prop him up in a better position.

He stops choking, but now has shortness of breath and his muscles are weak.

In a few minutes, Adobe regains his composure but does not open his eyes.

"Are you okay?" Murphy says gently.

Unable to speak, Adobe waves him away.

Murphy starts to bring out the Revert Document, which is still in his shirt—but now it is too wet to burn. A loud roar blends with the explosive thunder and abruptly stays his hand.

Large rocks crash down from above in front of the small cave, bouncing off the meeting area and rolling off the cliff. The men are out of harm's way, but the rockslide is covering her body. Then it stops as abruptly as it started.

"She is gone." Adobe barely gets the words out.

The rocks buried *La Guerrillera* in an unmarked grave in some far away, forgotten place.

63

Mady Rides Again

Nurse Denton makes her rounds. Mady waits, ready to have her day. The sadistic nurse stares in the small door window, pleased to see Mady in a fetal position, moaning in agony on her narrow cot.

"Shut up! Do you want to disturb the other guests?" she shouts.

Mady answers with louder moans. Predictably, this response causes Nurse Denton to enter Mady's cell to assert her authority. "I said, 'Shut up!'"

"I'm sorry. I'm dreadfully upset."

"Everybody's upset here," scolds Nurse Denton.

"My head hurts so much. This bandage is so tight," Mady moans.

In a rare moment of compassion, Nurse Denton leans in to adjust the bandage. Mady promptly smacks her in the head with the gun butt. Exhilarated, she says to the fallen, numb nurse, "How does it feel? Are you speechless? That is a first. Now you know *why* they call me Mad Mady."

She ties Nurse Denton with strips of torn sheets and stealthily leaves the room. She carefully checks right and left—clear in both directions. Now she seeks *Señorita Valdez.* It does not take long. As agreed, she is at the head of the corridor.

Valdez says with trepidation, "*Sígame por favor rápidamente.*" (Please hurry.)

Mady follows her outside the madhouse, where a large black mare waits in the shadows.

Valdez says, "*Aquí está su caballo.*" (Here is your horse.)

Mady says, "*Aquí está su dinero.*" (Here is your money.) She hands Valdez one hundred dollars.

Taking charge, Mad Mady Blaylock mounts up, ready to ride. She starts at a slow pace, then quickens and once at a safe distance from the asylum, she prods the mare into a trot. With the madhouse fading from sight, she breaks away in a full gallop and heads south. She reaches the lake and sees a tree with the letter C carved into the trunk and dismounts.

Wildly moving brush around, she finds a saddlebag containing clothes and boots. In seconds, Mady pulls on blue pants, a red shirt and a blue vest. Her trademark brown hat with a flat round brim and a flat round top is back on her head. She pulls the leather cord tightly under her chin.

Ready to resume the charge, Mady rides again. Galloping through New Mexico's land of enchantment, she ignores the environment and remains fixed on her destination. Adrenaline and a powerful horse propel her into the distance. Racing so fast, Mad Mady holds her hat with one hand to prevent it from flying away. Running at dangerous speeds, determination, not fear, is in her face.

64

Little Hill Top

It is possible that a coyote can teach humans to see death within life as a chance for rebirth. The magic of creation involves learning to use the cycles of life, the highs and lows to advantage. Humans tend to think that lows are not useful. The coyote could be a good teacher for Adobe, but not now. Adobe's world has changed. Now there is nothing for him except emotional pain. Today he finds a measure of comfort by sitting on Little Hill Top, immune to the cold winds of late autumn.

Adobe, inconsolable, feels dazed and guilty for not saving Gabriella. He stares at the mountains, angry about her irresponsible actions for a reckless cause.

Since returning to Circle C, he has had trouble sleeping, eating, concentrating and making decisions. He has given orders not to be disturbed. Even so, A.P. ventures to Little Hill Top on the second day.

"Boss, are you coming down later?"

Adobe shakes his head. The inquiry had broken in on his dark mood.

"Are you coming down today?"

"No."

"Are you ever coming down off this hill?"

Adobe ignores the attempt at humor and waves him away.

"Boss, you need more than fresh air. Come on; let's go to town for some chili."

"I thought I gave orders not to be disturbed. To be left alone."

"Yes, you did, but for what—to protect your solitude and sorrow?"

"A.P., I am wretched and as low as a man can get. I should have given her the Revert Document."

"Listen, I know you're grief-stricken. You can't change the past, but you can change your future. So deal with your loss; deal with your life, too. I can't imagine your pain. After holding on to a dream for so long, a tragedy ends some things, but not all things."

Adobe looks up, finally able to make eye contact.

A.P., sensing an opening, goes on, "Yes, not all things. You have the Circle C, and your position in Valtura, in the county, and in Santa Fe. Most everyone in Valtura embraces and respects you. They're ready to help you during this time of bereavement. Boss, you're a highly respected man. Women want to be with you, and men want to be your friend."

Men want to be your friend.

Those last words resonate with Adobe. At the colonel's grave, he made a solemn promise: *Goodbye, my friend. I will bring your killer to justice.*

A.P. continues, "And don't forget about statehood and your next trip to Santa Fe. You are expected at the capital on the fourth."

Adobe looks up. "What did you say?"

"You have a meeting in Santa Fe."

Following a period of silence, Adobe says, "Yes on the fourth… do me a favor, A.P."

"Sure, what is it?"

"Saddle up Patriot."

"Yes sir. Good to have you back."

Adobe rides hard to Valtura. The stallion races as fast as he can. So does the rider's mind. *I still don't know which chess pieces the colonel had in his hands. A king is nobility, a bishop is the church and pawns are commoners, but the colonel's message may not be about the killer's social position. It may be the quantity of the chess pieces. He held four pieces. Did he mean the fourth estate in reference to the press? Oh God. Johan had been visiting the colonel right up to the day he was killed. This is unthinkable, but I must go where logic leads me.*

Adobe arrives at the newspaper office. It is too early for Johan and Klara to be at work, yet the door is ajar. He enters, quickly looks around and sees the basement door is wide open. He walks down the steps and comes to a shocking and abrupt halt. Johan's body is slumped over the printing supplies, which are soaked with blood. Sometimes the sword is more powerful than the pen.

From across the plaza, Buster sees Adobe rush into town on Patriot. Entering the building, he calls out, "Sheriff, what's going on?"

Adobe, staring down at Johan's body in abhorrence, yells, "Come down."

Before Buster can reach the last step he exclaims, "Oh my God!"

Kneeling over the body, Adobe is staring at the colonel's watch with its image of a coyote and the initials CC engraved into its case.

"What happened?" Buster asks.

"He was murdered."

"Murdered? Why? Who?"

"I don't know, but he was shot at close range, just like the colonel. It says in the Good Book that the measure you give out, that same measure shall be given out to you."

He was a decent and hardworking man," Buster says.

"At least hardworking; I believe Johan killed the colonel."

"What? That is outrageous!"

Killed for not revealing the secret of Chaco Canyon, Adobe thinks, and says, "I'm not sure."

"What do we do now, Sheriff?"

"Wait outside and don't let Klara inside. Send her to my office and then deal with his body."

When Klara arrives, Buster takes her to Adobe's office and then leaves.

"What's going on, Adobe?" Klara looks concerned.

"Sit down, Klara—it's your father."

"I know he worked late last night and sometimes he stays at the office. He did not come home, and…."

"Klara, wait. Your father has been shot. He's gone."

"What? No! It can't be true!" she screams and collapses in Adobe's arms.

"I'm sorry, Klara."

Adobe refrains from accusing Johan of murder, but says, "Has there been anything unusual going on at the office lately?"

Klara is unresponsive.

"We can talk about it later," Adobe offers.

"There was an unusual visitor, a man with a heavy German accent. My father sent me away, but I heard them speaking in German."

"What was his name?"

"I don't know, but my father said to him, '*Call me Herr Morgenstern,*' before I left."

"Herr Morgenstern," Adobe repeats.

The night before, Johan, working late on *Freedom*, was having second thoughts about the wisdom of his actions on East Corona

Street. Ironically, his magazine's political philosophy was the polar opposite of the German government's bureaucratic structure. His willingness to help the fatherland discover the Revert Document suggests a personal conflict.

To Steiner and Hietmann, he is an abject failure. Steiner entered unannounced with a tense demeanor.

"Herr Steiner, what are you doing here?"

"I think you know. We discussed how your interviews with the colonel would be a natural way to extract the information we needed. But you failed to locate the Revert Document and engaged in a killing. All is lost for us."

"Herr Steiner, I assure you, it was self-defense."

"Self-defense against what?"

That night, Klara paces her house, obsessed with her father's death and his admonishments to her about women and guns.

65

MAD DASH

Mad Mady Blaylock rides through the colorful mesas and mountains that are unnoticed by the fast rider. On the second day, the swift sister reaches the Jemez Mountains, where ancient lava flows had created striking red rock mesas. She is close to Valtura.

Moving through the forested wilderness, rocky peaks, streams and waterfalls, Mady comes to the Pueblo of Jemez. The Pueblo is an independent sovereign nation. On any other day, she would have stopped for their famous Indian fry bread—but not on this day. Today, she continues her mad dash to Valtura and her saloon.

She rides past Linden Lake and close to the Circle C. With the ranch in view, Mady wonders if Adobe would mind an unannounced visit to his precious Circle C. It does not matter; she is bearing down on Valtura.

Mady stops at the top of a low hill and sees Valtura in the distance. The old familiar rectangle plaza and the surrounding buildings, including Mad Mady's Saloon, are a welcome sight.

66

Long Overdue Intervention

It is early morning in late fall and the cool moonlight is deceptively peaceful around the Circle C. The air is thick with tension as Adobe, A.P., and John Murphy wait to confront Mademoiselle Sharon and her co-conspirators. Any further delay would work against the interests of justice. Accordingly, the men ready themselves to invade the place they still call Mad Mady's Saloon.

Blackstone is back. They believe he will meet Sharon at Chez Beau Sharon after closing time. The time has come for a long overdue intervention. At 2:15 a.m., the men ride from Circle C to Valtura for a rendezvous at Calle De Valtura, one block north of Corona Street and away from the plaza. They arrive close to 3:00 a.m. and wait for Lieutenant Montero and his men.

A few minutes later, Montero and two rangers enter Valtura on horseback and join the other men to prepare to strike. They approach the target on foot with caution and encircle the building—Adobe, A.P., and John Murphy at the front door and Montero and his men at the back door.

They burst in with revolvers drawn. From upstairs, Sharon sees the action and rushes up to her room. Blackstone and four men are at a center table in the saloon. The invaders place themselves at a strategic distance, enveloping Blackstone's table.

"Bill Blackstone, you are under arrest for the killing of Berta Brandt. Surrender your firearm," Adobe demands, with his Navy Colt at the ready.

Blackstone snarls, "You found me, now come and get me."

Adobe announces, "Do it now or I will send you to hell."

Blackstone answers with hot lead, firing wide. His men jump up, draw revolvers and fire. Adobe moves sideways, shooting as he moves. Blackstone and his men fire their six-shooters, wounding A.P.

Adobe stops moving to his right and fires a shot that rips through Blackstone's chest. Montero's shots find their mark, hitting one of Blackstone's men in the chest. The man falls, badly wounded. Then Montero, hit in the leg, reels, stays up, and steps back, still shooting, hitting his target in the head. The man slumps over dead. Murphy and the two rangers surround the two remaining men and point their guns at the men's chests. It all happened fast—a fusillade of bullets, rapid close-range fire with men blasting shots in seconds.

When the gunfire stops, Adobe goes over to A.P. "You all right?"

"Sure, it's just a scratch."

Then he looks at Montero who signals that he is okay. The others rangers are fine, but Murphy is hurt badly. Adobe turns in the direction of one of the rangers and says, "Get help!"

Adobe leans over and says, "Hold on, Murph, we're getting help."

"I could use some right now."

From the second-floor railing, a Winchester aimed at Adobe is ready for killing. Sharon, who watched the gunfight from the shadows, is a second from pulling the trigger, but before she can, a pistol bullet hits her leg. Sharon collapses and is stunned when she looks up at the shooter, "Well look at what the coyote dragged in." Her voice drips with mockery.

"It's nice to see you too, Sister." Holding her leg but showing no pain, Sharon continues, "Welcome to Chez Beau Sharon."

"This is Mad Mady's Saloon!"

"Sorry, Mady, *Nous avons changé à une vie plus aisée ici.*" (We have gentrified the premises.)

"Who do you think you are, Madame Defarge? What do you know about running a saloon anyway? You've always wanted what I have. It was *never* enough for you to succeed; I had to fail. This time you found a way to do both at the same time. At least you think so! But think again, Sister. You are through."

"Oh, Mady, can't you handle a little sibling rivalry?"

"What? Are you forgetting murder and mayhem? You had me forced into the insane asylum and you stole my saloon."

Holding her bleeding leg, Sharon says, "The way you treated me, you should expect some repayment."

"Liar! And God knows what else you've done—it took every ounce of willpower not to aim my gun higher!"

"Calm down, Mady, you're hysterical."

"Hysterical? Hysterical? I'm not hysterical!" Mady screams at the top of her lungs.

"Mady," exclaims Adobe, as he and two rangers reach the top of the stairs, "How did you get out?"

"I overstayed my welcome and got tired of waiting for you!"

"Glad to see you back upstairs, Sheriff." Sharon says caustically.

Mady looks at Adobe; he turns to the rangers, "Get her the hell out of here."

Adobe and the two rangers came through the gunfight without a scratch. However, A.P. was shot in the arm, Murphy was hit in the shoulder, and Montero was grazed on the calf. Blackstone died where he fell with a mortal chest wound. One of his men, shot in the abdomen, was fatally injured and bled out, one was killed instantly and two men capitulated. Thirty minutes after the shoot-out, with the wounded, prisoners and dead bodies removed, Adobe sits with Mady.

"I am indeed glad to see you, Mady."

"Thanks, and for the first time, I'm *sure* you mean it."

Adobes smiles and says, "I thought you didn't like guns."

"I got over it."

Jane finds the courage to leave her room. She comes to their table and says, "Miss Mady, I'm sure glad to see you back."

"It's good to be back. Where's Berta?"

Jane looks down at Adobe.

"What is it?"

"Mady, Berta was killed. She defended you and paid for it with her life."

Mady breaks down in tears and Adobe hopes she doesn't ask about Mercy, at least not now.

"Berta's death and your abduction was part of a much larger plan. At the center of the plot is an old paper called the Revert Document that provided for the return of New Mexico and Arizona to Old Mexico."

"Revert Document? I only know that this saloon will revert to *me* starting now! But Old Mexico, I told you Sharon was there."

"She was involved as a government agent for Old Mexico."

"An agent for Mexico? That is shocking. I underestimated my sister."

"She and other agents tried to delay statehood by influencing delegates."

"Influence or seduce?"

"I'm no fool."

She stares and wonders, but drops her question.

"Mady, the colonel is dead. We believe he was killed for not revealing the location of the Revert Document."

"Oh, no, Adobe, I'm sorry to hear that. I know you were close. Who did it?"

"Brace yourself. I believe Johan Morgenstern killed the colonel."

"Oh my God! Have you arrested him?"

"He's dead too, killed by an unknown assassin."

"I *have* been gone a long time!"

"Klara may be in some kind of danger, so I have a man watching her house and following her to the Journal office—at a distance. I don't want her to know about it."

"Of course, you wouldn't want to upset her sensibilities.... Sorry."

Adobe offers no response.

"Sorry, how is she?"

"She's still grieving her father's death, but she's putting on a brave face. There's more. I went to Juarez to see an old friend—the woman in the photo."

"What? That's why you never returned to help me. Why did you ever..."

"Wait, Mady, she's dead. She was involved with powerful forces in Old Mexico."

Mady shakes her head to process the news and does not know what to say, but finally asks, "What happened?"

"I'll tell you another time." Adobe lowers his head. "We're going to the Territorial Insane Asylum for their day of reckoning."

"Good. There are at least two other women wrongly committed, including Kentucky Woman, who may have betrayed me."

"Kentucky what?

"Kentucky Woman, Lilly Sheldon. You knew her husband, Lane Sheldon of Bernalillo County. He was killed."

"Yes, we thought that was a random unsolved crime."

"I told you about women being held for killing their husbands. Well, his wife is there for murder."

67

LAST ACT AT THE ASYLUM

Three days later, Adobe, County Sheriff Manny Rodriquez, and two deputy sheriffs are ready to act against corruption. They intend to end the evil activities of the Territorial Insane Asylum, and arrest Dr. Trumble and his key staff members. The raid will end the conspiracy that has revolved around the Revert Document.

Under the current administration, Dr. Trumble abdicated responsibility by accepting and holding people unjustly, creating an atmosphere of exploitation. He detained women who were associated with statehood delegates and in the process supported political opposition against the United States.

The absence of safeguards allowed a poorly trained psychiatrist and hospital administrator with little or no medical ethics to rule. Even ethical personnel are obliged to accept anyone—insane or not—when escorted by a law officer. For now, Adobe and the men will make changes to prevent further harm or death. The territory needs new mental health laws to protect victims. Their work on this night is a short-term solution.

Two sheriff's deputies, empowered with a search warrant,

will confiscate papers, including notes, records and memoranda presumably made in the course of the conspiracy. They will not use a subpoena to get relevant material, which could have allowed the asylum to prepare a defense. Instead, based on the belief that Dr. Trumble would destroy evidence, Adobe rejected the subpoena and called for a search warrant. Given the assault on Mady, the authorities had reasonable suspicion that the asylum administration had committed a crime and had granted his request.

Adobe moves about in the saddle as he and the other men ride up to Loma Lake. They water their horses and look at the Territorial Insane Asylum in the distance. Then Rodriquez leads the men forward at a lope. Stopping about 100 yards from the big building, the horses fidget, but the men are calm and ready.

As hysterical screaming echoes through the dismal corridors, Adobe pounds on the heavy door. Nurse Denton, her head bandaged, appears and he declares, "We have a warrant for the arrest of Dr. Trumble and for the immediate release of women falsely committed and held."

A stunned Nurse Denton protests, "But you can't do that, you can't come in here."

"Stand aside or be pushed aside."

She holds her ground.

"Stand aside," orders Adobe."

"But Dr. Trumble is indisposed."

"Stand aside," orders Adobe. "It all ends today."

Nurse Denton moves aside.

"Come with us."

The men march through the halls with a sense that justice is about to be served. Adobe walks past the woman who had slipped him the note during his last visit to the asylum. "God bless you," she cries.

Ray Raton is staring wildly when Adobe, flanked by men,

approaches him and says, "Ray Raton, we have a warrant for your arrest."

Stunned but cooperative, Ray is more rational than Nurse Denton is and follows the two deputies outside. *Señorita Valdez* enters the area and Rodriquez takes hold of her arm.

"Let her go," Adobe says, "she helped Mady escape."

"Yeah, probably for a price," Nurse Denton snarls.

Now the men storm into Dr. Trumble's office and Manny Rodriquez declares, "I am Sheriff Rodriquez of Arriba County. We have a warrant for your arrest."

"What? What's the charge?"

Adobe interjects, "You mean *charges*."

Although they are in Rodriquez's jurisdiction, he defers to Adobe due to his personal involvement with Mady's ordeal.

"What charges? I demand to know!"

"You are being charged with conspiracy to commit murder, kidnapping, and assault and battery on Mady Blaylock."

"What murder?"

"You have the wives of murdered statehood delegates unjustly imprisoned here."

"I know nothing about any murder!"

"All the same, you are an accessory after the fact."

"I did not know that patients were unjustly admitted. I was just doing my job," he pleads.

"We're just doing *our* job."

"Everyone is brought here against their will."

"Tell it to the judge. You kept people here you knew were not supposed to be committed. The county attorney will sort out the counts of murder, kidnapping, patients committed wrongly and bribes."

Dr. Trumble's eyes search the room, looking for help. There is none. Adobe continues, "For good measure, after we examine your files we may have charges of falsifying documents, making false statements to the police, obstruction of justice and medical malpractice. Don't worry, Doctor. You'll find the accommodations at the territorial penitentiary much better than here."

"But, Sheriff Centori, I don't understand."

"If you don't understand, find someone to draw you a picture, because I haven't got the time."

Rodriquez takes Dr. Trumble outside. Adobe orders Nurse Denton, "Take me to Lilly Sheldon, Rebecca Taylor and Maria Otero. It will be your last official act here."

She stares in disbelief, unwilling to move.

"Now!"

68

Mad Mady's Saloon Redux

A week later, Adobe starts his day a little earlier than usual. Wearing a long duster against the cold December morning, he rides Patriot to Valtura. Bypassing his office, he goes directly to the south side of the plaza and Mad Mady's Saloon.

"Good morning, Mady."

"Right on time or even a little early," she observes, laughing.

"Mady, I'm glad to see you running your place again."

"It will be like old times around here, Adobe."

"Old times in a new world; New Mexico is the forty-seventh state and with Arizona becoming the forty-eighth, the map for U.S. states is complete."

"It has been quite a troubling year leading up to statehood."

"You know that more than most, Mady."

"It was no walk in the plaza for you either, but we are finally a state."

"Yes, Mady, New Mexico will have self-government, a long time in coming. But statehood is a bittersweet victory for me." *It was a year filled with mayhem, the betrayal by Ellison, Berta's death, Mercy, the fire, the possibility of war, the near loss of Patriot and the real loss of the colonel.*

The most devastating loss of all was the tragedy at Chaco Canyon. Adobe, lost in his thoughts, finds little comfort in Tennyson's words, '*Tis better to have loved and lost, than never to have loved at all.*'

"Adobe, *que pasa*?"

"Oh, sorry, Mady. So what about the fancy changes Sharon made here?"

"I am keeping most of them; call it payment for the trouble she put me through."

"No bad memories?"

"I will remember the good things about Sharon, our childhood years in New York. We had trips to Coney Island—the roller coaster, Steeplechase and Nathan's Famous. There were visits to Central Park—ice-skating and the zoo. It was all before she went 'round the bend. The only bad memory now is the thought of her languishing in the territorial prison. Sharon's criminal behavior could be lunacy, and they call *me* Mad Mady.

"So no bad memories. I like the changes. Besides, we are a territory no more. As a state, we deserve improvements in all things," Mady jokes.

"Agreed. Our economy should grow and prosper. In fact, I will remind Governor Jackson, and indirectly his powerful railroad friends, about extending the line into town. A railroad avenue will be a grand addition to Valtura."

"As a returning saloon keeper, that would be welcome news," Mady says.

"Yes, Mad Mady's Saloon will need to expand; perhaps you will compete with the Union Hotel."

"Oh, yes, Valtura will change. The saloon has changed, and after all that's happened, we have changed, too."

Adobe goes into high alert and calmly says, "No question, things are not the same."

"Well, with all the new optimism and positive talk for the future, will I finally see your precious Circle C Ranch?"

"Has the asylum made you mad, Mady?" he offers with humor.

"You are good at dodging bullets."

"Only way to stay alive."

Venturing beyond metaphor, she says, "So marriage will kill you?"

Remaining composed Adobe replies, "No, I enjoy our time and look forward to being here more often."

"Ever since I met you, you have avoided talking about *us.*"

"Only at times."

"Look, Adobe. I have been keeping my love for a long time."

Now that Gabriella is gone for good, Mady presses her advantage.

"Adobe, what if we…?" She does not complete the thought.

"What's that?"

'No…nothing." She senses those old boundaries are still in play; and they may be stronger now. Besides, mentioning *La Guerrillera* is poor salesmanship. Instead of bringing up a grief-stricken romance, Mady says, "Okay, you win for now."

Relieved, he quickly says, "Mady, are you going to the Territorial, I mean the special State Fair in Albuquerque?"

"That's weeks away, but no. I'll stay right here at good ol' Mad Mady's Saloon. It's good to be back in Valtura. But I'm sure Klara will be going with you," Mady probes.

"Klara is in Santa Fe, probably working against the new state government, and is planning to petition Congress about the women's vote," he says with a slight smile.

"Okay, Adobe, I hope you enjoy the fair."

"Thanks. I'll be travelling to Washington for the statehood signing. Hope you won't disappear while I'm gone this time."

"Don't worry," she says, laughing. "I will never again leave Valtura unwillingly, at least not alive."

"Has this place gotten too fancy for coffee, Mady?"

"Not likely. Rest assured, it will be black and strong!"

"Let me be the judge of that."

Mad Mady's Saloon is back in business on Valtura Plaza.

69

New Year's Eve 1911

Adobe and A.P. sit near the kiva fireplace in the Circle C great room, smoking cigars. The rhythm of coyote cries breaks the peacefulness of the clear, cold night.

Adobe turns to A.P. and says, "Thank you for another fine year at the Circle C."

"Sure, Boss, and quite a year it was."

"You did much more than run things around here."

"You're welcome."

Adobe smiles and reaches into his pocket and pulls out the colonel's watch. Coyote cries echo outside as he looks at the watch with the coyote image and the initials CC engraved in the metal. It is 11:58 p.m.

Adobe invites A.P. into his library and grabs a bottle of whiskey and two glasses. He pours, raises his glass and says, "Happy New Year, A.P."

A.P. smiles and says, "Boss, any wishes for the new year?"

"I don't know," he laments.

"Don't worry, you will find your way." A.P. says.

"Thanks, Pard."

"Happy 1912."

The next day, Adobe and the New Mexico delegation begin a long rail journey to Washington. The president is ready to sign the bill for statehood. When Valtura received the news, Adobe unfurled the American Flag at his office. In Santa Fe, the flag was unfurled at the Palace of the Governors.

70

STATEHOOD

As far back as 1848, General Kearney promised statehood, but it took more than sixty years for that promise to be fulfilled. Over the course of decades, there were many chances to adopt a constitution, but social, religious, political and economic issues prevented New Mexico statehood. However, as Victor Hugo said, "There is one thing stronger than all the armies in the world, and that is an idea whose time has come." Finally, after many obstacles, the time has come for New Mexico to become a full member of the United States of America.

Based on a congressional resolution promising statehood, a territorial-wide election held in November 1911 ratified the state constitution and approved the conditions imposed by Congress. New Mexicans then adopted a constitution and asked for admission.

New Mexico achieved new responsibilities at the ballot box. The election included choosing two congressional representatives and a new state legislature that subsequently appointed two U.S. Senators. The Corona County vote helped re-elect Governor Jackson.

Despite the rumors and the promising signs from the governor,

Adobe Centori was not appointed to the U.S. Senate. The people of Valtura said he was too honest for politics. Anyway, he may have had enough political adventure for a lifetime.

In accordance with the congressional provisions, President Taft proclaimed that the imposed congressional conditions on New Mexico's constitution were satisfied and should be sent to Congress. In the Senate, the final vote was unanimously in favor of statehood. The same thing happened in the House.

Statehood was a long time arriving, but finally New Mexico will join the Union as the forty-seventh state. The stage is set for statehood day, January 6, 1912.

71

WASHINGTON CITY

Delegate Centori is part of the three-man New Mexico delegation that will witness President Taft signing the historic proclamation. The train arrives in Union Station at 5:00 p.m., January 5, 1912. The delegates are excited about meeting the president and being part of the historical event.

It is Adobe's first time in Washington and he is determined to make the most of the experience. Dressed in his best clothing and his big tan hat, he steps down onto the platform and walks out of the station with the delegates. Most of the delegates, having never been east before, are amazed by Washington City. Adobe, born in New York, is nevertheless as amazed. They check into the Willard Hotel on Pennsylvania Avenue, two blocks east of the White House, and then gather in the main dining hall.

The next morning is New Mexico's moment of gaining self-government—the statehood bill is ready for official signatures. The process started with the territory's referendum vote for statehood, the petition to the U.S. Congress, the adoption of a constitution and now action by the House and Senate. The Congress, by a simple majority, voted for a joint resolution accepting New Mexico as a state. The House assembled and Speaker Champ Clark signed the bill. Then, Vice President James Sherman signed the bill in the Senate. From Capitol Hill, the bill arrives at the White House, where the clock reads 1:40 p.m.

Delegate Centori, two other delegates, four cabinet members, and key congressional representatives who were supportive of the bill, are at the White House.

President Taft has received the statehood bill for his official signature. The Postmaster General presents the president with a gold pen. Adobe hands the president a gold-banded quill taken from an American eagle in New Mexico. The president uses both pens to sign. Following centuries of colorful history and dozens of attempts over sixty years, the president signs the proclamation admitting New Mexico to the Union, ending the territorial era.

After signing, the president speaks to the delegates. "Well, it is all over," he says. "I am glad to give you life. I hope you will be healthy. New Mexico's long struggle for statehood is finally over."

With the ceremony and celebration completed, Adobe ventures alone to see the sights. The Capitol, the Washington and Jefferson Memorials and the Smithsonian Museum are all fascinating. Immaculate facades express the greatest of American democratic ideals.

The most meaningful sight to Adobe is not a building at all. One would think that he would have had enough of documents, but one parchment, located in the State Department building and sealed between two plates of glass, is first on his sightseeing list. The document is available for exhibition on special occasions and at the discretion of the secretary of state. Thanks to John Murphy's curious connections in Washington, Adobe has a special invitation.

Walking from the White House, Adobe arrives at the State Department Building, where an official leads him to an inner area.

"Take all the time you like, Mr. Centori."

"Thank you."

There it is before him, a document justifying U.S. independence: The Declaration of Independence adopted by the Continental Congress in 1776. After studying the document, his eyes come to rest on the second sentence—the most powerful words in American history:

> We hold these truths to be self-evident, that all men are created equal, that they are endowed by their Creator with certain unalienable Rights, that among these are life, Liberty and the pursuit of Happiness.

I have life and liberty. But did I really pursue my happiness? he wonders.

Thanking the official, Adobe leaves the building, making a mental note to buy Murphy dinner in Valtura for arranging the viewing. Walking along the National Mall, he thinks, *This entire city is a treasure dedicated to art and history, although one important structure is missing.*

Construction will be in an open area, previously swampland, but this site will be an inspiring part of Washington. In 1867, Congress created the Lincoln Monument Association and in February 1911, they authorized the memorial, but it has been almost a year with no progress.

Adobe grew up admiring and studying Lincoln's speeches, which had a profound impact on his perspective of the Union. He wonders if he will return to Washington to see the Lincoln Memorial when it is finished, not knowing it will be two years before the first stone is set. Eight years will pass before Chief Justice Taft and Lincoln's surviving son Robert dedicate the Memorial on the last Monday in May, Memorial Day, the day that honors Americans who died for their country or, as Lincoln said, "Gave the last full measure of devotion."

With Adobe's job done, it is time to reflect on the cost of statehood. The long train ride back to New Mexico provides more than enough time. *She has taken our love again, this time forever. I do not know if the price of patriotism was too high.* He remembers her challenge—the Circle C in *Nuevo Mexico*?

72

TERRITORIAL FAREWELL

By order of Governor Jackson and due to popular interest, the thirty-second Annual Territorial Fair, scheduled for September, was moved to January 20th. Politicians, businessmen and citizens gather in Albuquerque for the fair, an industrial exposition and festival promoting New Mexico commerce and, in recent years, statehood. This year is different: the Territorial Fair is now the New Mexico State Fair.

The fair provides a racetrack for horseracing, the Albuquerque Browns for baseball and the first airplane flights in New Mexico. The crowd expects Governor Jackson to attend the opening day ceremonies.

There is a private, indoor reception in the afternoon for Governor Jackson, his wife, local politicians and statehood delegates from Bernalillo and adjacent counties.

The governor holds a luncheon plate and stands next to his wife who is drinking tea from a cup and saucer. Mrs. Jackson, who wears a beautiful black and white gown, stops smiling when her husband starts flirting with two young women.

"Excuse me, William. I would like more tea," she says with a frown.

"But, I thought we had an arrangement," he whispers.

"We have *no* arrangement, only your derangement," she whispers.

After the reception, the governor delivers a political speech, and then proceeds to the public reception area. Delegate Block of Bernalillo and Centori of Corona go with him.

Jackson turns to Centori and says, "It's a great day for our *state* and our country, Sheriff."

"Yes, we finally have self-government. Our long journey is over. Let's hope the federal government will not overpower our state."

"Sheriff, let's put politics aside for today. I know your ordeal and personal loss have been extremely difficult, but today is for celebration."

With that, Jackson begins greeting a long line of people. All are smiling except one. Waiting her turn in line without emotion is Klara Morgenstern. As she draws closer, her eyes become fiery and focus on Governor Jackson. He has been shaking hands for about five minutes when she advances and faces him. Adobe, surprised, thinks, *Why did Klara come here alone? We could have driven together in the Ford.*

Jackson extends his hand, but before he can shake her hand, Klara pulls out a pistol. Adobe sees the sun reflect from the gun's barrel and grabs her wrist. Klara screams as Adobe's grabs her lower arm, pointing the gun upward. Then she goes down hard, as Charles Brock tackles her, trying to knock the gun from her hand. Klara's death grip on the pistol is iron-clad. Two more men fall on her, as the struggle continues. Adobe shouts, "Get the gun!"

Klara is fighting like a cornered lioness. Then, amidst the chaos, a single shot rings out. Klara Morgenstern instantly becomes still for all time.

She was an anarchist determined to write and speak against what she perceived as the tyranny of government. Today, she acted against a man with power over citizens. Although she failed to kill her target, she will never be a government prisoner. In that goal, she was successful.

The governor rushes to Adobe and says, "You saved my life, Sheriff!"

Adobe nods to Jackson as he stands over the dead body of a woman he may have loved. Although distrustful of women, he never lost the ability to hope within a life of romantic dissatisfaction. Through the emotional pain of his quixotic disappointment, he has tried to be open to other women. Klara's beauty and innovative mind gave him happiness in their brief time together, and in the end, she exposed her desperation.

Klara was against government force and control. Government force in a free society, she believed, should be used to defend against people who use force for criminal purposes. Federal and state authorities should not use force to confiscate private property, require government service or regulate morality. Klara strongly believed in personal rights. If a citizen does not use force against others, government should not use force against them.

Ironically, Klara used force against the perceived danger of statehood, ignoring her own criminal behavior. Early that morning, Klara had ridden on horseback to Albuquerque. About a mile from the city, she stopped to gaze upon a coyote standing on a boulder. People may feel disconnected from the coyote, not understanding the animal's purpose of taking care of humankind. If this is so, the coyote may resort to crafty plots to enlighten people. The coyote, as the creator, may not be placid in giving this lesson. If people disrespect the world, it could release the coyote's mean streak. *I wonder if that coyote is going to howl,* she thought.

73

FORTY-SEVEN STARS

In the beginning of 1912, Berlin recalled Ambassador Albert Hietmann to Germany with his political future in doubt. Emiliano Zapata challenged the Mexican government, while General Huerta, commander of the federal troops, imprisoned Madero and assumed his presidency. If Madero had recovered the Revert Document, he could have secured his presidency, but the mission failed, dooming him.

Some will argue that suppressing the Revert Document was wrong because it denied Mexico's legal claim to the border territories. Others will argue that plotting to delay statehood was wrong. In any case, Adobe never acted from aggressive instincts. Rather, in the essence of the matter, he sought to prevent war. Right or wrong, he worked to keep New Mexico part of America, without war.

On January 15, 1912, at the state capital, William Jackson was inaugurated governor of the state of New Mexico. Standing on the capital building steps in Santa Fe, he became the first leader of the new American state.

A new American flag with 47 stars will soon fly over Valtura

Plaza. New Mexico has been part of the Imperial Spanish Viceroyalty of New Spain, part of Old Mexico, a U.S. territory and now a U.S. state. The new flag will not last long; Arizona will soon become the 48th state.

One week later, Adobe is alone again at the Circle C and the coyotes around the ranch are sounding mournful. Earlier in the evening, at Mad Mady's Saloon, he consumed most of a tequila bottle and the worm. Now the solemn coyote wail fills the cool night air. The myth maintains that the coyote cannot die and will be the last animal on earth. As their song plays on, the lament becomes an apparent requiem.

Sitting in the stately Circle C library on a large leather chair with his feet on an ottoman, Adobe scans the bookshelves and stares at the kiva fireplace. The flames almost mock his loneliness. He prefers to call it aloneness. Either way, emptiness can play tricks on a man's mind, especially if the condition is chronic. The howl, the coyote's most significant quality, can warn of danger, call for help, remind people of primal connections or express loneliness.

Adobe thinks about the successes and failures of the past year and glances at the old World Series Program. This year, a fire swept through the Giants' ballpark, consuming the wood, but leaving the steel uprights in place.

He considers the year a great success for his beloved Giants. The team played in the Yankees' ballpark while rebuilding the Polo Grounds and rose from the ashes with their ballpark to win the 1911 National League pennant.

Reflecting on his role as a delegate, he calls to mind his involvement with the convention that framed state law and his voting on the proposed New Mexico state constitution. That honor was one of the proudest moments of his life. As he drifts to sleep, thoughts turn to doubts and doubts turn to dreams.

Did I make a positive difference in this world? I hope so, at least in some small way. I guess others will make that determination. His mind spins backward in time and in memory as the library fades.

Adobe's dream sends his mind whirling through time, remembering the hard winter of 1910/1911. It was indeed the closing years of the open range, an end of an era. His mind continues to spin, this time forward. *Sounds like the 6th Cavalry band is playing a dirge. Is that you, Murph? How could it be... he fought in a great European war. The unimaginably destructive war killed him—he is gone.* His dream turns to the present Mady Blaylock. *Soon it will be time for coffee at Mad Mady's Saloon. She deserves an invitation to the Circle C, but I must avoid the trap of the wrong woman.*

Then Havana—the sea, the fruit, the coffee, the tobacco and Gabriella, *"Mi corazón," would we meet today and walk the narrow streets and plazas? Maybe she will go to Washington to see the Lincoln Memorial with me. I wonder if she's happy or has misgivings.* For a second, he is back at their favorite place, in front of Havana's Cathedral. *I love you, from now and until the end of time.* Then in an instant, she is gone. All things are ephemeral, but his love for Gabriella transcends time and space, and carries him away. Alas, the love of his life was never a real part of his life.

Aldoloreto "Adobe" Centori's ancestral narrative began in Verona, Italy. His life started in New York City and flourished in Valtura, New Mexico. Adobe did not save the Union as Mr. Lincoln and his soldiers did, but he helped complete it. New Mexico became part of the United States, followed by Arizona, and now America is a true continental country. Centori's life story may be incomplete in some ways, but his country is not.

Dreams reflect a creative process, not finality, and show that the imagination is active. Life is always in a perpetual process of creation and inspiration.

"Boss, wake up. You will be late for the big day," urges A.P. "Are you okay? Did you spend the night in that chair?"

"Huh?" he mumbles, blinking his eyes. "Yes, I'm okay, just a few strange dreams," he says despite a big headache from too much whiskey.

"We're all saddled up. I've been waiting outside for you."

"Have we heard from John Murphy lately?"

"No, but he is due in Valtura today for the statehood ceremony."

"A.P., I had a disturbing dream that he was killed in Europe. It was Armageddon, a major conflagration, nothing at all like the war in Cuba."

"It was just a bad dream. Anyway, Europe's problems are an ocean away. No business of Uncle Sam."

"Not a bad dream, a horrible nightmare that seemed so real, A.P. Remind me not to eat the worm next time."

Beyond a nightmare, Adobe's premonition is upsetting and enervating. In an attempt to get him moving, A.P. says, "It may have seemed real, but not as real as flying the flag over the Corona County courthouse. Today will be a special, inspiring day. So let's get to gettin'."

Adobe manages to shake away the nightmare and says, "Okay, let's go to town."

The men step outside to mount Patriot and Minuteman and begin the six-mile ride. Typically, Adobe stops at a low hill on the outskirts of town to view Valtura, but not today.

Both riders enter town on East Corona Street and pass the shops and houses, including the colonel's house, which stands empty, or so they think. A woman who is originally from an upper class family in upstate New York purchased the colonel's old Victorian house. The new owner recently arrived from Albuquerque where she lived for several years. She will take control of the inactive Valtura Journal.

The extent of her involvement, as publisher, editor, columnist or reporter is unclear.

The colonel's nephew from Las Cruces handled the last will and testament and estate sale. Adobe inherited twenty-five percent of the house sale proceeds and placed the money in a Valtura Plaza beautification fund in perpetuity. In addition, he introduced a bill to the town council changing the name of Valtura Plaza to Antonio Santos Square. A plaque describing the colonel's public service and war record will appear on the gazebo. Adobe also received the colonel's antique weapons collection, hand-carved chess set and his timepiece.

Approaching the plaza, Adobe and A.P. see a town crowded with revelers. Red, white and blue bunting decorates the buildings. The plaza is jammed with about a thousand people and the temporary stands at National Street are overflowing.

They dismount and tether their horses. Adobe briskly walks to the courthouse and A.P. joins the revelers including Mad Mady Blaylock and John Murphy. They all share this time of excitement for New Mexico and are alive with patriotism.

As arranged, the Corona County delegate will have the honor of placing the flag on the highest building in Valtura and will raise two flags near the gazebo: the state flag and the new American flag.

The announcement, a grand, official declaration of statehood by President Taft ends decades of waiting. The mission bells peal and congratulatory telegrams click away throughout the state. Fireworks boom as Adobe climbs up into the courthouse cupola with the new American flag—with two new stars. He runs the flag up the pole and waves his big hat to the cheering crowd below—the people in Valtura are ecstatic.

When the crowd sees the new 47-star flag, the band in the plaza plays "My Country 'Tis of Thee." Even the children are waving flags and shouting, "Hurrah for New Mexico, the new state!"

As Adobe returns to the plaza, he moves through a whirlwind of congratulations. He arrives at the plaza and embraces A.P. "Great job," says A.P. "The flag looks great, too, all 47 stars."

"Thank you, pard," Adobe says.

John Murphy is next to offer his congratulations, "Adobe, I can think of no better man to raise that new flag over Corona County."

"Murph, I am really glad to see you. How's your shoulder?"

"Much better; it feels fine, especially today."

Then Mad Mady breaks in to give Adobe a hug and says, "You may be a great fool when it comes to women, but you're a great American who deserved the honor of raising the flag."

Knowing his strengths and weaknesses, he smiles, "Thanks, Mady."

Buster shakes his hand and says, "It is an honor to know you, Sheriff."

Smiling, the sheriff replies, "Buster, from now on call me Adobe."

That makes Buster's day. Adobe breaks through the crowd, bounds up the gazebo steps and stands there, waiting for the applause to stop. Finally, he gets to the center of the gazebo to start his speech.

The straight-talking handsome hero, in his familiar big tan hat, red shirt, and white bandanna, arrives amidst a large endowment of good will. At the sight of him, the excited crowd cries, "Adobe! Adobe! Adobe!" They see him as a fearless, rugged individual, a man who gets things done by self-reliance. Many people in Valtura know about his role in the statehood affair and that he had contributed in a big way. A few know about his involvement with the Revert Document affair. Attempting to quiet the crowd with little success, he surveys the audience and recognizes an old man dressed in black, staring with a slight smile. The aged man, who moves with a slow step and unnatural eyes, startles Adobe, compelling him to stop the speech.

The crowd, pressing against the gazebo, causes Adobe to lose sight of the old man. Finally, he is able to say, "Thank you for the warm welcome and kind words. Thank you all."

Once again, he waits for the cheering and applause to stop and goes on, "We are here today for Corona County's official statehood and flag-raising ceremony. During the long struggle for statehood, many people worked hard to achieve self-government. I hope my efforts contributed in a small way."

The loud applause from the crowd answers in the affirmative. He continues his speech. "Over the decades, as the statehood battle continued the political power here and in Washington shifted. We needed many people to organize political efforts to move from territorial status to statehood. The men in Santa Fe won support for the constitutional convention from many political factions throughout New Mexico. All of which led us to this significant day. After the heroic efforts of so many people for so long, New Mexico is admitted to the Union with the sovereignty that is the right of free men and women."

Another eruption of applause drowns out Adobe's voice, but he continues to extol the virtues of statehood, "After years of territorial status, New Mexico is a state with the most historic name in the U.S.—only Florida is older. Before Jamestown, New Amsterdam and Plymouth, there was a New Mexico."

More applause stops him for a moment. "With self-government, there will be many improvements in our lives. Already we can expect improved rail transportation right here in Valtura. Construction work on the railroad extension from the Valtura Station to Junction Street, a distance of five miles, will begin in the spring. Several east coast capitalists have agreed to finance the project, which will transport passengers from the station to town and enhance the free market, with more people driving the local, county and *state* economies. In addition, there are plans to build a moving picture theater just off the plaza. It will be called El Dorado."

There is an impromptu cheer from the raucous crowd, "Adobe! Adobe!"

He stops and waits for the chanting to end and sees the same old man, who is not cheering, but rather is calm and smiling with admiration. Adobe is transfixed as the old man dressed in black nods his head in approval. Tears begin to impair his vision as he watches the colonel touch his heart and fade back into eternity.

Pulling himself together, Adobe goes on, "People from across the country will observe the new 47-star flag and think of New Mexico. Statehood stands as a tribute to our commitment to the land, and the well-being and education of our citizens."

His speech concludes with, "Today, not only do we come together as Mexicans and New Mexicans, but we join together as Americans in the forty-seventh state of the Union."

Another eruption of applause signals an end to Adobe's speech. He moves from the gazebo and through the crowd again, slowly making his way to the commemorative marker between the flagpoles for the flag-raising ceremonies. About a thousand people stand at attention to watch Adobe as the flags slowly ride upward; a mild wind flaps the flags.

He adds, "Now, we must show that our new state is a commendable addition to America!"

Mady rushes to Adobe and hugs him then yells to the crowd, "Statehood celebration reception, right now at Mad Mady's Saloon. Let me say it again—Mad Mady's Saloon!"

EPILOGUE

VENUS OF VALTURA

Five hours later, the crowds are gone, Mad Mady's Saloon is dark and Adobe sits alone in his office smoking a cigar. Most people believe he is ingenuous and steadfast; the dramatic crowd reaction surprised him—and humbled him. He was a rock in the Spanish-American War, strong in managing the Circle C Ranch and fearless in running down the Revert Document.

Through it all, Adobe arrived at certain conclusions. He loves the Circle C, but remains alone. Regret does not consume him, but he imagines what marriage to Gabriella, a grand beauty, could have produced. Memories of a lost love are enduring, with that love's best feelings frozen in his mind.

His heart is open, but Adobe is uncertain about Gabriella's destiny—perhaps the good of the many does *not* always outweigh the good of the few. There are paradoxical situations in life and the struggle to reconcile contradictions can show a man's character. He remains optimistic about the new century and the new state of New Mexico.

Adobe started the year with a hard-hitting blizzard and violent forces of wind. Unknown to him, a far greater wind is coming. It is just a whisper but more powerful than the strongest storm or hurricane.

A cold wind sweeps the plaza. He decides to step outside to Corona Street and watch the gazebo flags whip in the wind under the moonlight. Then he looks up to watch the new courthouse flag wave. A stranger, with an affinity for strong leaders, whispers a compliment, "That was quite an acrobatic act on the top of the courthouse." Her voice is throaty, with confidently intoned upper-class elocution.

He stops. It is just a whisper but more powerful than the strongest storm. A low voice—perchance the whisper of love.

Intrigued by her alluring voice and seeing her classic beauty, he softly says, "Thank you, Miss."

A fine, high-collared purple dress drapes her five-foot, six-inch, 120-pound body and fits perfectly over a curvaceous figure. She wears a large hat with a wide face-shadowing brim. The lace and small pleats are the height of fashion. Holding a reporter's notebook, she says, "Your statehood speech was inspiring too. The eloquence moved everyone," she smiles.

"Thank you again, but it was just a few simple words."

"Those words overjoyed the crowd. You stirred their hearts with a great speech. They know you love our new state and new American flag. Have you considered running for mayor?" she smiles again.

Distracted by the mass of gleaming reddish-blonde hair that cascades and sways over her shoulders, he wonders, *Could that natural smile on her face convey romantic interest?*

"My name is Jennifer Prower," she declares with a regal manner.

Jennifer Prower, a majestic name, he thinks.

"I arrived from Albuquerque just in time for the statehood celebration."

Intrigued, he says, "I'm glad you did."

Although surprised by his forwardness, she offers another genuine smile.

Enthralled, he sees only the beauty in her exquisite face. Somewhere between blue and hazel, her eyes reflect substance and style.

"You don't sound like you are from New Mexico."

"Quite right. I was born in upstate New York, near Albany."

"I was born and raised in Manhattan. I've been up the Hudson River to Albany."

What is different about this woman? Such loveliness…but…?

"Sheriff, you may know, I purchased the Victorian House on East Corona Street."

"I know the house well, Miss Prower. The previous owner was a close friend." Adobe's eyes look down, but just for a second.

While touching her sparkling turquoise and silver necklace, she says, "Perhaps we can become friends as well."

Hope just checked into Valtura, New Mexico!

Adobe's heart skips a beat as he feels tightness in his stomach. His mind races, *What a beautiful woman.*

Smiling seductively, Jennifer says, "I will be running the Valtura Journal."

"That is great news. We need our newspaper."

"So, we will be neighbors on the plaza."

"Indeed!" Adobe, barely able to contain his excitement thinks, *I must not place her too high on a pedestal, beyond reach, but some angels belong in the heavens.*

At times, a man walks a tightrope between strength and sensitivity. A woman's perception on how those qualities should be reconciled can vary. Adobe, a man of great strength, will save his emotions for another day. "You will be most welcome on the plaza, Miss Prower," he offers an even smile.

"Please call me Jennifer," she says.

His breathing and heart rate accelerate. *Is this love at first sight? No—that only exists in fairytales.*

"Jennifer, Valtura can expect an early spring now that you are here."

Another smile says he did not go too far. "Well, Sheriff, I must get back to the newspaper. May I quote you?" she teases.

"Yes, of course."

With that, she closes her notebook with a definitive snap, turns with flowing tresses of luxurious, long hair moving gracefully, and walks away. He releases a deep breath, watches her every step and wonders about the encounter, the feeling of euphoria.

Standing in the moonlight he thinks, *What's different about Jennifer? She is self-confident, a woman in control and happy. She is the image of female perfection, perhaps the most beautiful woman I have ever seen.* Then it hits hard. *Is she unlocking the chains forged long ago in Cuba?*

The new statehood era may begin with the past no longer holding a mortgage on the future. Time will tell.

That evening, Adobe returns to the Circle C and thinks, *The ancient Greeks called love madness from the gods. Will I be mad enough to invite Jennifer to the Circle C?* He rushes into the library, knowing exactly what he is looking for: a poem—with exquisite words that express his new feelings:

> *"Grace was in all her steps, heaven in her eye,*
> *In every gesture dignity and love."—Milton*

Feeling exultant, Adobe closes the book, looks in a drawer and glances at a photo in a Woolworth's frame and an old water-damaged government document. He walks outside toward the mountain and gazes up at the constellations. The stars are especially bright and aligned this night. Then he notices a coyote on Little Hill Top, who seems to be smiling. Perhaps Adobe is projecting his mood or the bright moonlight is distorting the view and the coyote is not smiling at all. No matter, he tips his big hat, returns the smile and says, "That's right my friend, there are no regrets in the future, just promise."

With his eyes fixed on the brightest star of the galaxy, he dreams, *Beyond her physical, mental, and emotional magnetism, Jennifer opens the door to my soul. She reaches my deepest emotions that have been, for so long, unengaged. She is like Venus to me—Venus of Valtura.*

Acknowledgments

I would like to acknowledge the many enthusiastic friends and family in both New York and in New Mexico. Their interest in this project was generous and inspiring. Thank you for your efforts throughout the process. In addition, I acknowledge my Molloy College colleagues for their support.

Dr. Catherine S. Akel, Sheila Bush, Anthony C. Cillis, Esq., Madeline Pafundi and Professor Christine Sacco provided comprehensive assistance.

Special thanks to Nancy Maffucci for her wild idea that I write this novel and for her extraordinary efforts in joining the separate energies that created *Statehood of Affairs*.

New York, NY
November 2011

APPENDIX 1

REVERT DOCUMENT

Article X of the Treaty of Mesilla

WHEREAS a treaty between the United States of America and the Mexican Republic was concluded and signed at the City of Mexico on the thirtieth day of December, one thousand eight hundred and fifty-three; which treaty, as amended by the Senate of the United States, and being in the English and Spanish languages, is amended with this article as follows:

IN THE NAME OF ALMIGHTY GOD:

The Republic of Mexico and the United States of America desire to remove every cause of disagreement that might interfere in any manner with better friendship and to maintain the peace that prevails between the two republics and intercourse between the two countries, and especially in respect to the Treaty of Mesilla in the year 1853.

Therefore, the President of the United States has appointed James Gordon, Envoy Extraordinary and Minister Plenipotentiary, and the

President of Mexico has appointed as Plenipotentiary his excellency Don José de Bonilla, Secretary of State, and of the office of Foreign Relations.

James Gordon and José De Bonilla have full powers for this negotiation, who, having communicated their respective full powers, and finding them in proper form, have agreed upon the following amendment to the Treaty of Mesilla: Article X.

Article X

The Treaty of Mesilla grants property protection for Mexicans in the new United States territories, and, notwithstanding what was covenanted in the Treaty of Mesilla in the year 1853, additional interpretations have been urged to strengthen and more firmly maintain the peace.

In consequence, the United States hereby acknowledges that any ceded border territory that does not obtain American statehood by December 31, 1911, is subject to revert to the Mexican government immediately.

In testimony whereof, we, the plenipotentiaries of the contracting parties, have hereunto affixed our hands and seals, the first day of December, in the year of our Lord, one thousand eight hundred and sixty.

Now, therefore, be it known that I, JAMES BUCHANAN, President of the United States of America, have caused the said amendment to the Treaty of Mesilla and the article thereof, may be observed and fulfilled with good faith by the United States.

In witness whereof I have hereunto set my hand and caused the seal of the United States to be affixed. Done at the city of Washington, this sixth day of January, in the year of our Lord, one thousand eight hundred and sixty-one.

BY THE PRESIDENT:

APPENDIX 2

By the President of the United States of America

PROCLAMATION 1175 ADMITTING NEW MEXICO TO THE UNION JANUARY 6, 1912

WHEREAS the Congress of the United States did by an act approved on the twentieth day of June, one thousand nine hundred and ten, authorize the people of the territory of New Mexico to form a constitution and state government, and provide for the admission of such state into the union on an equal footing with the original states upon certain conditions in said act specified:

AND WHEREAS said people did adopt a constitution and ask admission into the union:

AND WHEREAS the Congress of the United States did pass a joint resolution, which was approved on the twenty-first day of August, one thousand nine hundred and eleven, for the admission of the state of New Mexico into the union, which resolution required that

the lectors of New Mexico should vote upon an amendment of their state constitution, which was proposed and set forth at length in said resolution of Congress, as a condition precedent to the admission of said state, and that they should so vote at the same time that the first general election as provided for in the said constitution should be held:
AND WHEREAS it appears from information laid before me that said first general state election was held on the seventh day of November, one thousand nine hundred and eleven, and that the returns of said election upon said amendment were made and canvassed as in Section Five of said resolution of Congress provided:
AND WHEREAS the governor of New Mexico has certified to me the result of said election upon said amendment and of the said general election:
AND WHEREAS the conditions imposed by the said act of Congress approved on the twentieth day of June, one thousand nine hundred and ten, and by the said joint resolution of Congress have been fully complied with:
NOW, THEREFORE, I, William Howard Taft, president of the United States of America, do, in accordance with the provisions of the act of Congress and the joint resolution of Congress herein named, declare and proclaim the fact that the fundamental conditions imposed by Congress on the state of New Mexico to entitle that state to admission have been ratified and accepted, and that the admission of the state into the union on an equal footing with the other states is now complete.
IN TESTIMONY WHEREOF, I have hereunto set my hand and caused the seal of the United States to be affixed.
DONE at the city of Washington this sixth day of January, in the year of our Lord one thousand nine hundred and twelve and of the independence of the United States of America the one hundred and thirty-sixth.

WILLIAM HOWARD TAFT